The Jackal Club

By Paul Mann

For Nancy, Jessica, Alexandra and Sarah.

Other books by Paul Mann

Season Of The Monsoon

The Burning Ghats aka The Burning Tide

The Leek Club

The Witch's Code

The Britannia Contract

The Traitor's Contract

The Beirut Contract

The Libyan Contract

Dirty Hit

Sweet Kill

Dark children of the mere and marsh,

Wallow and waste and lea,

Outcaste they wait at the village gate

With folk of low degree.'

- Beast and Man in India, Rudyard Kipling.

Chapter 1.

It had all gone horribly well and Sansi only had himself to blame. Sansi, Mukherjee and Associates was thriving. Billings were already up 20 percent on the previous year. The firm had a dozen full time employees; three paralegals, five secretaries, a managing office clerk, a billings clerk, an accountant, a receptionist and a pool of part time paralegals. Still they struggled to keep up with the caseload. They had appropriated the offices next door and across the hall and now occupied the entire top floor of Lentin Chambers, a creaky former shipping brokerage at Hutatma Chowk. Mukherjee was pushing Sansi to move the firm into one of the gleaming new tower blocks that were transforming the Mumbai skyline. But Sansi wasn't comfortable with his success. It was not the success he craved. What he wanted when he left Crime Branch was to set up a practice profitable enough to enable him to take on pro bono cases on behalf of the downtrodden and the dispossessed. But he had committed two unintentional masterstrokes. The first was timing. He would stick to the basics of family law; divorce, wills and property. He had been just in time to catch a wave of change that swept through Mumbai and transformed the practice of law in India's richest city. New money fueled a property boom that saw real estate change hands at dizzying speed. At the same time long repressed social pressures blew the lid off traditional Hindu family life, empowering women and triggering a massive increase in the divorce rate. Husbands, wives and children fought over assets and inheritances and lawyers who practiced family law found themselves inundated. This set the stage for Sansi's second masterstroke when he plucked Jeet Mukherjee from the roving herds of law school graduates who touted for business around the city's law courts. Mukherjee was ambitious and clever. He built up the firm's property division and moved aggressively into commercial property. When he passed the Maharashtra bar exam Sansi rewarded him with a junior partnership. Sansi hoped the promotion would motivate Mukherjee to do most of the work. It did. He brought in more business that required more employees and more of Sansi's time.

Mukherjee's ambitions were apace with Mumbai's soaring skyline. The new generation of moguls preferred to do their business with firms that occupied the same steel and glass world in which they operated. Increasingly Mukherjee wanted to focus on financial law where the big money was. Sansi couldn't blame him but it meant he was pressed to keep up with his share of the caseload. More and more he found himself handing off cases to the paralegals and assuming the role of supervising attorney. Instead of helping the downtrodden and the dispossessed Sansi found himself pandering to the pampered and the privileged. Mukherjee couldn't have been happier and Sansi couldn't have been more miserable.

It was almost noon and the *dabbawallahs* would come soon with tiffin boxes filled with hot lunches for the employees of Sansi, Mukherjee and Associates. To Sansi it felt later. He had taken off his jacket and loosened his tie and sat with his chair turned away from his desk, feet propped on the windowsill so he could ignore the growing stacks of legal folders and the computer with its silently importuning emails. As head of the firm he occupied a corner office that overlooked Dalal Street, Mumbai's Wall Street. The Manhattanisation of Mumbai might be well underway but the same scummy sea of poverty and corruption lapped at the feet of its shiny pillars. There was more money in circulation but it went to the same many handed gods of government and business. Sansi had spent his whole adult life in Mumbai and had never felt more apart from it.

There was a discreet tap at the door. Bansari, the receptionist, asked apprehensively: "May I interrupt you for a moment, Mr. Sansi?"

"If you must," Sansi announced.

The door opened and Bansari stepped inside and closed the door quietly behind her. An earnest young woman working her way through law school her eyes wore a look of perpetual surprise.

"There is a Mrs. Deshpande here to see you," she said.

"I don't recognize the name," Sansi said. "Does she have an appointment?"

"No, but she says it is very important...and she knows your mother."

A lot of people claimed to know Sansi's mother. Pramila Sansi was a former lecturer in Feminist Studies at the University of Mumbai and an acclaimed author. When people said they knew her it usually meant they'd read her books or heard her speak. Sansi was inclined to tell Bansari to make an appointment for Mrs. Deshpande but felt guilty that the day was half over and he had yet to do anything useful.

"It's alright, I'll see her," he said. He got up, fastened his tie and shook on his jacket.

Mrs. Deshpande entered the room cocooned in a sheen of affluence. A middle aged woman she wore a full green sari with gold trim and gold and silver bracelets on her arms. Her hair was pulled back into a braid and she was impeccably made up with a deep red bindi, a gold stud in her left nostril and heavy gold ear rings. When she spoke it was with the elevated cadence of the Brahmin.

"I do appreciate you seeing me at such short notice, Mr. Sansi," she said. "I know how busy you must be, I hope I'm not inconveniencing you too much."

"Not at all," Sansi said and offered his hand. Many women, especially upper caste women, shook hands with men in a business setting now. Mrs. Deshpande gave his hand the merest squeeze.

"May I offer you some *chai*?" he said.

"Yes, thank you, would it be too much to ask for a *sulemani*?"

As far as Sansi knew the tea the women in the office drank was *masala chai*.

"Black tea with lemon and sugar?" Bansari said.

"Yes, perfect," Mrs. Deshpande said.

Sansi gestured her to one of two visitor's chairs and she sat down with a waft of perfume and tucked her expensive leather purse in beside her.

"How can I help you, Mrs. Deshpande?" Sansi said returning to his own chair.   "First, Mr. Sansi, let me tell you how blessed you are to have Pramila Sansi for a mother, though I am sure you already know that," Mrs. Deshpande said. "A truly great and courageous woman she has done so much for the women of India. And she has never been afraid to lead by example has she? I was 14 when I first read 'The Fire Lotus.' I had to keep it hidden from my parents. I would have been in so much trouble with my parents if they'd known. It was the first book I read that gave me hope that one day women in India would be able to make their own decisions about their own lives. That we would no longer be the property of men. I still have it, the same copy. It has been my constant companion through the years."

"I will convey your appreciation to my mother and I know she will be very touched," Sansi said.

"Thank you, Mr. Sansi, that makes me so happy. When I knew I would need a lawyer I decided I could do no better than to come and see the son of Pramila Sansi."

"I am happy to be of assistance," he said.

"I have not had an easy life, Mr. Sansi," she began. "I know people look at someone like me and they think my life is nothing but luxury and fine things. I have servants who do everything for me and I have nothing to worry about. But for all the freedom I have had in the 28 years I have been married to my husband I might as well have lived my life in the *zanana*. I can't go anywhere without my husband's permission and when I do he is always checking on me. If he finds out I was here he will be very angry."

"He will not find out from us," Sansi said and wrote the word 'Divorce' after Mrs. Deshpande's name on a yellow legal pad. "At least not yet."

"I know I can rely on your discretion, Mr. Sansi."

"And what is your husband's name?" Sansi asked, pencil poised.

"His name is Parth Deshpande. He owns Deshpande Electronic Systems."

"Are there any children of the marriage?"

"Yes, we have two daughters. Both are married and out of the house. They could not wait to get away."

"I'm sorry to hear that. Are you in regular communication with them?"

"They call me on the telephone, they are very good like that. But they don't like to come to the house. It has too many bad memories for them. My husband treated them the way he treats me, like we were all his property."

Sansi wrote down their names. "Are there any grandchildren?"

"My eldest daughter has a boy, Balaji. He is two years old."

"Do you get to see him at all?"

"Yes, that is one of the few times my husband will permit me to leave the house."

"Does your husband see your daughters? Has he been to see your grandson?"

"No, my daughters won't have anything to do with him. When I have been to see them he doesn't even ask about them."

"Let me ask you this, do you have any life outside the marriage? Do you have the opportunity to meet with friends or to socialize with other people at all?"

"I sit on the boards of the Conservation Foundation and the Wildlife Protection Association. My husband gives them money so I know people through them but that's all really."

"That's all?"

"There are company events during the year, dinners and things my husband requires me to attend as the dutiful wife of the boss. Sometimes he will have me host a dinner party at home for his foreign business visitors."

"And you go along with this?"

"He bribes me. He gives me jewelry."

"How often would you say you speak to your husband, Mrs. Deshpande?"

"Oh, he speaks to me every day when he is home. He looks in on me before he goes to work in the morning and in the evenings when he gets back from work. I like it when he goes away on business, then I can go out. He is away in Japan now, that is the only reason I can come here."

"Forgive me for asking but when was the last time you had conjugal relations with your husband?"

"You mean sex?"

"*Acha.*"

"I haven't been to his bed in 16 years. We have lived separately under the same roof for 16 years. He doesn't need me for sex. He has his girlfriends."

"You know that beyond doubt?"

"Oh yes. He has had affairs all through our marriage. I confronted him about it a long time ago. He didn't deny it."

"One more thing," Sansi said. "Has he ever abused you, physically or verbally?"

"Verbally, yes. Not physically. I was too valuable an asset to be damaged."

"Has he ever insulted you or humiliated you in front of the servants or anyone else?"

"My whole life with him has been nothing but humiliation," she said.

Sansi leaned back and tapped the pencil against his lips. "You certainly have grounds for divorce. The question I have is why you haven't divorced him before now. At least after the children left home. It can't be a question of money. Once you are divorced he will have to provide for you."

"I don't want a divorce," Mrs. Deshpande said.

"You don't?"

"No, Mr. Sansi, I want everything."

"Alright." Sansi paused. "What does that mean exactly, everything?"

"Everything I have suffered for these past 28 years," she said. "The house. The company. The money. Everything."

Sansi took a breath. "I can understand why you feel this way, Mrs. Deshpande. But you have to understand, the law provides for an equitable division of assets not punitive action by one party against another. Not revenge."

"I am long past caring about revenge, Mr. Sansi. "I have no feelings for my husband at all. I want only what I am owed."

"You know, divorce settlements have a retributive element to them. It is generally acknowledged within the law that taking half of what a man has accumulated over a lifetime is punishment enough. Nobody gets it all."

"That is why I have come to you, Mr. Sansi. I want the kind of solution that only the son of Pramila Sansi can provide. I want a solution outside the law."

"Outside the law?" Sansi repeated. "I'm not sure what you mean by outside the law. You do understand that the law is not something that applies in certain places at certain times? That it is everywhere at once?"

"Yes, like God. But people choose when they want to follow God and they choose when they want to follow the law."

"I know what you're saying. And, yes, it is unjust that the law can be manipulated to the advantage of unscrupulous people. But that is something I have stood against my whole life and it is my firm belief that we make for a more just society when we all at least try to work within the law."

"That would be in an ideal world, Mr. Sansi. We do not live in an ideal world. Why is it alright for powerful men to pick and choose when they follow the law but it is not alright for a woman like me? My husband has lawyers who will do anything for him, inside the law or outside. I have money too. I can pay."

"Yes, but pay for what exactly?"

"You know people. All kinds of people. People who can help someone in my situation. I would like you to arrange an introduction."

"For what purpose?"

"Isn't it better you don't know?"

"In which case I have to assume it is for something illegal and not something to which I can be a party."

"I am speaking to my lawyer," Mrs. Deshpande said. "What we tell each other here is protected isn't it? Under the law?"

"I am not your lawyer yet and based on what you have told me I am not going to be your lawyer," Sansi said. "And I should caution you that if I am made privy to any information about illegal activity I am required to report that information to the proper authorities."

"Oh." Mrs. Deshpande tilted her head to one side. "It is going to be like that is it?"

"Yes, I am afraid it is going to be like that," Sansi said. "And it would be better for both of us if this meeting were to come to an end now."

"I thought, as the son of Pramila Sansi, you of all people would understand."

"I think I do understand and I am sorry there is nothing I can do to help you." Sansi came out from behind his desk to usher her from his office. "You will have to leave now."

"This is most disappointing," Mrs. Deshpande said. She got up, smoothed her sari and collected her purse. "You aren't at all the man I thought you were," she said.

On her way out she passed Bansari bringing her *sulemani chai.*

Bansari looked at Sansi. "No *chai* for Mrs. Deshpande?"

"No *chai* for Mrs. Deshpande," he said.

*   *   *

Sansi left work early and took a taxi to Malabar Hill. He let himself into the apartment he shared with his mother, threw his jacket over a chair and kicked off his shoes. Mrs. Khanna, the *bei*, was in the kitchen. When she heard him she came out and asked if there was anything she could get for him.

"Thank you, Mrs. Khanna but there is only one thing I need right now and I can get that myself," he said.

He went to the drinks cabinet, poured a generous measure of scotch into a tall glass and added ice and soda from the refrigerator to make a stengah, his father's favorite drink when he was in India. He padded out onto the terrace where a fresh breeze chased away the stale air of the city. His mother was going through her daily yoga regimen, bending backwards into an improbably steep position for a woman her age. She wore grey drawstring pants with a loose black top, her silver hair tied in a pony tail. If she was the kind of woman who cared about such things she could have dyed her hair and passed for 20 years younger. She ate healthier than her son, rarely touched alcohol and practiced yoga twice a day every day wherever she was. And she was as busy as she wanted to be. She had retired as chairwoman of the Department of Feminist Studies at Mumbai University the previous year and received more invitations as a public speaker than she could possibly fulfill. Sansi suspected she would outlive him.

He sat on a wooden slatted recliner and took a series of cooling sips from his stengah. She knew he was there but continued her evening ritual, one improbable position after another, till she concluded with her forearms flat on the floor, her chin touching the mat, her legs curled over her head.

"Now you're showing off," Sansi said.

She uncoiled herself into a cross legged position, plucked a towel off a nearby table and dabbed at her face.

"You're home early."

"Too many silly people with too much money and too much time on their hands," he said. "I had to get away."

"They're your clients."

"You don't have to remind me."

Pramila got to her feet, picked up a pitcher of lime juice on the table, poured some into a small glass, dropped in a pinch of salt and gave it a stir.

"I had a visit from one of your fans, a Mrs. Deshpande, wife of Mr. Parth Deshpande, owner of Deshpande Electronic Systems," Sansi said.

"I don't think I know her," she said.

"She loved 'The Fire Lotus.' Said it was a great inspiration to her. Apparently it inspired her to want to do away with her husband."

"Do away with...?"

"I had to stop her before she said anymore. I felt quite sorry for her but I draw the line at arranging contract killings for my clients."

"You think that's what she meant?"

"I had to stop her for her own good before she went any further."

"Oh dear."

"She said she expected more of the son of Pramila Sansi. She found me a great disappointment."

"Well I know how she feels. I'm going to have some curds and fruit. Would you like some?"

"I'll get something from the Delhi Durbar."

"You get the same thing every time. What is it, *rogan josh*? Too much meat will rot your insides."

"If I don't have a few pleasures life won't be worth living."

She stopped beside him on her way inside. "You're drinking too much."

"You sound like my *ma*."

"We've talked about this."

"No, you've talked about it."

"If I have to I'll throw out every drop of alcohol in this house."

He looked up but the sun was behind her so he couldn't see if she was serious or not.

"I don't drink anywhere near as much as you think."

"It's not just your liver I'm worried about."

"Well, I'll stop then."

She took the glass from his hand and tossed the contents over the parapet.

"I'll stop now," he said.

She stepped out of the sun and sat on the edge of a nearby recliner.

"You're not happy and you haven't been happy for a while."

"And here I was thinking I'd hidden it so well."

"You walked away from the job you always wanted, you were unfaithful to the woman you loved and all your spoiled and self-indulgent clients remind you of yourself - does that about sum it up?"

"I wouldn't have put it quite in those terms."

"No, because if you did you'd have to stop feeling sorry for yourself and do something about it."

Sansi had come to realize over time just how furious his mother was with him over his treatment of Annie Ginnaro, the American reporter at The Times Of India with whom he'd been in a close relationship. Pramila adored Annie and resolved that their friendship would not suffer because of her son's indiscretion. She continued to invite Annie to the teas and dinners she hosted regularly for her women friends. If Sansi had ever found it uncomfortable he knew not to look to his mother for sympathy.

"This isn't about money is it?" she asked. "You're not staying in it for the money?"

"We are making a ridiculous amount of money," Sansi said. "The only reason I stay on is for Mukherjee and everybody else. They deserve to make some money, I owe them that much."

"At least you're not just thinking about yourself."

"Are you sure you're my *ma*?" he said.

She got up to go inside and patted him on the head. "You were such a lovely boy and then you had to spoil it all by turning into a man."

*   *   *

Sansi arrived at the office at nine the next day to make up for his early departure the day before. Bansari was waiting with his messages. There were 15 of them. The most urgent, she said, was from a man by the name of Ravi

Samant in the office of Vijay Bahl, leader of the Bharatiya Janata Party.

"He didn't say what it was about," she said, "but he asked that you can him back at your earliest convenience."

Sansi leafed through the message slips as he walked to his office. Most were from clients or other attorneys in ongoing divorce cases and a couple were from paralegals seeking his instructions. The message from Vijay Bahl's office was the most intriguing. The Bharatiya Janata Party, or the BJP, sat in opposition to the ruling Congress Party in the state assembly.

Sansi took off his jacket and set his messages aside while he worked through the stack of daily newspapers Bansari left on his desk each morning. India was one of the few countries in the world where newspapers were booming. It was a country where only the affluent could afford personal computers but literacy was increasing among the general population and newspapers cost only a few cents. In a population of more than a billion the readership of newspapers was measured in the tens of millions. Mumbai alone had a score of English language dailies and many more in Hindi, Urdu and Marathi. Bansari brought Sansi his morning tea, a large cup of Assam with milk, which everyone agreed was the Englishman in him. He didn't see anything about Bahl but there was one major story that caught his attention. His former boss at Crime Branch, Narendra Jatkar, had pulled off something of a coup by capturing the most wanted sandalwood poacher in India, Sunni Shah. Joint Commissioner Jatkar had called a press conference to announce the successful conclusion to a year long undercover operation. The report said Shah was the only survivor of a shootout between the smugglers and the police. In each paper there was a photograph of a triumphant Jatkar with a sullen Sunni Shah beside him in shackles. Among the officers in the background Sansi recognized Chowdhary, his former head constable at Crime

Branch. Sansi didn't doubt that the effort that had gone into capturing Shah but it would have been officers like Chowdhary who did the work while Jatkar took the credit.

Sansi finished his tea and wondered what Vijay Bahl wanted with him. He didn't like dealing with politicians. They were all slippery. Besides, the political parties had their own lawyers and only recruited outside legal help for specialty work, sometimes of a dubious nature. Or it might just be that Bahl wanted a divorce. A matter of some sensitivity for a man in his position. Sansi picked up the phone and asked Bansari to get him Samant.

"I most appreciate you returning my call so promptly, Mr. Sansi," Samant said. "The leader himself, Mr. Bahl, has asked that I get in touch with you about a matter of some importance. It is not something that can be discussed on the telephone. Would you be able to come to the *Vidhan Bhavan* and meet with me in the next day or so?"

The *Vidhan Bhavan* was the Maharashtra State Assembly building at Nariman Point.

Sansi checked his schedule. On paper he was fully booked but he juggled appointments constantly. The *Vidhan Bhavan* wasn't far from Lentin Chambers and it was an excuse to get out of the office.

"I could see you around eleven if that works for you?" he said.

"Oh," Samant sounded surprised. "Yes, Mr. Sansi, that is most acceptable. I will leave your name at the front gate."

Sansi got in most of his calls before it was time to leave. He stopped at a stall outside Lentin Chambers and bought a *kulfi* for the walk. As he crossed the Mahatma Gandhi Memorial Park the *Vidhan Bhavan* loomed ahead with its 21 story tower and circular assembly hall that looked like a giant cake mold. The assembly was guarded by protective tiers that included crash barriers, razor wire and a multitude of armed guards. As Samant had promised a visitor's pass was waiting at the main gate. But he still had to go through a metal detector and submit to a pat down before he was allowed into the building. He rode an elevator up to the eighth floor where the offices of the leaders of the opposition were located. Coming out of the elevator he had to undergo yet another security check before he was escorted to Bahl's offices by a guard. A secretary showed him in to the office of Bahl's chief of staff, Ravi Samant.

Samant was a small, neat man who wore a long black vest over white *kurta pajamas*. He told his secretary to see that he and Sansi weren't disturbed. He gestured Sansi to a sitting area and offered him a glass of iced water. He tried to put Sansi at ease but he also seemed in a hurry.

"Have you seen the news of the past 24 hours, Mr. Sansi?" he asked.

"I try to keep up," Sansi said.

"You will be aware then of the capture of Sunil Shah. It has been all over the newspapers and television."

"I have seen some of the coverage, yes."

"Sunil Shah is a person of particular interest to us, Mr. Sansi. It will not come as a surprise to you that the reason he has managed to go free for so long is because of the influence he has over some of the legislators here at the *Vidhan Bhavan*."

"As you say."

"What we want to know is what has changed? Why now? Why have the protections he has enjoyed for so long been taken away from him at this particular time?"

"I could think of several possibilities," Sansi said. "Perhaps his bribes don't go as far as they used to. It is possible the police decided they'd had enough of him, that happens too. I think the most likely explanation is that there has to be an election in the next six months and this makes the Congress Party look strong on law and order."

"It has everything to do with the election, Mr. Sansi. But there is more to this than a public relations exercise to make Congress look good - it is also a distraction."

"From what?"

· "From something bigger than Sunil Shah. Something that could cost Congress the election."

"And that something would be?"

"That is where you come in, Mr. Sansi."

"With respect, Mr. Samant, so far you haven't told me anything," Sansi said. "It is beginning to sound like you want someone to go under the radar for the sole purpose of digging up some dirt on Congress and if that is the case I am not your man."

"We have the dirt, Mr. Sansi, what we need now is the analysis," Samant said. "It would appear that Mr. Shah has not only been providing members of Congress with gifts and money, he has also been providing them with underage girls. It is our understanding that at least one of these officials is a member of the Athawale cabinet." Madhava Athawale was the leader of the state Congress Party and the Chief Minister of Maharashtra. "We need an experienced and independent interrogator to talk to Sunil Shah to find out if any of this is true. But, this is something that has to be done at arm's length. So, if it blows up we don't get out fingers burned." He smiled. "Now that Shah is in prison we can get to him. He can confirm or deny what we have been hearing for years. And, because he has been deserted by his friends in Congress, he may be willing to talk. It is a unique situation that requires a person with unique qualifications. We would pay you well for your services."

"You know my mother is a Congress supporter and has been since Independence?" Sansi said.

"Yes and we are very much aware of your reputation, Mr. Sansi. Not everyone has your reputation for personal integrity."

"I don't know how much that reputation will be worth when it gets out that I have been taking money from the BJP," Sansi said. "There is something else you should consider. When you start something like this it can acquire a momentum of its own. You start by digging up some dirt and it quickly turns into an avalanche. If your information is correct you may find it is not only Congress Party members who are caught up in it but BJP members too."

"We know that and we are prepared for it," Samant said. "It is the party in power that has the most to lose."

"I'm not interested," Sansi said flatly.

He walked back across Gandhi Memorial Park deep in thought. There was much that troubled him about his conversation with Ravi Samant. It seemed to him both political parties were using Sunil Shah as a pawn in their own game. Sansi remembered his father, a General in the British Army, telling him how he feared for India after Independence. That India would not learn from the abuses of its Colonial rulers and once in power the Indian ruling class would slip all too comfortably into the excesses of the ruling class they had replaced. Sansi didn't trust either the Congress Party or the BJP. Each was as bad as the other. And he didn't have to play their game.

Chapter 2.

There were many beautiful women in the ballroom at the Taj Mahal Palace Hotel but the only woman to hold Sansi's eye was Annie Ginnaro. She wore a cream and gold sari with red trim that matched her hair. In the middle of her forehead was a gold flecked red *bindi*. She was with a man in a tan suit handsome enough to be a Bollywood star. Sansi had no right to be jealous but he was. He had accompanied his mother to the Taj to visit her friend, Shallu Jindal, one of India's most acclaimed classical dancers. Pramila was visiting with Shallu in her dressing room while Sansi meandered through the glittering crowd, a salt lime in hand, trying not to look lost. He wasn't sure Annie would be pleased to see him, especially when she was with another man, but she caught him looking and gave him a welcoming smile. He made his way towards her.

"I didn't realize you were a fan of Shallu Jindal," he said.

"I know who she is but I've never seen her perform," Annie answered in Hindi.

"Me neither," Sansi said. "And your Hindi has become quite fluent."

"People like it if you want something and you speak to them in their own language," she said. Turning to her companion she added: "George is an attorney. His mother is Pramila Sansi. I'm sure you know who she is." To Sansi she said: "This is Ajit Birla. Ajit is the publisher and managing editor of India Today and my new boss."

Sansi and Birla shook hands.

"I know the name George Sansi too," Birla said. "You were with Crime Branch at one time were you not? I recollect a case a few years ago that caused something of a stir between New Delhi and London."

"In another life," Sansi said. To Annie he said: "You've left The Times?" She had worked at the Times Of India since he'd known her.

"I had to," she answered. "It's getting harder and harder to do any real investigative journalism there. I made a call to Ajit and he gave me a job."

"A happy coincidence," Birla said. "We were looking for a seasoned investigative reporter to join our team in Mumbai and if Annie hadn't called us we would have called her. She did some very impressive work at the Times."

"She is fearless," Sansi said.

"We are counting on it," Birla said. "Indian politicians speak only two languages -money and shame."

"Give them enough money and they can live with the shame," Annie said.

Birla seemed to sense some reticence between Sansi and Annie and that his presence might be the cause. "I see someone I have to speak with if you will excuse me a moment," he said and melted into the crowd.

"I think he might be the most intuitive man I've ever known," Annie said, switching to English. "Among other things."

There shouldn't have been any awkwardness between them. She and Sansi continued to see each other occasionally but always in the company of other people. And this was the first time he'd seen her with another man.

"So, you've decided to stay," Sansi said.

"I have."

"You weren't so sure the last time I saw you."

"A few weeks in L.A. were enough," she said. "I loved spending time with mom and dad and my sister - who is married now and pregnant so I'm going to be an aunt soon. But after a few weeks I knew where I really wanted to be. Anyway, there's more job security here. American newspapers are closing all over the country. Another few years and all the afternoon dailies will be gone. They've cut back on their bureaus, they get most of their national and international news from news agencies. A lot of people I knew at the LA Times have been bought out. There's less money for serious journalism. It's all entertainment and gossip now."

"There is plenty of gossip here too," Sansi said. "You can't get away from it."

"It comes down to those few media owners still in a position to support real journalism," Annie said. "Lucky for me Ajit is one of them."

"I'm glad you came back," Sansi said. "I like having you here - and India needs you."

People had begun moving to their tables. Birla reappeared out of the crowd. "We should take our seats before the show starts," he said.

"Is Pramila here?" Annie asked Sansi.

"Of course," Sansi answered. "She's backstage visiting with Shallu."

"I should have guessed," Annie said. "I'd love to catch up with her afterwards."

"She is hosting an after show party for Shallu at Malabar Hill, you are both very welcome to come."

"We might take you up on that," Annie said.

"It was a pleasure to meet you," Birla said.

Sansi watched as Birla placed his hand familiarly on Annie's back and steered her to their table. As he made his way across the ballroom Sansi wondered how usual it was for the owner and managing editor of India Today to fly from New Delhi to Mumbai to take a new reporter to dinner and a show at the Taj. He thought Birla was married but that didn't seem to count for much anymore. It bothered him that Annie had used 'we' when she responded to his invitation to come back to Malabar Hill. It bothered him more later when they didn't show up.

*   *   *

The next morning Sansi took a taxi to Arthur Road Jail halfway up the lobster claw peninsula that was Mumbai. It was the oldest jail in Mumbai and held 3,000 prisoners in a space built for 800. Its crusty stone walls were reinforced by safety barriers and razor wire but the city pressed in on all sides with teeming alleyways and apartment buildings. Police patrols armed with automatic weapons circled the perimeter.

Sansi skirted a knot of khaki clad police officers outside the main entrance and made his way to a reception area where a guard ran a detector wand over him while another went through his briefcase. The admissions officer told him Sunil Shah was allowed official visitors only. Sansi explained that he was an official visitor and slid a couple of thousand rupee notes across the counter. The officer issued him a pass and had a guard escort him to Shah's cell. Sansi had been unable to get Shah out of his mind since his meeting with Samant. The poacher was hardly a sympathetic figure but he did not deserve to be used as a puppet by Congress, Jatkar and the BJP anymore than Sansi did. Risky as it was for Sansi to be seen helping Shah it was a risk he was willing to take on his own behalf. As Samant said, the opportunity to talk to a man like Shah, who knew as much as he did about politicians and the police, didn't come along often.

Most prisoners were housed in barracks rife with rape, HIV and exotic new strains of tuberculosis for which there were no known cures. But gangsters with money had their own cells and access to every amenity. Sansi followed the guard along a web of dusty pathways to Anda Block where the rich and connected prisoners were housed. The guard took him as far as the entrance to Anda Block and Sansi gave him 500 rupees. Inside the prison walls there was no further need for discretion. Bribes were no more than tips for services rendered. A block guard took Sansi inside. Anda block was shaped like a wheel with cells radiating out like spokes from a hub. If it weren't for the barred gates it could have been a hotel. It was clean and well lit and cells were stocked with snacks, cigarettes and liquor. All had hotel beds instead of prison bunks and most had their own bathrooms. The walls were decorated with posters of sports stars and Bollywood starlets. Stacks of empty tiffin boxes suggested inmates of Anda block didn't rely on prison food. Sansi knew these men had ganja, hashish and women delivered to their cells too. Even in maximum security *hafta* opened every door.

The block guard walked Sansi to Shah's cell where he found the poacher seated cross legged on his bed playing cards with a couple of goondas, muscle hired from the prison population. Inmates of Anda Block didn't wear prison uniforms and Shah wore blue kurta pajamas he'd had delivered. If he wasn't so well known he could have passed for a visitor. His two *goondas* wore loose white inmate uniforms. Unlike many cells his cell was locked for his own protection. The guard told Shah he had a visitor and, without looking, Shah put up a finger telling them to wait. Shah and his *goondas* were playing *Teen Patti,* a three card version of poker. He threw a couple of hundred rupee notes into a money pile on the bed and was called. He played the 6, 7 and 8 of spades but was beaten by three fives. With an oath he got off the bed, walked over to the gate and looked Sansi up and down.

"I don't know you," he said.

"No, but I know you and I know powerful people who have an interest in what happens to you," Sansi said.

Shah waggled his head as if to say it was about time. The guard unlocked the gate and Sansi stepped inside. One of Shah's *goondas* went to search him and this time it was Sansi who put up a finger. Shah told his hirelings to step outside for a smoke while he and Sansi talked. The guard locked Sansi in with Shah. From the open door of a cell across the corridor a man said: "Watch what you say to him, Sunni, he's a cop."

Sansi turned and recognized the squat, powerfully built man with a full black beard and a head as bald as a betel nut. Edi Bheru, a gangster who ran the airport rackets in Mumbai and continued to run them from prison despite a 30 year sentence for murder.

"Is that right, you're a cop?" Shah asked.

"I was a cop a few years ago," Sansi said. "I am a lawyer now." He took out his I.D. card and showed it to Shah.

"So you're a bigger crook," Shah said. He opened a half sized refrigerator and offered Sansi a cold drink. Sansi declined. Inside the fridge he saw bottles of beer and soda. On top of the fridge was a bowl of mangoes and bananas. Shah took out a bottle of Limca, twisted off the cap and flicked it into a garbage can. He sat on the bed, back to the wall, took a swallow of the fizzy lemon-lime soda and set the bottle on a bedside table where there were a couple of bottles of Bagpiper whiskey, one of them nearly empty, and an open carton of *bidis*. In a corner there was a mobile cabinet with a TV and above it shelves packed with DVD's. Sansi sat on a scuffed wooden chair and put his briefcase on the floor beside him. The two men studied each other. Sansi was struck by how small and slight Shah was despite his fearsome reputation.

"Who sent you?" Shah asked.

"Nobody," Sansi said. "I am here entirely on my own account."

"You said you know powerful people who can help me."

"I said I know powerful people who have an interest in what happens to you," Sansi said. "It is not the same thing."

Shah thought of the unanswered messages he'd sent to Bandhu Kulkarni, the Congress Party member of the state legislature for Pune. He'd paid Kulkarni and others countless lakhs of rupees over the years and now he needed them they were nowhere to be found.

"What are you doing here, looking for business?"

"You are a man in an unusual predicament," Sansi said. "There are two groups of powerful people in Mumbai who have completely different ideas about what to do with you. That could be made to work to your advantage but only for a time. I might be able to help you but that depends on what you tell me. What I will tell you is it is very much in your interest to be candid with me because you will not have this opportunity again."

"So what can you do for me?" Shah asked.

"Let me make something clear," Sansi said. "I don't like you and I don't like what you've done. The reason I am here is because of the way your situation has been turned into a political game between the government and the BJP. Congress wants to use you for a show trial to make them look good in time for the next election. The BJP thinks you know something they can use against Congress so they can win the election."

"There is an election?"

"There will be some time in the next six months. By putting you on trial and seeing that you are severely punished they can say they are cracking down on crime and that always plays well with the voters."

"I think I am liking the BJP better than Congress," Shah said.

"I thought you might," Sansi said. "The problem with the BJP is once they have what they want from you they will drop you like a hot coal."

"So you can make a deal for me," Shah said.

"There is a deal to be made here but I don't think it is a deal you are going to like."

"What kind of a deal?"

"A deal that gives me what I want," Sansi said. "What I want is for the government and the BJP to stop interfering in the judicial process so there can be a trial that is fair and is seen to be fair. But a fair trial won't give you what you want either. You will stay in jail, probably for a long time."

"You are right, I don't like it," Shah said. "And you can fuck your mother."

"Here is something else you are not going to like," Sansi said. "You don't have much of a choice so you really should try and keep on my good side."

Shah eyed Sansi sullenly. He got up, went to the refrigerator, took out a wad of *paan* and wedged it into his cheek, seeking a boost from the betel juice.

"I don't need you," he said. "I could go to the newspapers, tell them how the cops massacred my men in Karnataka."

"The official version is that there was an exchange of gunfire between your gang and the police."

"That is a lie."

"You can take your story to the papers if you want," Sansi said. "I am sure they will publish it and it will be the talk of Mumbai for a day or two. But I doubt it will make much difference to your situation because the only people hated more than the cops in India are *dacoits*."

"You don't care about a fair trial either, you're here playing your own little power game," Shah said. "Doesn't it seem strange to you that I was taken without a scratch but every one of my men was killed and not one cop was wounded? It wasn't just the local cops. The cops from Mumbai knew. They were there. The cop who brought me back, Chowdhary, he had to know what was going on. And Jatkar, the big boss at Crime Branch, he knew."

"Alright. "Sansi took a pen and legal pad from his briefcase. "Tell me what happened."

Shah chewed for a while, savoring the sweet and sour tang of the betel juice. "The cops were waiting for us when we came out of the forest. They said my men would not be harmed if I told them to give themselves up. So, my men put down their guns and came out and the police shot them down like dogs. Now I am Shah the traitor."

"How did you get away without being harmed?"

"There was a cop inside my gang, an informer. He was riding with me in the first truck. When we came to the roadblock he put a gun to my head and brought me out first."

"What happened then?"

"There had to a hundred cops, all of them armed. They were ready for something. The cop in charge, his name was Adiga, he said if I got my men to come out peacefully they wouldn't be hurt."

"Then what?"

"What could I do? I told my men it was okay, they could come out. The cops wouldn't hurt them. Then they turned me over to Chowdhary."

"To come back to Mumbai, straight back?"

"They had a car waiting to take me to the airport."

"So you didn't see what happened to your men?"

"They put down their guns and came out. I had just got to the car when the shooting started. I knew what it was. It was only coming from one side. They massacred my men and they knew in advance that was what they were going to do."

Shah knew Sansi was right when he said there was little public sympathy for *dacoits*. That didn't mean it was okay for the police to massacre them once they'd surrendered.

"If what you say is true..."

"It is true," Shah cut in.

"Were you questioned when you were brought back to Mumbai?"

"*Acha*, by Jatkar."

"What did you tell him?"

"I didn't have to tell him anything, he knew everything."

"That is his permanent condition," Sansi said. "Did you tell him what happened to your men?"

"I told him. He said I should consider myself lucky I was still alive. Then he paraded me in front of the newspapers and the TV cameras."

"Well, the way it stands now he has the testimony of an undercover police officer and a hundred other cops at the scene. There are no independent witnesses and only your word against his. You can complain about what happened to your men as much as you want and I can tell you now it won't go anywhere."

"Doesn't it bother you that they killed all my men?" Shah said.

"It bothers me a great deal," Sansi said. "But I am here to talk about what can be done, not what can't be done."

Whatever had brought Sansi to see him Shah knew now he would have to stay in jail longer than he thought. There was nobody on the outside who could help him anymore. Not the politicians he thought he had in his pocket, not the sons who would tell no-one he was their father. All he had now was the money he had hidden away. The hard part would be staying alive till the day came when he could use it to get out.

"You have to give me something that can be substantiated," Sansi said. "As I understand it you have firsthand knowledge of corruption in the government."

"I paid politicians for 30 years," Shah said. "I can give you the name of one who is still there in the *Vidhan Bhavan*. I can prove he took my money. I wrote the numbers down."

"Write his name down for me," Sansi said and proffered the notepad and pen.

Shah stared at them. "I can only do numbers," he said. "I can read a little but I can't write."

"Alright." Sansi leaned toward him. "Tell me his name."

Shah lowered his voice. "Bandhu Kulkarni. He is from Pune."

Sansi wrote it down though he didn't recognize it. "It is a start but it is not enough on its own. I have been told you did favors for Congress Party members all the way up to the Cabinet. That you provided them with underage girls."

"I never did that," Shah said. "I trade in sandalwood. I paid money to Kulkarni and gave him and some of his friends sandalwood but that was all. Sandalwood and money."

"What are you saying, Sunni?" A voice from outside intruding on their conversation. "What are you telling him?"

Edi Bheru had approached Shah's cell unnoticed.

Shah spat a jet of betel juice at him like a cobra spitting venom. Bheru twisted away cursing.

"You're going to have to give me more than this," Sansi continued.

Shah thought for a moment. "I can give you something more. It doesn't have anything to do with me but I can give you the names of two bigwigs in the government who have been taking bribes from the biggest developer in Mumbai. Is that the kind of thing you want?"

"It might be," Sansi said. "What are their names?"

Shah lowered his voice again. "One is Aadekar, the other is Dubade. Are they big enough for you?"

Gaurav Aadekar was the Minister for Housing and Hemant Dubade the Minister for Urban Development. Both were ministers in the state Cabinet and both wielded a lot of power in deciding which developers got their projects approved in Mumbai.

"They're good cards, hey?" Shah said. "Two jacks? Two kings maybe?"

"Can you prove they took money?"

"They didn't take money, it was something worth more than money. It was property. That is where the big money is in Mumbai today isn't it? They both got apartments for themselves in new apartment blocks. They put them in the names of their wives and kids but you can find that kind of thing, can't you? You can prove that?"

"What is the name of the developer?" Sansi asked.

Shah hesitated. "You know him. He is the biggest developer in Mumbai. Everybody knows his name."

"Tell me," Sansi said and leaned closer.

"If it gets out that I gave you his name he could get to me in here," Shah said. "He has enough money to buy the whole prison."

"Tell me and I might be able to arrange protection for you."

Shah smiled a bitter smile. "He will find a way."

"None of this is without risk," Sansi said. "To either of us."

Shah thought about it. Whatever happened he had no intention of growing old in jail. He leaned closer and whispered the name "Pujari."

Rushil Pujari was the head of Akasha Industries, a multi-national with branches throughout Asia. His construction company had been especially aggressive in the Mumbai property market in the past 10 years. If Pujari had bribed two Cabinet Ministers with free apartments they were bribes that could be measured in millions of rupees.

"Let me think on it," Sansi said.

Shah eyed him suspiciously. Sansi knew he was wondering if this lawyer was telling the truth or if he had his price too.

Sansi put his notepad back in the briefcase and called the guard to let him out. Across the corridor Edi Bheru glared at him.

"Try not to make too many enemies while you are in here," Sansi told Shah.

When he left the prison Sansi walked down to Sane Guruji Marg to get a taxi, heedless of the noisy swirling crowds. He was more alive than he'd been in years.

*   *   *

Back at Lentin Chambers Sansi found a sheaf of message slips waiting for him.

"Commissioner Jatkar from Crime Branch called about half an hour ago," Bansari said as she handed over the slips. "He asked that you call him as soon as you came in. He said this is his direct line."

Sansi asked Bansari to bring him some tea and went to his office. Somebody must have called Jatkar within minutes of Sansi leaving Shah's cell. Sansi drank half his tea before punching in the numbers. It rang twice.

"Jatkar." The same confident tone.

"George Sansi returning your call, Commissioner."

"George Sansi, legal confidant to Mumbai's rich and infamous?"

"Only if you are in need of a divorce," Sansi said.

"I couldn't afford your fees," Jatkar said.

Jatkar also had a lawyer in the family. His son had a law degree from Harvard and worked for a Mumbai law firm that specialized in financial law, the kind of firm Mukherjee would prefer to be with.

"How can I help you, Commissioner?"

"There is something I want to discuss with you person-to-person," Jatkar said. "Can you come to the house tonight?"

"Are you still at Cumballa Hill?"

Jatkar's wife, Malti, came from old money. Her father had given them the house on Cumballa Hill as a wedding gift 30 years ago.

"The same old place," Jatkar answered. "Come around seven."

The same old place, as Jatkar called it, wasn't the grandest house on Cumballa Hill but it was on a quiet, tree lined street and in Mumbai peace and quiet were priceless. Sansi arrived by taxi a few minutes before seven. The taxi driver dropped him off on the street because there was only one entrance to Jatkar's residence and it was blocked by a police car and a half dozen armed officers. More officers were posted at intervals in front of a spiked iron railing along the road and there would be others throughout the grounds.

Sansi strolled up the darkened driveway to where it looped around a grassy island where there was a lone toddy palm whose skirts rustled in the inshore breeze. The driveway passed under a broad portico that offered shelter from the sun and the monsoon. An elegant bungalow built in the 1880's for the chief engineer of the British consortium that built the peninsular railway it had been picked up for a song by a director of Tata Steel just before Independence. The house was dark except for a few lights in the portico and an inside hall. Broad stone steps led up to double doors flanked by a pair of green marble elephants. Jatkar's police guard had alerted him to Sansi's arrival and he was waiting at the top of the stairs. The Commissioner looked sleek and relaxed in white *kurta pajamas*. There was more silver in his hair since Sansi had last seen him but Sansi was older too.

"It's good to see you again," Jatkar said and patted Sansi's shoulder, a gesture as intimate as it was unexpected. "You've been here before haven't you?"

"Once, many years ago," Sansi said.

"More than that, surely," Jatkar said. "Come, we'll go through to the verandah."

The high ceilinged vestibule was flanked by open arches. Facing the front doors was a wood carving of Shiva poised in his wheel of fire. Jatkar led Sansi through rooms of imposing decor that had a museum quality about them. The house was quiet except for the whisper of ceiling fans. There was no sign of Jatkar's wife, Malti, and if there were servants they had been banished to their quarters.

Jatkar stopped at a small ornate bar in the corner nearest the doors to the verandah.

"Would you like a drink, you're a scotch and soda man aren't you?"

"Only the soda these days," Sansi said. "And a dash of lime if you have it."

"The restraints of moderation bestowed upon us by age," Jatkar said. He took a couple of chunky glasses off a shelf. "Would you like ice?"

"Thank you."

Jatkar poured some lime cordial into one glass, added ice and soda and gave it a stir. He poured a scotch for himself. He carried the drinks out to the verandah and Sansi followed. The verandah was at the back of the house, its lights invisible from the front. There was a jumble of rattan chairs and sofas littered with cushions, books and papers. It looked like the most lived-in room in the house. The bottom half of the outside wall was teak panels, the top half shutters. The shutters were open but wire mesh screens kept the mosquitoes out. A pair of swing doors led to a set of wooden steps and a gently sloping lawn enclosed by cassias, mango trees and a majestic banyan. Through the branches the lights of container ships queuing up to enter the Port of Mumbai glimmered like a bead necklace cast upon the sea.

"We can sit here." Jatkar steered Sansi to a round bamboo table. The two sat down and Jatkar raised his glass. "Cheers," he said. The Raj was long gone but the echo of empire still resonated among India's elite.

"How long has it been since we last saw each other?" Jatkar asked.

"Close to four years, I think."

"That long?"

"The free port in Goa."

"That's right, of course."

The Commissioner had asked Sansi to investigate a land sale racket in Goa linked to a Cabinet minister in Maharashtra. Sansi had expended a great deal of time and effort only to have Jatkar shut the investigation down when the minister was murdered. The free port was never built and corruption followed the course of least resistance to new opportunities.

"How are you enjoying the practice of law?" Jatkar asked.

"It has its rewards," Sansi said.

"If measured in money," Jatkar said. "But that is not you, is it, Sansi? Only you could land on your feet and hate every minute of it."

"How do you know I hate it?"

"I go to more bar association dinners than you do."

"I spend enough time with lawyers at work."

"When you were at Crime Branch you hardly ever went home."

"Perhaps there is something to be said for the company of honest criminals."

"Admit it, Sansi, you don't have the temperament for lawyering."

"I like being my own boss."

"A rickshaw driver is his own boss but he's still a rickshaw driver."

Sansi had a mental picture of himself pulling a rickshaw with Mrs. Deshpande in the seat behind flicking a whip at him.

"You've stayed with it longer than I expected," Jatkar said. "It must be that British stubbornness you inherited from your father."

Sansi was a child of scandal; an affair between his mother and General George Spooner in the turbulent last days of the Raj. He carried his father's genes in his blue eyes, a reminder that he lived on the cusp of two worlds.

"It is admirable in its way," Jatkar added. "But not when you are wasting your talents doing something you don't like and for which you are so eminently unsuited."

"And what am I suited for?"

"You are a policeman, Sansi, and you know it. You are a competent lawyer at best but a brilliant policeman. The best I have ever known. You can stay a lawyer and you will always be one of many. I can give you something more - the chance to make a difference. That's what you really want, isn't it? You had a career at Crime Branch before, you could have it again if you want."

"You are inviting me back to Crime Branch?" Sansi said, astonished.

"I am offering you power," Jatkar said. "You can't get anything done without power and there are only two institutions in India that can give you that power, the government and the police."

"You do remember why I left?" Sansi said. "It was because of political interference in police business. And from what I've seen these past weeks nothing has changed."

"You can't change anything from the outside, Sansi, you know that. You want change you have to be on the inside."

"Why should I believe that is any more possible now than it was before?"

"Because I am going to give Crime Branch to you," Jatkar said. "If you can't change it then you will have no-one to blame but yourself."

Sansi was so astonished he was momentarily lost for words.

"I have made plans," Jatkar smiled. "You could be an important part of those plans."

"What sort of plans?"

"In two to three years I will leave Crime Branch to take up a career in government. Before I go I want to make sure Crime Branch is in the hands of someone I can trust."

There had been speculation about Jatkar's political ambitions for years but, to the best of Sansi's knowledge, the commissioner had not shared those ambitions with anyone. And certainly nothing so definite as a timetable.

"Who else knows this?" Sansi asked.

"Only my wife," Jatkar said. "And now you. That should tell you how much confidence I have in you."

"I am more than a little surprised," Sansi said.

"That I trust you?"

"Actually, yes. We haven't always seen eye to eye."

"That is why I want you to replace me at Crime Branch. Whatever happens I can depend on you to always be you. You won't do anyone any favors, Sansi. Me or anyone else. You will annoy everyone equally. That makes you the perfect choice."

Sansi was too amazed to be offended.

"I will bring you back with your old rank of Inspector," Jatkar said. "Sometime in the next six months Athawale will call an election. My expectation is that he will be re-elected but if he isn't it won't make any difference. After the election I will promote you to Chief Inspector and begin my transition to Congress. Before I leave I will announce you as my successor at Crime Branch."

"You think the Commissioner of Police and the Director-General will view me as an acceptable choice?"

"The Commissioner will do what the Director-General tells him to do and the Director-General will do what the Chief Minister tells him to do," Jatkar said. "The Chief Minister will do what I tell him to do."

"Does Athawale know any of this?"

"Athawale knows what he needs to know."

Sansi knew Jatkar would not be speaking with such confidence if he did not already have the backing of Congress Party chiefs.

"This is a lot to consider all at once," Sansi said.

"It is also a very big commitment I am making to you, Sansi. This offer is between you and me. No-one else can ever know. I would like an answer in one week."

"I won't discuss it with anyone," Sansi said. "I must tell you, this is not the conversation I thought we would be having."

"What were you expecting?"

"I thought you wanted to speak to me about my visit to Sunni Shah this morning."

"I'm not worried about that," Jatkar said. "I think it would be a mistake for you to represent him if that is what you are thinking of doing but if you take my offer it ceases to be an issue."

"I don't know if there is much I can do for him," Sansi said. "The BJP asked me to speak to him. They wanted to see if he had any dirt they could use against Congress in the election. I told them I wasn't interested. My interest is that Shah gets a fair trial. That Congress doesn't turn it into some kind of political *tamasha*."

"He will get a fair trial, for all the good it will do him," Jatkar said. "The poaching charges are just the beginning. We will be bringing further charges of murder while committing *dacoity* and that is a capital offence. He and his gang killed police officers, Sansi. He is going to hang."

"You have already decided?"

"He is guilty a thousand times over," Jatkar said. "Believe me, Sansi, you don't want to dirty your hands on this one."

"What if he had something to offer in exchange for a guilty plea?"

"There is no plea agreement to be made here."

"That is for the public prosecutor to decide isn't it?"

"I would oppose a plea agreement for Sunni Shah with all the powers I have at my command."

"Do you want to know what he has to offer?"

Jatkar looked skeptical. "What?"

"He has information on two serving Cabinet Ministers who took bribes in the form of free apartments from Rushil Pujari," Sansi said. "He will give up the names and plead guilty in exchange for a lighter sentence."

"You are missing the point," Jatkar said. "We don't want to make a deal, we want to go to trial. Athawale is counting on it for his re-election. We're not going to throw that away."

"You don't care about the two cabinet ministers?"

"I didn't say that. My guess is he already gave you their names. Accept my offer and we can act on them anyway. You don't owe Shah anything."

"That is exactly the kind of attitude that would make me think twice about coming back."

"Sansi, make up your own mind," Jatkar said. "You usually do."

"Shah told me something else too. He said the cops in Karnataka shot his men after they put down their weapons and gave themselves up."

"He told me the same thing."

"Did you know ahead of time they were going to do that?"

"Of course not. I would never go along with anything like that."

"But you followed it up?"

"I debriefed Chowdhary when he got back from Karnataka with Shah. He told me nothing happened till after they'd left the scene. So Shah didn't see anything. He's looking for something he can grab onto. Anything he thinks might be negotiable. He's using you, Sansi, isn't it obvious?"

"What did Karnataka Crime Branch say about it?"

"I talked to Commissioner Adiga. He said it started with Shah's men. One of them panicked and started shooting and Adiga's men returned fire. I am inclined to believe him before I would believe Shah. And so will the court."

"He is well aware of that."

"Shah is not the popular figure he still thinks he is, Sansi. He ran out of friends a long time ago. You are the only man in India who cares what happens to him."

"Would it bother you if I try one more step?" Sansi asked. "If I take it to the Advocate-General?"

"To Deshmukh?" Jatkar said.

Advocate-General Abhay Deshmukh was one of the highest legal officers in Maharashtra and acted as a liaison between the state and the federal government on sensitive judicial cases.

"If that is what you want I will make the appointment for you," Jatkar said.

"Then we will have exhausted every avenue," Sansi said. "And we will both have clean hands."

Britain had taken much from India but had given much in return. One of those gifts was the High Court Of Bombay. Built in 1878 it was a High Victorian confection of towers, spires, arches, flying buttresses and colonnaded walks. It overlooked the Oval Maidan where several games of cricket were always underway and was within comfortable walking distance of Sansi's office. The clamor of the city fell away when Sansi entered the high walled courtyard and in the pillared halls the majesty of the Raj sounded in every footfall.

The office of the Advocate-General was on the first floor. It was Friday afternoon and Abhay Deshmukh wanted to get away early. His wife was throwing a birthday party for their eldest daughter and he wasn't pleased at having to extend his schedule to accommodate Sansi. But Jatkar told him it involved the high profile Shah case and his opinion would be valued. Sansi was shown into Deshmukh's office a little after four in the afternoon. The Advocate-General was a heavyset man with drooping eyes. He wore dark suit trousers with a snow white shirt and a pearl grey tie. His manner was formal. A black leather briefcase sat on his desk ready to go, a hint to Sansi if one was needed. Deshmukh motioned Sansi to a worn leather couch and the two of them faced each other from opposite ends.

"What can I do for you, Mr. Sansi?"

"I believe Joint Commissioner Jatkar has spoken to you about the Sunil Shah case," Sansi said. "I have met with Mr. Shah and he is prepared to save the state a great deal of time and trouble by pleading guilty to the charges against him in return for leniency. Mr. Shah is a figure of national notoriety and there is a very real prospect that the state will yield to the temptation of evidentiary overkill in its prosecution of the case, which would result in Mr. Shah not getting the fair trial that a person of lesser notoriety would receive."

"That is a discussion you should be having with the Public Prosecutor, Mr. Sansi, not me," Deshmukh said.

"Under normal circumstances that would be the case," Sansi said. "But these are anything but normal circumstances."

"Not normal to Mr. Shah perhaps," Deshmukh said. "But to the court they are perfectly normal."

"Mr. Shah is also in possession of information that would be of considerable value to the state in return for mitigation of his sentence."

"What kind of information?"

"Information about the bribery of two serving cabinet ministers in the form of free apartments provided by a major property developer in return for improperly issued permits."

"You want to use me to blackmail the government?" Deshmukh said.

"Sir, not at all," Sansi said. "My representation here today falls well within the bounds of correct judicial discussion. Mr. Shah's offer would expedite the legal process and avoid the kind of show trial that continues to breed cynicism among the public when they see men like Mr. Shah prosecuted while those in power who took his money for years go unpunished."

"You have more than Shah's testimony about the alleged corruption of these two ministers?"

"Sunil Shah is a uniquely qualified informant," Sansi said. "Investigations have been initiated on much less."

"But you have nothing to put before me today in support of Mr. Shah's allegations?"

"No, but..."

"Mr. Sansi," Deshmukh stopped him. "I agreed to see you today as a courtesy to Joint Commissioner Jatkar. Based on what you have told me I see nothing that would compel the intervention of this office. Sunil Shah's notoriety is of his own making. The state has accumulated a mountain of evidence against him and the prosecution is entitled to present that evidence to the court and to the public. I would have thought that you of all people, given your history, would approve of that. Now, if you will excuse me..." Deshmukh got up to indicate the interview was at an end.

Sansi left the precincts of the high court stinging under the Advocate-General's rebuke. Power was a walled city and Sansi was on the outside.

*   *   *

The next day Sansi called Shah in prison and told him the outcome of his meetings with Jatkar and Deshmukh. Shah was surprisingly fatalistic and Sansi returned to his regular caseload believing there was little more he could do. Until a few days later Bansari told him a man who would not give his name was calling for Sansi from a hospital in Byculla and it sounded urgent. Sansi told her to put him through.

"This is Sansi."

"I work at the J.J. Hospital," said the voice at the other end, the voice of a nervous young man. "Sunni Shah was brought in last night. He wants you to come to the hospital right away."

"What happened to him?"

There was a pause at the other end. "He was stabbed."

"What condition is he in?" Sansi asked but whoever it was had gone. An orderly or porter perhaps. Someone

Shah had bribed to get a message out. Sansi hurried outside to get a taxi.

Byculla wasn't far but traffic was barely moving and the taxi made such slow progress Sansi got out and walked the last two blocks. Shah was in a top floor room with three armed police officers at the door. At first they were reluctant to let him in but relented when he explained who he was. Inside, the window blinds were down so the room was dark. Shah was in bed, propped up against a stack of pillows. His torso and right arm were heavily bandaged and he was on a heart monitor and a drip. He might have been dozing but his eyes flickered open at the sound of the door opening. They registered relief when he saw it was Sansi.

"What happened?" Sansi asked.

Shah's response was breathy and labored. "Edi Bheru...he paid off my goondas...he had a sword...he came at me with a sword...he stuck me through the chest...but I was quicker...I stuck a bottle in his neck."

"Did you kill him?"

"You don't give a man...a second chance...to kill you in prison."

"They will probably charge you with his murder."

"I have a hole in my lung...but they tell me...I'll live."

"If it is any consolation the government wants you alive."

"Long enough...to hang me."

"What can I do for you?"

"I want to...tell you something."

Shah was weakening and Sansi had to lean in closer.

"I'm not going to cover...for those bastards anymore."

Sansi listened keenly.

"You were right about the kids...I didn't do it...but they did...kids...drugs...everything."

"Who do you mean by 'they?' " Sansi asked.

"You have to find Shiney Borkar...that's how you get to Pujari."

Rushil Pujari was the name of the developer Shah had given Sansi at their last meeting. The name Shiney Borkar was new to him.

"Who is he, how do I find him?"

"He does the dirty work for Pujari...he knows them all...in the government... he gets them what they want...women...girls...boys."

"Are Aadekar and Dubade in on it too?"

Aadekar and Dubade were the two ministers Shah said had taken apartments as bribes from Pujari. This was the first suggestion they had other appetites that were met within the Pujari empire.

"They're in it...but there are more...all through the government...Shiney has a business...Enticing Escorts...it's in one of Pujari's buildings...at Nariman Point...you go there...it's all there."

If Sansi had the resources of Crime Branch at his disposal he could raid Enticing Escorts, seize its records and bring its employees in for questioning. But not as a lawyer. Not on his own.

"I will see what I can do," he said. "Try and get some rest. You're safe here."

                    *   *   *

Sansi went back to the office and tried to work but his mind kept returning to what Shah had told him and what, if anything, he could do about it. When he got home Pramila was out and he told Mrs. Khanna he didn't feel like eating. He went out to the roof garden and watched the ice in his tonic melt while he went over the possibilities. In the end it came down to a single phone call. Annie picked up on the second ring.

"I would like to see you," he said. "I may need your help with something."

"Of course," Annie said. "When do you want to get together?"

He heard voices in the background and realized it was a TV drama in Hindi. He could see her in her apartment, barefoot, loose top, red hair brushing her bare shoulders.

"Is it alright if I come over now?"

She hesitated but only for a second. "Yeah, that's okay."

Sansi hadn't been to Annie's apartment in two years. It wasn't deliberate on his part but since their lives had taken separate paths there'd been no need. It hadn't changed much; a modest one bedroom on an upper floor of one of the older apartment blocks in Nariman Point where rents kept going up no matter how many new apartment blocks were built to meet demand. It was where she'd lived since she'd first come to Mumbai. She had a conservative streak, he'd learned, and when she liked something she stuck with it. He often wondered how many other things there were about her that he didn't know.

"Can I get you a drink?" she offered.

"Tonic water if you have it," he said.

"I have it," she said. "Sorry about the mess, grab yourself a seat somewhere."

He'd been wrong about what she was wearing. She wore white jean cut-offs that showed off her legs and a pale green T-shirt with the word 'Outsourced' on the front. There was a newer, bigger sofa and an elegant coffee table that hadn't been there when he last visited. A warm breeze ruffled gauzy curtains at the door to the balcony and outside the lights of new apartment blocks crowded in on what had been her view. She wasn't watching TV anymore and her laptop was open on the table next to the kitchen counter. That was where most of the mess was; notebooks, papers, a recorder and a pile of mini cassettes. He took a seat on the sofa.

"Am I keeping you from working?"

"Yes," she said, "but I haven't really got into it yet so it's fine."

She brought his tonic water and took a seat across from him, folding her legs under her. He wished he was there on personal business.

"I have a favor to ask," he said. "A big favor. Too big perhaps and I will understand if you say no."

"Well, you've got my attention now," she said, "let's hear it."

Sansi told her about Sunni Shah, how he'd talked to Shah at Arthur Road Jail, how Shah had been attacked and what Shah had told him in hospital. He told her about Rushil Pujari and the bribes of senior government figures but kept back the names of the two cabinet ministers involved. He told her what Shah had said about getting to Pujari through a goonda by the name of Shiney Borkar and his escort agency, Enticing Escorts. Annie listened without reaction, her eyes fixed on his.

"I have been told to let it go," he said. "But I can't. It is not the scale of it that bothers me so much. It isn't even the money and the greed, that's everywhere. It is the ordinariness of it. The casualness of it. The fact that it is a part of everyday life. Senior government officials using children as sex toys in return for construction permits. Children treated as if they were just another thing, a commodity to be bought and sold. I can't turn away from that. I can't pretend it is acceptable. I keep having the same thought over and over. The people who sell children for sex are evil. And knowing about it and not doing anything about it makes me as evil as they are."

At first Annie had no reaction, then she emitted a long drawn out sigh. "Oh boy."

"I can't get it out of my mind," Sansi said. "All I can think of is what should I do and how should I go about it?"

"You do understand if you start something like this there's a very good chance it will take over your life," Annie said.

"I know," Sansi said. "I wasn't looking for this, it found me. And now I can't walk away from it. I have to do something."

"And you want my help in breaking it?"

"Breaking it...?"

"As a news story through India Today."

"No, no, it is too soon for any of that," Sansi said. "First I have to know if Shah is telling the truth. If he is I have to get some idea of how it works today. I have to get a look inside the system. To do that I have to pose as a potential customer. I will take a room at a hotel as a visiting businessman and I will call Enticing Escorts and see if they will send me an underage a girl."

"So where do I come in?"

"Any child who is brought to the hotel room of a stranger is going to be terrified," Sansi said. "I want you to come with me as a friendly female face. I think you will be able to reassure a young girl better than me that she is in safe hands. Your Hindi is good enough now, you could do that."

"Then what?"

"We take her somewhere safe. We talk to her, see what she can tell us about what happened to her, how she got into a place like Enticing Escorts and whatever she can tell us about the people who run it."

"Yeah, you're right, this is more than any favor anybody else ever asked me," Annie said. "And you know, if we do this, we make ourselves responsible for this child, whoever she is, and what happens to her afterwards."

"Yes, I know that," Sansi said. "I can afford to help a child. I will find her a safe place to stay and get her into a good school. I am prepared to accept the responsibility for all of that."

"Where would we take her from the hotel?"

"Actually..." Sansi looked around Annie's apartment. "I thought it might be easier for her if she could stay with you for a few days."

*   *   *

Two nights after his talk with Annie Sansi checked into The Majestic Hotel on Cuffe Parade. It was known as a hotel for traveling businessmen. A call from there wouldn't arouse suspicion. He arrived around seven in the evening wearing a suit he'd retired years earlier. He carried one of his older suitcases in which there was a popular Mumbai sex magazine, 100,000 rupees and two cans of pepper spray. Smoky blue wall tiles, a grey stone floor and sickly lighting gave the hotel lobby all the charm of a railway station at two in the morning. There was a small shop and newsstand and a gloomy restaurant whose kitchen, Sansi knew, had a back entrance. Three men stood talking by the newsstand, their voices amplified by the tiled echo chamber. When the desk clerk asked for an identity card Sansi lowered his voice and said the purpose of his visit was "confidential." He gave the clerk two thousand rupees, enough for one night and a substantial tip. To sign in he used the name Bobde, a fitness instructor at the police training academy whom he'd never liked. The clerk handed Sansi the keys to a room on the third floor and wished him a pleasant stay.

The elevator was poorly lit and smelled of onion bhaji. Sansi saw his reflection in the mirror and thought he looked seedy, the kind of man who would come to a hotel like this. He got out on his floor and the smoky tile motif continued, many of them cracked or with corners missing. He tried to remember how long the Majestic had been in business. He'd seen it as a boy when he rode the bus from Malabar Hill to school at Colaba. Back then it might have been a reputable hotel. His room was predictably drab, the furniture old and worn. The floor in his room was stone too so the room felt cold. He dropped his suitcase on the bed and turned on the TV. A house channel came on showing an English porn film whose performers suggested it was made in the 1970's. He switched to Zee TV and left it on then called Annie on his cell phone and gave her his room number. He opened his suitcase, took out the magazine and flipped it open at the back where he'd circled an ad for Enticing Escorts and put it on the desk by the room phone. Then he stood with his hands in his pockets and watched Zee TV while he waited for Annie. He had no intention of sitting on the bed or any of the chairs. Annie arrived after about half an hour.

"Classy place," she said. "I got hit on four times between the taxi and the elevator."

She was dressed all in black; jeans, sensible shoes and a hip length leather jacket zipped up to her throat. Her hair was tucked up under a baseball cap. She threw a pink plastic duffel bag on the bed.

"Let's hope all we need is in there," she said.

"Are you sure you are alright with this?" Sansi asked.

"I'm here, let's go with that."

"*Acha*, we should get on with it."

He used a handkerchief to pick up the room phone and punched in the number for Enticing Escorts. It rang briefly and then a woman answered.

"Enticing Escorts, what is your pleasure?"

"I am calling about an escort...for the evening." He tried not to sound too rehearsed.

"Of course sir, do you have a particular type of escort in mind?"

"A girl. I want a girl."

"What kind of girl would you like? Indian girl, European girl, Asian girl, natural blonde?"

"Indian is alright. But I want young. She must be young."

"Which do you prefer, over 18 or under?"

"I want a virgin. She must be a virgin."

"You want a virgin?"

"Yes."

A virgin would cost more but customers were not just paying for novelty, there was also a much reduced risk of catching AIDS. That drove the price of virgins up while scarcity drove their ages down.

"A virgin is very special, very expensive."

"How much do you want?"

"Forty thousand rupee for virgin," she said. "We take American dollar, Australian dollar, pound sterling, Swiss francs. Cash only, no traveler's check or credit cards."

"I can pay forty thousand rupees."

"You are staying at the Majestic Hotel?"

"Yes," Sansi said. She had the hotel on caller I.D.

"Give me your name and room number. Someone will call you back."

Sansi gave his fake name and put the phone down.

"They are going to get back to me," he said.

"Just listening to that made my skin crawl," Annie said.

"Mine too," Sansi said.

It was a long 20 minutes before the phone rang. It was another woman, older, and she used Sansi's fake name.

"We have a girl for you," she said. "Indian girl. Very nice girl. Obedient. Clean."

"She is a virgin?"

"She is one hundred percent virgin guaranteed."

"What is her age?"

"She is eleven years old. Very pretty girl. Very nice."

"When can you bring her here?"

"Our man will bring her to you in one hour. You can keep her for 12 hours. If you want more you pay more. If you want her for wife we talk new price then."

"You will bring her in one hour?"

"You have the money with you."

"I have it."

"Have a very pleasant evening sir."

Sansi and Annie passed the next hour restlessly. He switched the channel to CNN and they watched the news from around the world; war, natural disaster, political crisis in an unending loop. With the hour almost up Annie took the duffel bag into the bathroom and waited there so it would look like Sansi was alone in the room. After another 15 minutes there was a knock at the door. Annie hid behind the bathroom door leaving it ajar so the bathroom looked empty.

Sansi opened the door to a blocky man with a heavy mustache and unshaven jowls. He was wearing a pale blue tracksuit with stripes on the sleeves and legs. With him was a small figure in an orange sari, her head bowed.

"Are you Bobde?" the man asked.

"Yes."

"This is Usha."

The man prodded her into the room and followed, closing the door behind them. He put a hand under the girl's chin and tilted her face up. A small nut brown face crudely embellished with make-up and an orange *bindi* in the middle of her forehead. Her eyelids were shaded blue with gold crests at the corners. She wore glittery ear studs and her long hair was braided and hung down her back. On her feet were cheap orange slippers. A woman in miniature made to look like a whore.

"You see, very nice girl," the man said. "You want to take her in there and look her over?" He pointed his thumb towards the bathroom.

"She looks...alright," Sansi said.

"You have the money?"

Sansi picked up a wad of notes from the desk and handed it to him. The man counted it quickly, frowning whenever he came to a note that wasn't pristine. He had no scruple about delivering a child to whatever fate awaited her but he was fussy about clean bills. He shoved the money into a pocket.

"You keep her for twelve hours," he said. "You want her longer you call same telephone number." He patted the girl in the back, pushing her at Sansi. "You go with uncle now," he said. "You be nice for uncle."

When he'd gone the girl stood in the middle of the room staring at the stone floor. She was trembling and seemed scarcely to breathe.

"I am not going to hurt you," Sansi said. "I am not going to touch you. Nobody is going to hurt you, I promise."

He knelt slowly in front of her keeping as much distance as possible between the two of them. His instinct was to hold her and comfort her but he knew if he put so much as a finger on her it would only add to the terror she was feeling.

"I know you are frightened," he said "I want you to know that I am here to help you and to take you somewhere safe."

But she wouldn't lift her head to look at him.

"I have brought a friend with me, a very nice lady," he said. "She is going to take you to a place where you will be safe. We will make sure nothing bad happens to you."

The girl didn't move.

"I am going to ask this lady to come out now," Sansi said. "Her name is Annie...An-nee. She is going to help you change out of those clothes and she is going to take you to a nicer place not far from here."

The girl said something but so faintly it was inaudible. Sansi got up and turned the TV off. The room filled with silence.

"I'm sorry, I didn't hear you," Sansi said. "Could you tell me again?"

She spoke again without looking up. "I want to go home," she said. "I want my ma and papa."

Almost certainly it was her parents who had sold her. A bargain that would typically have been struck days, perhaps weeks before. All the parents had been waiting for was the call that there was a customer for her. The goonda would have paid them a few hundred rupees then taken her back to the agency to be tarted up before he delivered her to the hotel.

"I can't take you home but I promise you I will take you somewhere where you will be safe," Sansi said. "You have to be brave, try and be brave for just a little bit longer. I am going to bring out my friend now."

She looked up with apprehension as yet another stranger entered her life. Annie knelt down, put the palms of her hands together and bobbed her head in a gesture of friendliness she hoped the child would recognize.

"Namaste, Usha," she said. Speaking slowly in Hindi she said: "My name is Annie. The people who brought you here are bad people and this is a bad place for little girls. I am going to take you away from those people. I am going to take you to a place where you will be safe."

Usha stared back at her.

Annie got up slowly and took her by the hand.

"I'm going to take you into the bathroom now and I'm going to give you different clothes to put on and then we will leave here to go somewhere safe."

Usha allowed herself to be led into the bathroom. Once inside Annie shut the door and shook the contents of the duffel bag onto the counter. There were a couple of pairs of jeans, T-shirts, sweatshirts, baseball caps and flip-flops.

"I want you to try these on and see which ones fit you," she said.

Numbly the child allowed the red haired stranger to remove her clothes till she was down to her underwear. When Annie looked at her she saw only the frail body of a child. There was no woman that had begun to emerge. But the customers in this trade didn't want a woman, they wanted a child. And if the child was scared maybe that added to the thrill. Annie ran some warm water into the sink and dampened a facecloth

"I'm thinking there's a little girl somewhere under all that make-up," she said. Gently she washed off the make-up and the *bindi* then patted her dry with a towel.

"Okay, let's see which of these will fit." She held a pair of jeans against Usha but they were too big. The next pair were long but they fit at the waist and the cuffs could be rolled up. Annie pulled a T-shirt and a sweatshirt over Usha's head and tucked her hair inside so it couldn't be seen. She eased the little girl's feet into a pair of flip flops then put a baseball cap on her head, adjusted it so it fit snugly and folded the peak down to hide her face. It wasn't a perfect disguise but it would be enough to get her out of the hotel.

Annie stuffed the discarded clothes into the duffel and went to open the door but stopped when Usha looked up at her and said:"I want to go home."

Annie bent down and spoke softly to her. "Usha, even if I knew where your home is I couldn't take you there. I'm sorry, sweetheart, but home isn't safe for you anymore."

The little girl looked at her, bewildered.

"I'm going to take you away from here now," Annie said. "I'm going to take you downstairs and we're going to go out through the kitchen and I want you to hold onto my hand all the way and not let go."

She opened the door and led Usha out. Sansi was waiting with his suitcase. He handed Annie a can of pepper spray keeping one for himself.

"Let's hope we don't need it," he said. "Give me ten minutes."

He took the fire stairs down to the ground level exit. The door opened directly onto the street but the hallway was blocked by stacks of chairs. It took him a few minutes to move the chairs and as soon as he exited onto the street he went in search of a taxi. There were several in front of the hotel but he didn't want to take the chance that the goonda who had delivered Usha had hung around. He skirted the honking mass of traffic till at last he found a taxi. He climbed in the back and told the driver to go around the block. When they came to the alleyway that led behind the Majestic Sansi told him to take it but the driver balked.

"Sir, is not good area," he said. "Too many bad people…drug people…bad people."

"I'll double your fare," Sansi said.

"Sir, is too dangerous," the driver persisted.

"I'll pay three times your fare," Sansi said. "If that's not enough I'll get another taxi."

The driver sighed. "Sir, I am not liking it but I am doing it."

The driver pulled into the alleyway lined with shanties and lit by dozens of small cooking stoves. Gaunt faces slid past, *bidis* glowed in the dark. The taxi drew closer to the kitchen door at the rear of the Majestic but the way was blocked by a crowd. Sansi jumped out and pushed his way through. Outside the kitchen door there was someone on the ground. A man was bent over the still form and for an instant Sansi thought he was trying to help but then he realized the man was going through the victim's pockets. Sansi grabbed him by the shoulders and heaved him away so violently he tumbled over the ground scattering the crowd. Annie lay partially on her side, an arm outstretched, blood seeping from a wound behind her ear. Sansi held two fingers to her neck. Her pulse was strong. He looked for other signs of injury but could see none. He lifted her up and cradled her head in his lap and made sure she was breathing freely. Her eyes were closed as if she were sleeping. The can of pepper spray he'd given her lay nearby unused. And there was no sign of Usha. Sansi picked Annie up and carried her to the waiting taxi.

"I tell you, sir, this is bad place," the driver said. "Bad people, bad place."

Sansi laid Annie on the back seat and got in beside her and told the driver to go to Mumbai Hospital. Annie's eyes opened as the taxi pulled up to the hospital's main entrance. She looked dazedly at Sansi then was suddenly aware.

"Where's Usha?"

"You have a head injury," Sansi said. "We need to take care of that before we worry about anything else."

Despair merged into confusion on Annie's face.

"We were at the back door," she said. "Something must have happened but I don't remember…"

"Somebody hit you, probably from behind," Sansi said.

"They took her, didn't they…the bastards took her…?"

A nurse shaved her hair around the wound and gave her a tetanus shot. A doctor cleaned the wound and sutured it shut. It took more than Sansi expected, 20 sutures in all. She was groggy and the doctor said she might be concussed so she should stay overnight and she could be examined again in the morning. As groggy as she was she was still upset about Usha and a nurse gave her a sedative to help her rest. Sansi sat by the bed and held her hand till she drifted off to sleep. He stayed till almost dawn then told a nurse he would be back in the morning. He took a taxi home, showered, changed and left before his mother or Mrs. Khanna were awake. He was the first to arrive at Lentin Chambers and he let himself in and took in the morning papers. He made a cup of tea and went to his office, newspapers tucker under his arm. The tea was just what he needed and he sipped it slowly. His eyes burned and he tilted his chair back and closed them for a while. He knew he wouldn't sleep. His mind kept turning over the events of the past 12 hours thinking about what he should have done differently. He should have hired a couple of men himself. It was foolish to think the agency wouldn't have somebody stay behind to keep an eye on their investment. He heard Bansari and some of the other women arrive and the office came to life around him. He drank the last of his tea and looked over the front page of the Indian Express. The headlines were about a bribery scandal in New Delhi involving a new military aircraft contract. The Prime Minister promised an unflinching investigation. Sansi looked down the page and was jarred into wakefulness. Armed men had broken into J.J. Hospital and overwhelmed Sunni Shah's police guard leaving one officer dead. The story said Shah 's eyes and tongue had been cut out. The gangland punishment of the informer. Sansi stared at the newsprint till it blurred. Then he picked up the phone and called the number for Joint Commissioner Jatkar.

Chapter 3.

Sansi took Mukherjee to the kind of restaurant he hated, a hole in the wall where most of the diners were *kulis* and *dhobi-wallahs* who ate off banana leaves.

"Indulge me," Sansi told Mukherjee. "This is the last time you will have to come here."

Sansi had a fondness for such places. They brimmed with the life and color of Mumbai. Places where the breathe of the city could be felt, not the sterile air conditioned towers that sprouted up around them.

"How long have you and I been partners?" Sansi asked. "Five, six years?"

"It will soon be six years, Sansi-ji," Mukherjee answered. He wore a pale grey pinstripe suit, a blue shirt with white collar and cuffs and a tie with a silvery sheen. He sat with his hands on his lap, afraid of dirtying his cuffs on the scratched tin topped table.

"*Acha*," I thought it was something like that," Sansi said.

Mukherjee eyed him curiously, wondering what was coming.

"I am most pleased with your contribution to the firm," Sansi said. "You have invested a tremendous amount of energy and initiative in building up the practice. The last two years especially you have embarrassed me by contributing so much more than I have." He paused. "I do not think it is fair to let things continue like this and I have come to a decision. It is time I stepped aside and turned over the firm to you. You can buy me out for a half share over whatever period of time works best for you."

It was a generous offer. Sansi had plucked his junior partner from the swarms of law school students who hustled for business outside the city courts and started him off with a 20 percent share of the firm.

"You will be free to leave Lentin Chambers whenever you wish and take new chambers in one of these skyscrapers you have wanted for so long." Sansi said. "Just make sure you don't move into one where they didn't mix the right amount of cement and sand." Every so often one of the new tower blocks would collapse because of shoddy construction. "You can take the firm in a new direction, put all your energy into financial law if you like. A few years from now you will be too rich to speak to me."

Mukherjee was scarcely able to contain his joy.

"Oh Sansi-ji that is most excellent news," he said. "When do you think you will be leaving?"

Sansi smiled. "We can make the announcement when we get back to the office if you like. I will leave it to you to draw up the papers. I will need two or three weeks to put everything in order and reassign my cases. But I would like to be gone by the end of the month if you are agreeable. I realize it is quite a sudden transition but I will make myself available for consultation as long as you need me."

"Oh yes, indeed, Sansi-ji that is most agreeable," Mukherjee said. He went to clasp Sansi's hands in gratitude but recoiled as a waiter came to wipe off the table. "Will you be retiring from the law or is there something else you are preferring at this time in your life?"

Sansi sometimes wondered how old Mukherjee thought he was. "I am going back to my old job at Crime Branch," he said.

Mukherjee looked puzzled.

"The same job you left behind?"

"Yes, the same."

"But why Sansi-ji? Why would you be returning to a job where you were having so many difficulties and making so little money?"

"Perhaps the best way to put it is that I have always felt I have unfinished business there."

The waiter returned with two steel cups filled with water.

"After so many years what business can you have left there?" Mukherjee said.

"The kind of business that cannot be accomplished in private practice," Sansi said. "For some things you must have the authority of the state on your side to get anything done."

The waiter slid a banana leaf in front of each of them. He was followed by another waiter with a trio of steel pots hanging from a hook. Sansi and Mukherjee each took a serving of boiled rice. Other waiters circulated past their table with more pots. Sansi took servings of *aloo paneer* and *pani puri*. Mukherjee ordered the *chaat*.

"Please, do not think me impertinent Sansi-ji, but every time you are speaking about Crime Branch it is how dirty the politics there are. Something very big must have happened to make you want to go back to that."

"I don't think anything has changed in that regard," Sansi said. He had no intention of telling Mukherjee about his arrangement with Jatkar.

Mukherjee prodded his food suspiciously. "If nothing has changed then why go back?"

Sansi formed a wad of rice in his fingers and used it to scoop up a gob of *paneer*.

"Perhaps it is me who has changed," he said. "Perhaps I am no longer quite so fussy about getting my hands dirty."

*   *   *

Pramila went with Sansi to the hospital to collect Annie. She had a concussion and her doctor wanted to keep her in an extra day for observation. While there was no dangerous swelling of her brain she was warned that nausea, dizziness and blackouts might persist for days, if not weeks afterwards. Pramila had decided she would look after Annie at Malabar Hill. Annie had given her the keys to her apartment and a list of clothes and other things she would need.

When Pramila and Sansi arrived at Annie's room she was seated on the edge of the bed, dressed and ready to leave. She had told the nurse to shave all of her head so her hair would grow back uniformly and there was a large dressing above her right ear. It made her look vulnerable and Sansi felt wretched over it. She'd just started an exciting new job and now she had to take medical leave because she'd been injured helping him.

Even the short taxi ride to Malabar Hill made Annie queasy. Pramila took her directly to the guest room, closed the windows and pulled the blinds so she could rest. Sansi took the opportunity to go in to Lentin Chambers and begin the process of offloading his cases. He spent much of the afternoon calling clients and reassuring them that his replacements would take good care of them. He resisted the temptation to tell them that anybody could charge them a fortune and hold their hands while they went through a divorce.

When he arrived back home he found Pramila and Annie under a shade umbrella in the roof garden drinking chai. Mrs. Khanna brought out a fresh pot and a cup for Sansi.

"Feeling better?" he asked Annie.

"Quite a bit better," she said. "I slept for five hours straight. I didn't get that much at the hospital."

"How much recovery time did the doctors say you would need?"

"Two, three weeks."

"Annie I am so sorry," he said. "I should not have sent you downstairs with the girl. I should never have involved you."

"It was my choice," she said.

"The goonda who brought her to the hotel must have stayed around."

"You have to get her back," Annie said. "I don't know how you do it but you have to find that child and get her back."

"I will do everything I can to get her back..." He was about to use the word 'promise' but stopped himself.

"Do you think they might have hurt her? Punished her for trying to get away."

"It is impossible to say but my guess is probably not. They will have frightened her so she won't try it again. But I doubt they would do more than that as long as she's worth money to them."

"How could anybody hurt a child like that?" Annie said, her voice wavering. Her injury had brought her emotions close to the surface.

"If you can help one you help one," Pramila said.

For a moment the only sound was the gulls squabbling over scraps along the shallows of Back Bay.

"I suppose this is as good a time as any to share some news with you," Sansi said.

The two women looked at him as if daring him to tell them more bad news.

"I have decided to go back to Crime Branch," he said. "Joint Commissioner Jatkar made me an offer and I have accepted."

"Well, it's about time," Pramila said. "You've been impossible to live with these past two years."

"Really?" Sansi said. "I didn't think I'd been that bad."

"You are so like your father," Pramila said. "Little things would drive him mad - little men with their little problems he would call them. But give him something big to manage and it was a different story. He loved the war, he was in his element then. He positively glowed when he was getting ready for a battle. He was the calm at the center of the storm."

"It's a good move for you," Annie said. "You're going back to what you do best."

"I think I can do more good there than cleaning up messes made by spoiled rich people," Sansi said.

"It will be different this time," Pramila said. "You know yourself better."

"You could have said something sooner."

"I tried to give you the occasional nudge in the right direction," Pramila said. "But you're a grown man, remember? You're supposed to make these decisions for yourself."

Sansi got up and kissed his mother on the top of her head. "Always good to have your support, *maa*, even after the fact."

"However long it takes to get you there?" Pramila said.

Sansi smiled. "I'm going to have a shower before dinner." Dinner wouldn't be for another hour but it had been an eventful few days and he needed to retreat to his room and shut out the clamor of the world for a while.

Pramila followed him inside.

"George?"

"Yes."

She placed her hand on his chest. "You find that child," she said. "I don't care what it takes, but promise me you'll find that child."

"I will," he said. "I will find her, I promise."

*   *   *

From the outside Mumbai police headquarters was the same grey provincial English town hall it had always been. Inside it had been transformed. India had come late to the digital age but was modernizing at a rapid pace. Offices that had been drab and dim and cluttered with old furniture were now clean, brightly lit and equipped with the latest Indian made computer ware. Jatkar's second floor office had the same hulking mahogany desk but instead of manila folders and overflowing wire baskets there was a single computer. Instead of his heavy wooden chair he had a springy roller chair that allowed him to wheel around. As any good politician must Jatkar had reinvented himself. Sansi was 10 years younger but felt he had some catching up to do.

"You'll notice some changes," Jatkar said. "I assume you've kept up with technology?"

"I still type with two fingers if that is what you mean," Sansi answered.

"*Bakwas*," Jatkar scolded him. "If I can learn to keyboard so can you."

"Is it really that important?"

"Not especially but it sets a good example to the men."

"In my experience computers are wonderful for communications and research," Sansi said. "But until India can deliver reliable electric power I think it is wise not to become overly dependent on them."

"We are the police," Jatkar said. "The power will go out at the *Vidhan Bhavan* before it goes out here."

Sansi wasn't due to start for a few days but Jatkar had asked him to come in early and get acquainted with the new Crime Branch.

"I've pulled Chowdhary from his former duty and reassigned him to you," Jatkar said. "I think the two of you worked well together before and he will help with your re-introduction to Crime Branch."

"I could think of no-one better," Sansi said.

"He has been promoted to Assistant Sub-Inspector," Jatkar said. "You'll also have two constables and a secretary working for you."

"That is twice the personnel I had before."

"You will need them for the work I have in mind for you," Jatkar said. "Come with me, I'll show you around."

Sansi followed Jatkar outside, along the second floor verandah and down to the ground floor. There was no sign of the shrapnel scars that had pitted the walls of the Crime Branch building after a car bomb exploded on the parade ground when Sansi had last worked there. The grey stone walls had been restored and the white trim freshly painted. Jatkar cut across the parade ground to a separate building he said housed the Crime Branch cyber crime unit. A long, low ceilinged room it was equipped with rows of computers where young uniformed constables, including several women, tapped busily at their keyboards.

"They could be wasting their lives in Bangalore providing technical support for American computer companies," Jatkar said. "Here they can use their computing skills to do something important in the real world."

An officer came out of a glass walled office and saluted Jatkar. On each epaulette was the single star of an assistant sub-inspector. The name tag over his right chest pocket said his name was Gabale.

"Is there anything I can assist you with, sir?" he asked.

"Gabale I'd like you to meet Inspector Sansi," Jatkar said. "He will be joining us next week."

"Welcome to the cyber crime unit, sir," Gabale said to Sansi. "Is there anything you would like to know?"

"I would not know where to begin," Sansi said.

Jatkar tapped the shoulder of a young man seated nearby.

"What are you working on, Constable?"

"I am tracing stolen credit cards, sir," he said.

"How are you doing?"

"I am working with three others, sir," he said and nodded at the constables seated along from him. "We have been tracking a gang working the big hotels."

"When will you have some actionable information?"

"We are closing in on several suspects, sir. We should be able to move on them soon."

"How soon?"

"Within the hour, sir."

"Fighting crime in real time, that is the big difference," Jatkar told Sansi. "You are coming back at the perfect time. Crime Branch Mumbai can hold its own with Scotland Yard and the FBI now can't it, Gabale?"

"Oh yes sir, that is most correct," Gabale said.

Jatkar led Sansi from the cyber crime unit and walked him over to forensics. It was in the same grim building with the same green walls and the same stench of chlorine that could never quite eliminate the undercurrent of putrefaction. The autopsy room had been expanded and two post mortems were underway but Dr. Vyankatesh Ranjana, the Deputy Coroner of Mumbai, was in his office working at his PC. He greeted Sansi warmly. Ranjana was a little heavier and his hair and beard a little greyer but there was the same vital spark in his eye.

"I thought you were making too much money stealing from little old ladies to come back to Crime Branch," Ranjana said.

"It was the hardest money I ever earned," Sansi answered.

"Well, it serves you right," Ranjana said. "It will be good to have you back."

"I never thought I would say it," Sansi said looking around, "but it feels good to be back."

"Have you been assigned any cases yet?" Ranjana asked. "They doubled my budget and gave me two new assistants and we still can't keep up with all the murder and mayhem in Mumbai."

"I have more than enough to keep him busy," Jatkar said.

From forensics they returned to the Crime Branch building where Sansi's old office had been. His office was the fourth door along on the ground floor but Jatkar went in the third door and once inside Sansi saw why. A dividing wall had been torn down and two small offices turned into one large office. He recognized Chowdhary but there were also the two constables and civilian secretary Jatkar had told him about. They all stood up as Jatkar and Sansi walked in and Chowdhary and the two constables saluted. Sansi went directly to Chowdhary and shook his hand.

"How have you been, old friend?"

"Most well, Sansi-ji, and I am most excited at your returning," Chowdhary said solemnly.

"Congratulations on your promotion," Sansi said. "I am looking forward to the two of us working together again."

Sansi shook hands with his two new constables, Agarkar and Nimkar and with the secretary, Kapale. The walls had been whitewashed, the furniture was new and there were air conditioners instead of the old ceiling fans. Jatkar gestured to a glass cubicle at the end of the room.

"This is your new office."

Sansi stepped inside and felt as if he was in a fish tank. Everything was new; desk, chairs, computer, phone, even a pair of filing cabinets. A lot of money had been spent on Crime Branch since Sansi had last worked there.

"We have the best of everything now," Jatkar said.

"I can see that," Sansi said.

"Technology is tools and gadgets but a policeman's most powerful weapon is still his gut. How he reads people. How he reads a situation." Jatkar turned to the others. "Inspector Sansi is one of the finest police officers I have ever had under my command. He will expect each of you to give your best and so will I."

Sansi told them he would see them again soon and followed Jatkar back up to his office. Jatkar sat at his desk, opened a drawer and slid a black leather wallet to Sansi.

"There is your new badge," he said. "We will get your picture taken Monday and issue your new identity card."

Sansi turned the badge over in his hand, it was heavier than he expected.

"Do you still have your uniform?" Jatkar asked.

"I do," Sansi answered. "But for some reason it feels a little tighter on me."

"We'll get you measured for a new set of khakis. Some of the insignia has changed, we'll make sure you're up to date."

It wasn't critical. As a detective Sansi only needed a uniform for official and ceremonial occasions.

"I've compiled a shortlist of cases," Jatkar said. "We can go over them now or on Monday and set some priorities. Which do you prefer?"

"I think we should discuss them now," Sansi said. "Before we commit ourselves to anything I want to talk about Rushil Pujari's influence on the government and the two Cabinet ministers who have been taking bribes from him in the form of new apartments. It turns out they have been taking more than apartments. They have also been taking underage girls. And they are not the only ones. There are scores, perhaps hundreds of them, all through the government.

"This is based on information from Sunni Shah?"

"*Acha.* I saw him in the hospital after he was stabbed. He asked me to come down and see him."

"A deathbed confession?"

"He did not know he was on his deathbed at the time. He was still trying to make a deal."

"You think Pujari had him killed?"

"I know you and Athawale wanted to see him stand trial but there were others who didn't and they got what they wanted and you didn't and that should be a matter of concern to you."

"It is of concern to me," Jatkar said, a touch defensive. "It was Shah who told you about the underage girls?"

"*Acha.*"

"Then I have to ask you the same question I asked you last time, the same question Deshmukh asked you - where is your proof? Where is the evidence? Sunil Shah was a desperate man who would say anything to save his life."

"He told me some of the girls were provided by an escort agency called Enticing Escorts. A man by the name of Shiney Borkar manages it for Pujari. I know they provide underage girls because I bought one."

Jatkar's way of registering shock was to register nothing at all. After a moment he said: "What did you just say?"

"I bought an underage girl from Enticing Escorts last week," Sansi said. "I registered at the Majestic Hotel, called the agency, paid 40,000 rupees and they delivered an 11 year old girl to my room. I was going to take her somewhere safe and see what she could tell me, but they got her back."

"They got her back from you?"

"*Acha.*"

"How?"

"I asked a friend to help me. A woman who could reassure the girl she was going to be safe. I went out to get a taxi while she took the girl out the rear entrance but somebody saw her and attacked her and took the girl away from her."

"What woman is this you are talking about?"

"Annie Ginnaro. You've seen her name, she is an American reporter."

"Yes, she is your girlfriend."

"Not for a while," Sansi said. "But she is a friend, a good friend. She was helping me and she was hurt in the attack."

"How is she?"

"Someone left her with a nasty head wound and concussion. The doctors don't expect she'll be ready to go back to work for several weeks."

"*Are Bapre.*"

"I want to raid Enticing Escorts," Sansi said. "All the proof we need is there."

"It is not the role of Crime Branch to assist you in your search for revenge, Sansi."

"No, but it is you who will benefit from it the most, not me," Sansi said. "When you lost Shah you lost the show trial you and Athawale were counting on. If we can bring down a child prostitution ring that caters to men at the highest levels of government it will be the biggest show trial in years. You have to admit, Pujari is a much bigger name than Shah. I admit that it won't do much for Athawale but it will be a law enforcement triumph for you."

"Politics, Sansi...you?" Jatkar said.

"Politics are the art of compromise are they not?" Sansi said. "What I am proposing gets us both what we want."

Jatkar didn't have to think about it for long.

"*Acha*, you can have your raid. When do you want to go?"

"I want to go now."

"Now? Tonight?"

"Yes."

"You had better be right about this, Sansi."

Sansi got up to go.

"There is one more thing you could do for me," Jatkar said. "Stop referring to them as show trials, would you?"

*   *   *

Sansi's staff were embarrassed to be found drinking *chai* and talking about him when he came back. For Chowdhary it was like old times. He had told his new colleagues Sansi was a man who liked to get things done.

Sansi tasked his two constables, Agarkar and Nimkar, with pinpointing the location of Enticing Escorts. There was no address in the sex magazine ads and there was no company by that name in the state's company listings. There were several phone numbers for the agency but none of them had a Nariman Point prefix or a Nariman Point address. Sansi had them cross check company names linked to Pujari and they came up with more than sixty, half of them with Nariman Point addresses. In the past it would have taken days to run through them all but with computers they did it in under an hour. What was left was a single Nariman Point location served by 20 separate phone lines. Pujari's corporate headquarters had only 50. With 20 lines and numbers relayed through other exchanges an illicit business like Enticing Escorts could rotate numbers every few weeks to keep people like Sansi from finding out where they were.

The address was a 26 story tower with the 16 lower floors commercial and the top ten floors residential. Eventually they were able to place the agency on the twelfth floor but they wouldn't know which office suite on the twelfth floor till they got there. Sansi put Chowdhary to work organizing a raid for that night that would require a Special Unit team of 20 men and 60 uniformed officers. While his staff applied themselves to their first all nighter under Sansi he dug up a police file on Shiney Borkar. It told the story of a young goonda who started out in the Mumbai underworld as a low level enforcer for money lenders and drug dealers. He had been charged with assault many times only to have the charges dropped when no-one would testify against him. His sole conviction was 11 years earlier for illegal possession of two handguns. He served an 18 month sentence and, officially, hadn't been in trouble since. The file notes told a different story. He was active in the drug trade until he decided Mumbai's property market offered more money for less risk and struck out on his own. He muscled in on the construction business and, after a series of clashes with the gangs running the city's building sites, emerged the winner. He was now believed to have his own 'Goonda Raj' of some 200 men to enforce his will. The file photo showed a man of around 30, thin faced and dark skinned, his hair swept back from his forehead. He stared through the camera lens at whoever was standing behind it. Those caught at their worst but who looked defiantly back at the world were often the most dangerous.

Sansi set the raid for 10 p.m. when pedestrian and vehicular traffic would be light. Shiney Borkar had a lot of manpower at his disposal and the last thing Sansi wanted was a bloodbath on his first raid in six years. He sat up front in the truck that led the police convoy out of police headquarters at 9.30. With him in the truck were 10 Special Unit men led by Commander Wagli, wearing full body armor and heavily armed. They were followed by a second Special Unit truck with the rest of Wagli's men and three police buses carrying Chowdhary and the uniformed officers. At the rear was a bus that would be used to ferry prisoners to police headquarters. When they reached the building the driver of the lead truck bounced up over the sidewalk, sending passers-by scurrying, and stopped within 20 feet of the front entrance. The Special Unit men spilled out and quickly secured the lobby to prevent security guards triggering an alarm. Behind them the police buses blocked the street while the uniformed officers set up a cordon around the building and occupied the garage and stairwells. Sansi and Chowdhary rode an elevator to the 12th floor with Commander Wagli and half a dozen of his men. The rest of Wagli's men and 10 uniformed officers followed them. When they were all assembled Sansi deployed armed constables to guard the fire exits at opposite corners of the building then led the way along the main hallway. Each office suite was occupied and its business clearly identified. Except for Enticing Escorts. The only office without identification was Suite 1205. Sansi pressed an ear to the door and listened to the ringing of telephones and the background murmur of many voices.

Sansi doubted Borkar himself would be inside but warned Wagli there could be anything from two or three goondas to a dozen and to expect all of them to be armed. What he could be sure of was that there would be women answering the phones and an unknown number of prostitutes waiting to go out on calls. He reminded Wagli that the purpose of the raid was to acquire information and to avoid the use of deadly force if at all possible. He stood aside for Wagli's breach man to open the door. There was no knocking, no shouted warning and no battering ram. The breaching officer used a shotgun to blow the lock off and kicked the door open. Wagli rushed past followed by the rest of his men in combat stance shouting at those inside to stay where they were and put their hands in the air. They were met by stunned silence except for the subdued commentary of a Mumbai versus Chennai night cricket match on a wall mounted TV. Six or seven men sat around drinking beer and watching the match. They stared at the cops, put down their beers and slowly raised their hands. A woman stood frozen in the doorway to the kitchen. She dropped a glass she was holding and it shattered on the floor. Women appeared from adjoining rooms, terrified.

The door to one room was slammed shut from the inside. A couple of Wagli's men went to force it open, several women screamed and it looked as though panic was about to take hold. A couple of goondas seized the moment to make a run for a back exit.

Sansi grunted his disapproval, went to a set of wall switches and turned them all off, filling the room with darkness. He left it dark for a couple of seconds then switched the lights back on and did the same thing two more times until the threat of panic passed. The only sound in the room was the soothing monotone of the cricket commentator. Everyone, including Wagli and his men, stayed where they were waiting for the next move. Sansi turned off the TV and took up a position in the center of the room.

"I am Inspector Sansi of Mumbai police and you are all under arrest," he said.
"We have the floor secured and the building surrounded and this will go a lot easier for everybody if you remain calm."

Almost on cue the two goondas who had tried to escape by the rear fire stairs were brought back inside by the officers who had been waiting there.

"Each of you will give your name, each of you will be searched and each of you will be taken to police headquarters for questioning," Sansi said. "Your cooperation is appreciated."

With order restored Sansi had the Special Unit cops separate the men from the women and put them in different rooms. From the attitude of the men three of them were goondas and the rest were drivers. Sansi was gratified to see among them the man who had brought Usha to the hotel. He wore a green tracksuit this time but he was the same man and from the look in his eyes he recognized Sansi. There were 41 women, all but three of them escorts. Two of those were phone operators and the third, by her manner, was the madam. There were no young girls. No Usha.

A search of the men produced an assortment of knives and one spring loaded baton. The baton came from the goonda in the tracksuit and Sansi had it bagged for forensics in case it was the weapon used on Annie. Sansi spread their wallets across the kitchen counter and went through their contents. When the female officers arrived they used a couple of bathrooms to search the women. They turned up no weapons, just an assortment of meager personal effects; purses with a few rupees in them, combs, lipsticks, compacts, breath mints and condoms. All the girls wore bracelets with charms of Hindu gods that were supposed to keep them from harm. According to her identity card the madam's name was Bhadra Lele, or Madam Lele as the girls addressed her.

Sansi put Chowdhary in charge of evidence. That meant taking out every computer, storage drive, floppy disk and CD, every filing cabinet and the contents of every desk drawer and waste basket. Sansi had Madam Lele open the office safe. Inside were an automatic pistol and what looked like hundreds of identity cards. There were also passports, print-outs, brick size blocks of rupees and thousands in U.S. dollars, Australian dollars, British pounds and Swiss francs. Sansi was struck by how there had been no attempt to hide any of it. Enticing Escorts had never been raided and it appeared neither Madam Lele or her employers had any reason to believe it ever would be.

When the evidence had been collected, sealed and removed for further examination Sansi unplugged the phones in the call room so he could use it for preliminary interviews of a few key suspects. He had the three administrative women brought in separately, Madam Lele first. She said Enticing Escorts was a legitimate escort service that provided upscale companions for businessmen, visitors and foreign dignitaries. She said the agency did not use underage girls and there had never been a girl there by the name of Usha. Her two subordinates weren't so sure of themselves but they held to the same story. All they did was take calls and make bookings, they said. They too said nobody named Usha had ever worked at the agency. Sansi decided it was time to speak to the one man who knew, the goonda who brought Usha to his hotel room. According to the contents of his wallet his name was Deepak Patel and he was from Alang, a gritty ship breaking town on the coast of Gujerat. After a place like Alang a job at an escort agency in Mumbai must have felt like heaven.

Patel was a head taller than Sansi and even though he stood between two constables with his hands cuffed behind him he still had plenty of swagger.

"Where is Usha?" Sansi asked.

"I don't know who you are talking about," Patel said.

"The girl you brought to me at the Majestic Hotel last month."

"I have never seen you before."

"And yet I know quite a lot about you," Sansi said. He threw the contents of Patel's wallet onto the desk.

The goonda barely glanced at them "Take me in if you want, I will be out in 24 hours."

Sansi wasn't sure what annoyed him more, Patel's matter-of-factness or that he was probably right.

"When you put it like that it hardly seems worth the paperwork does it?" Sansi said.

Patel smirked.

"I don't want to waste your time anymore than I want to waste mine," Sansi said. "In fact, why don't we forget the whole thing and I'll just let you go. That will save us both a lot of trouble won't it?"

He had the cuffs removed, the two constables stepped aside and Sansi returned Patel's wallet and contents to him.

"You can go," Sansi said.

Patel hesitated, sensing a trick, then stuffed his wallet into a pocket.

"Why don't I walk you out so there is no mistake," Sansi said.

He walked the goonda across the sitting area past Madam Lele and her girls.

"We appreciate everything you have done," Sansi said just loud enough for them to hear.

"What do you mean?" Patel said.

"You did everything we asked," Sansi said. "We could not have asked for more."

"I didn't do anything."

"You are not worried about them are you?" Sansi nodded in the direction of the watching women. "You will never see them again."

"Don't listen to him, he's lying," Patel protested. "I didn't tell him anything."

He was met with blank stares.

"You're trying to fuck me here aren't you?"

Sansi could see the gears turning. What would Shiney believe?

"Any problems you know how to reach me," Sansi said and turned to go back to the call room.

Patel scanned the faces of the women he'd taken to and from appointments for the past two years. Women who had plenty of reason to hate him. He could see from the look in Madam Lele's eyes he couldn't rely on her either.

"*Maderchod.*" He followed Sansi back to the call room.

"You have reconsidered your position?" Sansi said and closed the door behind them.

"I want money," Patel said. "I'll tell you what I know but I want money."

"That will depend on what you have to offer," Sansi said. "You can start by telling me what you did with Usha?"

His swagger gone Patel sat down, fists balled on his knees. "I didn't do anything with her. It wasn't up to me, it was never up to me. I was the delivery man, you know that."

"Where is she now?"

Patel took a breath. "After what happened at the hotel Madam Lele didn't want her here. She wanted rid of her as quick as she could. She found somebody who would take her out of the country."

"Who did she find?"

"They sold her to some Arab."

"An Arab? Are you sure?"

"I only know what I heard."

"Where did he take her?"

"I don't know. All I know is they found somebody who would take her somewhere far away. Ask Madam Lele, she runs the place. She knows everything."

"Was it you who snatched the girl at the Majestic?"

"Me and the driver. We were in the bar and we saw the red haired woman come down with the kid. We followed them out."

"Who hit the woman?" Sansi asked.

Patel stared at the floor.

"Did you hit her?"

"It was a job," Patel said. "I was doing my job."

"So am I," Sansi said.

*   *   *

It was almost dawn before the last prisoners from Enticing Escorts were shuttled to police headquarters but Sansi was just getting started. He began sifting through the evidence with Chowdhary. Agarkar took the seized hard drives, floppy disks and CD's over to the cyber crime unit and the passports and identity papers to the Central Forensic Science Laboratory. Nimkar was put to work trying to find a connection between Enticing Escorts and Shiney Borkar. Or better still, Rushil Pujari.

Sansi preferred to leave the computer work to the younger officers. He settled into his new office with a hot *chai* and worked his way through the wad of print-outs taken from the safe. The print-outs were transaction records for the past quarter. Each transaction recorded the date, client name, escort name, the location where the escort was delivered, the number of hours the client was with the escort and the money received. Most clients were identified by nicknames, probable aliases and sometimes symbols. More than half the payments were made by credit card and whoever kept the records had been thoughtful enough to include card numbers. Others paid by cash and some entries had no client name at all. Perhaps because no money had changed hands. Most transactions were for ten to twenty thousand rupees, the going rate for an escort in Mumbai. Much less than Sansi had been charged.

Sansi found his transaction under his assumed name, Bobde, which told him the entries were current. The date and the address were there for the Majestic Hotel. Instead of the name, Usha, there was a lotus symbol and the amount of money that had changed hands. It was less than the actual cash amount Sansi had paid. He had paid 40,000 rupees and the figure entered was 25,000. He leafed ahead and found more lotus symbols and entries for similar amounts. The lotus symbolized purity and purity didn't come cheap. Some weeks there were no entries, some weeks one or two. But there were no names. And, if the money Sansi paid had been skimmed, it was probable other payments had been skimmed too.

After 24 hours without sleep Sansi decided to give everybody a break. He told them to get something to eat and rest for an hour or two. He sent Agarkar out to the food carts clustered at the front gates to bring back some *misal*, *poha* and *parathas* for everybody to share. When he'd finished eating Sansi lay back in his chair, closed his eyes and slept. He hadn't lost the policeman's knack for napping just about anywhere. Chowdhary and the others followed his example. It might be a while before they got another chance. After an hour or so Sansi awakened feeling rested enough to continue. He went to the bathroom, splashed cold water on his face and combed his hair. He was willing to pit his stamina against the prisoners and wanted to start the interrogations while they were tired and disoriented. Before he could begin Agarkar told him a constable from the cyber unit had called with a preliminary report. The PC's taken from Enticing Escorts were a closed system. The hard drives, floppy disks and CD's held financial records that went back nearly eight years. Cold numbers that signified thousands of transactions, thousands of women and children bought and sold. But the cyber unit officer wanted to know if there was another hard drive to come. Sansi asked Chowdhary if there was another PC at the agency and Chowdhary said he'd only logged in three. Agarkar said the initial cyber unit analysis showed a one way flow of data from two PC's to a third PC inside the network. But data had also been sent from there to a separate location outside the network. Somewhere there was a fourth PC. Sansi wondered if his men had missed it somehow. Or perhaps it wasn't at the agency at all. Perhaps it was in Shiney Borkar's hands so he could see the money coming in. All that Madam Lele wanted him to see. First Sansi wanted to know what the women of Enticing Escorts could tell him about a girl called Usha.

He and Chowdhary took over one of three interview rooms. Each one 20 feet by 20 feet with high ceilings, whitewashed walls and a darkly stained cement floor. There were no windows or two-way mirrors. Just a steel

table cemented to the floor and four metal folding chairs.
Each room smelled of urine and disinfectant. Sansi and
Chowdhary took the chairs facing the door. In one corner
Chowdhary had set up a camera on a tripod. There were no
security cameras. Indian police rarely wanted a record of
the way they treated prisoners. Chowdhary also had a
notepad and pencil. The escorts were brought in one at a
time. Their ages ran from 18 to 35 though the older women
tried to look younger. Castoffs in the tide of girls that
flowed into Mumbai every year dreaming of becoming the
next Amrita Rao or Kareena Kapoor only to find
themselves relegated to the brothels instead. The younger
women wanted to be cooperative but none of them would
admit to seeing an eleven year old girl called Usha. Some
of them went further and said they'd never seen any
underage girls at the agency. The older women were cagier
but they too said they'd never seen underage girls at
Enticing Escorts. Either they had all been thoroughly
intimidated or they were telling the truth. The two middle
aged women who acted as Madam Lele's assistants said
they answered phones, made bookings and kept the office
running. But Madam Lele oversaw everything. From the
clothes the girls wore to the way they did their hair, their
make-up and jewelry and which girl went to which client.
They told Sansi only Madam Lele handled the money, kept
the books and had access to the safe. But when he asked
them about underage girls they both dropped their heads
and fell silent. It was the opening he'd been looking for.

"You know, under the Immoral Traffic Prevention
Act, as an accessory to the prostitution of a child, you can
go to prison for life?" Sansi said.

The two women eyed each other, neither of them
wanting to be first to speak.

"Let me give you a choice," Sansi said. "Whichever
one of you decides to cooperate will be safe from
prosecution. The other will go to jail."

It was like a dam bursting. Both women began babbling at the same time.

"You." Sansi pointed to the woman directly across the table from him. "Tell me what you know."

The woman next to her put her hands to her mouth and began to cry.

"We were told when those calls came in we were to pass them on to Madam Lele," the first woman said. "She was the one who made the arrangements."

"But you knew what those calls were about?" Sansi said.

The woman hesitated. "Yes."

"You knew the caller wanted an underage girl?"

"Yes."

"Did customers ask explicitly or was there some kind of a code?"

"They would just say what they wanted."

"And when did you tell Madam Lele?"

"We had to tell her right away."

"And if she was busy or she wasn't there?"

"She always has a cell phone with her. We would call her."

"And then?"

"She took over everything. We never saw the girls. They never came to the agency. Madam Lele kept them separate from the rest of the business."

"Where did she find the girls?"

The woman paused and it was enough for her friend to leap into the gap.

"She paid people to send girls to her. Sometimes the ma would call us asking if we would take their daughters, sometimes the papa."

"Then what happened?"

"We passed them on to Madam Lele."

"What did she do with the girls?"

"She would see if they were suitable," the first woman said.

"What did suitable mean?"

"Every girl who comes to the agency has to be approved by Madam Lele. She would have done the same with the young girls."

"Did she go to them or did they come to her?"

"She has an apartment in the building," the second woman interjected. "Two floors up from the agency. You should look there."

"Did she arrange for girls to leave the country?" Sansi asked.

"It was one of her services," the first woman said. "She arranged weddings, she took care of the travel papers."

One of the oldest rackets in Mumbai was the arranged marriage of young girls to foreign visitors, most of them Arab. Some customers dumped them the next day, others took them home. It explained why the safe in Madam Lele's office was full of unused passports.

"*Acha*," Sansi said. "There is a way the two of you can help yourselves."

The second woman suddenly looked hopeful.

"You can testify against Madam Lele."

Dismayed, the two of them fell silent.

"You mean in court?" the first one asked.

"Yes," Sansi said. "You would have to testify against her in open court."

"Would you give us protection?"

"We'll be killed if we speak against Madam Lele in court," the other woman said.

"Who would kill you?" Sansi asked.

"Shiney Borkar," the first woman said. "He is the big boss. Madam Lele runs the business but she runs it for him."

"How do you know Shiney Borkar is the boss?"

"He comes all the time and takes girls for free. He likes to try out the new girls."

"He was the *babu*," the second woman added. "He treated us like he owned us."

"And Madam Lele was afraid of him," the first one said.

"Did he ever take underage girls?"

"I don't know. If he did he would go to Madam Lele's apartment."

"You should look there," the second one said.

"Now will you give us protection?" the first one said.

"Only if you agree to testify against Madam Lele."

The two women eyed each other. They knew they had gone too far now to risk going back.

"I will testify," the first woman said.

"I will testify too," the second one added.

"I will see the two of you are put in a cell by yourselves," Sansi said. "If you continue to cooperate I will see that you are kept separate from the general prison population."

Both women looked relieved. When they had gone Sansi told Chowdhary to get a search warrant for Madam Lele's apartment.

"I want it ready by the time I am finished here," he said.

As Chowdhary left Nimkar arrived with a report from forensics. All the passports found in Madam Lele's safe were new, he said.

"The new ones, the old ones, they are all officially issued passports, no forgeries," Nimkar said. "It is the same with the identity papers. Some are used, some are new. They come from different states but they are all genuine."

Sansi gave the slightest waggle of his head. It was time to confront Madam Lele.

He had Nimkar re-start the camera and take over for Chowdhary except this time Sansi would take the notes. The guards brought Madam Lele in, shuffling with shackles on her wrists and ankles. She had been kept apart from the other prisoners and was the only one Sansi had ordered shackled. Her hair and clothes were in disarray but she looked more resentful than afraid. Sansi had found nothing in the police files about Madam Lele and he suspected it was her first night in a police cell. He had wanted it to be as uncomfortable as possible. He kept her standing while he reviewed Chowdhary's notes and made some notes of his own.

After a while she said: "I would like to sit down."

"By all means," Sansi said without looking up.

She shuffled around the chair and sat down with a grunt. When Sansi was ready he looked up and made a point of studying Madam Lele's features, searching for a trace of whatever it was that would lead her to sell children for sex. What he saw was a pudgy faced woman with dark pouches under her eyes and a spattering of sun spots along her cheekbones.

"Would you like some *chai*?" he asked.

"Yes, I would like some *chai*," she said.

Sansi signaled to a guard to bring her a cup of *chai* and had the other remove her shackles. She sighed as they came off and rubbed her wrists.

Have you had anything to eat?" Sansi asked.

"No."

"No breakfast or lunch?"

"No."

"Were you offered food?"

"I wouldn't feed it to dogs."

"You can have something brought in if you like."

"You took my money. You took everything."

"You can have someone outside send food in for you. Is there anyone you would like us to contact on your behalf?"

"I want to speak to a lawyer."

"Do you have one in mind?"

"His name is Lomate. Agira Lomate."

"Shiney Borkar's lawyer?"

She looked away.

"He has done work for Rushil Pujari too, hasn't he?"

"I'm not going to answer any questions until I have spoken to Lomate," she said.

"All I am asking is if you would like some food brought in," Sansi said. "You can probably have something to eat without incriminating yourself."

"I know what you're doing," she said. "You're trying to get me talking."

"Actually, you don't have to say anything if you don't want to."

"Then why am I here…actually?"

"You are here because you are being charged with 41 offences under the Immoral Traffic Prevention Act," Sansi said.

The guard returned with a steel cup filled with hot *chai* and set it down in front of her, its aroma perfuming the stale air. She picked up the cup with both hands and took several quick sips.

"We will contact Lomate and see that he gets a copy of the charges," Sansi said.

"When can I see him?" Madam Lele asked.

"When he is ready, I expect," Sansi said. "You know how lawyers are, never around when you need them."

Madam Lele retreated into silence.

"Enjoy the *chai,*" Sansi said and got up to go. As he left he told he guards: "Let her finish, then put the shackles on her and take her back to her cell. See that she doesn't see or speak to anybody."

*   *   *

Sansi arrived at Madam Lele's building with Chowdhary, Nimkar and half a dozen constables. He had the constables secure the lobby and put the building's security men under guard. He continued past the elevators to the building manager's office and entered without knocking. The manager had his feet up and was snacking from a bag of corn puffs while he watched *Hum Paanch* on TV. Sansi showed him the search warrant and told him to take them up to Madam Lele's apartment. The manager stared at Sansi, then at the warrant then back at Sansi. But he didn't move.

"Or I could charge you with obstruction," Sansi added.

Reluctantly the manager got up and took a ring of keys from a peg board on the wall. He had a trapped look in his eyes as he rode the elevator to the 14th floor. Madam Lele's apartment was on the west side facing Back Bay so she could enjoy a drink and watch the sun go down after a long day of destroying lives. As they approached the apartment they heard loud music coming from inside. The manager stopped some 20 feet from the door and refused to go any further.

"That's it," he said. He selected the right key on the ring and offered it to Sansi.

"You open it," Sansi said.

Chowdhary gave the manager a push but he wouldn't go any further.

"I can't," he said. "There is somebody in there."

"Who is in there?" Sansi asked.

"Two men."

"Who are they?"

"Two of them…there are two…"

"Do you know who they are?"

"No."

"Why did you let them in?"

"I...they...I don't know."

"What are they doing in there?"

"I don't know."

"I will ask you once more, what are they doing in there?"

The manager looked panic stricken. "I cannot say, I'm sorry."

"Is there any other way out of the apartment?"

"*Nehir*, only this door."

"Give me the key."

The manager handed over the key and Sansi told Nimkar to watch him. Sansi went to the door and listened. All he heard through the music was an occasional bump. Chowdhary drew his pistol while Sansi quietly unlocked the door. Sansi pushed the door open and sneaked a quick look. There was a short entrance hall that led to a living room on the right and an open kitchen on the left. Slashed cushions, splintered furniture and broken glass littered the floor. But he saw nobody. The music was louder and the bumps seemed to be coming from the direction of a bedroom accompanied by an occasional curse. Sansi took a few short steps to the living room and looked around. A sofa was tipped on its back and the bottom cut open, spewing out chunks of foam. The walls had been stripped of pictures which lay smashed on the floor. The kitchen had been ransacked too. Drawers and cupboards left open, cooking pots, bottles of oil, bags of rice, loose potatoes and onions strewn across the floor. Chilies, lentils, yellow split peas and multi-colored spices formed a drunken mosaic. The thumps were coming from the bedrooms to the rear of the apartment. Sansi eased his way down the hallway past an empty, wrecked bathroom. He looked in the first bedroom and saw a man with his back to the door using a carving knife to slash open a mattress. In his other hand was an open bottle of whiskey. The contents of a wardrobe and two chests of drawers were spilled over the carpet and a dresser mirror had been smashed. He was drinking whiskey and listening to music while he turned over Madam Lele's apartment. Sansi planted a foot squarely in the man's rump and pushed hard enough so that he sprawled forward cursing and spilling the whiskey. Before he could recover Sansi stepped on his wrist, took away the knife and stood back. The man scrambled to his feet, furious. He was in his early twenties and when he saw Sansi his expression turned from fury to bewilderment.

"You are under arrest, my young friend," Sansi said. "Put the bottle down and behave yourself."

Chowdhary had continued to a second bedroom where he found a similar scene. He had to tap the barrel of his pistol against the side of the other goonda's head to get his attention. The man spun around, thinking it was his friend playing a trick and found himself with a gun in his face. Sansi and Chowdhary led the two goondas out into the trashed living room. Both of them smelled heavily of liquor. Sansi switched off the stereo and called Nimkar to bring the manager in.

"You know these men?" Sansi asked the manager.

The goondas cursed the manager and he looked away.

"Did Shiney send you two over here?" Sansi asked them.

"We heard there was a party," one of them said and the other one grinned.

"Search them," Sansi told Chowdhary. "Put them out on the balcony till we're done here."

Chowdhary searched the two goondas and found on one a loaded nine millimeter Makarov. The other had a knuckle blade and a packet of Gold Flake with a couple of foil wrapped hashish pellets inside. Chowdhary waved them over to the balcony.

"Him too," Sansi said and nodded at the manager.

The manager protested but Chowdhary herded the three of them out onto the balcony and locked the sliding door behind them.

"Now, let's see what they missed," Sansi said.

He began by sifting through the debris in the living room. There was little of interest except for pictures of Madam Lele with friends or relatives; travel snaps and get-togethers in restaurants. There was also a professionally taken portrait of a younger and slimmer Madam Lele with a man, a former husband perhaps, along with what might have been brothers, sisters, nieces and nephews. Apparently Madam Lele had no difficulty separating her personal life from her business. The second bedroom was relatively undisturbed. In the closet were child size saris and slippers for little girls, trousers and clean white shirts for boys. A dresser was covered with brushes, combs, jars of make-up, lipsticks and mascara brushes. Gaudily lacquered jewelry boxes filled with cheap bracelets and necklaces. The drawers contained child sized *cholis* and underwear. It was where Madam Lele dressed the children and made them up before sending them out to whatever fate awaited them.

Sorting through the mess in Madam Lele's bedroom Sansi found a smashed PC. It took Nimkar only a minute to take out the hard drive. There was no safe in Madam Lele's bedroom but hidden behind a wall panel in the back of the closet was a compartment the size of a suitcase. That was where Sansi found Madam Lele's money. As much as half a million U.S. dollars in various currencies, he estimated. There was jewelry too. Real jewelry. Gold rings, bracelets, necklaces and a black velvet drawstring bag that held loose stones; emeralds, rubies and diamonds. There were also keys to bank security deposit boxes and five Indian passports in Madam Lele's name. All current. But what interested Sansi most was a ledger bound in red leather. He leafed through it and found what looked like every financial transaction from Enticing Escorts for the past year. A mirror image of the computer print-outs in every detail but one. The sum entered in his name was the actual amount he'd paid; 40,000 rupees. Not the 25,000 in the print-outs. If Madam Lele had skimmed every transaction in the book for the seven years the agency had been in business she had stolen millions from Shiney Borkar. But there was one thing missing. There was no record of a second transaction for Usha.

He was interrupted by a loud buzz from the intercom by the front door.

"Go and see who that is," he told Nimkar.

He kept looking through the ledger, Nimkar's voice in the background. He couldn't make out what was said. Then Nimkar called to him.

"You must come, Inspector."

Sansi went out to the living room followed by Chowdhary. Nimkar was staring at the balcony. Where there should have been three men there were now only the two goondas leaning over the rail looking down.

"They threw the manager off the balcony," Nimkar said.

"*Are Bapre*," Sansi breathed.

"It is how things are now, Sansi-ji," Chowdhary said.

Chapter 4.

"You have a decision to make," Sansi said. "Tell me where the girl is and I will recommend leniency. Or you can take your chances at trial."

Madam Lele sat across from him in the interview room. She was haggard from lack of sleep but her eyes were defiant.

"You don't impress me," she said. "I'm not Patel."

"I am offering you a choice," Sansi said.

"I told you, I want to see my lawyer."

"Lomate's office was closed when we called," Sansi said. "We left a message. We will let you know if we hear back from him."

"You will hear from him soon."

"I would not be so sure if I were you."

"I'm not saying anything until I have spoken to him."

"You do understand you will be going in front of a magistrate in the morning?"

"You can't do that."

"Actually, I can."

"Actually? Actually?" Her voice escalated. "Why do you keep saying that? Who do you think you are?"

"You won't have to enter a plea tomorrow," Sansi continued. "It is for a 60 day remand in custody. Just a formality, really."

"Lomate will come. He will get me out of here, you will see."

"The reason we haven't heard back from him, I suspect, is because he is talking to Shiney Borkar and Rushil Pujari about what to do with you. There is no reason for them to hurry. They are not sitting alone in a cell where every minute feels like an eternity."

"You put me in a cell by myself because you think it will be harder for me."

"We put you in a cell by yourself for your protection," Sansi said. "Child traffickers don't last long in prison."

"You think you're so clever, don't you?" she said. "You know what you are - you're a nobody."

· "You may be right," Sansi said. "But I am the nobody who can keep you here as long as I like. At least until this investigation is over - and I decide when it is over."

It wasn't true but he wanted to plant the seed in her mind.

"I have friends in the government," she said. "Important friends. More important than you."

"For a woman of your experience you have a surprising trust in the constancy of politicians," Sansi said. "You can take that chance if you want; a few years in jail or the rest of your life. It is up to you."

Madam Lele sat silently, calculating.

"I know where the girl is," she said. "But I will tell you only when you let me go. I want a guarantee in writing that I will not be prosecuted."

"I will set you free when the girl is safely back in our hands," Sansi said.

"What is it about this girl?" Madam Lele said. "Why does she matter to you?"

"She is a child of India," Sansi said. "I wouldn't expect you to understand."

"A child of India?" Madam Lele said derisively. "What does that mean? To be a child of India? She will have a better life where she is."

"Attending to the sexual demands of an old man in a foreign land?"

"Ask her parents why they sold her," Madam Lele said. "If India cares so much about its children, ask them."

"They are desperate people and you feed off their desperation," Sansi said. "You are a parasite."

"Big man," Madam Lele said scornfully. "Cops, judges, bigwigs, you're all the same. So *pukka*. So puffed up with your own importance. Put a little girl's *yoni* in front of you and you fall to your knees." She leaned forward as if to share a confidence. "You liked her, didn't you, uncle?"

Sansi saw amusement in her eyes, as if she knew something about him that he didn't know about himself. Sickened, he got up and stepped away from the table.

"Take her back to her cell," he told the guards. "Keep the shackles on her. Don't let her see anybody. Don't let her talk to anybody."

*   *   *

Exhaustion finally caught up with Sansi. After almost 72 hours in the same clothes he went home to clean up and get some rest before court the next day. He showered, put on a white cotton *kurta pajama* and filled a plate with chicken biryani left for him by Mrs. Khanna. He poured himself a tonic water with lime and went out to the roof garden where his mother and Annie were enjoying some after dinner coffee.

"I didn't think you were due to start work until tomorrow," Pramila said.

"Something came up," Sansi said as he sat down.

"It always does," Pramila said. To Annie she said: "Jatkar will work him to death and take all the credit."

"You look tired," Annie told Sansi.

"I have the burdens of virtue and few of the pleasures," he said.

It was a joke but as he said it he realized Annie might not find it so amusing. Their relationship had foundered on his infidelity. But she seemed not to notice, and why would she? She had a new man in her life. Ajit

Birla, rich, powerful and brilliant. He had more to offer her than Sansi ever could.

"How does it feel?" Sansi asked, gesturing to her head wound.

The dressing on the side of her head had been replaced with a narrow flesh colored strip.

"Probably looks gnarlier than it is."

"Gnarlier?" Sansi repeated. "Have you spoken to Ajit?"

"I talked to him the day after I got out. He told me to take as much time as I need. I think another week should do it. I'm going back to my place tomorrow."

"You know you are welcome to stay here as long as you like," Pramila said.

"I know." Annie put her hand on Pramila's arm. "You've been so kind. Believe me, I could get used to this."

"It has been a joy having you here," Pramila said. "As you can see George isn't much company."

"The humble man does not offend by his presence," Sansi said.

"Who's that?" Annie asked. "Tagore?"

"Sansi," Pramila said. "He does that now."

It was a warm clear night and the sea air was scented heavily with frangipani. Across Back Bay the city shifted with restless energy. Twenty million souls striving day and night for a piece of the Mumbai dream. Sansi ate his biryani. Annie and his mother talked about the coming election just announced by Chief Minister Athawali and the prospects of the Congress Party. He could have told them those prospects were worsening by the day. When he finished eating he dabbed his lips with a cotton napkin and poured himself a cup of coffee.

"And what has kept you so busy you couldn't call home?" Pramila asked.

"Isn't it bad enough that a 47 year old man has to live with his mother?" Sansi said.

"You can move out anytime you want," Pramila said. "I have plenty of other uses for your room."

"I have been trying to find our missing girl," he said. "I have made some progress but the news is not good."

"They didn't kill her, did they?" Annie asked.

"No, they didn't kill her," Sansi said. "But she has been sold into a life not worth living."

"What did they do with her?" Pramila asked.

"They sold her to an Arab man who took her out of the country," Sansi said. "They knew something was up after the business at the hotel so they got rid of her."

"How do you know this?" Pramila said.

"We raided the agency Friday night," Sansi said.

"Well done." Pramila rapped her knuckles on the table.

"We made 46 arrests," Sansi added. "We've been conducting interrogations and going through the evidence ever since."

"Do you know where she's been taken?" Annie asked.

"Could be Saudi Arabia, Yemen, the Emirates, any of those places."

"How can they get a girl that age out of the country?" Annie said.

"It is not as difficult as you might think," Sansi said. "Arabs have been coming to India for hundreds of years to buy women and children for sex and as servants. The agency provides the passport, it's all part of the service. Between 50,000 and 100,000 girls are taken out of the country each year. Nobody knows the real number."

"It must cost quite a bit," Annie said.

"It does," Sansi said. "But for a wealthy and well connected Arab price is no object."

"Virginity is one of India's most prized commodities," Pramila said.

"When you say it like that it sounds like something you can trade on the stock market," Annie said.

"It is a market," Pramila added. "An underground market but a market all the same. Gold and silver can be sold and re-sold many times but virginity is a commodity that can only be sold once."

"What happens in the case of a girl like Usha when she is taken out of the country?" Annie asked.

"That depends on the man who bought her," Pramila answered. "If he likes her he will keep her for a while. Arab men are allowed to have up to four wives. But when he tires of her he may sell her to his relatives or friends. Eventually she will be sold into prostitution in one of the hot spots of the Gulf like Bahrain or Dubai."

"Somebody from the agency must know who took her," Annie said.

"Somebody does," Sansi said. "Madam Lele, the brothel keeper. But she won't talk unless we give her immunity from prosecution."

"I don't know how these people live with themselves," Annie said.

"They live very well," Sansi said. "That is why they do it."

Pramila said: "If you have to give this Madam Lele immunity to get the child back you should do it."

"And then she goes back to selling children," Sansi said. "We save one but lose hundreds more."

"Then you charge her again," Pramila said. "And you keep charging her until she gets sick of it."

"I'm not even sure we can save Usha," Sansi said. "The Emirates passed a law a few years ago prohibiting men from bringing back child brides from India but it is not enforced. There is too much demand, too much money."

"Maybe it's time we shone a light on it," Annie said.

"You mean in India Today?" Sansi said.

"It's what Ajit hired me to do."

"No," Sansi said. "These are dangerous people. They wouldn't hesitate to kill you. I can't ask you to put yourself at risk again."

"You're not asking, I'm offering," Annie said.

"I'm still working on Madam Lele, let me see what I can get out of her first."

"If you have any trouble let me have a few minutes alone with the bitch," Annie said. "I'll get it out of her."

*   *   *

"You have been busy for somebody who wasn't supposed to start work until today," Jatkar said. "Forty six arrests and now the two goondas charged with murder."

"There will be more," Sansi said. "We have a mountain of evidence."

"Tell me, when you went in front of Magistrate Chandiwal this morning, did you choose him because he has daughters?"

"I think it prudent to know who is on the bench on any day," Sansi said. "Where a 60 day remand is involved." Jatkar said.

Sansi had come directly from the Magistrates Court where his application to keep Madam Lele and her employees behind bars for 60 days had been approved without demur. Madam Lele had tried to protest the conditions under which she was being held but Magistrate Chandiwal had her removed from the court, her complaints echoing along the corridor as she was taken back to her cell.

"I have already had a call from Dubade," Jatkar said. "I expect to hear from Aadekar before the end of the day and when they don't get anywhere with me they will call the Comissioner."

"Pujari will be putting pressure on Shiney and Shiney will be putting pressure on them," Sansi said.

"You've got them scared," Jatkar said. "But I need evidence to persuade the Commissioner."

"I have never seen a case where there is so much evidence," Sansi said. "A blind man could have gone to that agency and found enough evidence to convict a thousand people. I will give you something you can take to the Commissioner."

"How much time do you think this is going to take?" Jatkar asked.

"Three or four weeks, perhaps more."

"Two weeks and no more," Jatkar said. "You saw Athawale called the election? We have to move this thing forward."

"I think we are going to have to let Madam Lele go," Sansi said.

"Why? I thought we needed her testimony against Borkar and Pujari?"

"She won't testify against them, but her two personal assistants will testify against her and we can connect her to Borkar and Borkar to Pujari. If we put Madam Lele on the stand she will only hurt us."

"How?"

"She is a nasty piece of work," Sansi said. "I think she will try to incriminate me because I had the agency deliver a girl to a hotel room. I have to make a deal with her anyway. It is the only way I am going to get her to tell me where the girl is."

"What does it matter where the girl is if you already have enough evidence?"

"Madam Lele sold the girl to an Arab man who took her out of the country. I want to find her and get her back."

"Why? As a witness? We don't need her as a witness."

"No, not as a witness."

"Then why?"

"Because I am responsible for what happened to her."

Jatkar sighed. "No, no, no Sansi. You see what happens when you get personally involved? You don't need this kid. You don't need to worry about what happened to her."

"Shutting down Enticing Escorts isn't personal."

"You are making it personal now." Jatkar paused. "I don't want you jeopardizing this case because of the girl."

"She is 11 years old. A crime was committed selling her. A crime was committed taking her out of the country. Everything that happened to her was a crime."

"Where was she taken?"

"That is what I need Madam Lele to tell me."

"And what happens when you find out?" Jatkar said. "Wherever she is, to get her back we would have to go through New Delhi. Do you know how many cases the Government of India has like this in a year?"

Sansi went to speak but Jatkar stopped him. "No, no, this is where you listen, Sansi. None. That's how many cases like this India does in a year. And there is a reason for that. The reason is that it is too much trouble. It brings two governments together in confrontation. It creates diplomatic tension. What happened to this kid is terrible but it happens all the time and we can't resolve every case. And I know what you're going to say and the answer is still going to be no. This is not the case. This is not the one kid you bring back. This is the case we bring to trial in time for the election. Everything else is a distraction. If we don't need Madam Lele, we don't need her. But do not complicate this case unnecessarily, Sansi. Get me the evidence I need to reassure the Commissioner and come back to me in two weeks with enough to bring charges."

*　　　*　　　*

During the next two weeks Sansi and his team worked ceaselessly to process the evidence seized from Enticing Escorts. It helped that the cyber crime unit managed to salvage the data on the hard drive from the smashed computer in Madam Lele's apartment. In it were not only the names of Dubade and Aadekar but many more highly placed officials in the government, throughout the Congress Party and the Opposition parties. More than a hundred in all. It constituted the biggest child prostitution ring in the history of Mumbai and smashing it would be a triumph for Jatkar and Crime Branch. It would ignite a media firestorm and confirm Jatkar in the public eye as a man of courage and integrity. It would also serve notice to every politician in the state that he was a power to be reckoned with.

The cyber crime unit was still tracing credit card numbers that belonged to the agency's foreign clients. There were thousands from Europe, the United States and all over the Persian Gulf but nothing to tell Sansi which of them had taken Usha. The unit had more success tracking how much of the agency's cash flow Madam Lele had diverted into her personal accounts. So far it was U.S. $2.7 million. That didn't include what offshore accounts Madam Lele might have.

Sansi left her to stew in solitary. He had only one shot at getting her to tell him where Usha was. If he mishandled it he would get nothing. He would speak to her soon enough. First he and Jatkar had to organize the operation to pick up 118 suspects and somehow keep word of it from leaking out to Mumbai's voracious news media. It had been named Operation Garuda and it would launch in 36 hours. It was after dark again when Sansi went home in search of a few hours of peace before the storm broke.

If he hadn't been so absorbed by thoughts of what was to come he might have seen something strange in the absence of the security guards who protected his apartment building. There were never less than three, day or night. They took it in turns to patrol the inside and outside of the building but there was always one in the lobby. This time there were none. A couple of folding metal chairs at the back of the lobby where the guards rested were unattended. Sansi would curse himself later for assuming there was an innocent explanation. A policeman, he had missed the obvious. The moment he opened the door to the apartment was when he knew something was wrong. It wasn't the quiet, it was the weight of the quiet. A quiet that prompted a prickle of unease on the skin. He turned to leave as quietly as he had come in but found himself face to face with a man with a gun. A man with the confident manner of someone who was no stranger to violence. He must have been waiting in the closet beside the front door.

"Keep going," he said.

As Sansi walked down the hallway he smelled cigarette smoke, something his mother wouldn't tolerate in the apartment. In the living room were three more men, two of them standing behind a wide sofa where Pramila and Mrs. Khanna sat side by side. They seemed unhurt but Pramila held Mrs. Khanna's hand in a vain attempt to reassure her. Sansi saw the trails of dried tears on Mrs. Khanna's cheeks. A third man sat at the table across the room, smoking. The doors to the roof garden were closed but even with the air conditioning the fume of cigarette smoke suggested the men had been there a while.

"I'm afraid we have some unwelcome visitors," Pramila said.

Sansi recognized Shiney Borkar from the picture in his police file. His hair was receding but he still wore it swept back from his thin dark face.

"Did you check him out," Borkar said.

The goonda went through Sansi's pockets and delivered the contents to Borkar. The gangster picked through them with barely a glance at Sansi's police badge but he dropped Sansi's cell phone to the floor and smashed it under the heel of his shoe.

"You don't carry a gun?" he said.

"I have never felt the need for one," Sansi said.

"You know who I am?"

"I believe so."

"Then you know why I'm here."

Borkar got up, dropped his cigarette and ground it into the polished parquet floor with the others. He crossed the room with a lazy, self-assured manner and stood in front of Sansi. He was the same height as Sansi and his eyes held the same challenging stare they had in his file photo. He was thin and wore a yellow polo shirt with a shark grey suit that looked a size too big. His skin was the color of polished betel and in the hollow of his neck was a rind of scar tissue where he'd been stabbed when he was a young man. Sansi knew Borkar had other scars on him; two bullet wounds in the chest and another in the lower back. The bullet in his back had grazed his liver and he should have died but he didn't and it added to his reputation. He stared at Sansi, taking his measure.

"We had a girl with blue eyes once," Borkar said. "She made us a lot of money."

"Please, just tell us what you want and be on your way," Pramila said.

"*Maa*, it's better if I handle this," Sansi said.

This was why Sansi hadn't heard back from Madam Lele's lawyer. Borkar wanted to handle it himself.

"Your son knows why I'm here," Borkar said without taking his eyes off Sansi.

"I've had a lot on my mind lately," Sansi said.

"You took something from me" he said. "I want it back."

Pramila said: "I can tell you this now my son is home. We made a decision a long time ago that if we should ever find ourselves in a situation like this we would never give in to threats, even if it does put our lives at risk."

"*Maa*, please..." Sansi said.

"You people," Borkar said. "You never had to worry about money so you think if you are willing to die for something more important than money it makes you better than us. I never had that choice. My god is money and he has never let me down. What about the *bei*? Is she willing to die for what you believe?"

Mrs. Khanna whimpered and Pramila squeezed her hand.

"Leave them out of this," Sansi said. "It's me you want, not them. I'll go with you, wherever you want."

Borkar sauntered off to the kitchen. They heard him opening cupboards and pulling things out. He returned holding a spray can of oven cleaner and stood in front of Mrs. Khanna.

"Hold her still" he told the goonda behind her. "Hold her face up."

The goonda wrapped an arm around her neck and with his other hand grabbed a fistful of hair and yanked her head back. Mrs. Khanna let out a wail of terror.

"Don't you touch her," Pramila shouted and threw herself across Mrs. Khanna. But the other goonda grabbed hold of her and restrained her easily no matter how hard she struggled.

"Open her eyes," Borkar ordered the man holding Mrs. Khanna.

"Tell me what you want and I'll do it," Sansi said.

Borkar paused, the spray can inches from Mrs. Khanna's eyes.

"You shut down my business, you cost me money, you put my people in jail."

"What do you want me to do?" Sansi said, pleading.

Borkar shook the can and sprayed a jet onto the arm of the sofa and watched it bubble and foam as it burned into the fabric.

"You want Madam Lele, is that it?"

"That would do to start," Borkar said. "But there's still the money you cost me."

"I can deliver Madam Lele to you tonight, anywhere you want," Sansi said.

"Tonight?" Borkar said.

"Yes, I can get her to you tonight."

It was close to eight-o-clock, leaving him four hours.

Borkar put the spray can down.

"I'll take the *bei* to make sure you do what you say. There's a new apartment building going up on Colaba Causeway, 22 floors, yellow walls. You know the one?"

"I'm sure I can find it," Sansi said.

"You have Lele there by midnight," Borkar said. "If you're not there I'll kill the *bei*. If I see anybody with you I'll kill her."

"Don't, please don't let them take me," Mrs. Khanna sobbed.

"Take me instead," Pramila said. "Please, I'm begging you."

"You're getting what you want," Borkar said. "You made her life worth more than yours."

. Mrs. Khanna sobbed helplessly. Pramila put an arm around her and whispered: "Be strong, trust George, he'll bring you back safely."

Mrs. Khanna fought and screamed so much they had to gag her and tie her hands and feet to carry her out. Sansi watched feeling helpless. Pramila turned away, hands to her face. When they had gone Sansi called police headquarters and ordered a security detail of four armed officers over immediately to guard his mother. His next call was to Jatkar at home. He told Jatkar what had happened except how he intended to exchange Madam Lele for Mrs. Khanna.

"Borkar went to your home?" Jatkar said. "He knows where you live?"

"Somebody must have told him," Sansi said.

"Somebody inside Crime Branch?"

"There aren't that many people who know I'm back," Sansi said.

"*Maderchod.*"

There wasn't a police force in India that wasn't riddled with bad cops. Pay was poor and opportunities for graft plentiful. Taking bribes and selling information were easy ways to pad their income. They often ran their own rackets hand in glove with local goondas and beatings and torture were commonplace. To the poor people of India the local police were just another armed gang. Sometimes worse. The goondas dispensed favors and gifts to win over the population, the police didn't have to. But Crime Branch was supposed to be different. It was an elite investigative unit with a rigorous selection process intended to recruit a better grade of cop. An informer in Crime Branch was far more dangerous because of the secretive nature of the work.

"If Borkar knows about Operation Garuda he could undermine the whole thing," Jatkar said. "I'm moving it forward 24 hours. We go at first light."

Midnight was a little over three hours away. First light was five and a half hours after that.

"See me at Crime Branch in half an hour," Jatkar said.

"I can't," Sansi said.

"Why not?"

"I am not going to abandon Mrs. Khanna."

"You don't have time for that," Jatkar said. "I'm sorry, Sansi, you have to let her go."

"I will be at Crime Branch soon after midnight," Sansi said. As the words came out of his mouth he knew he and Mrs. Khanna might well be dead by midnight.

"I won't have you putting personal considerations ahead of this operation, Sansi," Jatkar said. But Sansi was gone.

His next call was to Chowdhary whom he told to get an unmarked car and meet him outside the police detention block. Lastly he called the guardhouse at the detention block and told them he wanted Madam Lele ready for release when he arrived. Before he left he kissed his mother on the cheek. Neither of them had words for the dread that gripped them. Sansi hurried down the stairs. There was no sign of the building security guards anywhere. He waited outside till the security detail arrived in a police truck. Sansi brought the senior constable up to date and told him to search the building for the missing guards. He rode back to police headquarters in the truck guilt gnawing at him for the harm he had brought into the lives of those he loved. First Annie, now his mother and Mrs. Khanna. Men like Shiney Borkar would always hold the advantage over men like himself, Sansi knew. Men like Borkar were never troubled by doubt.

Madam Lele was waiting in the transfer cage when Sansi arrived. She had eaten enough prison food to get by but her face was gaunt and the lines around her eyes were etched deeper. The *salwar khameez* she'd been wearing the night she was arrested had been returned to her but it hung loosely on her now. Her leg shackles had been removed and there were calluses on her ankles. She sat on a steel bench, her head bowed, her cuffed wrists on her lap. The poor diet and solitary confinement had sapped her energy and when she looked at Sansi her eyes had lost their fire.

"Get up," he said. "You are coming with me."

"Where?" she asked. "Where are you taking me?"

"You will see," Sansi said.

A guard opened the cage door and she came out, her sandals scraping the cement floor. Sansi walked her down a corridor of whitewashed brick to a final checkpoint. When the gate opened she hesitated as if afraid to leave with him.

"You can leave or you can stay, it's up to you," Sansi said with an insouciance he didn't feel.

She stepped out into whatever it was this man she so despised had in mind for her. After the stink of prison the night air smelled sweet. She stopped and breathed it in. Sansi let her savor it knowing that at any minute the first officers and men would be streaming in to assemble for the operation at dawn, Jatkar among them. With feigned confidence he led her to the unmarked car where Chowdhary waited. Sansi held the passenger door open for her. As she sank into the back seat a gust of stale sweat rushed up into his face. He walked around the car and got in beside her.

Chowdhary drove out through the main gates and nudged his way into the glittering maelstrom of L. T. Road. Honking cars, buses, taxis, trucks, swarms of motor rickshaws and scooters loaded with whole families crawled through Crawford Market. On the sidewalks crowds of strollers and shoppers navigated the *khau galis.* Food lanes where greasy *samosas* and *pakoras* were cooked on open air stoves. Hawkers sold peanuts, sugar cane and fried corn while sidewalk dentists, astrologers and *paan wallahs* competed for business. Fruit stalls were piled high with coconuts, papayas, pineapples and mangoes. At spice stands tows of tiered baskets brimmed with green and red chilies, curry leaves, turmeric root and tamarind pods. An endless succession of stalls sold sandals, hats, sunglasses, bracelets, bead necklaces, exotic birds and fish. Shawls, shirts and dresses swayed from plastic coat hangers like polychromatic palm fronds. Jewelry store windows blazed and clusters of shiny steel pots hung outside kitchen stores splintering the light into kaleidoscopic shards. Billboards proclaimed the latest Bollywood blockbusters and a crazed array of street signs promised everything from 'VD service' to 'Fantastic Trouserings.' A river of life rushing through canyons slick with light.

Sansi watched Madam Lele take it all in. The world going on without her, indifferent to her weeks of privation. Chowdhary turned south past Church Gate Station then west to the golden arc of Marine Drive and north to Chowpatty Beach with its crowds paddling in the shallows, taking pony rides and snacking on *bhelpuri*. Chowdhary turned east till they had come almost full circle and pulled over near the Bawarchi restaurant just as Sansi had asked him to do. The car windows had been left open so Madam Lele could smell the food cooking.

"I have made you two offers," Sansi said. "This is the last offer you will get. Tell me where Usha is and you can sleep in your own bed tonight. Refuse and you go back to your cell and stay there until the trial. And the trial will not begin for at least one year."

"If I tell you, you will drop the charges against me?"

"That is the offer."

"How do I know I can believe you?"

"Because what happens to that little girl matters more to me than what happens to you," Sansi said. "You can believe that."

Madam Lele gazed at the Bawarchi, at the happy faces of the diners eating delicious food.

"She went to Dubai."

"How did she get to Dubai?" Sansi asked.

"She went with a man."

"What is the name of this man?"

She hesitated.

"I want his name."

"I know him as Al-Habash," she said. "Akeem Al-Habash."

"Where can I find him in Dubai?"

"I don't know. I think he is with the government. I don't know where he lives."

"Did he pay by credit card?"

"No, he didn't pay."

"What do you mean he didn't pay?"

"She was a gift."

"From who? Borkar? Pujari?"

"Shiney told me to do it."

"This Arab, what is his age?"

"I'm not sure, around 50."

"What does he look like?"

"He looks like an Arab."

"Is he tall, short, fat, thin? Does he have a moustache or a beard?"

"Not tall, not short, not fat. Average. He has a small beard. Grey. He wears glasses."

How many times did you meet him?"

"I'm not sure, two times, maybe three."

"Was this his first time or had he been before?"

"He came once before."

"When?"

"Some years ago. I don't know when."

"Did he buy a girl then?"

She turned her face to the window.

"Have you sold other girls to this man?" Sansi said.

She mumbled out the open window but it was lost in the din.

"Look at me when I'm talking to you," Sansi snapped.

She turned away from the window and looked ahead through the windshield as if insufferably bored.

"If there were others they were before my time there."

"How long has it been since you sold this other girl to him?"

"Three years, four."

"How old was she?"

"She was young."

"The same age as Usha?"

"About the same. The age doesn't matter, it's the way the girl looks."

"Was she a virgin too?"

"You're a man. You know. All men like them young. The younger the better. They find a girl they like but she grows up and they don't want her anymore so they come for another one."

"What was her name?"

"I don't remember. And if I could it doesn't matter. Most of them it's not their real name."

"Where did this man go when he was in Mumbai?"

"I don't know. I only saw him at the agency. Shiney brought him. He picked out a girl he liked and that's all there was to it."

"Just another transaction?"

"Yes." She looked contemptuously at Sansi. "Just another transaction."

Sansi looked at his watch. It was past eleven. He knew he'd got as much as he was going to get out of Madam Lele. He tapped Chowdhary on the shoulder. "Colaba.".

Chowdhary restarted the car, pulled out into traffic and started south.

"Why are we going to Colaba?" Madam Lele asked.

"You will see," Sansi said.

Madam Lele stared at him with undisguised hatred then turned away.

The yellow tower that Shiney Borkar had mentioned was hard to miss. It was 22 stories high and floodlit top to bottom. A citywide curfew was supposed to prohibit construction between 10 p.m. and 6 a.m. but bribes bulldozed it aside and nobody listened to the complaints of the neighbors. The tower was the last tall building before the Mumbai Port Trust Gardens. Sansi told Chowdhary to pull over some 50 yards before the building.

"Why are we stopping here?" Madam Lele asked.

"This is where you go your way and I go mine," Sansi said.

He got out and opened her door. She looked around suspiciously as she got out. He took her by the arm and steered her across the street. She was a short woman and she had to walk quickly to keep up with him. The construction site was ringed by a corrugated iron fence. There was a wide, deeply rutted entrance where several heavy trucks were parked. Just inside the entrance was a site office that looked empty. Nor were there any security guards, which was unusual. Construction workers moved through a pall of grey dust and Madam Lele buried her face in her elbow. The lower half of the building was well advanced with workmen putting in windows and yellow wall panels. At the front of the building was a portico and a lobby where more workmen installed marble tiles. A tower of marble and gold. All fake. The Rushil Pujari brand. Appeal to Indian vanity but skimp on the materials. Sansi led Madam Lele under the portico where they could wait out of the dust. As apprehensive as Madam Lele might be it was she who had Sansi at her mercy now. He had nobody to help him if it all went wrong. And he was under no illusion that he could get himself and Mrs. Khanna to safety if Borkar had other plans for them. Somewhere behind the dusty glare of construction lights, probably on an upper floor, Borkar and his goondas would have watched Sansi arrive with Madam Lele. They would have seen his car pull over and watched him exit with Mrs. Lele and walk her across the road. They would have seen there was no police back-up.

When Sansi next looked at his watch it was past midnight. He expected Borkar to be late. He just wanted

Sansi to wait. A little after quarter past Borkar came around a corner of the building with two of his goondas, one of them supporting Mrs. Khanna because she had difficulty walking. Madam Lele knew immediately she was part of a hostage swap. Borkar had used this woman to force Sansi's hand and Sansi had used Madam Lele to get what he wanted. Everything he said had been a bluff, he was never going to return her to her cell.

"*Dogala,*" Madam Lele shouted at Sansi. It was Hindi for bastard. "You made a deal, you had to let me go."

She lifted her cuffed hands and went for his face but Sansi brushed them aside, grabbed her fiercely by the arm and spoke quickly to her before Borkar was close enough to hear: "If you ever sell another human being again, I will tell Shiney how much you stole from him."

"That's a lie," she shouted back at him.

"You know and I know it isn't."

"He won't believe you."

"Yes, he will."

Borkar came to within a few feet and stopped. "What's going on here?"

Madam Lele wrenched free of Sansi's grip and backed away. "Kill him, kill him," she shouted to Borkar.

Borkar looked from her to Sansi. "What did you just say to her?"

"He's a liar," Madam Lele screamed. "Kill him...kill him..."

Sansi said: "I told her if she ever sold another human being I would tell you she'd been stealing from you."

"He's a liar...he's a lying cop," Madam Lele shrieked.

"She has been skimming your business for years," Sansi said. "We found the money and a second of books in her apartment. She's stolen millions from you."

"He's lying..." Madam Lele screeched. "Kill him...kill him...kill him..."

Borkar took a pistol from under his jacket and fired a rapid series of shots into her. Madam Lele staggered under the impact and fell, arms and legs splayed. Workmen in the lobby stopped and looked. Mrs. Khanna moaned and slumped to her knees. Borkar signaled to one of his goons and the man went over to the lobby and told the workmen to get back to work. Then Borkar turned his attention back to Sansi.

"Let's say you're right," he said, tapping the warm barrel of the gun against Sansi's chest. "Now you have to get me my money back."

"I can get it," Sansi said.

"How much did she steal?"

"There are two million American dollars we know of," Sansi said. "The money in her apartment. But she has accounts all over, inside India, outside."

Borkar glanced disbelievingly at Madam Lele's body then told Sansi: "I will give you two days to get that money back to me. I'll hold on to the *bei* till then."

"I cannot do it that soon," Sansi said. "And I cannot do it all at one time. It is evidence now and it has been put in a safe in the evidence room. I can do something but only a bit at a time."

"A bit at a time?" Borkar repeated.

"It is a lot of money," Sansi said. "If I take too much at one time it will be noticed and that doesn't help you or me."

"I want the second set of books too and the bank accounts."

"I can get you copies of those," Sansi said. "But Mrs. Khanna comes with me now or there is no deal."

"You are not in any position to bargain," Borkar said.

"Let her go or you get nothing," Sansi said. "Kill me and you get nothing."

If only Borkar knew, Sansi thought. If he knew the operation that had shut down his escort service and cost him millions was just the beginning. That in less than six hours it would expand into something much bigger. Something that would wipe out much of his client base and all the connections it had taken him years to build up. If he had known any of it Borkar would have murdered Sansi where he stood.

"You are a very annoying man," Borkar said.

"You are not the first person to tell me that," Sansi said.

Borkar put his pistol back under his jacket. "We will talk again soon," he said. He told his men to let Mrs. Khanna go then had them retrieve Madam Lele's body. Sansi hurried to Mrs. Khanna and held her to reassure her she was safe now. She was shaking and too shocked to speak. It was several minutes before he could coax her to her feet and half walk, half carry her to the street. The whole time he had to keep from her how shaky his own legs were.

*   *   *

Police headquarters thrummed with activity. Jatkar had turned Crime Branch into the control center for Operation Garuda. He'd set up computer stations and brought in officers from the cyber crime unit to manage the operation. The unit's deputy sub-inspector, Gabale, was in charge of electronic tracking and he had his own command desk in front of a big screen TV monitor at the back of the room. The monitor showed a satellite map of Mumbai and would provide live streaming of the operation with the ability to zoom in on any location. Police headquarters hummed through the night as officers were formed into four man squads to pick up 118 suspects throughout the city. Jatkar had organized the operation so that each squad was assigned five or six names on the arrest list. Another nine suspects would be picked up by the state police in places like Aurangabad, Nagpur and Pune and a separate officer had been assigned to act as the Crime Branch liaison. As men and vehicles assembled on the parade ground it began to resemble an army base mobilizing for war. Sansi found Jatkar in his office going over the details with the squad leaders. He waited till they were finished and filed out of the office.

"You'd better have got the *bei* back in one piece," Jatkar told Sansi. "I don't want to hear it was a waste of time."

"I got her back," Sansi said. He decided it was not the time to tell Jatkar about everything else that happened.

Jatkar walked around his desk. "Next time you put personal considerations ahead of something this important I'll fire you," he said. "Now, you can help me finish putting this operation together."

Exhausted though he was Sansi somehow found the reserves to work through what remained of the night. By five-o-clock in the morning everything was ready and Jatkar went out onto the Crime Branch verandah to address the assembled strike force. He told the men they were taking part in an historic operation. This was the day they would strike a heavy blow against the corruption that crippled Mumbai, he said. A day they would remember for the rest of their lives. Sansi watched from inside. Seeing past the commissioner to the upturned faces on the parade ground Sansi knew he was witnessing the aspiring politician at work. Jatkar building the legend of a leader. When Jatkar was finished the men climbed into their vehicles and formed up in order of departure. Jatkar signaled the lead van to go and the strike force rumbled out through the gates and into the unsuspecting city.

Sansi and Jatkar went inside to have some *chai.* There would be a lull before reports of the first arrests came in and then they would become a flood. The two of them stood at the back of the room and sipped hot sweet *chai,* their eyes on the TV monitor. There were 20 computer stations in the room, an operator for each squad, including Sansi's constables, Agarkar and Nimkar. The atmosphere was calm but expectant. By the end of the day the government would be in uproar but Jatkar's name would be on everyone's lips and a step closer to becoming the people's hero.

"So, Sansi, now you are as popular as me," Jatkar said. "So popular you need your own personal security detail."

"Borkar will go to ground," Sansi said. "But he is not a patient man, he will want to get back at me."

"*Acha*, the key is to get him before he gets you," Jatkar said.

It would be no simple matter to get Borkar first. Mumbai's crime lords commanded immense resources. Years ago another infamous gangster, Dawood Ibrahim, had fled to Dubai from where he masterminded a massive attack on Mumbai. His men had planted 13 land mines around the city, the explosions killed 350 people, wounded 1,200 and destroyed the Mumbai Stock Exchange. Shiney Borkar could prove just as elusive and his reach just as long.

A female operator at the front of the room signaled deputy sub-inspector Gabale she had a report coming in. The home of Gaurav Aadekar, the Minister for Housing, was closest and it had been hit first. A modest townhouse in the Khetwadi area it went with the modest image he had cultivated for himself.

"Aadekar is in custody," the operator said. "No resistance."

A little green bubble containing the number one popped up at Aadekar's address on the big screen map of Mumbai.

"I hope they all come in so easily," Jatkar said. He wanted the two biggest names picked up first. Hemant Dubade, the Minister for Urban Development, was next. A few minutes later an arrest report for Dubade came in and a number two went up on the map. Dubade too had surrendered peacefully. Sansi thought it would be a miracle if every arrest went so smoothly. Cabinet ministers didn't get to where they were without thick skins and an ability to deny everything. Lower level *babus* didn't have the same gall and some men would rather die than be as exposed as a child molester.

The first two squads brought their VIP prisoners in for processing then went out for the next names on their lists. Jatkar had set up a system whereby prisoners would be processed as they arrived and placed in holding cells until there were enough of them to be shuttled to Arthur Road in prison vans. It wasn't long before a call came from the detention block to tell Jatkar that both Aadekar and Dubade were demanding to see the officer in charge.

"Tell them they will be treated like every other prisoner," Jatkar said.

The pace of arrests picked up, reports flowed in and the room filled with chatter. One green bubble after another popped up on the screen. There were 29 before the first blue bubble appeared signifying a failed arrest. If a suspect wasn't at home each squad was to go to the suspect's workplace and arrest him there. If that failed the arrest warrant would be considered non-executable, a red bubble would go up and the squad would move on to the next name on the list. By noontime there were 63 green bubbles onscreen, five blue and three red. Relatives of those arrested had begun to gather at the front gates. The first calls from newspapers, TV and radio stations were coming in. Jatkar had his aide tell them he would make a statement at the end of the day. A call came in from Chief Minister Athawale's office and Jatkar had his aide tell Athawale's aide the same thing.

Commissioner Singh stopped by soon afterwards but he didn't say if it was in response to a call from Athawale's office. A burly Sikh with a full beard Singh was unreadable. He exchanged courtesies with Jatkar and Sansi, watched the action on the big screen for a few minutes then left without another word. This was Jatkar's show and the credit or the blame would be all his. If Singh's visit told Sansi anything it was how much autonomy Jatkar had acquired within the police service. In the years Sansi had been away Jatkar had become a power unto himself.

By seven-o-clock that evening the operation was winding down. There were 101 green bubbles on the screen and 17 red; suspects who could have been ill, away on business or on vacation. They would be picked up later. A few suspects had resisted but most had been taken by surprise. Like Madam Lele they had assumed they were protected by Shiney Borkar's extensive web of corruption. There were a few minor injuries due to rough handling by the police but nothing serious. By any measure Operation Garuda was a success. Jatkar was exhilarated and went around the control room doling out praise. When he came to Sansi he put his hands on Sansi's shoulders and told him: "This is a great day for us. For Crime Branch, for the police service, for the people of Mumbai. And for the government, even though they might not appreciate it yet. And none of it would have been possible without you, Sansi. You are the man behind Operation Garuda. I am the public face, that is all. You see, I was right. You and I together - we are a winning combination."

Jatkar ordered his aide to schedule a press conference for 8 p.m. and invited Gabale to join him. Then he retreated to his office to shave and put on the clean uniform he wore for special occasions. Sansi and Chowdhary stayed behind to wrap up the operation. The last two arrests came within half an hour. Gabale thanked everybody and went off to join Jatkar. Officers shut down their work stations and got up to stretch and move around. A couple gave each other shoulder massages and some went outside to smoke. Others stayed for a last cup of *chai* and to ease the adrenalin out of their blood. Two of them were Sansi's constables, Agarkar and Nimkar. Sansi told them they could go home but they preferred to stay, to enjoy the moment. Days like this were rare. There was a distinct feeling that they were part of history.

Agarkar lowered his voice and told Sansi: "It should be you with Commissioner Jatkar at the press conference Sansi-ji, not Gabale."

"Gabale earned his share of the credit," Sansi said and left it at that. He had no desire to make his face known to the local media.

A few minutes before eight an officer tuned the big screen TV into the press room so they could watch Jatkar's press conference. The camera was trained on an empty table with a battery of microphones. By the buzz of voices in the background the press room was full. Jatkar was late and when he appeared with Gabale and a press office constable it was to a blitz of camera flashes. A barrage of questions followed. Jatkar held up his hands in an appeal for quiet then sat at the table and gestured Gabale to the seat beside him. The questions began anew and this time Jatkar simply waited for quiet. Finally, he said he would read a short statement and then take questions. He began reading into the expectant hush.

"Today, Crime Branch delivered a heavy blow to the forces of corruption in Mumbai. Starting this morning at dawn we launched a series of raids under Operation Garuda, an operation to bring to justice the clients of one of the biggest prostitution rings in the city. Operation Garuda is the largest operation of its kind in the history of Mumbai. Raids and arrests continued throughout the day. I can report to you this evening that we have taken 101 individuals into custody. These include two highly placed members of the Government of Maharashtra; Gaurav Aadekar, the Minister for Housing, and Hemant Dubade, the Minister for Urban Development."

The room erupted in frenzy and once again Jatkar said nothing and waited for calm. His manner was stern and his speech carefully parsed and Sansi could see how Jatkar played the crowd the way a conductor would play an orchestra.

"Other individuals arrested include department heads and officials at all levels of government," Jatkar continued. "Charges include illegal solicitation and soliciting sex from minors."

The media mob erupted again with repeated questions about Aadekar and Dubade and if they had been charged with soliciting minors.

"All suspects will appear in court on Monday," Jatkar said. "Charges are still being finalized and the investigation is ongoing." He put down his notes and looked directly into the eyes of his audience behind the cameras. An audience that could be measured in millions. "Operation Garuda sends a clear message that no-one is above the law. Whoever you are, however high and mighty you may be, if you break the law in Mumbai you will answer for your crimes."

Standing next to Sansi Chowdhary said: "He always plays forward."

It was a cricketing term for a batsman playing a fast ball. Chowdhary bowled for the police team and had probably bowled against Jatkar.

"How do you bowl to him?" Sansi said.

"He has a good eye so you can't be too predictable," Chowdhary said.
"I have had my best luck against him when I bowl an off spinner. If it catches him
wrong it will spin in and hit the off stump or the middle stump. Sometimes I bowl him a
bouncer and get him low. But it is not easy, he is a good player."

"One of your sons plays cricket doesn't he?" Sansi asked. "A bowler too as I remember."

"Raman," Chowdhary said. "He has been picked up by Mumbai as a replacement bowler."

The Mumbai cricket team was the premier cricket team in Maharashtra and its best players often went on to play for the Indian National Cricket Team.

"That is wonderful news," Sansi said. "Why didn't you say anything."

"Oh, he is a modest boy, Sansi-ji," Chowdhary said. "He does not like me to boast about him."

"I can't imagine where he gets modesty from," Sansi said. After a pause he added: "Would you mind stepping outside with me for a moment, there is something I have been meaning to ask you."

He led the way to the farthest end of the second floor verandah where he and Chowdhary couldn't be overheard. He positioned himself so he could see Chowdhary's face in the light.

"I have been thinking about what happened in Karnataka," Sansi said. "When you went to the Western Ghats to pick up Sunni Shah, did you know what the Karnataka Task Force was going to do?"

"*Nahi*, Sansi-ji," Chowdhary said impassively. "I did not know."

"Did Jatkar know?"

"I cannot say if he knew," Chowdhary added. "But he did not say anything to me."

"And where were you when the task force shot Sunni's men?"

"I was with Sunni in the car. We were leaving the scene. I did not know what happened for sure until I was back in Mumbai."

"But Sunni knew," Sansi said. "Sunni knew at the time it happened."

"Yes, he knew," Chowdhary admitted.

"You were there when he surrendered?" Sansi said.

"Yes."

"And you were there when he told his men to put down their weapons and come out and they would not be harmed?"

"Yes."

"You were leaving with Sunni in the car but you were close enough to hear the guns firing? Sunni heard them so you must have heard them too?"

"Yes, Sansi-ji."

"What did you think was happening?"

"I thought the same as Sunni," Chowdhary said. "But he went crazy and I had to subdue him."

"Who told you when you got back to Mumbai?"

"It was Commissioner Jatkar."

"What did he say?"

"He said the task force had cleaned up Sunni's gang."

"He used those words - cleaned up?"

"Yes."

"What did you take those words to mean?"

"That the task force had executed Sunni's gang."

"Didn't you think that was a little extreme?"

"Nobody said anything to me about executing prisoners, Sansi-ji. I didn't have any dealings with the

Karnataka officers, my dealings were with Deputy Commissioner Adiga. I was from Mumbai. I was there for Sunni Shah. When they handed him over my part was done."

"It had to have been planned in advance."

"Nobody told me about any plans."

"You didn't hear the men talking at the scene? You didn't hear them say anything?"

"Not about killing prisoners. It looked like a completely professional operation."

"It was certainly efficient," Sansi said. "How was Jatkar when he told you?"

"He said it was Karnataka's business, not ours. The important thing was we had Sunni."

"It wasn't important that one of our men was at the scene of a massacre?" Sansi said. "And by saying and doing nothing we might be complicit?"

Chowdhary looked pained. He hated any kind of disapproval from Sansi.

"I believe you," Sansi said. "And I don't think there was anything you could have done to prevent it. But whether we like it or not we are part of the cover-up."

Months had passed and Sansi hadn't seen anything in the news since the initial reports of Shah's capture and the official account of the shootout. Whether Jatkar knew of the fate of Shah's men in advance or not it had been decided between him and Deputy Commissioner Adiga that the matter of Sunni's gang would be handled locally. The bodies would have been disposed of before the end of the day. And in Mumbai Jatkar would get credit for the capture of Sunni Shah. It was the way things were now. Sunni Shah had been telling the truth.

*   *   *

Sansi had reached that eerie twilight between obsession and exhaustion where he thought he might never sleep again. His body ached and his eyes burned but his mind was too busy to let him rest. Instead of going home he stopped by Annie's apartment to tell her about Usha - and to warn her away from Malabar Hill until the danger from Shiney Borkar had passed.

"You look like you haven't slept since I last saw you," she said.

"When was that?" he said.

It had been long enough for Annie's hair to grow in so it lay flat against her scalp and the scar was all but invisible.

"Would you like something to drink?" she asked. "*Chai* or something?"

"I don't think I could look at another cup of *chai.*"

"How about some mango juice, I made some fresh about an hour ago?"

"Perfect."

"Go grab a seat before you fall over," she said and went to the refrigerator.

Sansi dropped his jacket on a chair and sank into the sofa. He felt buzzy, as if a little drunk. He didn't like it.

"How is the new job going?" he asked.

"They're a good crowd," she said. "Young and sharp, of course, but I think I'm going to like it. You want ice?"

"Just as it comes."

She set the glass of mango juice on the coffee table in front of him and took a chair opposite.

"You're not having anything?" he asked.

"No, I'm good."

He took a sip of juice and it tasted so good he kept drinking till the glass was half empty.

"I think I need some of this injected directly into my bloodstream," he said.

"It's full of good stuff," Annie said. "Drink up, I have plenty."

"Thank you but I can't stay long," he said. "You may have noticed, we have been quite busy at crime branch but I have some information about Usha I want to share with you."

"You got that bitch to talk?"

"If she is telling the truth Usha has been taken to Dubai," Sansi said. "Madam Lele also gave me the name of the Arab man she says took Usha there. She said he works for the government of Dubai."

"So that's what, a government to government thing?"

"We can't approach the Dubai authorities on our own, we have to go through New Delhi," Sansi said. "I discussed it with Jatkar but he says it's not something New Delhi has done before. And he made it very clear that Usha may be a priority to me but she isn't to him."

"Prick."

"In the meantime we had a bit of unpleasantness with Shiney Borkar to contend with. He's Madam Lele's boss and he came to the apartment with some of his men and took Mrs. Khanna hostage. I had to give up Madam Lele to get Mrs. Khanna back."

"Oh my god," Annie said, shocked. "How is she, is she alright?"

"Truthfully, I don't know," Sansi said. "She is very shaken up."

"And what about Pramila, how is she?"

"She was more upset for Mrs. Khanna than she was for herself," Sansi said. "But the situation now is that Shiney Borkar has more reason than ever to come after me and until the situation has been resolved I think it best you stay away from Malabar Hill."

"I'm going to call her," Annie said. "And I'm going over there."

"Didn't you hear what I just asked you?" Sansi said. "There is no need for you to put your life at risk as well. All that does is give me more to worry about."

"That's sweet," Annie said. "But I'm going over there."

"Call her first," Sansi said, thinking Pramila might have more success than him in persuading Annie to stay away.

"What happens next with this Shiney Borkar character?" Annie asked.

"I'm going to bring him in before he can do any more harm to the people I care about." Sansi said.

"How are you going to do that?"

"By making him angry at me."

"He was already mad at you. I'd say it's gone beyond that now, wouldn't you?"

"Angry people make mistakes."

"So do tired people," Annie said.

"It is nothing that a good night's sleep cannot cure," Sansi said.

"Okay, let me try something," she said. She got up and knelt on the sofa beside him. "Lean forward with your back to me so I can get at your shoulders."

"I should be going," he said.

"That's fine," Annie said. "Let me see if I can get some of that tension out of you first."

Too tired to argue he turned his back to her and leaned forward, one arm resting on the arm of the sofa. She put her hands on his shoulders, spread her fingers and began probing the muscles to the base of his neck, gently at first then deeper.

"Oh boy, you are so knotted up," she said.

She began kneading the muscles in his neck and shoulders. He felt the heat of her, the confident touch of her hands.

"Work with me here, I guarantee you this is going no further," she said.

He tried to relax, dropped his head forward so she could get at the tension in his neck.

"How long have you been like this?" she said.

"I don't know."

"You should do something, make time for a daily massage, take up yoga, something."

"I don't have time. My job is not predictable."

"Yeah, well, I can predict you're going to have a stroke or a heart attack if you don't do something."

"I will try."

"You lying piece of shit."

Sansi let her work on him. He moved his head from one side to the other so she felt the tendons in his neck crunch.

"You need days of treatment," she said. "Weeks."

"I do not think Ajit would like me to be the cause of you spending even more time away from work," he said.

"Nope, I don't think he would either."

"I am happy for you, Annie," Sansi said. "Truthfully, I am happy for you."

"You think Ajit and me are involved?" she said. "I knew you'd think that."

"I'm sorry, I didn't mean to upset you..."

"You know, even though I knew you'd think that it still pisses me off," she said. "Ajit is married, you know that, don't you? You think I'd have an affair with a married man? My boss? After everything I've been through?"

She dug her fingers deeper and he winced. Chastened, he fell silent. Gradually the tension eased out of his neck and shoulders. A soothing warmth spread downward through his body. He closed his eyes to rest them for a moment. His hand slid off the arm of the sofa and he began to snore. Annie stopped and got up, careful not to wake him. She leaned him back on the sofa and put a cushion under his head then took off his shoes and put his feet up. Then she went back to her laptop on the kitchen table and worked for another hour until she was ready for bed. She closed the curtains and turned out the lights and before leaving she stopped for a moment and watched him while he slept. He was no longer snoring, he was breathing deeply and rhythmically. He looked serene, untroubled in sleep.

"Dick," she said.

*   *   *

Sansi woke up feeling tired and sore. It was a moment before he realized where he was. He was in Annie's apartment. He'd fallen asleep while she was giving him a neck massage and now he felt even stiffer. The curtains were closed but the sun was burning brightly outside. Annie was at the kitchen table tapping at her laptop. She looked fresh in a pale lemon *salwar khameez*. She had been up for some time.

"You should have sent me home," he said.

"I don't think I could have woke you up," she said without taking her eyes from the screen of her laptop. "And I wasn't going to carry you downstairs."

"I'm sorry," he said.

"You want coffee?"

"What time is it?"

"A little after ten a.m."

"I should call in, they will wonder where I am," he said.

What he wanted was to go back to Malabar Hill, shower, put on clean pajamas and crawl under the cool cotton sheets of his own bed. He swung his legs off the sofa, reached for his jacket and found his cell phone. He called his mother first to let her know he was safe but he didn't tell her where he was. Then he called crime branch and said he'd be about an hour. Annie brought him a cup of coffee from the kitchen. It was hot, sweet and creamy.

"I am sorry to be a nuisance," he said. "I shouldn't have come here in such a state of collapse."

"No problem," she said. "I have to go in to the office. Help yourself to whatever you want. Make sure the door's locked when you let yourself out. Tell Pramila I'll call her."

She snapped the laptop shut, slid it into its case, said goodbye and was gone.

Sansi sipped his coffee, savored its restorative sweetness and felt better. When he was done he went to the kitchen and, like any good guest, washed and dried his cup and put it with the others. Then he went to the bathroom, splashed cold water on his face and ran his fingers through his hair before going downstairs to get a taxi. He arrived home to find his security detail had been strengthened on Jatkar's orders to two men on the street, two in the hallway and two on the roof garden. There was no sign of Mrs. Khanna and he thought she might be in her room still recovering from her ordeal. His mother was in the garden, seated by herself away from the parapet where the two officers stood guard. Sansi knelt beside her and put his hand gently on her arm.

"How are you today?" he asked.

She looked at him wearily. "I've had a phone call from Oxford," she said. "Your father died."

Chapter 5.

Sansi watched raindrops jitter across the window as the Air India flight from Mumbai to London began its descent through a sodden layer of cloud. The pilot throttled back, the engines groaned, the plane shuddered and slowed. Pramila gripped her son's hand.

"I don't mind the take-off and I quite enjoy the flight," she said. "But I don't like this part very much."

When Pramila went to speaking engagements in India she flew only when she had to. She preferred to travel by rail. She said the views and the people were much better. But when the call came from General Spooner's solicitor in Oxford that the old man had died there was no question that she and George would fly to England to attend the funeral. It was not unexpected. The last time Sansi had seen his father was six years before and while the old man was still sharp mentally he had been very, very frail.

The plane landed with a bounce and a spurt of spray and quickly decelerated. Pramila gave Sansi's hand a parting squeeze and let go. It was Pramila's first visit to England. Relations between her and General Spooner's family were such that she hadn't even gone to Oxford to see Sansi graduate. And, even though he had warned her of the interminable miles of underground tunnels at Heathrow she hadn't expected they would have to cart their bags as far as if they were at an airport in India. Sansi had a British passport but stayed with his mother while she went through foreign passport control. After they cleared immigration and customs they decanted with a stream of passengers into a cold and cavernous arrivals terminal. Through the windows Pramila saw palm trees, a consequence of climate change, cowering under a lashing rain.

"Oh, they have the monsoon here too," she said. She pulled her cashmere shawl tightly around her against the cold. "And they must be English palm trees."

Sansi pushed their luggage cart through the waiting crowd searching for their driver among the many who held up cardboard signs. At last he saw the name 'Sansi' on a card held by a man in a grey suit with grey curls under a grey cap.

"I think you are looking for us," Sansi said.

"Mister Sansi?" the driver said.

"Yes," Sansi said, "and this is my mother, Ms. Sansi."

"Very pleased to meet you sir, ma'am," the driver said and touched the peak of his cap. "My name is Kevin. Here let me take that for you."

Before Sansi could say anything Kevin had taken the luggage cart and was pushing off through the crowd.

"Stay close to me, we'll get you sorted," Kevin said. "Have you out in a jiffy."

"What is a jiffy?" Pramila asked Sansi.

"It means he is taking us to our car," Sansi said.

Sansi and Pramila followed the driver outside to a waiting area for limousines. Pramila began to shiver. Kevin stopped by a black Mercedes, pulled a collapsible umbrella from his pocket and opened it up. He popped the rear doors on the Mercedes and held the umbrella for Sansi and his mother even though there was just a sliver of rain between the pavement and the car. "Let's get the two of you inside and warmed up," he said. "This must come as quite a shock after Indian weather."

Sansi slid into the rear seat beside his mother and Kevin closed the door after him. Then Kevin got in the front seat, started the engine and turned the heat up.

"I'll get your bags loaded and we'll be on our way in just a jiffy," he said.

"Another jiffy?" Pramila said. "Why do we need two jiffies?"

"Beg pardon, ma'am?"

"*Maa*, a jiffy means something will be done quickly," Sansi said.

"You said he was taking us to our jiffy," Pramila said. "I thought you meant a motor car. It sounds as if it should be an English motor car."

Kevin loaded the bags, closed the boot and scurried around to the driver's side without the protection of the umbrella.

"Weather's been diabolical," he said. "Hasn't stopped raining since last Wednesday. We'll be growing fish scales if this keeps up. Got our seatbelts on have we? Got to have our seatbelts on. The law is very strict about that. Warm enough for the two of you? Would you like some music or just some peace and quiet after your flight? It's a long way from Bombay isn't it?"

"Yes, yes, no music and yes," Sansi said.

"As you say, sir," Kevin said. "And we're going to the Randolph in Oxford is that right?"

"Quite right" Sansi said.

"You speak very good English, if I may say so, sir, hardly any accent at all," Kevin said. "Though I quite like the Indian accent, I must say. Very pleasant to the ear. A singsong sort of accent, isn't it, if you don't me saying so? Did you grow up in England or were you educated here?"

"Educated here," Sansi said.

"At Oxford by any chance?"

"Yes,"

"Well, there you are then. No better is there, sir? No better education in the world than an English education. Are you warm enough back there? Are you warm enough ma'am? I can turn the heat up a bit more if you like?"

"I'm quite comfortable now, thank you," Pramila said.

"I can put the partition up. Have some privacy if you'd prefer. There's a heat control switch back there too. The two of you just sit back and make yourselves comfortable and leave the rest to me. We'll have you in Oxford in no time at all."

"In a jiffy," Pramila said.

"Right you are, ma'am, right you are, we'll have you there in a jiffy," Kevin said.

Kevin pulled out into the great grey labyrinth that was Heathrow and turned on the wipers against the pelting rain. They drove through a dizzying sequence of tunnels, underpasses and intersections. The traffic was stop and go and there seemed to be a roundabout or a traffic light every hundred feet. Gradually they pulled away from the rain swept mass of London and were on the M40 with neatly laid out fields on each side punctuated by grim clusters of densely packed housing. The pace of the traffic picked up until they reached the exit for the A40 and slowed down again. They soon passed a black and white sign that announced they were entering Oxford.

"*Are Bapre*," Pramila said. "Are we here already?"

"It doesn't take long," Sansi said. "England is a small country."

"Yes it is, sir," Kevin agreed. "But the English are a great people, don't you think so, sir? And a good hearted people?"

"I do, indeed," Sansi said.

"Thank you, sir, most kind of you to say so."

"It's all so different and so familiar at the same time," Pramila said as tightly packed rows of terrace houses yielded to the historic buildings of the university and the city centre. "I feel as if I were here in another life."

"Me too," Sansi said.

*   *   *

The Randolph was a venerable old maid of a hotel but comfortable and situated in the middle of Oxford, which made it convenient for everything Sansi and Pramila had to do in the short time they would be there. Once they were in their rooms Sansi placed a call to Gerald Patterson, his father's solicitor. It was Patterson who had called Pramila and told her of General Spooner's death and the General's wishes that she and their son attend his funeral. Sansi arranged for himself and Pramila to meet Patterson the next morning at ten.

Sansi and Pramila ate in the hotel dining room and retired to their rooms soon after. Sansi took a hot bath to relax himself before turning in but still slept poorly and woke up early. He showered, dressed and went out to walk off some of his restlessness. He borrowed an umbrella from the front desk and set off into the city centre. The rain had eased but low clouds cast the city in a dismal light. Blurred figures scurried along the footpath dodging puddles and the splash of passing cars and buses. Sansi hadn't gone far when he realized that, even with an umbrella, he would soon be soaked. He took refuge in an organic cafe called The Jolly Parrot. It was a little after seven and the café was half empty so he had no trouble finding a table. He ordered black tea with toast and settled into the murmuring quiet. A few discarded newspapers lay around and he picked up a recent copy of The Oxford Times and was surprised to come across a full page obituary for his father. He shouldn't have been because, even though he and his father had been close, his father was also a public figure and this was the side of him the rest of the world would know. The photograph showed General Spooner in full dress uniform with a chest full of campaign ribbons and medals that included the Military Cross, an OBE and the India Service Medal. Sansi hadn't seen the picture before but he thought it was most likely the year the General retired from the army when he was 60 years old. The sober expression and distracted gaze suggested a man more aloof than the man Sansi had known.

The obituary was extensive and flattering. It told how George Spooner was the youngest of three children and the only son of a Presbyterian Minister and his wife who moved from Richmond to Oxford in 1916. Spooner went to Oxford High School for Boys where he excelled in science and sports. From there he went to Sandhurst where he graduated with the rank of second lieutenant. Posted to the Oxfordshire and Buckingham Light Infantry his aptitude for logistics saw him promoted to first lieutenant in regimental operations. After performing well there he was promoted to captain and assigned to the office of the Adjutant-General at the War Office in London. While in London he married Audrey Lippmann, the only daughter of Walter Lippmann, a prominent merchant banker. Craving something more exotic than the musty corridors of Whitehall he persuaded his wife to agree to an overseas posting. In 1933 he was assigned to British Army Headquarters in New Delhi as assistant quarter master in the Quarter Master General's office. Audrey went with him and for five years they enjoyed the pleasures of the Raj at its imperial height. Those pleasures came to an end with the approach of the Second World War. Audrey was pregnant with their first child and it was agreed that she would return to England. Spooner was not to see his son, Eric, until the boy was six years old. War brought swift promotion and by 1941 Spooner had been promoted to the rank of Colonel and was second only to the Quarter Master General for the entire British Army in India. A series of devastating defeats by the Japanese saw British and Indian forces pushed out of Malaya and Burma back into India. As the Japanese prepared to invade India orders came from London that India was to be held at all costs. Colonel Spooner was tasked with ensuring that British forces had all they needed. He oversaw the reinforcement and supply of British and

Indian units on the border with Burma and visited the front lines regularly to make sure supplies were going where they were most needed. In 1944 the critical battle was fought at Imphal just inside the Indian border. If the British lost here it would be the end of the British Empire in Asia. The battle raged for five months and at its peak Spooner found himself trapped in Imphal by the encircling Japanese. It was here that he won the Military Cross for taking personal command of soldiers moving replacement artillery to the front lines under heavy enemy fire. The result was a major British victory that resulted in the annihilation of the invading Japanese army. The end of the war saw Spooner promoted to Brigadier General and put in charge of the British Army's western command headquartered in Mumbai. Audrey joined him there with their young son but any expectations that Mumbai would be a comfortable peacetime command were shattered by the escalating violence of the Indian drive toward independence. Audrey returned to England after just a few months and gave birth to their second child, a daughter named Hillary. With India coming apart at the seams Spooner struggled to preserve the peace until Indian Independence on August 15, 1947. He returned with the last British troops to leave India in February of 1948 and remained with the army until his retirement. The obituary described him as "a devoted husband and father and a supporter of numerous charities who had endowed a scholarship at Oxford Law School for outstanding candidates from throughout the Commonwealth." He was predeceased by his wife, who succumbed to breast cancer in 1968, and was survived by two children, Eric and Hillary, five grandchildren and one great grandchild. It was the story of a dutiful man who lived an extraordinary life that encompassed some of the greatest events of the 20th century. And it was true as far as it went. But it wasn't the whole story. It barely hinted at the complexity of the man and was oblivious to the personal drama that surpassed anything in his public life. If Sansi was certain of anything it was that George Spooner loved Pramila Sansi and his Indian family.

The obituary gave no real sense of how bad things were in India in the months leading up to Independence. It was a time when train loads of butchered refugees, Hindu and Muslim, arrived daily on both sides of a border between India and Pakistan that would not come into effect until August of 1947. A time when British authorities feared they would leave the country awash in the blood of its people. A time when British and Indian troops struggled to contain the slaughter in the streets while official dinners and receptions were conducted in the palaces and pavilions of the Raj in pretence of a civilized handover. It was in the midst of all this turmoil that General Spooner met Pramila Sansi.

Their first meeting did not go well. Pramila was at a reception at Government House in Mumbai with her father and two older brothers. Her father was a shipping agent who made a great deal of money transporting men and equipment from England to India during the war and back again when the war was over. At the same time he was trying to effect promising new relations with senior figures in the Congress Party who would head up the new government. Like her father Pramila believed the British departure from India was long overdue and told Spooner as much when she was introduced to him. There wouldn't have been a second meeting if it were not for an extraordinary event that took place a few days later. A demonstration on the *Maidan* turned violent and a Hindu mob set out for the Muslim quarter. Spooner ordered every available man onto the streets but it wasn't enough. Fresh tragedy on a scale that could happen only in India threatened. Spooner went out in a staff car to see for himself and realized that there were only two ways to turn the mob back; he could authorize the use of deadly force -

or he could ask them politely. Accompanied by a squad of 20 men he had his driver nudge the staff car through the crowd until he reached the head of the mob. He told the driver to position the car across the road and ordered his men to form a line behind it, rifles shouldered. The leaders of the mob paused, bewildered by the spectacle of a lone British General in an open car with a mere handful of soldiers. The General got to his feet, one hand on the windshield to steady himself, faced the mob and waited. If they had surged forward then they would have trampled him and his men into the dust. But there was something about him standing there for all to see, unarmed and unafraid. He had committed his fate to whatever happened next and was clearly at peace with it. And they began to quiet. When they had quieted enough he spoke to them. He didn't speak in the haughty voice of Empire. It wasn't the voice of command or rebuke. It was the voice of reason. Britain's time was over, he said. India was in their hands now. It was up to them to show the world what kind of country their India would be. That was all. And it was enough. The moment for violence passed. The mob was no longer a mob. Of their own will they turned back. And Pramila, who had watched from a tailor's shop with her mother where they had been trapped by the crowd, thought it the bravest and noblest act she had ever seen.

Two days later Pramila went to see General Spooner on her own. She wanted to apologize for what she had said to him at the reception and to thank him for putting Indian lives before his own. He invited her to take tea with him and before they knew it much of the afternoon had slipped by. When Pramila left Spooner knew he had been in the presence of a young woman of extraordinary intelligence and insight. And Pramila could not understand why she felt so drawn to a man 26 years her senior. A man who was, in every way, unsuitable for her. Over the next few months they found excuses to spend more and more time together until, that August, they had to acknowledge what had become abundantly clear - they were in love with each other. That December Pramila learned she was pregnant. She decided against telling Spooner. There was no prospect that he could ever leave his wife for an Indian girl. It was her mistake and she would accept the consequences. She told her mother and her mother wept. When her mother told her father he became incensed. He attacked Pramila in a rage and would have strangled her if her brothers had not intervened. He disowned her and put her out of the house that night. She had only the clothes she wore, a suitcase her mother sneaked out to her and what little money she had in her own name. She moved into a cheap hotel until she found a job as a language teacher at the Anglo-Indian School and was able to rent an apartment on the property.

Consumed by preparations for the British withdrawal Spooner surmised that Pramila had decided to end their relationship. He understood why. She had to make a life for herself in the new and fiercely nationalistic India. An improper dalliance with a British General could only have harmed her. He might never have known the truth were it not for a few chance words from a friend's child at a garden party who mentioned Pramila's name. Spooner went to her intending only to wish her well and to tell her that if she was made to suffer in any way for their relationship he would help her however he could. Her tears and silence told him the rest. Despite her protests he insisted that he would bear his share of responsibility for supporting her and their child. He bought the apartment on Malabar Hill in her name and settled sufficient funds on her to pay her hospital bills and cover any other expenses for several months.

The day before Spooner was due to lead his men through the Gateway to India and onto a ship bound for home he and Pramila stood on the broad terrace of the apartment on Malabar Hill and said their goodbyes to each other. Spooner promised he would return when their child was born. It was a promise he was unable to keep. The demands of duty kept him from returning. In the meantime Pramila took comfort from his letters, hired a day nurse for her son, and became the first woman to enroll at the University Of Bombay. She studied political science with the intention of going into politics. Her own experience told her that women would need someone to speak up for them in the new India.

George Sansi was two years old when his father first came out to see him. He stayed for 10 days. He came out the next year for two weeks and the year after that and the year after that. When he retired from the army his visits lasted two months and more. Sansi had vivid memories of his father from an early age; teaching him to swim at the Breach Candy Pool, showing him how to wield a cricket bat on the *Maidan* and dinners punctuated with laughter on the terrace that Pramila had decided to turn into a roof garden. Spooner's wife, Audrey, knew about Pramila and Sansi but took the same view as Rudyard Kipling: East was east and west was west and as long as the two didn't meet there wouldn't be a problem. After Audrey died and Sansi reached college age Spooner encouraged him to apply to Oxford University. When Sansi was accepted the General insisted he stay at the family home at Goscombe Park. What he did not expect was the rancor Eric and Hillary displayed toward Sansi. They blamed Pramila for what they saw as their father's betrayal of their mother and resented everything he'd ever done for her. As a living symbol of that betrayal they detested Sansi even more. Sansi put up with it for his father's sake but now their father was dead he was under no illusion how they would react to him and his mother coming to the funeral. Sansi did not care so much what his step brother and step sister might say to him. What worried him was that they would be cruel to his mother.

Overshadowing it all was the disposition of the General's will and the pent-up passions that would release. Sansi knew the reason for his restlessness that rainy Oxford morning. A reckoning was at hand that had been in the making for a lifetime.

*   *   *

When Sansi got back to the Randolph he found Pramila in the lobby chatting with a middle aged Indian couple there to visit their son who was taking physics at Oxford. The wife had recognized Pramila and was talking to her about her books. Pramila beckoned Sansi over to introduce him and when the woman asked what brought them to Oxford Sansi said something about revisiting his alma mater.

"Once an Oxford man always an Oxford man, is that it?" the woman said.

"Something like that," Sansi said. To his mother he added: "I'll see you in the dining room."

Pramila chatted with them a few minutes longer then joined Sansi.

"I know you're tired but that is no excuse for bad manners," she said.

"I'm sorry, *maa*," Sansi said. "I have a lot on my mind."

"I'm well aware of that," Pramila said. "But your father used to say good manners are the first bulwark of civilization. You should remember that, especially now that we are in England."

Sansi drank more tea while Pramila had her usual breakfast of fruit and yogurt. When she was finished he passed her the copy of The Oxford Times he'd pilfered from the café open at the page with his father's obituary.

"I thought you might like to see this."

When she had read it over she said: "It's good to see your father getting the recognition he deserves."

"I am sure it is what Eric gave to the papers," Sansi said. "As far as he's concerned we don't exist."

"How we feel is unimportant," Pramila said. "We are here as servants of your father's last wishes. We will come and go without leaving so much as a ripple."

After breakfast Pramila returned to her room to get a thicker shawl but as soon as she stepped outside she began to shiver.

"This is colder than Ooty," she said. "There's no damp like English damp is there?"

"The solicitor's office is only a few minutes away," Sansi said as he opened the umbrella over her. "When we're done there we'll stop in at Debenham's and get you a proper raincoat."

Sansi had checked out Patterson's office on his walk earlier, a smart Georgian townhouse on the next street. Even so, by the time they got there Pramila's shivering was worse.

"Oh you poor dear, come on over here and get warm," the receptionist said when she saw Pramila. She led Pramila behind the reception desk to where there was a warm air blower. "This weather is absolutely atrocious, it gets right into your bones."

"You are very kind, thank you," Pramila said.

The reception area was smallish with a couple of leather couches and pictures of sunlit English countryside. Sansi shook out the umbrella, dropped it into a cluttered umbrella stand and told the receptionist they were there to see Gerald Patterson.

"Yes, he's expecting you," she said. She buzzed Patterson and told him his ten-o-clock had arrived. When she'd hung up she asked if Sansi or his mother would like a hot drink. "Honestly, it's no bother, it won't take a jiffy," she said.

They both declined and Sansi caught an amused smile from his mother.

A florid faced man with untidy white hair and a woolen suit the color of mossy stone came out of his office and introduced himself.

"Delighted to meet you at last," he said and shook hands with Sansi and Pramila. "Sorry it has to be under such sad circumstances. General Spooner spoke of the two of you with great fondness."

He showed them into his office, which would have felt cramped were it not for two tall windows that overlooked the street. On one wall bookshelves were crammed with law books and on the other prints of English game birds. Photos on the windowsills showed Patterson with a shotgun crooked over one arm. Another showed him kneeling with a golden retriever and an array of downed pheasants before them. Sansi found it curious that Englishmen liked to celebrate the creatures they killed.

"Dreadful weather isn't it?" he said. "Even for the time of year."

"I thought the English would be used to it by now," Pramila said.

"English weather is why you find Englishmen all over the world," Patterson said. "Whether we are wanted or not."

He had the terse speech of a man used to distilling complex situations down to a few sentences. A terseness often mistaken for rudeness by those not familiar with English ways.

"Did you get an invitation to the funeral yet by any chance?" he asked.

"A formal invitation?" Pramila said. "No."

"I told Eric before I called you in Mumbai it was his father's expressly stated wish that the two of you be invited to the funeral. I take it you've heard nothing from him then?"

"We have had no contact from Eric whatsoever," Sansi said.

"I was afraid that might be the case," Patterson said. "And so was the General. In the event of which he instructed me to provide you with invitations from this firm." He opened a desk drawer, took out two white envelopes and handed one each to Pramila and Sansi. "As I said on the telephone the memorial service will be held at 11 a.m. on Saturday in the Goscombe Park Chapel. There's to be an informal reception at the house afterwards. I'll pick you up at the hotel in my car and personally accompany you to the service to make sure Eric doesn't make a prat of himself."

"Eric is nothing if not consistent," Sansi said.

"I had hoped he would find it in himself to adopt a slightly more conciliatory tone for the short space of time it will take to honor his father's memory," Patterson said.

"A family coming together in shared grief?" Sansi said. "No. Eric will use my father's death to divide this family even further than it is already."

"It is most unfortunate," Patterson said. "I have to say your father had no illusions about Eric. That is why he made me the executor of the will - over loud and protracted opposition from Eric I can tell you."

"I can only imagine," Sansi said.

"You know, it puzzles me how a man like your father can have one son so utterly devoid of similarity in any respect and another so exactly like him. I look at you and I see your father looking back at me. I've never seen that with Eric. I don't see any of your father in him at all."

"Eric had a lot of resentment toward George," Pramila said. "I think he believed his father liked George more than him."

"I think that's probably true," Patterson said. "But it's not something I would have told the General. He did what he could to accommodate Eric's demands but it was never enough. When he talked about Eric it was with, I hate to say it, resignation. Despair even. But when he talked about George here he was transformed. You could see the pride he felt. I don't think I'm telling you anything you don't already know but behind that reserve he was rather a sentimental man. Only when he could let his guard down, mind you. And he couldn't do that at Goscombe Park. He spent his last years there surrounded by people who, for the most part, were just waiting for him to die."

"I wish there was something we could have done," Sansi said.

"I know, I'm sorry for mentioning it," Patterson said. "Please forgive me."

"I understand it was my father's wish that he should be cremated?" Sansi added.

"Yes," Patterson said. "I told the funeral home to hold off until after you arrived. I thought you might want to view the body."

"Where is he being kept?" Sansi asked

"It's called Evergreen," Patterson said. "It's on Banbury Road and it's one of those places where they'll cremate you in a cardboard box or plant you under a tree. Your father didn't want a big, showy funeral. He couldn't stop Eric going ahead with a memorial service but that's more about Eric than your father. Your father thought Hindus had the right idea; burn the remains and scatter the ashes." Patterson paused and clasped his hands on the desk in front of him. "That brings me to the matter of what happens after the service. The General wanted you take his ashes back to India with you and scatter them in the sea from Malabar Hill. He said the days he spent with the two of you there were the happiest days of his life."

Pramila caught her breath.

"That is why he wanted us here," Sansi said. "To take him back with us."

"He wanted you here because you were the only two people in the world he was sure loved him for who he was," Patterson said.

Sansi looked at Pramila and saw tears on her cheeks. It was the first time he had ever seen her cry. She reached into her purse for a tissue at the same time Sansi and Patterson offered their handkerchiefs to her. She half laughed as she dabbed at the tears.

"*Are Bapre,*I thought I'd prepared myself."

"We were his escape, his refuge," Sansi said. "But duty always came first with him, to country, to family. The times he was with us were the only times he could be himself."

"He *was* a dutiful man," Patterson said. "He belonged to a different generation, a different time. Men like your father didn't think of happiness the way people today think of it, as if it was some kind of right. They were taught that life was a serious business. It was about hard work and sacrifice. You did what was expected of you and you didn't complain. If there was time left over for a bit of personal relaxation, well, that was the most you could hope for. But pleasure for the sake of pleasure, that was for ne'er-do-wells."

"Of course...of course we'll take his ashes home with us," Pramila said.

Patterson reached back into his desk drawer and took out a large sealed brown envelope.

"General Spooner also set funds aside to cover the expense of your coming here and of transporting his ashes to Mumbai." Patterson placed the envelope on the desk in front of them. "There are 20,000 pounds in there, it should be enough to cover your airfares and other expenses. If you need more let me know."

"We didn't have to be paid to come," Pramila said.

"I understand," Patterson said. "But I think the General knew if he asked you to come you would, regardless of the expense. And he had a good idea that when you were here you would agree to take his ashes back to India with you. I should tell you that no-one else in the family has any knowledge of this."

"No-one in the rest of the family knows my father wanted his ashes taken to India?" Sansi said.

"He had no intention of telling them and neither do I," Patterson said. "I intend to carry out your father's instructions to the letter and I expect that is a wound neither of you has any desire to open with the family either."

"Not at all," Sansi said.

"Good, I'm glad that's settled," Patterson said. "Once you've viewed the body I'll tell the funeral home to proceed with the cremation. I'll be at the crematorium to take charge of the ashes. I can bring them to you if you wish but if you would allow me I will see they're removed to a secure place until your return flight to Mumbai."

"Of course," Pramila said.

"Won't the family expect General Spooner's ashes to be at the memorial service," Sansi said.

"They will expect an urn with some ashes in it," Patterson said. "I will see to it that they get one."

"With whose ashes?" Sansi asked.

"I had one of my gun dogs, Maxie, cremated last year," Patterson said. "This will be her way of performing one final service for me."

"Did the General know this?" Sansi said.

"Yes," Patterson answered.

"Did he approve?"Pramila asked.

"He did," Patterson said. "Very much so."

"Well," Pramila said, "it was worth coming all this way just to hear that."

Patterson asked: "When would you like to go to Evergreen and view the body?"

"I won't be going," Pramila said. "I prefer my memories of George Spooner the way they are."

"I'll go," Sansi said. "As soon as we leave here."

"I'll call ahead and tell them you're coming," Patterson said. "But before you do there is one more matter I must discuss with you and I fear the solution won't be anywhere near as simple. I've sent Eric and Hillary their copies of the will and I have copies for each of you to take with you today. You should read it carefully. It's not long but it is very specific and it is important that you understand everything in it. If you have any questions you can get back to me and I'll be pleased to answer them for you. What I can tell you now is your father divided his estate equitably between Eric, Hillary and the two of you. There are provisions for the settlement of some modest sums on his three grandchildren, a great grandson and the housekeeper, Mrs. Chappell, but the broad intent of the will is to see that his heirs each get an equal one fourth share of the estate. He specifically mentions his three direct heirs and Pramila Sansi. Eric has already told me he intends to take legal action to overturn the will."

"I expected something like that," Sansi said.

"Yes, I did too," Patterson said. "But he'd be a fool to try. Legal precedent in this country attaches great weight to the intentions of the deceased. If Eric does proceed with a legal challenge the terms of the will would be frozen until decided by the court. That could take a year or more and it could be expensive if you decide to fight him."

"He doesn't believe in making it easy does he?" Sansi said.

"More than that," Patterson said. "What he doesn't seem to appreciate is that a freeze on the assets of the estate would have a calamitous effect on the business side of Goscombe Park. Your father hired a first rate estate manager some years ago, a good man who has built it up into a highly successful cattle breeding enterprise. In the event of a legal challenge everything would come to a halt. Nothing could be done without the unanimous approval of the heirs and the court. You could make life very difficult for Eric if you chose to do so."

"We have no desire to compromise the financial viability of Goscombe Park," Sansi said.

"I've tried to make him see reason but he is a man who tends to be governed by his emotions," Patterson said. "He's already threatened to take the legal business of the estate away from this firm. I suspect he'll do that regardless."

"It sounds as if we will have to engage a solicitor of our own," Sansi said.

"I'm afraid so," Patterson said. "I have taken the liberty of discussing the situation with a colleague at a law firm here in Oxford. His name is John Lilley and he's a highly experienced probate solicitor. He knows you are here for a limited time and if you like I can set up an appointment so you can get some idea where you stand in terms of your legal options. Certainly I would advise you to meet with him before you commit to anything - and I'm not supposed to advise you on anything."

Sansi looked at Pramila and she gave the slightest tilt of her head.

"Would the Monday after the memorial service work?" Sansi said.

"I'm sure it will," Patterson said. "I am just so dreadfully sorry that you have to go through all of this. You deserve better."

"It is quite alright," Sansi said. "We are patient people."

*   *   *

The rain was falling heavier than ever. Patterson's cheery receptionist called a taxi and Sansi dropped Pramila at Debenham's so she could pick out a raincoat and clothes for the memorial service. Hindu mourners wore white at funerals but she had decided she would wear traditional English mourning clothes rather than risk provoking the General's family. Sansi continued on to Evergreen's which was an oasis of light on a wet and dreary street, a frosted window with the name of the firm and underneath an acorn nestled in an oak leaf cluster. Inside was a medley of tranquil beiges and greens. A woman with platinum hair worked at a desk in a bright and slightly clinical reception area. In a corner a wicker basket was filled with dried rushes and reeds.

"Hello, I'm Sally," the woman said and came out from behind the desk. "You must be Mr. Sansi."

"What gave me away?" Sansi said.

She smiled the enthusiastic smile of someone running a health spa rather than a funeral service. Her face was young and unlined but her voice put her in her late forties or early fifties. She offered her hand which was warm and soft.

"You'd like to see your father," I believe.

"I would."

"He's resting downstairs," she said, as if the General was relaxing after a session of water aerobics with a refreshing glass of algae. She flicked a switch on the intercom and asked Tony to come and watch the front office while she looked after Sansi. Tony was young with longish black hair and an air of sly familiarity that suggested he and Sally might be lovers. Sally escorted Sansi down a hallway past a couple of consulting rooms and a larger room that looked as if it was used for all-denominational services.

"We met with your father twice before he passed," Sally said. "He was very clear and precise about what he wanted. A real military man. He approved everything right down to the shroud."

"Shroud?" Sansi said.

"To use his words he said he didn't want any 'damned nonsense'," Sally continued. "He said a shroud would do perfectly well considering what was going to happen to it."

There was an open area at the back with an industrial sized lift big enough to carry two body trolleys at a time. Next to it was a staircase that led down. At the bottom was an open area where trolleys were moved between the lift and a set of double doors that led to a garage. Past the garage doors was an unmarked door Sally said was the way to the crematorium. The floor tiles were heavily scuffed by trolley wheels. Opposite the stairs was a corridor with two doors, the first marked "Resting," the next marked "Transition." The temperature in the basement was noticeably cooler and there was a vaguely floral scent.

"Do you do any embalming or chemical preservation of the body?" Sansi asked.

"We don't do embalming, physical restoration or any inorganic preservation of any kind," Sally said. "The only method we use for preserving the body until the funeral is refrigeration."

"Have any other family members been to see him?" Sansi asked.

"Yes, his eldest son, I believe, Eric. And a daughter, Hillary. It was the day after the GP issued the death certificate and released the body. They wanted to have him transferred to a more traditional funeral company but that was directly against your father's instructions. They weren't pleased with your father's choice of funeral service."

She opened the door marked Resting and Sansi found himself in a room with tiled walls and cold enough to see his breath. In the middle of the room was a trolley with a body wrapped in a linen shroud. It could have been a Hindu funeral shroud except for the cloth ties at the neck, middle and feet.

"We bathed and disinfected him but that's all," Sally said. "He's not dressed or made up. We don't do that and he didn't want any of that either."

"He is free to do as he wishes now," Sansi said.

Sansi thought of the roof garden at Malabar Hill and the happy times he and Pramila had shared with the General there and hoped they were the last thoughts his father had had.

"Will you be attending the cremation?" Sally asked.

"No, my father's solicitor, Mr. Patterson will be here for that," Sansi said. "He has everything very much in hand and my mother and myself have full confidence in him. I think all you've been waiting for is for myself and my mother to get here and my mother has no wish to view the body."

"I understand," Sally said. "Would you like me to open the shroud?"

"Please," Sansi said.

Sally unfastened the cloth bow at the neck and pulled back the shroud to reveal the face. It was thin, drawn and pale blue. The eyes were closed, the hair dullish white, the jaw clenched tight.

"Would you like to be alone with him?" Sally asked.

"For a moment, yes," Sansi said.

She closed the door quietly behind her and Sansi was alone with his father. Or with the earthly vessel that had carried his father's spirit. Sansi had seen enough of death to be unmoved by it. There was nothing left of the man, his complexity, his passions, his gentle humor. Sansi passed two fingers over his father's brow, site of the *ajna*, or the third eye, then lightly touched the top of his father's head.

"May your breath be with the breath of the immortals and your spirit be at peace for all time," he said. It was a reference to the Upanishads and the completion of a soul's journey. Sansi wasn't a religious man but he believed his father had done more than enough good in his life to deserve eternal peace.

Then he opened the door and asked Sally to come back in.

"I wonder if you would do something for me," he said.

"Of course, if I can," she said.

"Would you draw two vials of my father's blood, one for me and one for Mr. Patterson when he comes? And would you certify that each vial contains blood drawn from my father's body on this date."

She hesitated. "I can, but I'd like to know why."

"For identification purposes," Sansi said.

He read her eyes, saw her calculate the family dynamics at play and reach the conclusion he wanted her to reach.

"Alright," she said. "Do you want to wait here or upstairs?"

"I will wait here," he said.

She left and returned a moment later wearing rubber gloves and carrying a small steel tray that held a syringe, two glass vials with sticky labels and some wipes. She set the tray down then opened the shroud further and pulled one side down to give her access to the naked body. There was a pronounced lividity where the blood had settled. She took the syringe, loaded one vial and inserted the needle into the bottom of one buttock. The blood came out slowly and as black as tar. She switched the first vial for the second, filled that too and withdrew the needle. She used a wipe on the puncture point so there was no residual blood to stain the shroud. Next she wrote the name of the General, the blood type and the date drawn on the two labels and wrapped them around each vial. She put one in a plastic bag and gave it to Sansi and the other in a bag for Gerald Patterson.

"Will that do?" she asked.

"That will do perfectly," Sansi said. He put the bag containing the vial in a pocket and registered briefly how cold it was.

Upstairs Sally had Tony call a taxi for Sansi. When the cab arrived Sansi ran through the drenching rain and jumped into the back seat. The sky was so dark it could have been early evening.

"Where to, sir?" the driver asked.

"Goscombe Park," Sansi said.

*   *   *

The house looked as it had always looked. A grey Georgian manor with high chimneys and 22 attic windows that Sansi counted when he first arrived there a lifetime ago. Built in 1738 by a West Indian sugar baron it had passed through the hands of several owners until acquired as a bankrupt estate by Walter Lippmann in his quest to become an English gentleman. He intended it to be a country retreat but rarely used it because his wife refused to leave their London townhouse. When Lippman died his widow would have sold Goscombe Park had their only daughter, Hillary, not pleaded with her to keep it so she and her husband could raise their family there. Following the death of her mother Hillary kept Goscombe Park and sold the townhouse. On General Spooner's return to England Goscombe Park became the family home. Their son, Eric, not only grew up at Goscombe Park he moved his wife, Joyce, in when they married and raised their children there too. Eric had never known any other home. His younger sister, Hillary, married a London barrister by the name of Baxter and they had their own house in Kensington but visited Goscombe Park with their children for the occasional weekend and family occasion. It was Hillary's daughter who had provided the General with his first and only great grandchild.

The taxi crunched to a stop beside the front entrance.

"I don't know if I am going to be here a few minutes or a few hours," Sansi told the driver. "Whatever it is I will pay you for your time."

He ran through the rain, up the broad stone steps and rang the door bell. He was about to ring again when the door was opened by Mrs. Chappell, the housekeeper. She was greyer than when he'd last seen her but her face was still as pink and as shiny as a rosehip. She seemed shocked to see Sansi.

"Oh, my word, it is you, Mr. Sansi," she said. "I wondered if you'd be coming."

"And here I am," Sansi said. "Is it alright if I come in?"

"Of course it is, come in, come in," Mrs. Chappell said.

Sansi stepped in out of the rain and brushed off the rain drops.

"I am here to see Eric, is he at home?"

"Well, in a manner of speaking he is," Mrs. Chappell said. "He's out with the estate manager at the minute and I'm not sure when he'll be back."

"Would it be alright if I wait?" Sansi asked.

Mrs. Chappell lowered her voice. "You have as much right to be here as anybody, Mr. Sansi, but I should warn you things have been a bit funny the past few months. I'm not sure how Mr. and Mrs. Spooner, or Hillary for that matter, will take to you being here, if you catch my drift. It could be a bit awkward."

"I will have to take that chance," Sansi said. "I am here to smooth things over if I can."

"Well, I wish you the best of British luck with that, Mr. Sansi, I really do," Mrs. Chappell said. "I'll see if I can find out where Mr. Spooner is and let him know you're here."

"Would it be alright if I wait in the library if nobody is using it?" Sansi asked.

"I should think so," Mrs. Chappell said. "Hardly anybody uses it anymore."

As Sansi accompanied Mrs. Chappell across the entrance hall to the library lively voices spilled out of the front drawing room.

"Everybody's here, including all the children," Mrs. Chappell said. "They're all grown up now, except for the little one, of course. Did you know Miss Hillary's daughter had a baby boy?"

"I read something about it in the newspaper," Sansi said.

At that moment Joyce Spooner came out of the drawing room.

"Oh," she said when she saw Sansi.

"Hello Joyce," Sansi said. "I gather you weren't expecting me."

Joyce quickly regained her composure.

"No, I wasn't," she said. "There's no reason for you to be here, no good reason."

"Only my father's dying wish that I attend his funeral," Sansi said.

"You still shouldn't have come. I'm sorry but you're just not welcome here, George. There is nothing and nobody here for you anymore."

"I am well aware of that," Sansi said. "I hoped that Eric and I might be able to make peace for the duration of the funeral, that is all."

"Did you bring your mother with you too?"

"Yes, my father asked that she come to the funeral too."

Joyce gnawed at her bottom lip. "That's not good."

"I can assure you we are here only for the funeral," Sansi said. "We will come, we will not say a word and we will leave."

"Yes, but it raises all sorts of..." she paused "...well, I'm not going to get into that with you now. Wait here. I'll call Eric on the mobile and tell him you're here."

"I'll wait in the library," Sansi said. "I don't want to be in anybody's way."

Mrs. Chappell opened the door to the library, looked inside and said: "There's nobody in there."

"Huh," Joyce said, half sigh, half exasperation, and returned to the drawing room. Sansi saw several people looking his way. Nieces and nephews his father had mentioned, all of whom he'd never met, all wondering who he was.

"Can I bring you a cup of tea while you're waiting?" Mrs. Chappell asked.

"I don't think I am going to be here long enough to drink it," Sansi said.

She stepped into the library after him, the door at her back so she couldn't be overheard.

"I hate what's been going on here these last months, " she said. "I promised the General I'd stay with him to the end but as soon as the funeral's over I'll be handing in my notice."

"I am sorry to hear that," Sansi said. "You've been a part of the life of this house a long time."

"Nearly 40 years," she said. "It's time I retired, it's never going to be the same."

"You've earned your retirement," Sansi said and clasped her hands in his. "I'm sure you made my father's last years as comfortable as you could and for that I thank you."

"You stick to your guns about going to the service," she added. "They don't know I'm going to be there either but there's nothing they can do to stop me."

She left and closed the door behind her leaving Sansi alone in the library where he'd spent so many hours of happy exploration when he was studying at Oxford. The air was stale with neglect. There were bookshelves on three sides and windows at the front that overlooked fields where cattle grazed forlornly in the rain. The Edwardian era furniture had never been replaced; heavily brocaded chairs and sofas, brass table lamps and a marble fireplace guarded by the figure of Diana the Huntress on the same brass fire screen. The bookshelves held books that went back a hundred years and more. A wealth of knowledge too great to be known by any one man. It had been Sansi's favorite room when he lived there. It was where he and his father invented their own game of bluff in which each of them in turn would present some preposterous historical 'fact' and the other would have to prove it true or false.

But Sansi had no time to dally. Eric could arrive at any minute. In a corner was a panel that opened into a backstairs passage. He pushed and prodded but it mustn't have been used in years and wouldn't budge. There was nothing to do but give it a hefty shove with his shoulder. It shifted with an alarming crack and swung inward. Sansi stepped through and closed it behind him. The passage connected with others that converged on a cellar where a much older tunnel ran under the fields to where there had once been a stand of trees. That tunnel had been sealed off years ago and on the cellar door there was a padlock that rust had fused into a single lump. The passage carried on to what had once been the servants quarters but was now used for storage. There was also an unused kitchen, pantry and scullery and a wider corridor that led to a tradesmen's entrance at the rear of the house. Between the kitchen and the back entrance was the door to a staircase that led to the upper floors. It wasn't locked but the hinges were rusted tight and Sansi had to force this door open too. It yielded with a crack and a puff of dust and Sansi had to bury his

face in the crook of his arm to stifle a sneeze. When it had
passed he continued up the stairs to the next floor and a
utility room that was still in use with a sink, mops, brushes
and a vacuum cleaner. The door opened onto a narrow,
thinly carpeted corridor that ran the length of the house.
Sansi had to tread lightly to keep the sound of his footfalls
down. If Eric had kept the same room it would be the third
door along. Sansi put his ear to the door and, hearing
nothing, opened it and peaked inside. The room was much
bigger than he remembered. Eric must have had it
expanded when he married Joyce. There were two walk-in
dressing rooms now and two bathrooms. The first bathroom
belonged to Joyce. Sansi went to the next and quickly
found what he was looking for; a hairbrush. The hairs in it
were short and sandy grey and could have belonged to
nobody but Eric. Sansi took half a dozen, wrapped them in
his handkerchief and put it in his jacket pocket. When he
was done he retraced his steps to the utility room, down the
stairs and through the passage back to the library. Pausing
only to make sure it was still empty he stepped inside and
closed the panel behind him. There were a few flakes of
plaster on the floor and he pushed them under a chair with
his toe. He pulled a book randomly from the shelves so if
anyone came in he'd look as if he'd been browsing. It was a
compendium on the butterflies of India, not a book he
might otherwise read to pass the time. He put it back and
strolled down the shelves looking for something that might
offer a genuine diversion. The Greek and Roman classics
were still there along with the collections of all the great
English writers, long undisturbed. As might be expected it
was a collection heavy on military biographies and histories
that went back to the wars of ancient Mesopotamia. Many
shelves were filled with books on India; not just the epics
like *Ramayana* and the *Mahabharata* but the works of
Prasad, Khatri, Premchand and Tagore. There were
histories of the Indian states, their peoples and their rulers,

agricultural surveys and government reports on banditry. It was an extensive collection for a military man and wholly reflective of the General's appetite for knowledge. Sansi recalled Pramila saying his father had told her that to govern a people you had to understand them and to understand them you had to know their culture. Every so often, as Sansi worked his way along, he would find tucked between the *Galpaguchchha* and the *Bhagavad Gita* some raffish gem like "A History of the Pirate Kings of Madagascar" or "Harem Life in the Courts of the Ottomans." But it was a shelf hat held a series of India Office reports from 1858 to 1908 where Sansi lingered. Ostensibly the dullest of reading choices it was a compilation of reports on 50 years of the Raj. But Sansi knew behind those fading brown covers could often be found the most astounding information cloaked in the driest of terms. It was one of these that caught Sansi's eye, a thin volume dated 1902 and titled: "A Report on Social Clubs, Organizations and Secret Societies of British India."

Sansi teased it out and opened it carefully, its pages as thin as onion skin. It was prepared by an undersecretary in the India Office identified as Marlowe Price and printed by the government printing office in New Delhi for official distribution. It was 120 pages long and on first examination little more than a list of social clubs used by British military men and colonial officers with a descriptive paragraph or two underneath each listing. Most were branches of masonic lodges and social clubs for high ranking officials of the Raj. Bastions of colonial snobbery but otherwise harmless. Except for one which stood out from the rest because of its name: The Jackal Club of Mumbai. According to the report it was formed in 1871 as a club for British only polo players. It quickly became notorious for the excesses of its members; dinners where the meals were served by naked prostitutes and drunken polo matches which on at least one occasion spilled over onto the streets. It was a pattern of recklessness that finally went too far when a groom was beaten to death by a club member.

The stench of privilege wafted up from the thin pages. Colonial officers lived lives of splendor in India on a scale that was not available to them in England. They were princes in a country where human lives were in inexhaustible supply and every vice could be indulged at whim. Food, drink, hashish, opium and human beings were passing pleasures to be savored without conscience. Club members called themselves jackals for a reason. They were proud of their depravity, they flaunted it as a right over a subjugated people. The rules that governed life in England did not apply. When the Governor of Bombay was made aware of the manner of the groom's death he ordered the club disbanded. Its principals were cashiered and returned to England, the rest were scattered among faraway postings. But no-one went to jail and the harm they did went unpunished. The Raj was eventually swept away in the cataclysm of independence but the stain of British rule could not be erased from the fabric of Indian life. India was a nation built on caste and the British had merely imposed their own caste system on top of it. The sordid legacy of the Jackal Club endured. It could be seen in the greed and extravagance of Indian moguls who held themselves above the law and *babus* who demanded their appetites be met too. Jackals still roamed the streets of Mumbai, only the color of their skin had changed.

"The bloody gall," a voice said behind Sansi. "Of all the unmitigated bloody gall."

"Hello Eric." Sansi turned to face his half brother who stood in the doorway to the library.

In a tweedy flat cap and oilskin jacket Eric looked every inch the squire. He'd been in such a hurry to respond to Joyce's phone call he still had mud on his boots. He also looked considerably older than the last time Sansi had seen him. He had gained weight and his complexion was a mottled red though some of that might have been due to his present temper.

"I gather you're under the impression you'll be attending my father's funeral on Saturday," he said.

"He's my father too," Sansi said. "He specifically requested that myself and my mother attend. In the absence of an invitation from you he left instructions for the invitations to be issued by his solicitor."

"Gerald Patterson?" Eric said disdainfully. "He doesn't have any say in this." Eric stepped inside and closed the door behind him. "There's never been any proof that you're my father's son and I will not have you and that tart you call your mother parading yourselves at the funeral on Saturday as if you were a legitimate part of this family. You do not belong here, you are not welcome here and I will not allow you to flaunt my father's failings in the faces of my children. You've had a wasted trip. The sooner you get on back to Mumbai the better."

Sansi tapped the book absently against his thigh.

"That's the real issue here, isn't it?" he said. "You haven't told your children about us and you're afraid that when they see us on Saturday they'll want to know who we are. And you'll have to tell them this deep dark family secret you've tried to keep hidden all these years."

"Our children don't know about you because there's no need for them to know," Eric said. "As difficult as it may be for you and your mother to understand, you simply don't matter. You don't mean anything to the rest of us, you never did."

"Neither my mother or myself have any desire to embarrass you, Eric. I came here today because I wanted to see if we might reach some sort of accommodation concerning the funeral."

"Well, you've wasted your time," Eric said. "There's no accommodation to be had. Your days of sponging off this family are over. The money tap has been turned off."

"With or without your approval my mother and I will be at the service on Sunday, Eric," Sansi said.

"Then you should know I've ordered security for the funeral," Eric said. "And if you and your mother do try to come I will have you physically removed - do you understand?"

Sansi gave a reflexive waggle of his head and he saw that even that irritated Eric.

"If that should be the case there is something you should know," he said. "You turn us away on Saturday and my next step will be to go to the newspapers and tell them all about this family secret of ours - the branch of the family tree you'd prefer to forget. I understand the newspapers in this country are quite keen on anything that shows the upper classes in a poor light. Then you won't just be embarrassed in front of the family, you'll be embarrassed in front of the whole country."

Aghast, Eric stared at Sansi.

"And you have the nerve to say you're here because of what my father means to you?" Eric said. "You'd do that to him? To his memory? To his reputation?"

"I wouldn't be doing it to him, Eric, I'd be doing it to you," Sansi said. "My father wasn't ashamed of us. He was discreet for the sake of your mother and the rest of you, but he was never ashamed. It wouldn't bother him if the whole world knew about us. It is only you who has never been able to accept us for who we are."

"You bastard," Eric breathed. "You sneaky wog bastard."

"One more thing," Sansi said. "I don't care what you say to me or about me but if you say one unkind word to my mother on Saturday, if you give her so much as a dirty look, I will go to the newspapers anyway. Now, do we understand each other?"

He went to leave without waiting for an answer when he remembered the book in his hand.

"Just so you know, I'm taking this with me."

"That's all you're here for really, isn't it, to see how much you can steal?" Eric said. "Keep it. It's the last thing you'll ever get from this house."

*   *   *

When he left Goscombe Park Sansi had the taxi driver take him back into Oxford to the university administration offices, an ugly cement box in Wellington Square. A helpful young man at the front desk told Sansi where he would find what he was looking for. Minutes later the taxi was swishing through the rain to Roosevelt Drive on the southern outskirts of Oxford and the Centre for Personalised Medicine. A low slung brick and glass building set back from the road behind trees and lawns it was eerily quiet inside and apparently deserted. A wall directory told him where the genetics laboratory was. He walked down the empty hallways and into the laboratory unchallenged before he encountered another human being, a young man with chin stubble who appeared to be transferring information from a large microscope into a computer. The brightly lit lab stretched out behind him with a dozen or so people working in silence.

The young man at the PC didn't see Sansi until he was beside him.

"Oh, hullo," he said. "Are you lost?"

"Not if this is the genetics laboratory," Sansi said.

"We're one part of it," the young man said. He looked Sansi up and down.
"Are you with the university?"

"Not anymore," Sansi responded. "I suspect I graduated before you were born. I was told you do DNA analysis here."

"Yes, it's one of the things we do."

"I wondered if I might have some genetic samples tested."

"We don't do that here," the young man answered. "We're not a public laboratory, we're a research laboratory."

"I understand, but this is a matter of some urgency and it is not something I could entrust to a public laboratory," Sansi said. "Is there someone in charge I could speak with?"

The young man studied Sansi for a moment assessing his nuisance potential. He got up with a sigh. "Wait here a minute would you?"

He went off down the lab and spoke to a middle aged man with a grey goatee who returned with him.

"I'm Jim Lessing, the assistant laboratory director," he said. "And you are?"

"George Sansi." Sansi showed Lessing his I.D. "Detective Inspector George Sansi of Crime Branch in Mumbai."

Lessing took it and examined it closely before handing it back.

"Well, Inspector Sansi, what can we do for you?"

"As I was telling the young man, I have some genetic samples I would like tested," Sansi said.

"I'm sure you'll find the Metropolitan Police more than happy to assist you as a matter of professional courtesy," Lessing said. "But, as my young colleague here told you, we are a research facility, we do not do work on request."

"I appreciate that," Sansi said. "But I am not here on official business so that option is not available to me. I am here on personal business but I can assure you it is no small matter. The results, whatever they may be, would answer a question that has bothered me all my life. You would be doing me a great favour and I would be happy to pay for your time and for any laboratory costs."

"We're not allowed to accept money directly," Lessing said. "Now, please, you shouldn't be here, I'm afraid you'll have to leave."

Sansi saw his opportunity slipping away.

"Please, permit me to me ask you just one more thing," he said. "I have an English first name and if you look at my eyes you will see they are blue. I am an Indian man with a white English father. What I don't know for sure is if the man I have always been told is my father is in fact my real father."

Lessing tilted his head to one side. Scientists were not unlike policemen. They were problem solvers too and Sansi knew the opportunity to resolve a mystery as easily as this must be tempting. And DNA analysis at a laboratory as well equipped as this one would be cheap and quick.

"Please, just knowing would give me the peace of mind that has eluded me my whole life," Sansi said.

Lessing eyed his younger colleague who just shrugged.

"You say you're an Oxford alumnus?" Lessing said.

"Yes," Sansi said. "I graduated from the law school here in 1969."

"From the law school?" Lessing said. "Well then, you should understand if we do do you this favour it would be completely unofficial," Lessing said. "You would not be able to use the results for any legal purposes."

"I want to know only for myself," Sansi added.

"Alright," Lessing said, "let's see what you've got."

Sansi reached into his inside jacket pocket and took out the vial of blood from his father and the hairs from Eric's hairbrush.

"Where did these come from?" Lessing asked.

"The blood is from the man I believe is my deceased father," Sansi said. "The hairs are from...someone else."

"Yes, well, I suppose the less we know the better," Lessing said.

The research assistant took the vial and hair samples and put them in separate specimen trays.

"We'll need a sample from you too," Lessing said. "A hair with the root attached or a drop of your blood."

"Do you have a pin?" Sansi asked.

The research assistant produced a needle and a small vial. Sansi pricked his forefinger and squeezed a few drops of blood into the vial.

"It shouldn't take long," Lessing said. "You can wait or come back in an hour or so."

"I have waited all my life to know this, another hour won't matter," Sansi said.

"There's a visitor's lounge with tea and coffee just down the corridor," Lessing said. "One more thing, you mention this to anybody and I'll have your balls in a Balti."

*   *   *

Gerald Patterson pulled up outside the Randolph in his rain slicked Range Rover to find Sansi and Pramila waiting in the lobby. A doorman with an umbrella escorted them to the Range Rover. Pramila wore a knee length black coat over a black dress with black stockings, shoes and gloves. She also wore a hat with a brim and a veil, all of which she expected to wear only once in her life. Sansi wore the charcoal grey suit he'd brought with him.

"Are we all ready?" Patterson asked.

"As ready as we can be," Sansi said. He hadn't told Patterson about his threat to Eric and would know soon enough if it had worked.

The rain drummed furiously on the roof as they rode out to Goscombe Park. On the way they passed waterlogged fields where new ponds were forming. They'd been in England five days and the rain had eased at times but never stopped.

"They've issued flood warnings for the Thames Valley," Patterson said. "The government has sent troops in to start sandbagging."

"You should visit us in Mumbai," Pramila said. "Our monsoon is over."

"I might take you up on that," Patterson. "If only to reassure myself that the sun is still shining somewhere."

He slowed as they approached Goscombe Park and joined the procession of vehicles going in. Sansi counted three security guards at the entrance checking invitations. Patterson lowered his window as they pulled up to the gates.

"Morning sir," a guard said. "Can I see your invitations please?"

Patterson produced the three black edged invitations, the guard glanced at them then inside the Rover and handed them back. "Thank you, sir," he said and waved them through.

They followed the procession up the driveway to the gravelled area in front of the house, which was full of cars. More guards directed traffic around the house to the rear. Patterson parked as directed and he and Sansi and Pramila got out to walk the short distance to the chapel. Patterson put a long black raincoat on over his black suit. He'd brought two umbrellas and carried one for Pramila while Sansi followed. They walked along a gravelled path beneath bedraggled ash trees, the fallen leaves slick underfoot. The chapel was a simple building but it was built of Cotswold stone which gave it grandeur. It was in the shape of a cross and while its arms were short and there was no bell tower its walls were high. The wall behind the altar was curved with three stained glass windows to represent the holy trinity. The chapel pre-dated the house by a hundred years and had been absorbed into the estate by the original owner of Goscombe Park when he acquired the surrounding land.

The chapel had room for perhaps a hundred people and, seeing the stream of mourners, Sansi thought it would be full to capacity. It was to be expected. His father was an eminent man. Under the porch Sally and Tony, both in formal black, greeted mourners and directed them inside where ushers showed them to their seats. Despite the modern relaxation of dress codes at funerals most of the mourners were closer to the past and wore black. Those who wore blue or grey suits wore black ties and armbands. Patterson had told Sansi and Pramila that as well as General Spooner's children and grandchildren there would be friends and neighbours from throughout the county and representatives from the university and the Ministry of Defence. Inside, the pews were three quarters full and the chapel smelled of human steam. Sansi, Pramila and Patterson were shown to the last row of pews on the side away from the family.

"Bloody Eric," Patterson said under his breath. "He's just about got us out the door."

Pramila put a gloved hand on his arm. "It is quite alright, I prefer these seats."

Sansi saw Eric and Joyce with their grown-up son and daughter, their spouses and children in the front row. In the row across from them were Hillary with her husband and their daughters and spouses, one of them holding the General's great grandson. A few rows behind them Sansi saw Mrs. Chappell. When she looked around and saw him she got up and left her seat to come and sit next to him.

"You've done it now," Sansi whispered to her.

"Doesn't matter," she said. "I handed in my notice yesterday."

In the Chancel were two of the most prominent churchmen in Oxfordshire, one of them the Archdeacon of Oxford, the other the chaplain from University Church. There was a third cleric whom Patterson said was a military chaplain. There was no live music but a tape deck played Elgar's 'Nimrod' in the background. Behind the Chancel was the altar on which sat a brass urn. On one side of the urn was a portrait of General Spooner in full dress uniform and all his medals and awards. On the other was a portrait of his wife, Audrey. Both portraits were bordered with black crepe.

When all the seats were full Sally and Tony closed the doors. Sally whispered to the young man operating the sound system in the rear of the chapel and the music faded away. Then she signalled the Archdeacon at the front that he could begin the service. The Archdeacon stepped up to the lectern and welcomed the mourners. He followed with a prayer of penitence then led the first hymn, 'Abide With Me.' Sansi hadn't attended a Christian church service since he'd been at Oxford and had forgotten the constant standing up and sitting down with its attendant coughing and shuffling. The Archdeacon then stepped aside for the university chaplain, who spoke of the General's involvement with the university, his charitable support and his educational endowment. He followed with a prayer of thanks for the life departed and concluded with 'The Lord is My Shepherd.' He yielded the lectern to the Chaplain General from the Ministry of Defence who spoke about General Spooner's long and distinguished military service and concluded with Kipling's 'Recessional.' This was followed by a taped version of 'Soldiers Of The Queen' by the Queen's Regiment which inspired images of scarlet tunics and white pith helmets bobbing across a burning plain. The Archdeacon then returned to the lectern and called on General Spooner's "cherished only son" to deliver the eulogy to his father.

Eric walked to the lectern and, with great solemnity, began to read the eulogy he had composed. Those who preceded him had paid tribute to his father the soldier and the public figure, he said. He intended to speak of George Spooner the man, husband and father. He spoke of the love and devotion his parents had for each other. He spoke of his father's love of family. How his father could be severe and aloof but also funny and kind. He spoke of his father's unfailing humour. He spoke of the demands the world had made upon his father and how he always returned gratefully to the bosom of his family. He concluded by acknowledging that his father was not a perfect man, but his love of family was "unconditional and eternal."

Eric's eulogy was personal and sincere. Even if it did overlook a major part of the General's life it was how Eric chose to remember him. He had imposed his view on the rest of his family and in this version Sansi and Pramila simply didn't exist. He finished with a heartfelt: "I love you, dad. God bless."

The Archdeacon returned to the lectern and read a passage from Ecclesiastes that declared: "For everything there is a season, and a time for every matter under heaven." He then led a heartfelt version of 'Jerusalem." At the conclusion he retrieved the brass urn from the altar and handed it to Eric for interment in the family crypt. Eric cradled it as the precious family icon that it was. His entire relationship with his father had been a lie and now he would take that lie to the grave.

*   *   *

Sally and Tony pushed open the chapel doors and Sansi, Pramila, Patterson and Mrs. Chappell were among the first to leave. Before they could venture back out into the rain they were approached by an elderly man in a long black coat who walked with the aid of a cane, a middle aged woman supporting his other arm.

He came directly up to Sansi and in a voice as frail as he looked said: "You wouldn't be George Sansi by any chance would you?"

"As a matter of fact I am," Sansi said, surprised.

"I thought so," the elderly man said. "I'm Arthur Bryant and this is my daughter, Helen. I've known your father for more than 60 years. We were at the War Office in London together and then in New Delhi. We tried to keep in touch but it wasn't easy the past few years, the two of us getting on as we were." Looking to Pramila he said: "Am I correct in presuming this lady is your mother?"

"Dad," his daughter said with a nervous smile. They had to step aside to make way for departing mourners, some of whom gave them curious glances. Nonetheless, Pramila pushed back the veil attached to her hat and said: "You would be correct."

"You may not remember, but we met once in Mumbai," Arthur Bryant continued. "It was at an Independence Day ball at Government House. I was on temporary assignment. Georgy boy introduced you as some VIP's daughter but I thought there was more to it than that. He came clean when we were both back in England. You were a looker then and if I may say so you're still a looker now."

"Dad!" his daughter said.

"I remember," Pramila said. "You had red hair and freckles and a terrible sunburn."

"Yes I did, by golly," Bryant said. "You remember."

"Georgy boy?" Sansi said.

"It's what some of his friends called him," Pramila said. "He wasn't very fond of it."

"Quickest way to get his goat," Bryant added.

"How did you know it was us?" Sansi asked.

"An Indian man with Georgy boy's eyes?" Bryant said. "Wasn't much of a guess. And I didn't much care for that business in there about 'his cherished only son.' I thought that was insensitive."

Gerald Patterson leaned between them and said: "This probably isn't the best place to have this conversation."

"Are you staying for the lunch?" Pramila asked Bryant.

"I'd be bored to tears," Bryant added. "George Spooner was everything they said he was in there but there was more to him than that, a lot more."

"We're staying at the Randolph," Pramila said. "Why don't you meet us there for a drink?"

"I think I'd like that very much," Bryant said.

They regrouped an hour later in the Randolph's clubby bar. Sansi and Arthur Bryant's daughter, toasted the General with tea, Pramila and Mrs. Chappell with sherry and Patterson and Bryant with good scotch. For the next hour they immersed themselves in another world; a world of historic events, epic upheavals and great men. A world of drama and intrigue, of glamour and romance, a world that few could remember. But Pramila and Patterson and Arthur Bryant remembered. And, to an extent, so did Sansi and Mrs. Chappell. For a while they made the past come alive, a vivid place of people and personalities, of textures and smells, of moments and feelings. And when it came to an end they felt the bittersweet burden of its loss.

*   *   *

Patterson was prepared. He sat at his desk with a cup of tea, the door to his office ajar. It was almost ten and the meeting with Eric and Hillary was the only appointment of the morning. He didn't expect a long meeting but had allowed the extra time just in case. As it happened they were a few minutes early. Eric was discernibly tense. Patterson came out to greet them as they shed their raincoats and umbrellas.

"No Sansis?" Eric said, looking around.

"They had other plans." Patterson said.

"That's something, at least," Eric said and relaxed a little.

"Please, come in, make yourselves comfortable," Patterson said. "Would you like some tea or coffee?"

Hillary declined but Eric said he would have coffee.

"Milk with two sugars."

The receptionist went to get Eric his coffee while Patterson closed the door to his office and returned to his chair. He had the original copy of the will on the desk in front of him and beside it a letter. There was to be no reading of the will, that was a melodrama confined to the movies. This was a meeting at which the primary parties to the will could make their positions known but did not have to be there in person.

"You've both had time to give this some thought," Patterson began. "Do you have any questions?"

"You know my position," Eric said.

"Yes, I do," Patterson said. "Hillary - you?"

Eric's younger sister, pale and pinched, shook her head: "No, I stand with Eric on this."

"Very well," Patterson continued. "As you're both aware your father divided his estate between four parties, his three direct heirs and Pramila Sansi. I met with Pramila Sansi and her son, George Sansi, last week and gave them their copies of the will. After due consideration they retained the services of another law firm in Oxford, Lilley and Partners. I have a letter here from John Lilley setting out their position, which I received by courier yesterday. I will read that letter to you now."

"This ought to be good," Eric said.

Patterson began: "This firm represents Pramila Sansi and George Sansi out of Mumbai, India in a matter concerning the last will and testament of George Alden Winfield Spooner of Oxford. In reference to the three direct heirs identified in the will information has been received by this firm indicating that Eric Spooner is not a direct heir of George Spooner. It is requested, therefore, that Eric Spooner produce proof positive that he is a direct heir of George Spooner. If he is unable to do so he will forfeit any and all claim to the aforesaid will."

"What the bloody hell is this about?" Eric sputtered. "Is this their idea of a joke?"

"No joke, I'm afraid," Patterson said. "On receiving this letter I called John Lilley myself and he tells me they are in complete earnest."

"It's a ruse, it's a bloody ruse of some kind," Eric said. "Some kind of legal trick to tie things up so they can get themselves some bargaining power. Who is this John Lilley anyway? What sort of legal charlatan is he?"

"John Lilley is the most experienced probate lawyer in Oxford," Patterson said.

"Well I've never heard of him," Eric said. "What sort of information could they possibly have? It's nonsense. Let's take the buggers to court, we'll have it out with them in front of a judge."

"I asked John Lilley what information they have," Patterson continued. "He said they have been made aware of DNA evidence that shows distinct similarities between George Spooner and George Sansi but there are no similarities whatsoever between George Spooner and Eric Spooner. They also sent this by messenger."

He produced a thickly padded envelope and removed from it a vial whose contents were identified by the Evergreen funeral service as a sample of the General's blood.

Eric eyed the blood vial suspiciously.

"It's preposterous," he said. "The whole bloody thing is a put up job, obviously. Let's call their bluff, take them to court and see what they've got."

"We can do that if that is how you choose to instruct me," Patterson said. "But if they produce credible evidence in support of their claim the court will very likely require you to submit to a DNA test to settle the question."

"I am my father's son and that's all there is to it," Eric said. "If they want proof I'll give them proof."

"That's not all there is to the letter," Patterson said. "Would you like me to continue?"

"Oh, I'm sure there's more," Eric said.

"In order to reach an amicable settlement in the matter, Pramila Sansi and George Sansi are willing to waive all rights as set out in the will in exchange for..."

"Here we go..." Eric interrupted "...now we get to the meat of the matter...now we find out what the blackmailing bastards really want."

Patterson continued "...in exchange for the full, entire and complete contents of the library at Goscombe Park, to be shipped to George Sansi in Mumbai, the cost of which is to be deducted from his share of the inheritance."

Patterson put the letter down and folded his hands on top of it. He looked first at Eric and then at Hillary, whose mouth hung open.

"What about me?" she asked.

"There is no question of the legitimacy of your parentage, Hillary, and no mention of you in the letter," Patterson said.

"Oh well, of course, everybody but me is legitimate and I'm the bastard," Eric said.

"You don't have to make a decision right here and now," Patterson said. "My advice to you would be to take the time to give this proposal your most earnest consideration. I'll be available to answer any questions you might have."

"You can't seriously think this has a snowball in hell's chance of succeeding in court," Eric said.

"I would not attempt to predict what a court will do," Patterson said.

"They're not going to get a penny more out of this family, not a penny more," Eric said.

"Eric, think about it for a minute," Hillary said. "Think of what it will cost to fight them. All they want is the books and they'll be out of our lives forever. Give them the books and be done with it."

"That's not the point," Eric said. "There's a principal involved here. I'm not the bastard - that bloody wog, he's the bastard."

"Eric, please, I wish you wouldn't talk like that," Hillary said.

"Oh, what? You're going to take his side now?"

"No, it's that language. You shouldn't call people names like that. It's not proper."

"Bloody wonderful." Eric got up out of his chair, raised his arms and let them fall by his side. "As if they hadn't made enough trouble for this family, now they're turning us against each other."

There was a timid knock at the door, it opened a fraction and the receptionist peaked in.

"Mr. Spooner's coffee?" she said.

"Now might not be a good time for that," Patterson said.

She retreated and Eric raised his arms and let them fall by his sides several more times.

"I'm speechless," he said. "Absolutely bloody speechless."

"As your solicitor I would suggest that the proposed accommodation might actually be the best outcome for you."

"Oh, yes, and you're completely impartial about this aren't you. What did you do? Did you put them up to this?"

"Get a grip on yourself, man," Patterson said sharply. "If you don't accept the proposal the will and the distribution of the assets will be held up in litigation for a very long time, perhaps years. And, if you lose, you lose everything. You will be removed from the will and you'll have ruined the estate in the process."

"I won't lose," Eric slammed his hand down on Patterson's desk. "I am my father's son. That...other...bloody...man...is... a...fraud!"

"Then perhaps the best course of action for you is to arrange for a DNA test yourself," Patterson said. "That way you'll know before you ever have to go to court."

Eric looked despairingly around. "I can't believe I'm hearing this."

"Eric, that's what you should do," Hillary said. "Then at least we'll know."

"And if the results go against you nobody else will know," Patterson said.

"Unbelievable," Eric said. "Absolutely un-bloody-believable."

"Let it go, Eric, for god's sake just let it go," Hillary said.

"And what does that say? That my mother had an affair too - just like my father?"

"What difference would it make at this stage in our lives?" Hillary said. "You'll still be my brother, you're still part of the family."

"Oh, well, thank you for that vote of confidence, Hillary. How very kind of you - and by the way our mother was a tart!"

"Before this gets any more heated might I suggest you take the information home and talk it out between you," Patterson interjected. "Let me know how you intend to proceed."

Eric left muttering, Hillary behind him with a copy of the John Lilley letter. They put on their coats and retrieved their umbrellas in the silent pall of Eric's fury. The receptionist watched the door close behind them with her hand to her mouth. When she put her hand down she was smiling. She looked at Patterson and gave him a thumbs up. Patterson went back into his office, closed the door and poured himself a scotch. He stood at the window, watched the pouring rain and raised his glass. "Rest in peace, Maxie," he said. "Rest in peace."

*   *   *

Four and a half thousand miles away Pramila Sansi sat in her roof garden on Malabar Hill and enjoyed the feel of the sun on her skin. On a side table was a glass of *chai*, on the other side a chair and on it a bronze urn. Gerald Patterson had shipped General Spooner's ashes in a plastic bag inside a wooden box that could be opened by security personnel to show that it contained nothing dangerous. Pramila had picked out the urn that morning. Apart from the police guards in and around the apartment she was alone. Mrs. Khanna had yet to return from her sister's home in Kerala and George had gone in to Crime Branch to catch up on what had happened while he was away. General Spooner had requested his ashes be scattered in the sea off Malabar Hill but Pramila had decided against that. She found his presence comforting. She would keep him with her until she died. When she was cremated their son would comingle her ashes with the General's and scatter them into the sea together.

"It's a beautiful day, *Baba*," she said, using her pet name for the man she'd loved for more than half a century. "Sunny skies and a nice breeze. The jasmine is out. The kind of day you'd love." She caressed the smooth curve of the urn. "I have to speak to the Business Women's Association next week and I have no idea what I'm going to say. Perhaps something on the need for more women to go into politics? What do you think?"

Chapter 6.

Sansi was glad to be back in the sunlit chaos of Mumbai. After a week in England it was like seeing the world in color again. He waited in Jatkar's office drinking *chai* and browsing The Hindustan Times. The fallout from the vice raid continued to spread. Chief Minister Athawale had promised full cooperation with the investigation but the opposition parties had fastened onto the government like pi dogs onto a sickly goat. The investigation would run for months and the trials that followed for years. But there was nothing in the papers about Shiney Borkar or Rushil Pujari.

Jatkar arrived accompanied by Babala, his imperturbable aide. The vice commissioner looked as if he'd stepped from the pages of GQ India. He wore grey suit pants with an open neck white shirt, sunglasses and his jacket slung over one shoulder. A steel Rolex gleamed on his wrist, an improvement on the gold Rolex he'd decided was too showy. Jatkar was also the most celebrated man in Mumbai and Sansi had helped put him there.

"How was England?" Jatkar said as he handed his jacket to his aide to hang up for him.

"Damp," Sansi said.

"Did you give your father a proper send-off?"

"Actually, we brought him back with us, his ashes at any rate."

"Whose idea was that?"

"His," Sansi said. "He wanted his remains scattered in the sea off Malabar Hill."

"Some of them loved it here, didn't they?"

"I think it had something to do with the place and the people."

"Of course."

Jatkar told Babala to bring some *chai* and looked inquiringly at Sansi who held up his cup to show it was still half full.

"Reading my newspapers?" Jatkar said. "You can't wait to sit in this chair, can you?"

"You can be assured I am in no hurry."

Jatkar turned on his PC and while it booted up he asked Sansi: "Do you have any thoughts on Shiney Borkar?"

"I had hoped, after a couple of weeks in custody, we would have got something out of the goondas who threw the building manager off the balcony."

"They are afraid of Borkar more than they are afraid of us."

"I will talk to them, see if I can get somewhere," Sansi said.

"You're welcome to try but Borkar has already had far too much time to think about what he wants to do next. We have to put pressure on him. We may not know where he is but we know where he does business. We have to squeeze him, choke off his money supply, flush him out into the open."

Babala returned with a cup of *chai*. Jatkar took a sip and said he and Sansi were not to be disturbed. The aide withdrew, closing the door soundlessly behind him.

"While you were away I worked with Commander Wagli to form a Special Action Unit to bring Borkar down," Jatkar said. "He picked 24 of the best men under his command and I had them moved to a secret location to protect the security of the operation. The only people who know about them are me, Wagli and now you."

"What about Commissioner Singh?"

"Not Singh, he is Athawale's man."

"He is still the Commissioner."

"We already have the authority to use deadly force when circumstances demand."

"Who decides when circumstances demand?"

"The man closest with his finger on the trigger."

"That gives a lot of discretion to each man."

"The men in this unit are the best of the best, Sansi. Highly professional, highly trained."

"And highly motivated to kill Shiney Borkar?"

"I thought you would be the last to worry about what happens to him."

"I hate him, probably more than I have ever hated anybody," Sansi said. "That is why it should not be up to me what happens to him."

"Shiney Borkar invaded your home, he threatened the lives of you and your mother and kidnapped the *bei*."

"Don't try to make this about me," Sansi said.

"It isn't just about you anymore, Sansi. If Borkar is prepared to do that to one of my senior officers he poses a threat to every police officer in Mumbai. When we find him we're not going to be taking any chances."

"What does that mean exactly?"

"It means any officer who believes himself to be under imminent threat has the right to shoot to kill."

"Are they your orders?"

"Nobody is going to shed any tears over Shiney Borkar."

"At the risk of sounding overly cautious I think somebody has to support the rule of law in Mumbai and that should probably be the police."

"He'll get his chance to surrender if that's what you're worried about."

"How much of a chance?"

"That's up to him."

"I am not comfortable..."

"Comfortable?" Jatkar interrupted. "The person sitting in this chair has to make life and death decisions every day, there is nothing comfortable about it."

"That is just an excuse for taking the easy way out."

Jatkar's eyes flared.

"What do you want, Sansi?"

"I would like to see a change in the operational orders for this Special Action Unit of yours."

"To what?"

"To something that says all reasonable effort should be made to detain the suspect before the use of deadly force is employed."

"All reasonable effort?" Jatkar said. "That would do it for you?"

"And notify Wagli."

"And notify Wagli."

"And the men in the unit. In writing. Copied to me."

"Don't push me too far, Sansi."

"That is all I want."

"And when Shiney Borkar is dead you will have clean hands."

"We will all have clean hands," Sansi said.

*   *   *

Annie called Sansi at Crime Branch late the next day and asked if he could come to her apartment that evening for a meeting with Ajit Birla. She wouldn't go into detail but it could only mean one thing. Her idea for a series about child prostitution in Mumbai had met with a positive response from Birla. Sansi was ready for something positive. He had spent most of the day working the two goondas who had tossed the building manager off the balcony of Madam Lele's apartment. He'd tried turning them against each other with promises of protection for whoever gave up Shiney's location. But, it was just as Jatkar said. They had nothing but scorn for Sansi's promises. As long as they didn't talk Shiney would look after them in prison. And if they did talk there was nothing Sansi could do to protect them. Of that they were certain.

Sansi arrived at Annie's apartment around dinner time with a bottle of La Reserve, a well regarded Cabernet Sauvignon from Bangalore. Annie had put out some *samosas* and *bhajjis* and a selection of chutneys on the coffee table. She set the wine aside for another time. She and Birla were drinking beer. Sansi asked for tonic water with ice.

Birla may have been used to grander accommodations but he'd made himself at home in Annie's apartment. His jacket was draped over a chair at the kitchen table, he had unloosened his tie and he sat on the sofa with his bare feet propped on a cushion. Sansi found himself a little irritated. His irritation waned as Birla inquired about the Enticing Escorts investigation and asked how it would affect the upcoming election. As they talked Sansi was increasingly impressed by Birla's political acumen and his appetite for factual information. He was clearly no figurehead at India Today. Sansi also realized that Birla's informality wasn't an excess of familiarity on his part. It came from a personality utterly free of affectation.

After a while Birla said: "Annie has been telling me about this child, Usha, that you attempted to rescue and the circumstances surrounding her disappearance. I have decided to run a major series about the child sex trade in Mumbai. I know tens of thousands of girls are sold into prostitution each year but I think the best way to approach it is by focusing on this child, Usha. We will tell the story of the many by focusing on the one. We will make her the example that will shame India before the world."

"Now..." he swung his feet down and leaned forward as his enthusiasm took over. "...I believe you know the identity of the man who took her to Dubai - he's connected to the government of Dubai somehow?"

"That is all I know," Sansi said. "I have had no opportunity to investigate it any further."

"Well, we have to find him in order to find the girl," Birla said. "When we know where she is we will go to Dubai and bring her back to India."

It took Sansi a moment to absorb what Birla had proposed and he decided the India Today publisher had no idea of the difficulties involved.

"My boss at Crime Branch thinks it is a waste of time. Even with his support anything that involves government to government contact moves very slowly."

"We are not going to wait for the government to act," Birla said. "We will run our own private extraction operation. I will take a business trip to Dubai using the company plane. We go there often so the plane will not attract attention. We will get the girl and bring her back on the plane so she avoids the authorities at both ends. There will be no government involvement. The government won't know anything about it until it is over."

"When you say 'we will get the girl,' who do you mean exactly?" Sansi said.

"We can't do any of this without you," Birla said. "I have people who will run the Dubai end of things. They will locate the girl, monitor the location and conduct the extraction. But we need somebody who knows the girl. Somebody who can identify her and at the same time somebody she will recognize and trust."

"I don't know how much she will trust me considering all she has been through," Sansi said. "She might see me as the man responsible for everything that has gone wrong."

"We have to expect that she will be damaged, physically and psychologically," Birla said. "That is not the reason we should not to do this - it is the reason we should do it. We must get that child back to India."

"It's a mindfuck isn't it?" Annie said. "It took me a minute or two to get my head around it."

"It is one of the more unorthodox proposals I have had lately and I have had a few," Sansi said. "If I agree, how much time are we looking at for this extraction operation?"

"We will be in and out in 24 hours," Birla said.

"It won't be easy for me to get away even for that amount of time," Sansi said. "Jatkar already thinks I have been away too much."

"I am sure you will find a way to handle Joint Commissioner Jatkar," Birla said. "Do you have a passport that doesn't identify you as a police officer?"

"I thought the authorities weren't going to be involved?" Sansi said.

"We will enter and exit Dubai legally," Birla said. "It's the girl we don't want them to know about."

"You are going on this operation too?"

"Of course," Birla said. "I wouldn't ask you to do anything I am not prepared to do myself."

"My passport identifies me as an attorney," Sansi said.

"Excellent, you can be a company lawyer for the purposes of our visit."

"There is one thing," Sansi said. "Even if it goes as you think - especially if it goes as you think - the Government of India and the Government of Dubai are not going to be happy about it. No government likes to be embarrassed internationally."

"You'd think they would be used to it by now," Birla said. "And you should know, Sansi, the higher the stakes the more likely the parties are to negotiate."

"You may also find yourself negotiating from the inside of a prison cell."

"It is a price I am willing to pay to watch the Government of India explain why they wouldn't lift a finger to help an Indian child sold as a sex slave and taken out of the country illegally. I have discussed it with my attorneys and in the end it comes down to a battle of credibility between me and the government. This situation arises directly out of the failure of the government to enforce the law. We, on the other hand, will not have broken any laws in either India or Dubai. In the absence of parental guardianship the Government of India is the child's guardian. The more they protest the worse they look. And if they want to be difficult about it my lawyers will file lawsuits on behalf of tens of thousands of children for official negligence."

"These people you have on the ground in Dubai, are they dependable?" Sansi asked.

"Very dependable," Birla said. "The team leader is former British special forces. He started by extricating rich people out of Iran after the Revolution. He knows his way around the Gulf."

"How well do you know him?"

"I have used his services several times before," Birla said. "He has never let me down."

"The last thing you want is something to go wrong on the ground in Dubai," Sansi said. "If anybody gets hurt you lose whatever moral and legal protections you might have had."

"This man is well aware of that."

"And when is all of this due to happen?"

"My man and his team are standing by," Birla said. "As soon as you give me the information we need they will go into Dubai and begin the surveillance part of the operation."

"And when your man is ready you call me and I drop whatever I am doing and get on your plane?"

"*Acha,*" Birla smiled.

"And what do we do with Usha when we get her back?"

"We put her somewhere safe. Annie will interview her and we will tell her story to the world."

Annie asked Sansi: "Do you want to know what we're going to call the series?" Birla said: "The front cover will be a close up of her face and the header will be: A Child of India."

"They're your words, remember?" Annie said. "I don't think there's any better way to say it."

"In a country of more than a billion people it is the story of the one that tells the story of the many," Birla said.

*   *   *

Sansi went to Lentin Chambers early the next morning to see Mukherjee. The door was open and the offices were in disarray with moving boxes everywhere. Bansari and the others greeted Sansi warmly.

"You will find Mister Mukherjee in your old office," Bansari said.

Sansi thought Mukherjee had wasted no time but instead of sitting behind his old desk Sansi found him in jeans and T-shirt packing his old law books. Indian fusion played loudly from somewhere but Sansi couldn't tell from where. He rapped sharply on the door and Mukherjee stood up with a start.

"I am away for just a few weeks and already the place has gone to the dogs," Sansi said.

Mukherjee brushed his hair from his eyes and reached over to a little box on the desk and shut the music off.

"What is that thing?" Sansi said.

"It is an MP3 player," Mukherjee said and held up the sleek silver box little bigger than a cell phone. "The very latest."

"It makes a lot of noise for such a small device," Sansi said.

Mukherjee wiped his palms on his jeans and offered his hand to Sansi.

"It is so good to be seeing you again, Sansi-ji," he said. "Can I get you something to drink? *Chai*, coffee, water?"

"No need, I can't stay." Sansi said.

"I have been seeing your exploits on the news," Mukherjee said. "You are being a very busy man."

"That is why I am here," Sansi said. "I have to ask you a favour - but I can see you are busy too."

"*Acha*, we are moving to new offices," Mukherjee said. "But I am always finding time to do you a favour, Sansi-ji."

Sansi took a sheet of paper out of his pocket and handed it to Mukherjee. On it was written the name of the Arab man Madam Lele had given to Sansi: Akeem Al-Habash.

"I wonder if you could find this man for me," Sansi said. "He lives in Dubai and I believe he works for the government there but that is all I know. I would like you to find his home address and anything else you can find out about him and I need it as soon as possible. You can't tell anybody about it, especially not at Crime Branch."

"It is no problem, Sansi-ji," Mukherjee said. "We are not moving until next week. I am just wanting to get an early start."

"Where are your new offices?" Sansi asked.

"I have got most favorable terms at a building on Colaba Causeway," Mukherjee said. "Very tall, very beautiful - like a tower of gold - very prestigious."

"The new 22-storey building covered in yellow panels to make it look like gold?"

"That is it, Sansi-ji, you know it?"

"You can't go there, Jeet," Sansi said. "Moving into that building would be the biggest mistake you ever made."

"But why, Sansi-ji?" Mukherjee said.

"It is a Rushil Pujari building and if he uses it like he uses his other buildings he will use legitimate tenants as a front for his illegitimate businesses and tenants. Your neighbors will be brothels, pimps and goondas." He paused. "You say you've been following the news?"

"*Acha*, Sansi-ji."

"The escort agency we raided was in one of Pujari's buildings at Nariman Point. A woman by the name of Madame Lele ran the agency for Shiney Borkar who controlled it on Pujari's behalf. They all lived in the same building along with crooked politicians who were given apartments as bribes by Pujari to use for their fun and games with prostitutes and underage girls. We are building a case against Pujari and when we move against him all his assets will be frozen while we investigate every business and every tenant in every one of his buildings. You don't want to be caught up in that."

"But you know we are an honest law practice, Sansi-ji," Mukherjee protested.

"I am trying to protect you now by keeping you from making that mistake," Sansi said. "Have you signed a lease?"

"Yes, Sansi-ji, for three years. We are telling all our clients, we are ordering new letterheads, new phone lines, new furniture."

"*Are Bapre*," Sansi sighed.

His cell phone buzzed in his pocket while Mukherjee stared dazedly at him. Sansi put the phone to his ear. It was Agarkar.

"We think we know where Borkar is," he said. "The boys picked up some cell phone chatter between Borkar and his people."

"Where is he?"

"Chembur district," Agarkar said.

It was a heavily industrialized area east of Mumbai.

"Have you told Jatkar?"

"Not yet."

"Call him, tell him I'm on my way."

Sansi shut off the phone.

"Do not move into that building," he told Mukherjee. "Write it off as a business loss. Stay here till you find somewhere else - and check with me first."

*   *   *

Sansi arrived back at Crime Branch in time to see Jatkar leaving in a jeep at the head of a convoy of police buses. Jatkar signaled Sansi to fall in behind and Chowdhary swung the car around and tagged onto the end of the convoy. Commander Wagli and the Special Action Unit would be converging on Chembur from a separate location. Traffic was so bad it took nearly an hour to get to Chembur. Once clear of the city the police convoy turned southward to the coast onto a road that led to the Bharat Petroleum Refinery, a sprawling matrix of processing plants, pipelines and storage tanks in a landscape of blackened mud flats. By the side of the road scores of tanker trucks waited to fill up with fuel and a short distance away tanker trains at a massive rail yard shunted in and out of the giant refinery.

The police convoy came to a halt and when Sansi got out to see why he saw Jatkar talking to Commander Wagli who was pointing in the direction of the refinery whose main gates were visible at the end of the road. Wagli's men in their specially equipped trucks had arrived ahead of Jatkar. The Special Action Unit would spearhead the police assault on Borkar wherever he was. After a minute Wagli trotted back to his truck, Jatkar climbed back into his vehicle and Sansi did the same. This time when the convoy started up it accelerated quickly. Moments later they barreled through the main gates of the refinery while security guards stood aside, bewildered. Wagli must have had a firm GPS fix on Borkar's presumed location, Sansi thought, because he seemed to know exactly where he was going. The convoy came to a careening stop and armed officers spilled out of the buses. Sansi hurried up to the front in time to see the Special Action Unit, divided into four teams of six men each, closing in on a two storey brick building set back from a car park that was half full. Some kind of administration building, Sansi guessed. A hundred yards away flame and smoke boiled from a battery of steel chimneys blotting out the sun and giving the scene a foreboding light. Jatkar ordered the support officers to hold back while the Special Action Unit secured the building. If there was a warning to those inside Sansi didn't hear it. The SAU men kicked in doors and windows and lobbed in stun grenades to clear their advance. Seconds after they entered firing broke out inside. A few sharp cracks at first then a crescendo of gunshots. Panicked men and women burst out the front doors and scattered. Jatkar told the waiting support officers to get the civilians to safety. Shooting flared at a rear corner of the building and Sansi worked his way around to a better vantage point. Several cars were clustered by an emergency exit and men had taken cover behind them. Borkar's men. The SAU teams closed on that corner of the building and poured a stream of fire onto the men behind the cars. The cars bucked and bounced and stray bullets howled off into the nearby pipes and chimneys. Sansi heard urgent calls to cease fire as others saw the danger too. The firing faded and it was all Borkar's men needed. Some of them used women as hostages as they scrambled into a couple of cars least damaged by gunfire and sped off down a road that led to the harbor a half mile away.

Sansi saw Jatkar come into view around the opposite corner of the building.

"Shoot their tires out," he yelled to the SAU men. "Shoot their tires out."

"No," Sansi shouted but no-one heard him.

A couple of SAU men dropped to their knees and aimed at the departing cars. They fired a series of rapid single shots but to no effect. Then a rear tire on the last car blew out. It shimmied and the driver regained control but then it swayed and slewed off the road toward a chain link fence which was all that separated the road from a row of storage tanks.

Everybody watched, hypnotized, until the car burst through the fence. Then they turned and ran. Sansi ran for the administration block to put it between him and any explosion. He threw himself to the ground beside the front wall and covered his ears with his hands. Some followed his example and others kept running as fast as they could go. No-one but those in the car saw what happened next. The car hit the storage tank and bounced back, throwing its occupants around like puppets. They slumped in their seats, stunned. For a moment there was nothing. Then flames flickered under the car. Someone in the car screamed and tried to get out but the door was jammed. A woman struggled through a window and fell heavily to the ground. A flame ran from the back of the car to the front and reached for the storage tank like a pointing finger to a thin spray of fuel that hissed from a single crack in the wall of the tank. The tank erupted in a volcanic mass of flame. The air itself recoiled as the explosion sucked all the life out of it. Sansi felt the silence to his bones. The ground shook as the blast wave rippled outward followed by the roar of destruction. Sansi's breath was sucked from his lungs and his ears threatened to burst. Dust filled his mouth and throat and he was pummeled mercilessly from head to toe. The explosion was too great and he was too close to survive.

He realized he'd lost consciousness when he revived. An uneven weight pressed down on him and there was a pain in his lower right leg. He opened his eyes and shut them quickly against a stinging pall of dust. He coughed and tried to expel the dust from his mouth but he had no saliva. His stomach convulsed and he vomited, which had the effect of clearing his airway. He cupped his hands over his mouth and nose and tried to breathe without inhaling more dust. He heard shouts and cries for help. The shouts came nearer and pieces of a crushing jigsaw puzzle were lifted off him. He groaned as unseen hands pulled at him and propped him against a wall. Someone spoke but the words were muffled and distant. There was a splash of water then a cloth wiping his face. He tried to open his eyes but they stung too much. A bottle pressed against his lips and he sluiced the water around his mouth and spat out a foul sludge. He drank some more and spat and retched as he cleared the dust from his throat. As he got his breath back he felt his strength return but when he tried to speak he couldn't. Someone spoke to him again. This time he heard the words. "Do not try to move, sir. Help is coming."

Whoever it was splashed more water on his face to flush the dust out of his eyes. Sansi blinked, trying to see. Everything was blurred and it was a minute or two before he could focus. A face and form materialized gradually out of the haze. Someone kneeling in front of him. Chowdhary.

"Please, sir, stay where you are," he was saying. "Ambulances are on their way."

Sansi felt around his face and head with his fingertips and everything seemed to be as it should. But his body ached and the pain in his lower right leg was worsening and he was sure he could feel blood under him. He had to move. He looked around and saw that he was in a pocket formed by the rubble, which must have given him some protection. The front wall of the office block was mostly intact but there were gaping holes where the windows had been and the roof was gone. All around him was the carnage of the battlefield, body parts strewn among the shattered brick, glass and furniture.

Sansi asked Chowdhary to help him up but all that
came out was an unintelligible croak. He took hold of
Chowdhary's forearm and tried to pull himself up but
everything began to spin and he slumped back.

"Oh no, sir, please," Chowdhary said. "You might
be hurt inside."

"I might be bloody well hurt on the outside too,"
Sansi tried to say, though again it was nothing but a series
of croaks. He waited a minute then tried again despite
Chowdhary's pleas. Seeing how determined his boss was
Chowdhary helped steady him as he got to his feet. He
couldn't have been out for long. It was the immediate
aftermath of the explosion. Against the roar of flame from
the burning tank he heard approaching sirens. He looked
down at himself and saw he was coated in black dust. His
clothes were shredded, he'd lost a shoe and his right leg
was bare from the knee down. He turned to look closer and
saw there was a jagged gash in his calf that was weeping
blood steadily.

"I see it, sir," Chowdhary said. "Lean against the
wall. I will take care of it."

Chowdhary doused the wound in water then took
off his shirt, tore it into strips and tied them tightly around
the wound.

"That will stop the bleeding for now, sir,"
Chowdhary said.

Before Chowdhary could say anything more Sansi
took him by the arm and gestured that he wanted to move
away from the building. Chowdhary helped Sansi hobble a
few paces then Sansi stopped and turned to survey the
scene. All that remained of the office block was a hollowed
out facade. The interior and the back wall had been reduced
to rubble. In the near distance the storage tank burned
furiously filling the sky with clouds of oily smoke that
drifted toward the city. Out in the open the heat from the
fire was terrific. Everything in Sansi wanted to get away

from it as fast as possible. Then he saw Jatkar with a couple of officers poking around in the debris at the other corner of the office building. Sansi signaled to Chowdhary to help him over to Jatkar. As they approached one of the officers stood up with a look of triumph on his face and something in his hand.

"Here it is, sir." He walked over to Jatkar and handed it to him. Jatkar took it, wiped it clean and examined it closely. Then he held it to his ear and listened. After a minute he gave a grunt of satisfaction and slipped it on his wrist. His Rolex.

*   *   *

Sansi spent the night in hospital. His leg wound was cleaned and dressed and he was shot full of antibiotics. He'd ingested an unhealthy amount of dust and his doctor told him he'd be coughing up black sputum for days but there should be no permanent damage to his lungs. He had multiple cuts and bruises but nothing was broken and his voice was coming back. Pramila spent the afternoon by his bedside and Annie came in that evening.

"Try not to get yourself killed," she told him. "I was just starting to like you again."

He was released the next morning with the doctor's caution that that he needed several days of bed rest before he could go back to work, a prospect that filled Sansi with impatience. Chowdhary drove him home and helped him up to his room. Then Sansi had Chowdhary give him the preliminary numbers on the disaster. Chowdhary obliged in his flat and unemotional manner. More than a hundred were known to be dead with 200 injured and another 50 or 60 missing. Counted among the dead were three police officers, two of them from the Special Action Unit. Another 23 officers had been injured. It wasn't known if Shiney Borkar was dead or alive but the one car that had got away had been found abandoned at the harbour. It was too early to estimate the cost of the disaster but it was on a scale that seemed only to happen in India.

Sansi slept a little in the afternoon but when he switched on the evening news it was to see that Chief Minister Athawale had called a press conference. Athawale announced there would be a commission of inquiry into the disaster. The commission would be relentless in its pursuit of the truth, he said, and those responsible would be made to pay. It was an echo of the promise Jatkar had made in announcing the investigation into government corruption. Jatkar had gone after Athawale and now Athawale was coming after him.

Chapter 7.

"I think you might want to open that," Pramila said and dropped an envelope on the breakfast table for Sansi.

He was at the breakfast table enjoying a lightly spiced *paratha* Mrs. Khanna had made for him. The letter was from Gerald Patterson in Oxford and was addressed to Sansi and his mother. Sansi dipped a piece of the *paratha* in a dish of yogurt, popped it in his mouth then wiped his fingers and picked up the envelope. His mother sat down opposite him to go through her morning mail. Sansi used a knife to slit the envelope open. The letter inside contained a single paragraph:

"I have the pleasure to inform you that Mr. Eric Spooner and Mrs. Hillary Baxter, have agreed to the terms proposed by you concerning the reconciliation of all claims related to General Spooner's will. Please advise when and where you would like the books in your father's library to be shipped."

It ended with a handwritten: "Sincere congratulations."

Eric had done had acknowledged the unthinkable. Sansi was General Spooner's legitimate male heir. Eric was a bastard on his mother's side with no claim on his father's estate except that which Sansi and Pramila cared to give him.

"Hmm," Sansi said.

"That sounds like a very self satisfied 'hmm'," Pramila said.

"It is," Sansi said. "It appears that Audrey Spooner was unfaithful to my father long before he was unfaithful to her."

"I wonder if he knew," Pramila said. "He never said anything to me."

"He was a gentleman," Sansi said.

"What are we going to do with all those books?" Pramila asked. "We don't have room here."

"I might have something in mind," Sansi said and left it at that. He knew exactly what he wanted to do with the books but he wasn't ready to tell his mother. Not yet. He finished his breakfast then got up and took his tea out onto the roof garden. He limped but that was due more to overall soreness than the wound on his calf, which was healing well. He sat down slowly and sipped his tea in the warm sun. A week had passed since the explosion at the refinery. Jatkar had issued a statement expressing regret for the loss of life and put all the blame on Shiney Borkar. Jatkar was also recuperating at home though his injuries were less severe than Sansi's. It allowed him to stay out of the public eye and avoid questions about Athawale's commission of inquiry while he decided how to survive this latest crisis.

Sansi picked up the Indian Express he'd been reading before Mrs. Khanna called him in for breakfast. The refinery explosion had been pushed off the front page by floods in the Punjab that had killed 2,000 people. In New Delhi tainted cooking oil had poisoned 300. In Assam attacks by indigenous tribes on Bangladeshi refugees had left a thousand dead and forced thousands more from their homes. It didn't take long for one disaster to be replaced by another in India.

Sansi heard someone at the front door and recognized Mukherjee's voice. Mukherjee had called the day before to say he thought he had acquired "useful" information about Akeem Al-Habash.

"Sansi-ji, it is most encouraging to see you looking so well," Mukherjee said as he stepped out onto the roof garden.

Mrs. Khanna inquired if Mukherjee would like something to drink and he asked for a glass of water. Sansi waved him to a nearby chair and he set his briefcase on his knee.

" I want to thank you for saving me from making a great mistake," he said. "Rushil Pujari is a very bad man." He opened his briefcase took out a sheet of print-out and handed it to Sansi.

"Akeem Al-Habash is with the Dubai Department Of Economic Development," he said. "He is an administrative deputy of the licensing and registration division, which is making him something of a bigwig. His residence is on Al Zahir Street in Al Rumailah. Because you are telling me of his connections to Rushil Pujari I am thinking Pujari is doing business in Dubai too. When I look I am finding many projects by Pujari companies; office buildings, a shopping mall and housing developments." Mukherjee took a second print-out from his briefcase and handed it to Sansi. There were names and addresses for 17 projects controlled by Pujari owned companies.

"It is a business model that has worked well for him in Mumbai," Sansi said. "We should not be surprised that he is getting away with the same thing in Dubai."

"I also looked to see if there were other sources of information on Pujari's business interests in Dubai and found a most amazing amount of material."Mukherjee pulled a sheaf of papers from his briefcase and passed them to Sansi. "These are from British newspapers and magazines, American, French, German, Italian - and online stories from CNN. Pujari's companies have been supplying Indian workers to Dubai for many years. It is all here, thousands of Indian migrant workers go there every year. He is not providing good accommodations for them and their wages are very poor. The suicide rate among Indian migrant workers in Dubai is very high. You will see in these articles, the Indian consul in Dubai is dealing with at least two suicides a week."

"And nothing about it in our press," Sansi said as he perused the copies of articles from The New York Times, The Guardian and Newsweek. "The news media in other countries reports on it more than we do. It's right under our nose but we ignore it because we've grown used to it." He sighed. "This is the great problem facing India, Mukherjee. Institutionalized corruption. Everybody knows what is going on and nobody does anything about it."

Mrs. Khanna brought Mukherjee a glass of water and he drank most of it in one swallow. "Is there anything else you would like me to be doing, Sansi-ji?" he said. "I am most pleased to be helping you."

"You have done everything I asked and more," Sansi said. "Don't forget to send me the bill."

"Oh, most definitely not, Sansi-ji," Mukherjee protested. "You are the father of our law firm and it is my honor to assist you."

"You won't get rich giving your time away," Sansi said.

"I am thinking of all the time and money you have saved me already, Sansi-ji,"

After Mukherjee had left Sansi called Annie but she didn't pick up so he left a message on her voice mail telling her to call him. When his cell phone rang a moment later he thought it must be her. But it wasn't. It was a woman who identified herself as Chief Minister Athawale's personal assistant. She said Athawale wanted to meet with Sansi at the earliest opportunity. Sansi was inclined to say no but he couldn't turn down the Chief Minister without risking his wrath. Nor was he willing to bind his fate so closely to Jatkar. Sometimes in a life karma was negotiable. He said he could meet the Chief Minister Saturday afternoon.

*　　　*　　　*

There were two reasons why it was convenient for Sansi to meet with Athawale on Saturday afternoon. That Saturday was a scheduled government half day - and Sansi and Athawale were practically neighbors. It was one of the benefits of owning property on Malabar Hill since before Independence. The Chief Minister's official residence, Varsha, was an easy walk from Sansi's apartment. He was restless after a week of confinement and thought a walk might unstiffen his legs. A couple of guards accompanied Sansi the short distance to Neapean Sea Road to the park like setting of the government bungalows where the Chief Minister lived.

Sansi left his guards with the guards at the front entrance to Varsha and was escorted up to the white walled house with its distinctive red roof tiles where there were more armed guards. A senior constable reported Sansi's arrival to someone inside and a secretary came out and told him the Chief Minister was in the garden. Sansi followed the secretary through a bungalow that was charming enough but modest for the most senior minister in Maharashtra. Out the back was a small lawn enclosed by palm trees. Athawale was alone at a green wicker table surrounded by matching armchairs. He wore rimless glasses and was reading what looked like official papers. The only other person was a servant who stood watchfully by a serving table. The secretary announced Sansi and Athawale looked up from the papers and peered at him through his glasses.

"Forgive me if I don't get up, Inspector, my legs aren't as young as they were," he said.

"Please," Sansi said.

He knew Athawale was in his eighties, perhaps his late eighties. Unlike the West age was not a barrier to high office in India where wisdom and experience were venerated. A Saraswati Brahmin Athawale wore white *kurta pajamas* and projected an image of scholarly elegance.

"Sit where you like," he said gesturing to the empty chairs. "As you can see I am a man with few friends."

Sansi took the chair nearest Athawale.

"Can I offer you something to drink?" he asked.

There was a steel pitcher on the table and a frosted glass near Athawale.

"Water will be fine, sir," Sansi said.

"You can have something else if you like. Fruit juice? Whiskey? You don't have to be an ascetic like me - and please, don't call me sir."

"Thank you, but I am quite content with water."

Athawale signaled the servant who brought Sansi a glass and filled it with iced water from the pitcher.

"Help yourself," Athawale said and prodded a small bowl of roasted cashews toward Sansi. "These are one of the few vices my doctors still allow me."

He set the official papers aside, removed his glasses and massaged his eyes for a moment. He was thin with parchment skin and a high forehead and had been in politics longer than Sansi had been alive, which was a testament to his cunning.

"I have had the pleasure of meeting your mother on several occasions," he said. "A remarkable woman and a credit to India. I have recommended her for the *Padma Shri* twice now but you know how difficult everything is with New Delhi."

"She would be flattered to know," Sansi said.

"Please give her my regards."

"I will."

"I understand you suffered some injuries recently in the service of the state?"

"Nothing serious. I am ready to go back to work."

"And Joint Commissioner Jatkar, how is he?"

"He is well, I believe."

Athawale waggled his head affably. "I am glad to hear it. He is a fine officer and I think he wants what is best for the state. So do I, but it would appear we disagree on how to get there. We find ourselves cast as adversaries and that is not only regrettable it is a waste of time and energy for both of us."

Sansi remained silent.

"In the course of my life I have seen many ambitious men," Athawale continued. "Able men, dedicated men and for the most part good men. Some have fulfilled their potential, most have stumbled and fallen. Those who fall almost invariably do so due to over confidence. I am afraid Joint Commissioner Jatkar is in danger of overplaying his hand. That is why I asked you to come and see me today. You could do Jatkar, myself and the state a great service by impressing upon him the need for patience. He has a future in politics, I see that, and I will be happy to support him in that endeavor when the time is right but that time is not now. If he continues on the path he has begun he will succeed only in wrecking this government and with it our chances of re-election. This is not the time to push, this is the time to be patient. By all means, proceed with the investigation. It will only strengthen us to weed out these perverted individuals who disgrace the name of the Party. The danger is that it is going too fast and will acquire a momentum all its own. A momentum none of us can control. All I ask is that he slow things down a bit. Give the government credit for the steps it has taken in cooperating with the investigation. Show the voters that the police and the Party are working side by side in the war against corruption. Because it is a war, Sansi. A war that will not be decided by a single battle. There are plenty of battles to fight without us fighting each other, don't you agree?"

"I cannot speak for Joint Commissioner Jatkar," Sansi said.

"I understand that, but do you agree that it would not be wise for my office and Crime Branch to dissipate their energies by fighting each other?"

"I agree that we should approach the investigation as allies rather than adversaries," Sansi said.

"That is what I want too," Athawale said. "It is my understanding Operation Garuda was your idea."

"I brought information to the attention of Joint Commissioner Jatkar and he agreed that it should be pursued," Sansi said. "Operation Garuda could not have gone forward without his support and leadership."

"Was it this investigation that brought you back to Crime Branch or was it something else?"

"There were several reasons."

"Tell me, I'm interested."

"I had reached the point in my law practice where I no longer found the work fulfilling," Sansi said. "This situation presented itself and I decided to accept Joint Commissioner Jatkar's invitation to return to Crime Branch."

"It is easier to get things done when you have the power of the state behind you," Athawale said. "Because, as I recall, your departure from Crime Branch was not amicable."

"There were disagreements on both sides."

"Between yourself and Commissioner Jatkar?"

"Yes."

"But there was one particular case, wasn't there? High profile. Quite controversial at the time as I recall."

"It was a murder investigation," Sansi said. "The chief suspect was a senior official in the British Foreign Office. The British Government and the Indian Government colluded to block the investigation."

"Yes, I remember discussing it with Governor Jejeebhoy," Athawale said. "He wasn't very happy about it either, you know. But that's how these things are. He could have resigned in protest, of course but that would have achieved nothing. But you resigned?"

"Yes."

"Why, when you knew it wouldn't make any difference to the outcome?"

"Because I found myself in a situation where what I did didn't matter."

"And you resigned so you could take matters into your own hands?"

"Yes."

"And what makes you think coming back now will be any different?"

"It won't be in some cases and I have to live with that. But I am prepared to compromise on some matters in order to move forward on others."

"Ah, so you have decided to play politics like the rest of us."

"Not quite like the rest of you, I hope."

"And what makes you think you can trust Commissioner Jatkar to compromise when something comes along that matters a great deal to you?"

"It is a risk I am prepared to take."

"So was I and look where that got us," Athawale said. "Jatkar must have offered you something very valuable to bring you back. What did he promise you - that you can have his job when he has mine?"

Sansi hesitated and it was enough for Athawale.

"I thought so," he said. "Obviously Jatkar sees something in you that he can use to his advantage and as long as he thinks that way you will be safe. But when the day comes that you are no longer of any use to him, that is when you will discover what his promises are worth."

"Then you can consider me suitably warned," Sansi said.

"I have heard you are an honorable man, Inspector," Athawale said. "Be careful how close you stand to Joint

Commissioner Jatkar. I would hate to see his impetuosity tarnish your name as well as his own."

"I appreciate your concern, Chief Minister."

"Then you will do me the favor of considering my words carefully," Athawale said. "When you leave here today I want you to know you have a friend in this office and you can speak to me on any matter at any time."

*   *   *

Sansi spent the rest of the weekend thinking about his conversation with Athawale. If the Chief Minister was trying to drive a wedge between Sansi and Jatkar his timing could scarcely be better. Sansi was worried about Jatkar too, especially his apparent disregard for high casualty rates among the civilian population. It was one of many reasons why the police were so despised in Mumbai. It not only went against Sansi's ideas of judicious policing it made it impossible for him to give Jatkar the loyalty he demanded. Nor did he want to be stuck in the middle of a power play between Jatkar and Athawale. One consequence of Sansi's conversation with Athawale was the idea that Mumbai might be better off with Jatkar gone. If that were the case Athawale was the only man who could facilitate Sansi's promotion to head of Crime Branch. It would destroy Sansi's relationship with Jatkar. And where would that leave him if Jatkar should succeed Athawale as Chief Minister anyway? Scandal hadn't kept anybody out of politics, the *Vidhan Bhavan* was full of crooks and con men.

When Sansi went back to work on Monday morning his first priority was to meet with Chowdhary, Agarkar and Nimkar to review the progress of the investigation while he'd been recovering from his injuries. He was pleased with the job they had done in his absence. They had confessions from Aadekar, the Minister for Housing, and Dubade, the

Minister for Urban Development, admitting they had taken bribes in cash, property and sexual favors from Rushil Pujari. The bribes included an apartment for each of them in Pujari owned buildings in Mumbai. They had confessed in exchange for promises of leniency but had held off signing their confessions till they knew just how lenient Joint Commissioner Jatkar was prepared to be.

After meeting with his team Sansi went upstairs to see Jatkar. They had spoken on the phone since the events at the Bharat Refinery but hadn't met face to face. Sansi found Jatkar worse for wear. His eyes were deeply bruised and his face reflected the discomfort of several cracked ribs. Sansi had no sooner sat down when Jatkar took a bottle of pain killers from his top drawer, popped a couple in his mouth and swallowed them with a drink of *chai*.

"Are you on these?" he asked.

"I take them when I need them," Sansi said.

"I need them all the time," Jatkar said. "My doctors say it's my ribs but there's something wrong with my back too. I can't sit or stand or lie down, I'm uncomfortable all the time."

"You should get a second opinion."

"I'm going in for more X-rays tomorrow," Jatkar said. "First I want to get something moving on Pujari. We need something to take everybody's mind off this wretched business."

Pujari was not only a bigger fish than Borkar he was easier to find. It was also the closest to an admission of failure Sansi was likely to get from Jatkar. The day after the refinery explosion he had issued a short statement describing the death toll as "regrettable" and putting the blame for it all on Borkar.

"You think these confessions from Aadekar and Dubade are enough to bring Pujari in?" Jatkar added.

"Not just to bring him in - to arrest him and pull search warrants," Sansi said. "Once we're inside his organization we should find enough to hang onto him."

"Offer them five years. You can go as low as two but nothing less."

"Pujari is out of the country at the moment," Sansi said. "We can be ready to move on him as soon as he gets back."

"Where is he now?"

"He is in Singapore and there is a flight plan for his plane from Singapore to Kuala Lumpur on Thursday," Sansi said. "We will track him all the way back home."

"Put a list together," Jatkar said. "As soon as we have him in custody I want raids on every one of his properties in Mumbai."

He pushed his chair back and got up with a grimace. "Do you mind if we walk a little? I feel better when I walk."

Jatkar took the stairs down to the parade ground slowly, Sansi behind him. Sansi would have offered his arm but thought Jatkar might be offended. When they reached the bottom the Joint Commissioner hobbled in the direction of the main gates.

"What did Athawale want with you on Saturday?" he said.

"He wanted to talk about you," Sansi said. He wasn't surprised Jatkar knew about his meeting with Athawale and intended to tell him anyway.

"Should I be worried?" Jatkar said.

"About me?"

"About the two of you."

"He knows you want his job."

"He *thinks* I want his job - and he went to you to find out."

"No, he knew it before he talked to me. He said you are too impatient. He tried to convince me that I should act as some kind of moderating influence on your ambition."

"With my best interests at heart, of course," Jatkar said. "What did you tell him?"

"I told him we are all on the same side."

"I'm at least three years away from taking his job and he is afraid I am moving too quickly."

"He also knows you promised me your job when you get his."

"Does he, indeed?" Jatkar said. "His network of informants is better than mine."

"That is what I think the real purpose of his invitation was, to add me to his network."

"What did he say?"

"Nothing overt. He wanted me to know that he knew what was going on and the door to his office would always be open to me."

"And who do you trust most, Sansi, him or me?"

"That is the same question he asked."

"Well, you are just going to have to make up your mind whose side you are on, aren't you?"

"Do I have to decide now?" Sansi said.

Jatkar managed a fleeting smile. They had passed through the main gates and out onto the street with its twinkling food stalls.

"I think I am going to have a falooda," Jatkar said. "Would you like one?"

"Yes, I think I would," Sansi said.

They stopped by the khulfi falooda stall and Jatkar ordered two.

"You know, Sansi, I don't mind that you want to be your own man, it is one of the reasons I brought you back," Jatkar said. "But you are not the only man in Mumbai with a conscience. If you do not believe I am working for the greater good you shouldn't be working for me at all."

"You know why I came back," Sansi said. "And I think you know how much I want it to work. I didn't expect it to be the same. I knew there would be changes and some of those changes have been good. The improvements in technology make us more efficient. But we seem only to have improved the way we do things, not why. In fact we seem to have gone backwards. There is so much emphasis on force now as the answer to everything. And force is not the answer to what is wrong in India. People will never trust us as long as we treat them as if they don't matter. There was a time when we showed the world how the politics of peace can overcome the politics of violence. But we seem to have forgotten the lessons of our own struggle."

The falooda walla handed two brimming paper cups to Jatkar. He gave one to Sansi and they turned back toward Crime Branch. Sansi used a plastic spoon to stir the mixture of ice cream, noodles, basil seeds and rose syrup together and spooned it into his mouth.

"You know what I am going to do when I am Chief Minister and you are Joint Commissioner of Crime Branch?" Jatkar said. "I am going to increase the police budget. More men, more training, more pay. Then you can run it the way you want and take all the credit." He wagged his spoon in the air to make a point. "The real question here is not whether you can trust me, Sansi. It is whether I can trust you."

*   *   *

Sansi began the week well when the disgraced Aadekar and Dubade, acting on the advice of their attorneys, each settled for two years in prison in exchange for signed confessions that identified Rushil Pujari as the man who had bribed them by providing them with free apartments in his buildings. Sansi had interviewed them separately and each of them, with an arrogance typical of senior ministers, had held out for no prison time. They caved when Sansi told them if they refused the offer on the bribery charges they would face further charges of unlawful sex with a minor. After this early success the rest of the week dragged as Sansi's team tracked Pujari's movements to see when he would leave the Malaysian Peninsula and return to Mumbai. The evening he was due back his departure from Kuala Lumpur was delayed. Sansi left Crime Branch late when it became clear that Pujari's plane would not land before morning. Too wired to sleep he sat in the roof garden alone in the dark and enjoyed the solitude, so rare in a city like Mumbai. Eventually he felt tired enough to go to bed and fell into a deep sleep. He awakened with a start when the phone rang after what felt like only minutes. It was Chowdhary to tell him that Pujari's plane had landed and he was on his way home to Akasha Tower. Sansi saw bright sunshine behind the blinds and the bedside clock said 9.25. He had slept almost five hours.

"Pull the warrants and pick me up here," he told Chowdhary. "Let Joint Commissioner Jatkar know we're on it and tell Commander Wagli we will meet him and his men at Akasha Tower."

He showered and dressed quickly and was waiting outside when Chowdhary arrived. The warrants lay on the front passenger seat awaiting Sansi's attention. There was one arrest warrant and one search warrant for Akasha Tower. There were 27 other search warrants for Pujari properties around the city and they would be executed at Jatkar's command when Sansi called him to confirm that Pujari was in custody.

The arrest warrant was in order except for the signature at the bottom. It was from a judge whose name Sansi didn't know.

"Who is this Judge Giridhar," Sansi said. "Why didn't you go to Chandurkar or Gudi."

"They weren't available," Chowdhary said. "I called Joint Commissioner Jatkar's office and Judge Giridhar is on the list."

In a city full of spies Crime Branch relied on its own list of judges who could be trusted to sign warrants without breaching police confidentiality and no names were added without Jatkar's approval. Sansi didn't like seeing a new name on such an important warrant but it was too late to do anything about it now.

Akasha Tower was visible from everywhere in Mumbai. Built by Pujari three years earlier at a reported price of US$2 billion it continued to dominate the Mumbai skyline. A glittering shaft of white granite it rose 85 stories above the city - three stories higher than the next tallest tower built by a Pujari rival. The lower half was occupied by Pujari's corporate offices and the upper half by his private residence. At the time TV reporters gushed over it as a "palace in the sky." Rooms in the residence had ceilings 20 feet high. It had three helipads, two swimming pools, several gardens, its own temple, gymnasium, yoga center, nightclub, ballroom, fully equipped theatre and cinema and a six level parking garage for the Pujari family's fleet of vehicles. The family and their guests were fed by the cooks of five kitchens and attended by a staff of 200. The name, Akasha, was Hindi for the elements of the astral world that formed the nucleus of all things in the material world. A spiritual name for a monument to vulgarity.

By the time Sansi arrived officers had thrown a security cordon around the building and were putting up barriers to hold back the crowds. Sansi found Wagli waiting outside the front lobby with his team.

Sansi told him: "We're here for Pujari. Wherever he is in this building we don't leave without him."

Sansi, Chowdhary and Wagli entered the lobby and were met by a man wearing a smart suit and a bemused smile. The other occupants of the lobby were a receptionist, a few security guards and several visitors who watched in various attitudes of apprehension.

"Gentlemen, I am head of security for Akasha Tower," the man in the suit said. "What can I do for you?"

"You can tell us where Rushil Pujari is," Sansi said.

"Do you have an appointment?"

"We do not need an appointment," Sansi said. "We have an arrest warrant." He held up the warrant for Pujari's head of security to see.

"Let me call his office, sir, and I will see if he is in today," the man said.

"He is in," Sansi said. "You can either take us to him or you can get out of the way."

"I can take you to Mr. Pujari's office." He eyed the phalanx of heavily armed special unit officers behind Sansi. "These other gentlemen, sir, are they necessary?"

"Yes," Sansi said.

"Very well, sir," the man said. "Come with me."

He turned and led Sansi, Chowdhary, Wagli and the special unit men to a bank of elevators. He took them directly to the last elevator which he needed a key to open. He ushered Sansi and the others inside but the elevator filled up quickly and he said: "I think some of your men will have to wait for the next elevator."

The elevator hummed upward and stopped at the 52nd floor with a bounce. The doors opened to reveal two more of Pujari's men in suits who, apparently, were expecting them. They and Pujari's head of security led Sansi and the others across a creamily marbled vestibule. The boots of Wagli's men squeaked on the floor. Pujari's men obligingly held open the doors to a reception area where the creamy motif continued. For those obliged to await an audience with the great man there were divans and chairs with silk cushions, marble topped coffee tables and a buffet stocked with tea, coffee, fruit drinks and mineral water. Two women in saris stood at a reception desk and they too seemed unsurprised by the arrival of a group of heavily armed police officers. The older of the two women picked up a phone and spoke softly.

"We will show ourselves in," Sansi said without waiting. But when he went to open the doors that led inside they were locked. The woman at the desk finished speaking into the phone and told Sansi: "You can go in now." She touched a button, the doors unlocked and Sansi led the way in. He and Chowdhary and Wagli and their men immediately found themselves confronted by floor to ceiling windows that took up the entire back wall and presented a 180 degree view of Mumbai from 52 floors up. It was like standing close to an Imax screen and it took their breath away.

"It can be a little disturbing at first but you get used to it," a voice said, cultivated and solicitous. "Please, come this way." The voice was far enough away and the room so huge it took Sansi a moment to locate the source. There were two men on the opposite side of the room, silhouettes against the brilliant backdrop. One of them was coming toward Sansi. The other, seated at an enormous black desk behind a bank of computer screens, had to be Pujari.

Details materialized on Sansi's periphery as he and the man coming towards him converged on each other; sculptural shards of metal and stone, massive contemporary paintings, irregularly shaped furniture. Everything had to be modern to show that Mumbai could hold its own against New York and Shanghai. Wagli and his men fanned out behind Sansi, eyes wide at a world they would never inhabit. The man approaching Sansi spoke first.

"Inspector, my name is Tambe," he said. "I am head counsel for Akasha Industries and personal attorney to Mr.

Pujari." He eyed the warrant Sansi was holding. "I'll be happy to take that off your hands."

"This is an arrest warrant for Rushil Pujari," Sansi said and put out an arm to move Tambe aside. He continued toward Pujari, who was on the phone, talking. Not so much talking but chatting, relaxed and unhurried.

"That sounds like an excellent idea," Pujari was saying. "We should have done it sooner. Would you like me to call you?"

"Inspector..." Pujari's attorney caught up with Sansi. "...none of this is necessary. Mr. Pujari is happy to meet with the authorities at any time..."

Sansi ignored Tambe and skirted the polished obsidian slab that was Pujari's desk with its clustered computer monitors that stood like ramparts between its occupant and the outside world. Sansi came within two feet of Pujari and held out the warrant.

He said: "Rushil Pujari, I am Inspector Sansi from Mumbai Police Crime Branch and this is a warrant for your arrest on charges of corruption."

Pujari looked at the warrant and then at Sansi.

"I know who you are, Inspector," he said.

Pujari was smaller than his photographs suggested but many famous people were smaller than their public image. He had been a playboy in his youth but had grown pudgy in middle age and his bottom lip was fleshy and pendulous. He also had the assuredness of immense wealth, an assuredness that said nothing in his life happened without his approval. Sansi found his relaxed indifference insulting.

"Hang up the phone and stand up and put your hands behind your back," Sansi said.

"If you would make an appointment Inspector I would be happy to answer any questions you might have," Pujari said. "And your men can put down their weapons, I can assure you I am not dangerous." He still held the handset of the phone and whoever was on the other end said something. Pujari put the phone to his ear and listened. "It is beginning to look that way," he said.

"Mr. Pujari hang up the phone," Sansi said. "This is the last time I will ask politely."

He let go of the warrant and it fluttered down into Pujari's lap like a wounded bird. Then he took a pair of steel manacles from his pocket. He could have used plastic ties but he wanted something menacing and final.

"Would you like to speak to him?" Pujari said into the phone. "I think that might be best, otherwise it is starting to look like I may lose the best part of my day." He got to his feet and offered the phone to Sansi. "Governor Thakare would like to speak with you."

"Governor Thakare?" Sansi said.

"Yes," Pujari said.

All eyes in the room were on Sansi as he took the phone.

"This is Inspector Sansi."

"Inspector, this is Governor Thakare," said the deep and distinctive voice at the other end. "I believe you have warrants for the arrest of Mr. Pujari and also to search his premises."

"Yes, I am in the process of executing those warrants now," Sansi said.

Pujari watched with his arms folded and a smirk on his face.

"Inspector, those warrants have no authority over Mr. Pujari," Thakare said. "You and your men are to leave Mr. Pujari's premises immediately and you are to return to him any materials you or your men have seized."

"With respect, Governor, these warrants were issued by a judge of the High Court," Sansi said. "They cannot be overruled except by a decision of the court."

"Inspector, your warrants were issued by the High Court of Maharashtra," Thakare said. "Mr. Pujari has a national security classification by order of the President. As you know these are constitutional powers vested in the President as head of the central government, the judiciary and the military."

"The President of India?" Sansi said, aware of how stupid he sounded.

"Yes, Inspector, the President of India," Thakare said. "Whatever evidence you have concerning Mr. Pujari you can send to me and I will forward it to the President for his consideration. But for now you are to leave..."

Sansi didn't want to hear anymore. He handed the phone back to Pujari, put the manacles back in his pocket and stepped out from behind the desk.

"Perhaps Inspector Sansi should have this back," Pujari said and handed the arrest warrant to his head counsel.

"Mr. Pujari is happy to cooperate with the authorities on any matter, Inspector," Tambe said. "We could have spared you this embarrassment if you had given us some advance warning." He passed the useless warrant back to Sansi.

"It seems to me you had all the warning you needed," Sansi said.

*   *   *

Sansi rode back to Crime Branch in silence. He would neither look at Chowdhary nor speak to him. When they reached headquarters he went directly to see Jatkar.

"They were expecting us," Sansi said, as angry as he was humiliated. "They had the Governor waiting on the phone when we got there. We had to stand down the whole operation."

"Thakare doesn't have that kind of power," Jatkar said.

"No, but the federal government does," Sansi said. "Pujari has the Governor and the President in his pocket. He got himself a national security classification."

"National security...?" Jatkar trailed off. "Military housing," he said. "Pujari has military contracts to build housing for the Indian Army. He got himself classified as an essential provider to the military."

"Building houses and apartments on military bases doesn't rise to the level of national security," Sansi said. "They gave it to him because he bought them. He bought everybody."

For once even Jatkar seemed at a loss.

"It doesn't end there," Sansi said. "Thackare told us to send everything we have on Pujari to him so he can forward it to the President - so Pujari and his lawyers can pick over it at their leisure."

"We're not sending anything to Thackare," Jatkar said. "There's a way around this, there has to be a way around this."

"Pujari knew we were coming," Sansi said, too agitated to sit. "Somebody told him. What do you know about Judge Ghiradhar?"

"The name is familiar," Jatkar said. "But I cannot say where I know it from."

"Did you put him on the warrant list?"

"I haven't added anybody to the warrant list in two years," Jatkar said.

"Chowdhary had Ghiradhar sign the warrants this morning," Sansi said. "He told me Ghiradi's name was on the list."

"Chowdhary said that?"

The two of them stared at each other. In any other circumstances Sansi would never have suspected Chowdhary. But he had begun to have doubts about his second-in-command. Chowdhary was not the same man Sansi had known before he left Crime Branch. The new

Chowdhary seemed more cynical than before, more callous. His response to the massacre at Karnataka, his attitude to the two goondas who had thrown the building superintendent off the balcony. According to Chowdhary it was the way things were now. Hadn't Sansi himself just said Pujari had bought everybody? Police pay was poor. Money didn't go far in Mumbai. Like every other government official cops took bribes, so why should Chowdhary be an exception? Did he owe Sansi any special loyalty when Sansi had been away from Crime Branch for so long? Circumstances changed and so did people. Perhaps Chowdhary was just looking out for himself now the way everybody did.

"Let me talk to him before we do anything," Sansi said.

"*Acha*," Jatkar said. "I think you should."

*   *   *

When Chowdhary pulled up in front of Sansi's apartment building Sansi told the guards to get out and wait for him. Then he asked Chowdhary to turn off the engine. Both men sat in silence for a while, neither one looking at the other.

"How long have you and I known each other?" Sansi said.

"Much time, sir," Chowdhary said. "Much time."

"I could always rely on you in the past and I thought it would be that way again," Sansi said. "I never thought I would be having this conversation with you. But, as you say, times have changed. People have changed. Perhaps you have changed too."

Chowdhary's Adam's apple bobbed in his long thin neck.

"We were so close," Sansi said. "If we'd had him for a few hours, just a few hours. Even if we had to let him go at the end of the day we would have had a day inside his computers and that would have been enough. Everything would be different. Now I don't know if we will ever be able to get him."

"I am most sorry, sir," Chowdhary said. "I did not know it would end like this."

"Why didn't you call Chandurkar or Gudi?"

"Their names were not on the list."

"What do you mean their names were not on the list?" Sansi said. "We have used them for years. If their names had been removed from the list I would have known."

"Their names were not on the new list, sir."

"What new list?"

"The new warrant list. I got it from Joint Commissioner Jatkar's office."

Why didn't you use the warrant list in our office?"

"I couldn't find it, sir. I looked but I couldn't find it."

"And Judge Ghiradhar was on this new list?"

"Yes, sir, it was the first name on the list."

"You should have known something was wrong. You should have called me. If you had called me we would have found another judge. Instead you took this warrant to a judge who is not known to me or Joint Commissioner Jatkar. In the name of God, Chowdhary, you have been part of this investigation from the beginning, you knew what was at stake. And you still went ahead and sabotaged the whole investigation."

"That was not my purpose, sir, I swear to you," Chowdhary said.

"Do you know someone has been feeding information to Pujari or his people since I came back to Crime Branch? Since I began this investigation?"

"Yes, sir, I had heard that."

"So you know how this looks?"

"Sir, I am not the informer. I never do that to you. Never."

"Then why Judge Giridhar? What do you know about him?"

"I also know nothing about him," Chowdhary said. "I tell you the truth, his name was on the list."

"The new list?"

"Yes, sir, the new list."

"According to Joint Commissioner Jatkar there is no new list," Sansi said. "He knows nothing about Giridhar. He hasn't added anyone's name to the list in two years."

"Sir, I swear to you by the *Lord Mahadeva* I saw it there with my own eyes. That is the reason I went to him."

Sansi was silent a moment. "Where was Giridhar when you saw him?"

"He was at home at his apartment on Marine Drive. He agreed to signing the warrants so I went to him and then I come straight to you."

"When you spoke to him on the phone, did you tell him who the warrants were for?"

Chowdhary looked miserable. "Yes, sir, I told him who they were for."

"What time was it when you spoke to him?"

"It was a little before eight-o-clock. As soon as I knew Pujari's plane had landed and he was on his way to Akasha Tower."

"So Judge Giridhar knew we were going to arrest Pujari for almost an hour before we arrived at Akasha Tower," Sansi said. "Somebody told Pujari's people we were coming for him and if it wasn't Giridhar that only leaves you."

"It was not me, sir and if it was Ghiradhar I am most sorry. I went to him only because his name was on the list."

"And Joint Commissioner Jatkar says it couldn't have been."

"It was there sir," Chowdhary insisted. "I could not find the list so I called Joint Commissioner Jatkar's office and asked them to send me the list by email to save time."

"Who did you speak to in the Joint Commissioner's office?"

"I don't know, sir, it was someone on his staff."

"Man? Woman?"

There were eight people on Jatkar's staff, six male officers, one female officer and a female secretary.

"It was a man?"

"And you didn't recognize his voice?"

"No sir."

"It is a simple matter to find out," Sansi said. "And if I look at the email on your computer I will find the list with Giridhar's name on it?"

"Yes sir, it will be there, I swear to you."

"*Acha*," Sansi said. He turned so he could look at Chowdhary directly. "Look at me, Chowdhary. I want you to look at me when I ask you this."

Chowdhary did as he was told, his long face sloughed in despair.

"This is between you and me now, man to man," Sansi said. "Have you ever taken money from Pujari or his people?"

"No, sir. I never take money from anybody. Never."

Sansi searched Chowdhary's eyes for the truth but all he found there was torment. The torment of a guilty man cornered or the torment of an innocent man wrongfully accused. Sansi sat back in his seat. "There has to be an investigation, Chowdhary. And you are a primary suspect. As of now I am putting you on suspension. You should return to Crime Branch and surrender your warrant and you will remain at home until the investigation has been completed."

"No!" Chowdhary shouted and launched himself at Sansi. He took Sansi around the neck and forced him to the floor. Sansi felt all the air squeezed from his lungs so he was unable to cry out for help. Chowdhary kept pushing him down and Sansi was astonished at how quickly he might be suffocate. There were shouts from the guards but no-one came to his aid. Then he heard the clatter of gunshots nearby and the ugly clang of bullets striking metal. The car windows shattered and Chowdhary jerked with each bullet that hit him but he clung determinedly to Sansi. Chowdhary never made a sound when the bullets hit him. Not a moan or an involuntary cry of pain. All Sansi felt was the unexpected heat of Chowdhary's blood as it washed over him. The firing went on like it would never end, the tempo rising and falling but never ceasing. Chowdhary stopped moving and Sansi worked a hand up the driver's side door to the handle. He pulled the handle, the door opened and he wormed his way out onto the footpath. The guards from inside Sansi's building came out to join the fight. All was clamor and confusion, people running, screaming, falling. Dust spurted from instant pockmarks in the front of Sansi's building shattering the windows of his neighbors. A glittering spray of glass filled the air. One of Sansi's bodyguards was crouched behind a rear wheel clutching an arm streaming with blood, his weapon useless beside him. He stared in dismay at Sansi soaked in blood. Sansi took cover behind a front wheel and peaked out at the street. There were two cars in the middle of the road, doors open and a dozen men trading shots with Sansi's guards, the two sides separated by mere yards. Behind one car Sansi saw Shiney Borkar, an AK-47 in one hand, shouting orders. One of Shiney's men went down and then another as the superior discipline of the guards took over. As abruptly as it had begun the attack broke off and Borkar and his men tumbled into their cars and sped away leaving their dead and wounded behind.

A guard rushed over to Sansi and knelt beside him, not knowing where to start. "It's not my blood," Sansi said. Other guards came to his aid, hoisted him to his feet and rushed him into the building. The last image Sansi had of Chowdhary was him face down in the front of the car, his back ripped open by bullets.

* * *

Pramila gasped when she saw Sansi. She'd heard the shooting outside and when Sansi's guards brought him in covered with blood she feared the worst. He tried to tell her he was unhurt but she wasn't convinced till he'd emerged from the bathroom showered and wearing clean clothes. She patted him with shaky fingers looking for any sign of injury. When he told her Chowdhary had died protecting him she had to sit down. It seemed the madness of India was beginning to wear even her down.

Sansi's guards remained in the apartment and in the outside hall were more guards with uniformed officers and frightened neighbors demanding answers. There was a sudden lull then the sound of Jatkar commending the guards for repelling the attack and saving Sansi's life. A guard opened the door for Jatkar who looked as if he'd been interrupted during an evening out.

"How are you?" he asked Sansi.

"I am alright," Sansi said.

Jatkar turned to Pramila. He and Pramila knew each other at a distance but until now they had never met.

"Madam Sansi I am most sorry that I have to come into your home in circumstances such as these," Jatkar said. "I will see that your protection is increased and I assure you we will do all that is necessary to apprehend those responsible and put an end to this as soon as possible."

"Just try and keep my son alive, commissioner," Pramila said. "I am rather fond of him."

"Believe me, Madam Sansi, the safety of your son is a top priority," Jatkar said. "If you will excuse me, I must speak to him now."

"Of course," Pramila said. She told Mrs. Khanna they should make some *chai* for their guests and went to the kitchen to help her.

Jatkar took Sansi aside.

"Borkar?"

"Yes."

"You're sure it was him?"

"I saw him."

"All the years I have been with Crime Branch I have never seen it like this," Jatkar said. "These men have no regard for anyone."

"That is what Chowdhary said," Sansi responded. "You should know it was Chowdhary who sacrificed his life to save mine until the guards could get me in here. Somebody inside Crime Branch told Borkar I was on my way home but I don't think it was Chowdhary."

"Were you able to speak to him about what we discussed?"

"We were talking about it when we were attacked,"

"Did he tell you anything useful?"

"He told me the list with Ghiradhar's name on it came from your office, in an email."

"Did he say who sent it?"

"He said he spoke to someone on your staff, a man, and asked whoever it was to send the list. He said it was a new list that replaced the list we'd been using."

"And I told you there was no new list."

"I know."

"What do you want to do?"

"I am going to Crime Branch now to look at Chowdhary's computer. He said the email with the new list was on there."

"Call me with what you find," Jatkar said. "Tonight."

Jatkar said he would stay on a bit longer in case he could be of some comfort to Pramila. Even at a time like this he wasn't about to overlook the opportunity to make a political ally.

The street outside swarmed with police. Chowdhary's body had been removed but the car was still there, his blood sticky on the front seat. The wounded guard had been taken to hospital and so had Borkar's two wounded goondas. An officer said two dead goondas had been taken to the morgue at Crime Branch. A forensics team had begun sectioning off areas of the street to be examined. Shell casings littered the pavement and broken glass crunched underfoot. At Jatkar's insistence Sansi returned to Crime Branch accompanied by two carloads of guards. On the way he called Agarkar and Nimkar and told them about Chowdhary. He also told them to stop whatever they were doing and go to the scene and interview every witness they could find. There was no time for grieving. Like every other cop he would lock it away inside and deal with it later.

Crime Branch was never quiet. Even at night when there wasn't an operation underway there was always an officer on duty and lights burned late in several offices as detectives worked long hours to bring new momentum to investigations that had stalled. But Sansi's office was empty and he wanted it that way. It was why he had sent Agarkar and Nimkar to the scene of the attack. He let himself in, turned on the lights and went to Chowdhary's desk. It was as spare and functional as the man himself. One of the qualities that made Chowdhary a good officer was his ability to stay focused under pressure and regardless of distraction. Sansi booted up Chowdhary's PC and waited. At last the Windows 95 desktop appeared, remarkably free of icons. Sansi clicked on the Inbox and looked through the

30-plus emails Chowdhary had received around the time he said he got the warrant list from Jatkar's office. There wasn't any email from Jatkar's office, there was no list and no mention of Judge Ghiradhar. Next Sansi tried Outlook Express and looked through all the email files for the past 24 hours. The system was sluggish and the program kept freezing. "We must be able to come up with something better than this," Sansi said to himself.

After an hour he had opened and examined every email received, saved, sent and deleted by Chowdhary over the past 24 hours and there was nothing to support his desperate protestations to Sansi in the car. Sansi sat back and absently tapped his forefinger on the mouse. Then he picked up the phone and called Gabale, the cyber unit commander, at home. Gabale had seen news of the attack on TV and was astonished to hear from Sansi. Sansi assured Gabale he was unharmed and said: "I want you to tell me something about computers."

"Whatever I can," Gabale said.

"When an email is deleted is it gone forever or is there still a trace of it on the computer somewhere?"

"*Acha*," Gabale said. "An email that has been deleted, like any other document that has been deleted, leaves a record in a file somewhere on the hard drive. The tricky part is writing the program that can find it."

"How would you do that?" Sansi asked.

"You need a codeword of some sort, something specific to the email and you search for it."

"Like a name?"

"*Acha.*"

"It sounds as if it would be time consuming."

"It is," Gabale said. "Why, what are you looking for?"

"Could you come into my office early tomorrow and take every PC to the cyber unit?" Sansi said. "I will tell you then what I am looking for."

Gabale hesitated. "How many PC's do you have in your office?"

"Five," Sansi said. "Including mine."

"What time do you want me there?"

"At nine, when everybody starts work," Sansi said. "I want them all to know what you are doing."

"*Acha.*"

"Then I want you to remove every PC in Commissioner Jatkar's office."

"Do you have Joint Commissioner Jatkar's approval for that?" Gabale asked.

"Yes," Sansi said. It wasn't true but it would be in the morning.

"How many PC's are there?"

"I am not exactly sure, nine or ten I think," Sansi said. "I will be there to make sure you get every one."

"That is around 15 PC's," Gabale said. "You do understand if I assign an officer to run a hard drive analysis on every one you will be taking up half the operating capacity of the cyber unit?"

"This investigation has priority over everything," Sansi said. "How long do you estimate it will take to examine every computer?"

"It's hard to say, a day, perhaps two."

"I will see you here in the morning."

*   *   *

Sansi didn't warn Agarkar, Nimkar or his secretary they were losing their computers for a day or two until Gabale arrived to take them. They watched in trepidation as Gabale's men loaded the computers onto a flatbed truck to be driven across the parade ground to the cyber unit. Before they left Sansi made a point of telling Gabale in front of his team that he was looking for anything that had Judge Ghirabhar's name attached to it. Then Sansi went up to

Jatkar's office while Gabale did the same there. Jatkar had approved Sansi's course of action after Sansi told him the night before he had been unable to find anything with Ghirabhar's name in it on Chowdhary's computer. Sansi watched the faces of Jatkar's staff as their computers were taken away. Jatkar's staff numbered around 10 but there were also part timers and temporary workers who came and went so if anything incriminatory was found on any those computers it would be harder to narrow down the suspects. After Gabale's men had removed all the computers he went to unhook Jatkar's PC.

"Mine?" Jatkar said.

Gabale looked uncertainly from Jatkar to Sansi.

"I am afraid so," Sansi said.

"I am the only person who touches my computer," Jatkar said.

"You don't know that," Sansi said. "I had them take mine too."

Jatkar seemed about to protest further then thought better of it. "Well, take it then," he said grudgingly. When Gabale had left Jatkar said to Sansi: "Now what am I supposed to do with my day?"

"Wait till I come back from seeing Judge Ghiradhar," Sansi said. "That should give us something to talk about."

*　　　*　　　*

Judge Giradhar was a rumpled man with a trim white goatee. He opened the door to his apartment personally to Sansi and welcomed him inside. The apartment was a one bedroom but with a glamorous view of Back Bay. It was comfortably furnished and gave the impression of a modest man.

"May I offer you a cup of chai?" the judge offered.

"Thank you but no," Sansi said, unable to disguise his coolness.

The judge gestured him to a pair of amply cushioned sofas that flanked a marble topped table by a pair of doors that opened onto a tiny balcony. The sound of traffic drifted up from the street 11 stories below. As he looked around Sansi got the impression that Giridhar lived alone. There were no family photos, no sign of a wife or any other partner.

"I am here to talk to you about Sub-Inspector Chowdhary," Sansi said. "He is the officer who came to you yesterday morning to get your signature on some warrants."

"*Acha*," Giridhar said, "I thought it might be something to do with that. I saw the news last night and I am most dreadfully sorry about what happened to Sub-Inspector Chowdhary...dreadfully sorry."

"Do you have any idea why he came to you?" Sansi said.

"I was curious about that myself," Giridhar said. "He said my name was on a list of judges available to sign warrants."

"Do you know why your name was on that list?" Sansi asked.

"I didn't know it was," Giridhar said. "To the best of my knowledge the only list I am on is the reserve judges list. I have been retired for two years but I make myself available to sit in on short cases for judges who have to be away for reasons of illness or some other emergency. It came as a complete surprise to me when Sub-Inspector Chowdhary called but I am happy to help when asked."

"Were you aware that Crime Branch had been conducting an investigation into Rushil Pujari for some time and that Rushil Pujari is the owner of this building?" Sansi asked.

"I only became aware of the investigation yesterday when I was shown the warrants," Giridhar said. "And no, I didn't know Pujari was the owner of this building. But I think I can see now where you're going with this."

"You tell me," Sansi said.

"I am not a financial associate of Mister Pujari if that is what you want to know."

"Have you ever met him?"

"No."

"What do you know about him?"

"Only what everybody else in Mumbai knows about him. Or perhaps a little more because of my position."

"Which is?"

"He is a highly successful businessman with all the attendant notoriety that attaches to such a reputation."

"Judge Giridhar, did you make any calls yesterday after you signed the warrants?"

"I don't believe so."

"Do you know or not?"

"Inspector, I am doing my best to assist you here, there is no need to take such an aggressive tone, I can assure you."

"Did you or did you not call anybody in the hour after you signed those warrants yesterday?"

"I didn't call anyone."

"So when we look at your phone records we won't find any calls?"

"I did not call Mister Pujari if that is what you are suggesting."

"Did you call anybody?"

"No, I don't believe I did," Giridhar said. "My short term memory is not as good as it was but I am quite sure I didn't call or speak to anybody after I signed those warrants."

"Not even to tell a friend or some judicial colleague?" Sansi said. "As you said, it was an unusual event, it would be surprising if you didn't mention it to someone."

"Well, I didn't," Giridhar said firmly. "You can look all you want. In fact, I invite you to do so." He seemed to scent Sansi's mistrust. "Inspector, I can appreciate the difficulty of the position you are in," Giridhar said. "It seems to me that you knew Sub-Inspector Chowdhary well and you are quite naturally distressed by his death. But I would caution you not to let emotion cloud your judgment. Please, proceed with your investigation. I will make myself available to answer questions or assist you in any way I can. The sooner you exclude me from your investigation the sooner you can move ahead with it."

Even the shrewdest observer could never really be sure when someone was lying but, Sansi was inclined to believe Giridhar. On the drive back to Crime Branch Sansi wondered why Chowdhary would invent such a disprovable fiction. To divert suspicion from himself? To buy time? It wouldn't have bought him much. Or had Chowdhary told the truth? Had someone in Jatkar's office sent him a list with Giridhar's name on it then hacked into Chowdhary's computer afterwards and removed all trace of it? The real informer perhaps, trying to set Chowdhary up? Or was it a mistake? Had someone in Jatkar's office confused the warrant list with the list of reserve judges with Giridhar's name on it and sent that to Chowdhary instead? Had Chowdhary been in too much of a hurry to realize he'd been sent the wrong list? Had Sansi, in his anger at Pujari's escape, wronged the most loyal friend he had in the police service in the moment of his death?

Sansi returned to Jatkar's office to find the Commissioner dictating letters to a secretary writing into a notepad. He paced as he dictated as if to burn off some of the nervous energy that accrued from computer withdrawal. It was barely a decade since computers had been introduced to everyday life and already people were dependent on them.

Jatkar interrupted himself when he saw Sansi. "What did Giridhar tell you?" he asked.

"Not much at all," Sansi said. "I'm afraid we will have to wait and see if Sub-Inspector Gabale can come up with something."

It wasn't quite noon and Gabale had told Sansi it could take a day or more to examine the hard drives on the computers he'd taken so when he left Jatkar's office Sansi was surprised to encounter Gabale on the stairs. The young officer held a bunch of papers in one hand.

"You found something?" Sansi said.

"Yes," Gabale said. "I thought you would want to see it right away."

Sansi turned around and walked Gabale into Jatkar's office. "Apparently the Cyber Unit found something."

Jatkar stopped what he was doing and told the secretary to leave. He closed the door to the outer office behind her then closed the verandah door to his office. He gestured Sansi and Gabale to two empty seats and sat at his desk. "Well?"

Gabale unfolded the papers in his hand to reveal several computer print-outs.

"Once we had the program I prioritized the search by starting with Chowdhary's computer and yours, sir," he told Jatkar. "We found Judge Giridhar's name on the hard drives of both. His name was on an email sent from your computer to Chowdhary at 7.46 a.m. yesterday. Both emails were subsequently deleted at 12.55 p.m. yesterday. Whoever did it knew enough about remote access to use the computer here to get into Chowdhary's computer downstairs and use DOS to wipe the document from the files of both. It suggests a rudimentary knowledge of DOS but whoever was responsible apparently did not know the documents would not be removed from the hard drives themselves. Or they knew but did not have time to remove the hard drives and do what we did today."

"Did it say what the title of the list was?" Sansi asked.

"Title?" Gabale said.

"Was the name of the list the warrant list or the reserve judges list?"

"It said warrant list." Gabale handed the print-outs of his findings to Jatkar and Sansi.

"I don't understand," Jatkar said after he had read the print-outs. "Nobody but me has access to my computer."

"Somebody did, obviously," Sansi said. "Where were you at 7.46 a.m. and 12.55 p.m. yesterday?"

"I was here in my office, at work" Jatkar said.

"Did you leave the office around either of those times?" Sansi said.

Jatkar paused to think. "Not for long. I was here from the start to the finish of our operation against Pujari."

"Did you know Chowdhary called here at 7.46 a.m. to ask for the warrant list?" Sansi said.

"No."

"Somebody was in your outer office to take the call and whoever it was used your computer to send the wrong list to Chowdhary as the new warrant list and used your computer again to delete both messages around lunchtime."

"Nobody but me has..." Jatkar began then stopped himself. "Babala."

Jatkar's personal aide. Babala, the man Jatkar no longer noticed.

"He's been with me for 11 years," Jatkar said. "He's like a member of the family."

"How do you want to handle this?" Sansi asked.

Jatkar got up, went to the door to the outer office and summoned Babala then walked back to his desk and waited. Sansi and Gabale both got to their feet.

Babala appeared at the door, his head bowed.

"Come in, Babala," Jatkar said. "Close the door behind you."

Babala looked at the three of them as if looking at his executioners. He swung up his right hand with a pistol he'd concealed by his side and fired at Jatkar.

"I am not a *kuli*," he shouted.

The first bullet hit Jatkar on the right side of his body and spun him around so he fell behind his desk. It was what saved Jatkar's life as bullets smashed into the bookshelves where he'd been standing. Babala advanced into the room with single minded purpose, firing with each step. Bullets tore into Jatkar's beautiful mahogany desk seeking the man on the other side. Babala seemed not to care about Sansi or Gabale. He wanted Jatkar dead, the man he'd served for the last 11 years. Sansi scooped up the first thing on the desk he could put his hands on and flung it at Babala's head. A small painted statuette of Lakshmi it had no real weight and it hit Babala's shoulder and bounced away. It was enough to distract Babala just for a moment, enough time for Gabale to grab a chair and thrust it legs first at Babala. It stopped him in mid-stride and he seemed puzzled to find himself pinned within the legs of the chair. Gabale shoved hard and wrenched the chair to one side so that Babala lost his balance and fell on his back with Gabale using the chair to hold him down. The impact jolted the pistol loose from Babala's grasp and as he scrabbled for it Sansi stamped on his wrist and held it fast. Jatkar got to his feet, a hand pressed to his bloodied side and stared at Babala in disbelief.

Again Babala shouted at him: "I am not your *kuli*,"

Chapter 8.

Mumbai Police turned out in strength for Chowdhary's funeral. Two hundred armed officers kept the crematorium cordoned off and an armored car guarded the entrance. Inside were mostly high ranking officers; Commissioner Singh, Sansi and Jatkar with his ribs bandaged and his right arm in a sling from the effects of Babala's bullet. It was the first time Sansi had worn full dress uniform in years. To one side stood a police honor guard with rifles. Chowdhary's family and his many relatives - some of whom had come long distances - were gathered around a bamboo platform garlanded with marigolds and jasmine where Chowdhary's white shrouded corpse lay. There was a photograph of him in uniform at the head of the platform. It had to have been taken in the last few months because it showed him in his assistant sub-inspector's uniform with his wife and sons standing proudly beside him. Chowdhary's widow, Hardika, was flanked by their five sons. Sansi recognized Raman, the eldest, immediately. He had the same lithe build as his father and the same solemn looks.

The crematorium was equipped with the latest gas burners but Chowdhary's family wanted a traditional funeral. The only difference was that instead of expensive sandalwood he would be burned with mango wood. A Hindu priest led the prayers intended to speed the release of Chowdhary's soul to a better world. When the prayers ended Raman and his brothers lifted their father's body off the bamboo platform and into an iron cremation crib atop a pile of logs. Raman placed the stone of life, known as the *jeev khada*, on the ground which he and his brothers touched with their left foot before circling the crib counter clockwise while the priest chanted. Raman carried a clay pot filled with water which he poured around the unlit pyre in a symbol of purification. Raman saved a cupful to pour into his father's mouth then used the *jeev khada* stone to break the pot. Next he placed a cloth on his father's face and sprinkled *ghee* on the body to purify the corpse. His brothers helped pile the remaining logs on top. Then Raman took a torch lit by the priest and touched it to the pyre. Flames flared up and the mourners drew back from the sudden heat. They watched in silence as the flames devoured Chowdhary's body and reduced him to ash and bone. Finally Raman stepped forward with a heavy bamboo pole, brought it down swiftly and cracked open his father's skull.

A bubbling grey sludge hissed in the flames and Chowdhary's soul spiraled skyward in a plume of sparks. The police officers saluted and the honor guard raised their rifles and fired a volley into the sky.

Before leaving, Commissioner Singh, Jatkar and Sansi paid their respects to Chowdhary's widow, Hardika, and their sons. Sansi thought he saw reproach in Raman's eyes but he couldn't have known what had happened between his father and Sansi in the last moments of his father's life. When Sansi went to Hardika she pressed his hands in hers.

"He was so proud to be working with you again," she said. "He looked up to you. He said you were the kind of man every honest police officer should want to be."

Sansi left feeling as empty as a ghost. He couldn't bear to go back to Crime Branch so he went home instead. When Pramila saw him she knew he was to be left alone. He closed the door to his room, sat on the edge of the bed, put his head in his hands and wept.

*   *   *

He awakened to the sound of his cell phone. It was almost midnight and he lay back on the bed still wearing his uniform. He fumbled for the phone and put it to his ear. It was Birla.

"Sorry to call so late," Birla said. "We're going to Dubai tomorrow. Be in front of your building at six a.m. Don't forget your passport."

Sansi removed his clothes and showered. It neither revived nor relaxed him. He felt a corrosive anxiety inside, a gnawing sense of failure. When he looked in the mirror he looked as if he'd aged 10 years in the past week. He lay on his bed and tried to sleep but kept replaying the events of the past few days in his head. After an hour he realized he was awake for the night and got up. He went to the kitchen, poured himself a glass of coconut juice and walked out onto the roof garden. His mother was there, a dark and tiny silhouette against the reflected glimmer of the sea. She turned when she heard the scuff of his bare feet.

"Can't sleep?" she said.

"My mind won't let me." He took the chair beside her. "I hope you're not sitting up worrying about me."

"I can't sleep either," she said. "It happens more often as I get older. And I like it out here. It's peaceful this time of night."

The two of them sat in silence and enjoyed the warm breeze on their skin.

After a while Pramila said: "It is important to have these moments. To remind ourselves what a gift life is."

"At times," Sansi said.

"The pain will pass, it always does."

"I am not so sure," Sansi said. "Not this time."

"Then accept it," Pramila said. "Live it. Live through it."

He couldn't tell her. He didn't know if he'd ever be able to tell her.

"I have to leave early in the morning," he said. "I will be away 24 hours, perhaps longer."

"Where are you going?"

"Dubai."

"To bring Usha back?"

"You can't mention it to anyone, not even Mrs. Khanna."

"That is where all this started, isn't it?" Pramila said. "If you can bring that child safely back to Mumbai it will all have been worthwhile."

"We need some good to come of it," Sansi said.

Sansi was in front of the building at six. He told the guards he wouldn't need them for the next 24 hours but said he wanted them to remain at the apartment and keep his mother and the *bei* safe until he returned. He took only his passport and was careful to leave behind anything else that might identify him as a police officer. Four guards waited with him but he had never felt less important in his life. The guards raised their weapons as a black Mercedes SUV swung into the street and pulled up at the curb. The windows were tinted and the guards kept their weapons ready until one of Birla's men, riding beside the driver, got out with his hands in the air. He opened the rear door, Sansi slid into the air conditioned interior and the door closed behind him with a heavy thud.

"Good morning," Birla said, casual in gray slacks and an open necked pin striped shirt. He patted a silver hard shell attaché case on the seat between them. "This is your briefcase. Every lawyer has a briefcase."

"Is there anything in it?" Sansi asked.

"The company's annual report and a couple of business magazines," Birla said. "It is unlikely anybody will ask you to open it."

On the floor between them was another identical attaché case.

"Is that yours?" Sansi asked.

"Not exactly," Birla said. "It contains half a million Euros in the event we might have to spread some money around quickly."

In the event...things went bad. How much worse could they get, Sansi thought? Then he answered his own question; the operation could fail, they could all end up in prison and a child could be forever lost.

Traffic was light at this time of day and the drive to Chhatrapati Shivaji Airport took only half an hour. They pulled up at gate number eight, which allowed vehicular access to the private jet terminal. Birla's man up front handed the security guard a packet and he waved the Mercedes through. They drove to the private jet terminal and parked outside. Birla's man collected the passports and disappeared inside. He returned a few minutes later. A dozen or so security guards lounged around but nobody came out to see who was in the Mercedes. Birla flew in and out often and his visit today was nothing out of the ordinary. There was an authoritative ease about Birla's man that told Sansi he had a broad job description. The driver too. Sansi thought it likely they were both armed. They drove a short distance to a hangar where a sleek white Gulfstream 550 was parked out front. The plane was unmarked except for its registration number. Birla, Sansi and the aide got out and the driver parked the SUV beside the hangar to await their return.

The co-pilot and a flight attendant waited by the plane to greet their passengers. Birla trotted lightly up the steps, Sansi, the aide and driver behind him. The cabin was equipped with eight white leather armchairs and a couple of divans and looked like it could accommodate a dozen passengers comfortably. While Birla leaned into the cockpit to speak to the pilot his aide directed Sansi to a seat. A moment later Birla took the seat across from him while the aide and driver made themselves comfortable at the rear of the cabin. For long flights Sansi guessed the divans could be screened off and used as beds.

"What kind of range does this plane have?" Sansi asked.

"We're fully fueled so we could fly from here to New York non-stop," Birla said. "It means we won't have to re-fuel in Dubai. The less we have to do with anybody on the ground the better."

The pilot retracted the steps and the co-pilot secured the cabin door while the flight attendant fussed over her passengers' seat belts then took a seat by the rear galley as the plane began its taxi to the runway. There was a short wait before the pilot announced they were cleared for take-off. Sansi watched Mumbai slide away as the jet surged down the runway, lifted steeply into the air and wheeled westward across the Arabian Sea. Sansi checked his watch. It was a few minutes before seven. Birla said the flying time from Mumbai to Dubai was about three hours. There was a 90 minute time difference which would put them on the ground in Dubai at around 8.30 a.m. local time. The flight attendant pulled out a table between the two of them and offered them drinks. Birla asked for coffee and Sansi the same.

"I'm guessing you didn't have time for breakfast?" Birla said.

"Actually I couldn't go back to sleep after you called," Sansi said. "I had some curds around five so I am not particularly hungry."

"I'm sorry about that," Birla said. "The nature of operations such as these is you have to go when the time is right. I was awake all night too. I spent most of the time talking to my man on the ground in Dubai, making sure everything is ready. I would suggest you have something to eat now while you can. I don't know when we might get to eat again."

The flight attendant returned with their coffee and at Birla's request ran through the breakfast menu for Sansi. There was an impressive choice of cooked *parathas, rotis* and *akuris,* all of which could be heated in a microwave.

Sansi had a *palak paratha,* a savory pancake stuffed with spinach and Birla had scrambled eggs with chopped chilies.

"You've been living dangerously since we last saw each other," Birla said.

"I seem to have developed an aptitude for it," Sansi said.

"A dull life is an unlived life."

"I don't worry so much for myself," Sansi said. "I do worry about those around me."

"Your mother? Annie?"

"Neither of them would want me to hold back on their behalf but what happens to them does weigh on my decisions now and I don't know how that is going to work."

"Annie told me about Borkar getting into your home. It sounds like he's inside your head too."

"Yes. And I can't get him out unless..."

"Unless he's dead?"

"That is Jatkar's preferred solution."

"But you're not comfortable with it?"

"No, I am not comfortable with summary execution by the police. I would still like to apprehend him, put him on trial and see him punished by the courts."

"He is not a man who will allow himself to be subjected to that kind of humiliation," Birla said. "He would rather die first, but before he does he will try to take you down and everybody dear to you."

"And the only way to stop him is to be just like him."

"Men like Borkar thrive on the revulsion of civilized men," Birlar said. "They reject the civilized world. They refuse to follow its rules and sneer at those who inhabit it for their weakness. Every crime they commit shows they are stronger than us. But do not forget for one minute that it is Borkar who brought us to this point. He is the one who set the city on fire. He is the one who engages the police in bloody shootouts in the streets. He is the one who has brought you to the point where the only reasonable course of action is to kill him."

"Criminals are so much quicker to violence now and the violence is more extreme," Sansi said. "It used to be they would beat up a man to spread fear. Now they kill him. Nobody is safe from them; old, young, women, children...nobody."

"I have seen the same thing happen in business," Birla said. "There is more money in the world now than at any other time in history. And everybody wants a piece of it. If you are willing to lie, steal and kill you can get your hands on quite a lot of it. So, there is no scruple anymore, no shame. There is only winning."

"And no fear of consequence," Sansi said.

"I have been making enemies of powerful and dangerous men much longer than you," Birla said. "Would you like to know how I deal with it?"

Sansi waggled his head in assent.

"It might look as if I have everything I want in life," Birla said. "I was born into wealth. I have never had to worry about going hungry or having a roof over my head. I could have chosen any career I wanted. All I had to do was buy the right education to get it - and I could have got around that if I'd wanted. The only choice I didn't have was to be lazy. My father wanted me to follow him into publishing but if I had wanted to be a lawyer, an architect or a pilot that would have been acceptable to him too. As it turned out I had the same interest he did in publishing and politics. I also happen to live in the country with the biggest and freest print media in the world. I saw the possibilities at an early age. And I won't lie to you, I saw the power too. I saw the influence my father had over political leaders and I saw what could be done with it. So I went to America and took journalism at Columbia and then a Masters in business administration at Harvard.

"When I came home my father gave me a job as a reporter in the business section at India Today. He took me to the Business Editor and told him not to do me any favors just because I was the boss's son. Which was bullshit, we all knew that. But I wanted to work my way up and it was important to me to earn the respect of the people around me. I was also in my mid-twenties and my parents were pushing me to find a wife and start a family. I was a good catch: Kshatriya, money, promising future, not bad looking. Some of the best families in India were lining up to arrange a match between me and their daughters and one by one I drove them away with just the right amount of rudeness and arrogance. My parents were quite frustrated with me. My father asked if I was gay. Eventually they stopped pushing. I was 31 when I met Madi. I think by then my parents had given up on me ever getting married. My younger brother was married and so was my sister. But my brother had no interest in publishing. He wanted to start his own tech company and it was the right move for him because it has done rather well. My sister is an entirely different personality, very social. I realize that may sound odd coming for me but most of my social activity is obligatory, my sister actually enjoys it. My father put her to work in the advertising department and that was precisely the right place for her. Her husband is a lawyer and my father gave him a job too but in the legal department. He is a nice enough fellow but no imagination. So it all kept coming back to me as the son who would take over the family business. My father just would have preferred me to be a respectable married man with children when I did it. So, you can imagine how happy he and my mother were when I met Madi. It helped that she was educated outside India, like me. She went to school in Switzerland and then to the Parsons School of Design in New York where she studied fashion."

Annie had told Sansi that Birla's wife was now a successful fashion designer with her own label.

"We dated as if we were Americans," Birla said. "It drove our families mad but it gave us time to get to know each other. Madi was seven years younger than me but it didn't make any difference. What was important was that we could talk to each other about everything. I was very honest with her about the life I wanted. I told her I did not believe power was worth having unless it was used for change. That means getting involved in politics and that means making enemies in high places. And in India that means risking your life; my life, the life of my wife and the lives of my children. And still she married me. My wife is a very courageous woman, Sansi, much more courageous than me. She knows the danger we are in and she entrusts the lives of our family to me every day."

"Have you talked about this with your children?" Sansi asked. He knew Birla had two children; a son, Bisaj, and a daughter, Malli, both in their teens.

"As soon as they were old enough to understand," Birla said. "All rich people live with the threat of kidnapping. We take security measures, we have bodyguards and the children know why. And is it really any better to know your life may be taken for money rather than principle? We love our children, Sansi, and we are fortunate to have the resources to protect them. But does that mean the lives of our children are more precious than the lives of poor children? The answer to that, of course, is yes. And that one fact is responsible for most of the misery in the world." He took a sip of coffee. "Every child is born innocent. Every child is born helpless. Every child is born with infinite possibility. And whose responsibility is it to protect those children? The adults who brought them into the world. And what do these adults do? They neglect them, they beat them, they sell them, they rape them and they murder them."

He leaned forward.

"Do you remember a few years ago there was a man in New Delhi who used children as slave laborers in his clothing factory? When they became troublesome, when they could no longer work he killed them and used their bones to make buttons."

Sansi remembered. The man had been sentenced to life in prison and within a year he had been murdered by other inmates. But nothing else had changed.

"If people would just stop for a moment and think about that," Birla said. "We live in a country where we use our children up and when they are no longer of any use we grind their bones to make into buttons. History has never been kind to children. Every generation betrays the generation that comes after it. The point is...it is not history. It is still going on today. And Indian sweatshops aren't alone in their guilt. The monsters who get rich off the backs of children run some of the biggest clothing companies in Europe and America. And whenever their connections to the slave trade are exposed they act as if they knew nothing about it. They come here and make deals with the sweatshop owners then go back to their luxury hotels and have a child prostitute delivered to their room. Madi and I have discussed this at length and she is with me all the way. Because she is in the garment business herself she is very careful to make sure her clothing lines are made in properly run factories with real employees who are paid real wages. She doesn't sign a contract with any new factory owner until she has inspected the premises and spoken to the workers herself. And I can tell you her company makes a very respectable profit.

"And what does the justice system do to protect our children? You must have seen it yourself in Mumbai.

Judgments handed down every day in cases involving children. I see it in New Delhi and the same goes on all across India. Crimes against children are punished less than crimes against adults because crimes against children are crimes of lesser consequence. Gangsters mutilate children to make them better beggars; cut off their hands, gouge out their eyes, cripple their legs. We see it every day. It's just an economic fact of life. A man beats a child to death and is sentenced to two years. A man rapes and murders a child and is sentenced to five years. Because, apart from raping and murdering this child, he was a good man. A man of good standing in his community. It takes a particular kind of evil to destroy the life of a child. A determined, soulless evil. Because that is what happens when a crime is committed against a child. Even if the child should live the life is still destroyed."

Sansi thought of the tens of thousands of children sold as sex slaves ever year in Mumbai and how reluctant Jatkar was to help just one of them if they didn't fit in with his plans.

"Can you imagine the thousand hells that are inflicted on the mind of a child when that child is raped?" Birla said. "Yet judges routinely impose more lenient sentences for crimes committed against children than they do for crimes committed against adults - or property. When what they should be doing is handing down more severe sentences. And what do we see when there is a crackdown on child prostitution and child pornography? We see politicians arrested, businessmen, sportsmen, policemen and judges. How many of those judges who hand down lenient sentences do so because they are sympathetic to the molesters or because they are molesters themselves?

"People look away because it is too terrible to contemplate. And what can be done about it anyway? It is too big, it would be like trying to sieve all the salt out of the sea. How many rich kids are there in the world, Sansi? A few million? And how many poor kids - five hundred million? A billion? And still we tolerate these great wrongs. We never confront them. We treat children as raw material, an infinite resource to do with as we wish."

He leaned back. "That is why what we are doing today is so important. That is why we are going to Dubai. That is why we are spending all this money, all these resources to rescue just one child. Because by doing this we say the life of every child is precious, not just the children of the rich."

Sansi had wondered how much Birla was spending on the operation to rescue Usha. Half a million dollars? A million? The answer apparently was whatever it took.

"The sexual enslavement of children is the great crime of our times," Birla said. "That is why we are doing this, Sansi. That is why the people we love and who love us in return support us. Because they are on this journey with us. Because, like us, they are prepared to risk everything. Because if we don't do it we have no right to call ourselves civilized."

*   *   *

The Gulfstream 550 tilted to one side and described a long curving descent into Dubai. From his window Sansi saw blue sea, brown desert and a glittering ribbon of buildings in between. Jutting above them all was the most famous building in Dubai, the Burj Khalifa. Tethered to the shore were a series of man-made islands sculpted into the shape of palm trees ringed by artificial sandbars. Further out was an even bigger conglomerate of even more preposterous fake islands. The plane descended over a patchwork of dusty browns and greens that gave way to lush suburbs with sprawling homes and swimming pools, parks, multi-lane highways and all the great buildings of a modern city. Surprisingly, to Sansi, Dubai International

Airport was located in the middle of the city despite the open desert that reached to the western horizon. The plane scuffed the runway, slowed and taxied for what seemed like a long time to the private jet terminal. Or, Sansi thought, it might be the apprehension that accrued naturally from the awareness that he was about to embark on something extremely dangerous. When they stopped rolling Sansi took his cue from Birla who remained seated while all the necessary landing arrangements were made for him. The co-pilot came out of the cockpit, opened the forward cabin door and lowered the steps. In an unspoken routine Birla's driver and aide got out first and boarded an airport shuttle cart that came to pick them up. They disappeared into the terminal to present passports to local officials and returned after a few minutes with a black stretch limousine.

Sansi was used to the heat of the tropics but was shocked by the fierce blast of air that greeted him when he stepped outside. A merciless heat that stung his skin and shriveled the hairs in his nostrils. He hurried after Birla to the air conditioned relief of the limousine.

"I think I may need a hat," he said.

"You won't be here that long," Birla said.

The limousine was big enough to accommodate twelve comfortably. The windows were tinted against the sun and allowed the passengers to see out without anybody seeing in. Birla's driver made sure everybody was on board then swung away from the plane and across the blistering tarmac to a guarded gate in a chain link fence. Beside the gate was a hangar and inside Sansi saw long lines of what looked like Indian men in chains, squatting on the floor and guarded by armed soldiers. Migrant workers who had committed some offence in Dubai and were awaiting their deportation to India.

"They have to chain them like that?" he thought out loud.

"Arabs have always been fond of keeping others in chains," Birla said.

Sansi had thought there was little to like about Dubai from afar and from first impressions he liked it even less.

They pulled out of the airport onto a multi-lane highway and drove south through a fantasyland of gleaming new buildings, gleaming new cars, gleaming new everything. The emirs of excess had thrown billions of dollars at every architectural firm in the world to create the most stupendous buildings in the world. They had turned a scrubby strip of land between the desert and the sea into a mad mixture of Las Vegas and New York. Dubai was also an international crossroads where crooks, con men and spies from Russia, eastern Europe and all Asia could amuse themselves with every vice the human mind could devise. The ultimate bazaar of gold, gems, arms and sex for those who were unencumbered by conscience.

The limo pulled into the Jumeirah Creekside Hotel. When he got out Sansi could still see the airport.

"When we leave we'll be leaving in a hurry," Birla said.

Birla's man went to the front desk and confirmed the booking arrangements. He had reserved a top floor suite in his own name for one night. After he had checked in he called Birla's driver and gave them the room number so they could go directly to the room. Sansi was reassured to find the lobby bustling with tourists and businessmen checking out so that no-one would notice them as they strolled through the crowd to the elevators. The suite was luxurious and impersonal with views of a golf course and Dubai Creek with its fleet of tourist dhows.

Birla's man offered drinks but Sansi and Birla declined. They settled down to wait. Sansi knew what was expected of him but he knew nothing of the operational details. Birla told him they would come from his mysterious man on the ground. Sansi admired Birla's motives but he wasn't comfortable putting his life in the hands of a man he didn't know. If anything went wrong the rescue attempt would fail and they would become hostages in an ugly diplomatic incident between the governments of both countries. They waited in uneasy silence for half an hour before the room phone rang. Birla answered, whispered a few words of confirmation and hung up. Moments later there was a tap at the door. Birla's man took out the automatic Sansi suspected he carried, looked through the spy hole and opened the door. A man with short cropped brown hair flecked with grey stepped inside. He and Birla's man greeted each other as if they'd worked together before. He wore a dark blue polo shirt with blue jeans and sneakers. There was a spatter of small pink scars on the lower left of his neck that extended under his shirt. He wasn't muscular but there was a sinewy toughness about him and he moved lightly on his feet. With him was a bigger man in jeans and T-shirt, heavily built with stubbled jowls, untidy hair and wary eyes.

"Good to see you again," Birla said. "How are things here?"

"So far, so good," the first man said.

"What time do you want to go?" Birla asked.

"Soon. Traffic is lighter after ten," the man said. "The home is out at Jumeirah Islands. Al-Habash leaves for work around seven. I have a man watching the house and he confirmed that Al-Habash left this morning at his usual time. I'd like to run through the procedure with your man now."

The man was British, as Birla had said, but there was a trace of another accent, Scottish perhaps.

"This is George Sansi," Birla said.

The man assessed Sansi with stony eyes.

"What do I call you?" Sansi said.

"John," the man said. He turned to Birla. "I have to speak to him alone."

Birla gestured to an adjacent bedroom. 'John' led the way and closed the door behind Sansi.

"Here's how it's going to work," John said. "We have a van waiting by the service exit of the hotel. It's in the name of a well known Dubai air conditioning company. We'll take you down and we'll change into company coveralls in the van. Then we drive to Jumeirah Islands. They're not islands, they're houses on a man-made lake. We'll be driving slow and steady and it should take around 30 minutes. Drivers in Dubai are from all over the world and most of them are mad. We don't have back-up, if we're in an accident the operation is scrubbed.

"The house is one of 16 in a circle on one of the islands. There are mature trees around all the houses which will give us some cover. We've had it under surveillance for two weeks and we know there are eleven people inside. In addition to Al-Habash there is another adult male, a brother or brother-in-law, and a boy of about ten or eleven. There are five adult females and three younger females of varying ages. As far as we can tell two of the adult females are servants, possibly Indian. The remaining females are either related to Al-Habash or they're his wives. The girls are aged anywhere from ten to fourteen. They rarely go out and when they do they're in a single van. We've only seen the van exit with the younger females on two occasions. Each time they were accompanied by the older females and each time all of them wore full burqas so we have no idea what the Indian girl looks like. When we get to the house we'll look like we're delivering a new air-conditioning unit. As soon as we gain access we'll secure the house and restrain the occupants. We'll be carrying weapons for intimidation purposes only, they won't be loaded."

Sansi was relieved. The less force that was used the easier it would be to negotiate their release if things went bad.

"The goal is to have the house and occupants secured within two minutes," John said. "How fast we get out depends on you but I'd like to be in and out in five minutes. The females won't be covered up because they're at home. Your job is to identify the Indian girl and persuade her we're there to take her to safety. She has to trust us enough so we can put her in the empty box without her panicking about it. It's only till we get her in the van but we can't have her kicking and screaming all the way. We'll drive directly to the rendezvous point just outside the airport and hand the girl over there. As soon as the transfer is done we go our way and you go yours. Clear enough?"

"It is clear," Sansi said. It sounded easy enough in the clipped and confident manner of a military man but once they entered the Al-Habash home Sansi knew any one of a hundred things could go wrong. Among the worst was that Usha might not even be there.

"Good," John said. "Leave your passport and anything else that can identify you with Ajit."

For the next hour Sansi sat in the living room and read a hotel magazine without taking in any of it. Birla stood at a window sipping from a glass of water, looking out at the city in the sand. John announced he would have "a little nap" and lay on a bed and immediately fell asleep. The big man sat in an armchair in a corner with his head tilted back and his eyes closed as if he too were taking a nap. A few minutes before ten John awakened from his nap without prompting. "Alright," he said as he came out into the living room. "It's time we were on the road." To Birla he said: "We'll see you at the handover point in about 90 minutes."

The big man got up with a grunt. "Time we got this show on the road," he said. An American, Sansi realized.

The three of them rode the elevator down to the lobby and took a rear exit to a service entrance where there was a row of empty parking bays except for a van with the name 'Gulf Air Systems' in frosty letters on the side. The engine was running and behind the wheel was a sparsely bearded Arab looking man in company coveralls and a peaked hat. John got into the front passenger seat and closed the door after him. The American opened a rear door and told Sansi to get in. The back of the van had benches on each side and between them was a large cardboard box with a picture of the air conditioner it supposedly contained. On the sides of the box were several air holes. Sansi assumed it was reinforced to hold the weight of the girl but the air holes meant if she was screaming her voice would be heard by anybody nearby. On one of the benches was a pile of coveralls, each with the company name on the back. The American tossed a pair to Sansi and they all pulled them on and zipped them up.

"All present and correct then?" the driver said in a Cockney accent.

"Ready when you are," John said.

The driver pulled out and drove around the hotel to a service road that led to the twelve lane highway out front. They headed south to a clover leaf interchange that took them onto the main highway past a lush green golf course and onto a bridge. No-one spoke. Everybody seemed to know where they were going and what they were doing. Everybody but Sansi. The highway turned north and took them toward the downtown area. New residential blocks, office towers and hotels added to the ever expanding skyline, among them signs for 'Akasha Construction Dubai.' No doubt Al-Habash, as an administrative deputy of the licensing and registration division of the Dubai Department Of Economic Development, helped smooth the way for Pujari's many projects in Dubai. Sansi watched the gleaming cityscape slide by and thought of the corruption that made it all possible. The road was busy but traffic was moving freely. The skyline dwindled to two and three storey buildings then vacant lots that awaited the developer's eye. They drove past a long and nondescript industrial estate on one side and open desert on the other. Police sirens came up on them fast and a green and white blur streaked past them.

"That gave me a bit of a turn," the driver said.

"The police in Dubai drive Ferraris?" Sansi said.

"You know what some of them are like," the driver said. "Give them a bit of money and a flash car and they think they own the bloody world."

They came to an area of palm studded suburbs laid out in a fanciful array of squares, circles and crescents. The driver slowed and they turned onto a side road then onto a palm lined highway that led them to the fake lagoon adorned by dozens of fake islands and red roofed homes set amidst unnaturally green lawns and parks.

"Place is a fucking maze," the American said.

They drove past several island clusters on both sides then turned into a circle of large houses with a small park in the middle. A silver Audi was parked at the side of the road just inside the entrance. The van stopped, the driver lowered his window and the driver of the Audi lowered his.

"How's it all look in there, sunshine?" the Cockney Arab driver asked.

The driver of the Audi smiled and said something in Arabic and the van driver responded also in Arabic. Then they closed their windows, the van continued and the Audi pulled out behind. In a place like Dubai a silver Audi in the suburbs was unremarkable.

"Says he hasn't seen anybody leave so they should all still be in there," the van driver said.

Sansi's apprehension swelled. Months had passed since he had last seen Usha. Everything that had happened since was because of her and the next few minutes would decide whether it had been worth it. If she was gone she was gone forever. He watched keenly through the windshield, looking for potential problems. There were plenty of trees but there were also people; a couple of kids on bikes and in the driveway of a house a man washing a car. They came to the fifth house along and turned into the driveway. The Audi pulled up beside the curb on the street where the driver could watch for trouble. The van stopped nose to nose against a black BMW. There was a two door garage but the doors were closed. John got out and waited, a toolbox in his hand. The driver came around the back of the van, the American pushed open the doors and climbed out followed by Sansi. The big man grabbed the empty air conditioner box and the driver helped him lift it out so it would look heavy to anyone who might be watching. John led the way up the path to the front door while the American and the driver manhandled the box after him. Sansi was last.

They put down the box at the door, John made brief eye contact with each of them then pushed the door bell. Chimes sounded inside and they waited but there was no response. He rang again and this time they heard women's voices calling to each other inside. A moment later the door was opened by a woman in a plain brown *salwar khameez.* She was in her late 20's and looked Indian. The housemaid perhaps, Sansi thought. The van driver spoke to her in Arabic and gestured to the air conditioner box. She looked puzzled and turned to call inside and the van driver stepped in behind her, put his hand over her mouth and his arm around her waist and walked her into the entrance hall. John followed with the toolbox and he and the driver quickly duct taped the woman's mouth, hands and feet. They lifted her into a sitting room on one side, laid her on the carpet and closed the door after her. At the same time the American carried the air conditioner box into the hallway and set it down. When Sansi was inside the big man closed the door behind him. Then John took three pistols from the toolbox and gave one each to the big man and the driver.

"You wait here," John whispered to Sansi. Then he and the American hurried down the hallway to the back of the house where voices could be heard. The van driver scampered upstairs, gun at the ready. A door opened with a crash toward the rear of the house then shouts and screams and through the noise threats unmistakable in any language.

Sansi heard a man pleading: Al-Habash's brother or brother-in-law. There was the sound of a struggle, something breaking, then silence. Sansi stared down the empty hallway, waiting. The driver appeared at the top of the stairs slid one legged down the stair rail and landed nimbly on his feet.

"How we doin' so far - alright?" he said and disappeared down the hallway after the others.

To Sansi each second was agonizing but then John appeared at the far end of the hallway and beckoned to him. "You're on," he said.

Sansi followed him down the hall to a sharp turn where one door opened onto a large kitchen and another led into what looked like an entertainment room. In the kitchen someone had been preparing food, broken dishes and vegetables were scattered on the floor. A kitchen phone had been ripped out of the wall and a cell phone lay smashed into pieces on a kitchen counter. In the entertainment room a big screen TV was tipped on its back and the screen broken. The adults lay on the floor, mouths, wrists and ankles taped. The man's hair was awry and there was a welt forming above his right eye. He was breathing hard through his nose. The American stood in the doorway with his gun trained on them. The three youngest females remained in the kitchen, terrified.

"Which one is ours?" John asked Sansi.

While none of the girls wore the hijab they all had their heads bowed so Sansi couldn't see their faces.

The van driver said something in Arabic but they didn't respond.

"Speak to them in Hindi," John told Sansi.

Sansi stepped towards the girls and all three of them flinched.

"Please, don't be frightened," he said. "Nobody is going to hurt you. I am looking for an Indian girl by the name of Usha. Which one of you is Usha?"

There was no reaction. Then, slowly, one of them raised her head. Trying to be as unthreatening as he possibly could Sansi gently moved her hair away from her face. There were dry white tear trails on her cheeks and her eyes brimmed with fear.

"Are you Usha?" he asked. "Do you remember me from Mumbai?"

She stared blankly back at him. It could have been her but her hair was different, straighter and longer. The way she looked at him she had no idea who he was.

"My name is Sansi," he said, coaxing her as if he had all the time in the world. "I tried to help you in Mumbai some time ago. I had an American woman with me. She had red hair and her name was Annie. But then some bad men hurt her and took you away and we've been looking for you ever since."

He thought he saw something in her eyes, a hint of recognition.

"I have come to take you home," he said. He gestured at the armed strangers who surrounded them. "These men are here to help me take you away from this place. To take you home to India. Please tell me...is your name Usha?"

She hesitated then, in a voice so soft it was barely audible, she said: "My name is Gamilah."

Sansi felt the bottom drop out of him. Then he realized she'd answered him in Hindi.

"My name before was Usha," she said.

Sansi wanted to put his arms around her and hold her close but he couldn't. He could only guess what she must have been through. Slowly he reached out to her and gently curled a finger around her hand.

"We never stopped looking for you," he said. "Never."

"Is this her?" John said behind him

"This is her," Sansi said.

"You're sure?"

"Yes, I'm sure."

"Alright, let's get her out of here," John said.

"You are safe now, you are going to be alright, I promise," Sansi told Usha. Then he realized he'd said that the last time only for her to be snatched away. "I promise you this time I won't leave you, not for a single second. I'm going to be with you all the way back to Mumbai."

She stared back at him and slowly, tentatively, she put her hand in his.

"It's time we weren't here," John said with increased urgency.

Sansi led Usha out of the kitchen to the front hallway. John was in the lead then Sansi with Usha and behind them the van driver and the American. John opened the door a sliver and peered outside. Sansi knelt down again so he could look Usha in the eye.

"We have to hide you inside this box," he said with a glance at the air conditioner box. She looked alarmed and he hurried to reassure her. "It will only be for a minute. It is so nobody can see you when we leave. There is a van outside and as soon as we are inside the van you can come out. But I need you to be brave enough to hide in the box - can you do that for me?"

She opened her mouth to say something but there was a loud crack from the far end of the hallway followed by a bellow of pain from the American. Usha screamed and buried her face in Sansi's chest. He looked down the hallway and saw the big man on his knees, a grimace of pain on his big meaty face. At the end of the hallway a boy was holding a pistol. They'd forgotten about the boy. He raised the gun to fire again. John ran at him to try and close the distance between them before he could get off another shot. The American was blocking the hallway and it seemed there was no way John could reach the boy in time. But, without slackening his pace, he leaped up at the wall and with one foot launched himself at the other wall and from that back to the other wall while the boy stared at him. Before the boy knew it the gun was kicked from his grasp and he was on his back. John quickly taped and gagged him then grabbed a fistful of shirt and heaved him into the room with the others.

"Now stay in there and behave yourself you little bastard," he said and slammed the door shut behind him. Then he came back to attend to the American who was on all fours, the right leg of his coveralls soaked with blood.

"Where are you hit?"

"I think it's my right ass cheek."

"Only a flesh wound then," John said. "Can you walk?"

"Help me up."

John hooked the big man's arm around his shoulder and heaved him onto his feet. The American groaned and with John's help limped to the front door.

"Try not to bleed so much in front of the kid will you," John said.

"Sorry," the big man said, then over his shoulder to Usha, "sorry about that."

Sansi waited till John and the American were on their way back to the van then pried Usha away from him.

"I know that was frightening, but it's over now," he said. "Now, let us get you inside this box and we can get you out of here."

She looked solemnly at him then put out her arms so he could lift her into the box. Once inside she sat down, her arms wrapped around her knees, all the while looking up at him with trusting eyes. Sansi closed the box flaps over her and he and the van driver lifted the box and carried her outside and down the path to the van. The driver of the Audi stood in the driveway watching anxiously. He'd heard the shot and if he'd heard it others must have heard it too.

"Hurry, hurry," he urged Sansi and the van driver.

Inside the American lay sprawled on a bench on his left side while John pressed a T-shirt against the wound to stanch the bleeding. Sansi and the driver place the box in the back of the van and pushed it inside. Sansi climbed in after it while the driver shut the doors and hurried around to the front. Sansi helped Usha out of the box and sat her on the bench beside him. She clung to his arm, her fearful gaze on the wounded man across from her. The driver started the engine, backed out of the driveway and headed back the way they had come. The sudden movement jostled the American and he swore.

"No swearing in front of the kid," John admonished him.

"No bleedin', no swearin'," the big man grumbled. "How about dyin', any dyin' allowed around here?"

"No dying unless I say so," John said.

Sansi remembered they'd left the front door of the house open but there was no time to go back and close it. He decided not to say anything to the others. The van driver drove with deliberate care, the Audi following in case it had to run interference. The man who had been washing the car had gone but the two kids with their bikes stood at the side of the road and watched the van pass with undisguised curiosity. When the van pulled out onto the main highway the driver accelerated to a safe cruising speed and John took out a cell phone. He punched in a number and after a few seconds said: "We have the delivery and we're en route." Then he snapped the cell phone shut and turned his attention back to the American's wound. Sansi tried to distract Usha from the scene inside the van by pointing to various sights along the way but her eyes kept returning to the blood that ran down from the bench and sluiced back and forth in the runnels of the van floor. There seemed to be more of it now. The American had been muttering under his breath but was quiet now.

They passed back through downtown with infuriating slowness until at last they crossed Dubai Creek. They turned onto the airport perimeter road toward the private jet terminal but before they'd gone far pulled onto a road that led to a closed cargo gate where Birla's limousine waited. To Sansi the area was too open but there was little traffic. The driver backed the van right up to the limousine so all that was needed was to pass Usha across a few feet of open space. Birla's aide opened the van doors and hesitated when he saw the amount of blood on the floor.

"Come on, take her," John snapped at him. Sansi climbed out first then helped Usha after him and got into the back of the limo with her. Birla sat across from them. Usha stared around her, bewildered. Birla's aide lingered a moment talking to John. Then he turned back to the limo and tapped on the window to speak to Birla.

"The American has been shot, they want to take him to the nearest hospital."

"They can't do that, they'll be arrested," Birla said. He got out, looked in the back of the van and told John: "Leave the van here, you're coming with us."

"It's three hours to Mumbai, I'm not sure he'll make it," John said. "He needs a transfusion now."

"I never fly without a trained nurse," Birla said. "We have medical supplies, plasma and saline on board.

We can take care of him till we get to Mumbai. Stop arguing and get him into the car."

John and the van driver helped the big man out of the van and into the limo but he was barely aware of his surroundings. As soon as the doors were closed the limo driver pulled away leaving the van driver and the Audi driver behind.

"What happens to them?" Sansi asked.

"They go clean out the safe house," John said. "By tonight they'll be across the border in Oman."

Minutes later the limo pulled up at the entrance to the business jet terminal. The guards at the gate barely glanced at the passports proffered by Birla's aide before waving them through. The plane was parked beside a taxiway, at the bottom of the steps were the co-pilot and flight attendant, whom Sansi now realized was also a nurse. Instead of stopping at the terminal first the limo driver drove to the bottom of the steps and parked between the plane and the terminal so nobody from the terminal could see the passengers exit the limo.

Sansi took Usha by the hand and walked her up the steps. The flight attendant tried to put her at ease and took her to a seat across from Sansi and got her settled. Somehow, John, the co-pilot and the limo driver got the American up the steps and into the plane. The flight attendant had them put him on one of the divans in the rear of the plane. With an efficiency that could only come from a medical background she cut away the big man's clothes to expose the ugly pucker of the bullet hole in his right buttock. There was no sign of an exit wound but surgery would have to wait. She went to the galley, opened a steel cabinet that looked as if it might have held dishes and returned with a couple of pressure pads doused in a powerful antiseptic.

"Hold them against the wound and press down firmly," she told John. She returned a moment later with a tray on which there were a couple of syringes. Antibiotics and a coagulant, she said. She injected both into the big man's buttock. Next she clamped a drip arm onto a bulkhead rail and hung a bag of plasma from it. She poked around for a vein in his arm and inserted the transfusion needle.

"That should help stabilize him," she said. "When we're airborne I'll see if there's any more we can do about the wound."

At the same time Birla's aide and limo driver returned the limo to the parking area beside the private jet terminal then disappeared inside to confirm the departure of Birla's plane. Sansi watched for them thinking of the open front door at the house. All it would take was for one those kids with the bikes to wander up the path to see what had happened. At any moment police cars might come racing across the tarmac towards them. Finally Birla's men emerged from the terminal and strolled back to the plane chatting as if they had all the time in the world. As soon as they were on board the co-pilot retracted the steps and the pilot started the engines. As the plane taxied out to the runway Sansi thought of the bloodied limo and van that had been left behind for the Dubai police to find. It was just as well Birla had no plans to return to Dubai any time soon. At last the plane was cleared for take-off. They swung out onto the runway, the pilot gunned the engines, the plane leaped forward and Usha gasped as she was pressed back into her seat.

"Don't be afraid," Sansi said and reached out to pat her hand. "This is what it is like in a smaller airplane."

They sped down the runway, the plane tilted steeply and leaped into the air. They climbed into a pale blue sky and banked eastward toward India and home. Sansi watched Dubai fall away behind them. He thought he saw a string of flashing lights on the approach road to the airport but they might have been the sun reflecting off passing cars. He smiled at Usha, relieved. He'd kept his promise.

*   *   *

"Well, young lady I have been waiting to meet you for a long time," Ajit Birla said as he knelt beside Usha's seat. "This must all seem very strange to you - and a bit frightening. You are a very brave little girl."

Usha shrank into her chair.

"It is alright," Sansi said. "This is Mister Birla and he is a friend of mine. This is his airplane and as soon as he knew you'd been taken away from India he wanted to come here and take you home."

"Would you like something to eat or drink?" Birla asked. "Something cold? *Kulfi* perhaps? We have coconut, strawberry, rose mango, we even have pistachio."

She stared wordlessly at him.

"Have you had *kulfi* before?" he asked.

"I don't know," she said.

"Well, we will have to put that right won't we?" Birla said. "Why don't we try them all?"

He got up and disappeared to the galley and returned after a few minutes with a tray on which there were several dishes of different flavored kulfi and two spoons. He pulled out a table, set the tray down and gave one spoon to Usha and kept one for himself.

"Let's try this one first just because it's pink," he said and stuck his spoon into the rose mango. He dug out a spoonful, put it into his mouth and opened his eyes wide. "Oh, my goodness, you must try this, it is so delicious." Some of the *kulfi* dribbled from a corner of his mouth and he had to wipe his chin before it dripped, which made Usha smile.

"Here, let me help you," he said. Gently he took her hand, guided her spoon to the *kulfi* and helped her dig out a small mouthful. She put the spoon to her lips, tasted it, then a little more and smiled again.

"You see, I told you it was good," Birla said. "Now, I want you to taste all the others and then tell me which one you like the best."

She took a spoonful from each dish and when she had tried each one Birla asked if she had a favorite. When she said no he said she would just have to try them all again. Sansi cautioned Birla that it would not do for Usha to get sick from overeating kulfi when she had only been in their care a couple of hours but in the end she made the decision for them. After one more spoonful of each she said she liked the strawberry best. And then she put down her spoon and said she was full.

Birla took away the tray of unfinished *kulfi* and Sansi thought Usha seemed a little more relaxed. She asked: "What will happen when I get home?"

"We will take you to a place where you will be safe," Sansi said.

"To ma and papa?" she asked.

For a moment Sansi wasn't sure how to answer. "You remember Annie, the lady with the red hair in Mumbai?" he said.

He had used Annie's name at the house to try and jog Usha's memory but he wasn't sure now how much she remembered.

"Annie has been worried about you," Sansi said. "She feels very bad because you were with her when you were taken away by the bad men." It was impossible to know what Usha made of all that had happened to her. Most likely, he thought, she didn't understand any of it. "Annie will be waiting for us in Mumbai. She is going to take you to a place where you will be safe. A place where nobody can hurt you."

"Will ma and papa be there?" she asked.

Sansi hesitated before answering. "No, I am sorry, Usha, they won't."

Guilt flickered in her eyes. "Are ma and papa angry with me for being a bad girl?" she said.

Sansi felt the bottom drop out of him. "No, no Usha, you mustn't think that. You are not a bad girl. What happened to you was not your fault. You are a good girl...you are a good girl..."

There were no words for what he wanted to say. How could he explain to her the ultimate betrayal? What had her child's mind made of it all? That her parents had sent her away so it had to be her who was to blame? How did he tell her she was blameless? By destroying her last illusion? He stared mutely at her and was suddenly afraid the inadequacies that assailed him might be mistaken by her for doubt. Or worse - disapproval.

"I have to speak to someone," he said. "I will be back in a minute."

He got up and went to the back of the plane. Birla and John were standing at the rear of the cabin talking softly while the flight attendant-nurse tended to the American behind the curtain. Birla glanced at Sansi as he passed but said nothing. Sansi locked himself in the bathroom and splashed some water on his face. His skin felt prickly, he was flushed and light headed and he had to hold onto the wash basin to steady himself. He looked in the mirror and saw a man whose confidence had been shaken to the core. When he stepped out Birla was waiting for him.

"Are you feeling alright?"

"*Acha*, I will be fine."

"You don't look fine."

"I...she asked when she could see her parents," Sansi said. "I don't know what to tell her."

Birla took a breath. "There is no easy answer for that. We wait until we have to tell her - and I don't know when that time will be either."

"Every grown-up she has ever known has lied to her," Sansi said.

"We will be kind," Birla said. "We will show her what kindness is. That is all we can do."

"And she is only one," Sansi said.

"But she will be the one who changes everything," Birla said.

*   *   *

It was early afternoon when they landed in Mumbai and an ambulance was waiting on the tarmac. The American had regained consciousness and while he was still weak he looked better than when he'd been carried onto the plane. Birla's flight attendant-nurse had decided not to try and remove the bullet but she'd stopped the bleeding, staved off any infection and restored his fluids. Once the bullet was out, she said, he should make a full recovery. Birla and Sansi accompanied the Briton while he followed the ambulance men as they loaded the American into the ambulance.

"I want to thank you again for your superb professionalism," Birla said. "I'm sorry your man was wounded."

"Just another scar for him to brag about," John said.

"In all the years I have known you, you have never let me down," Birla said.

"Funny you should mention that," John said. "I was thinking before I took this job it might have to be the last one."

"You're going to retire?" Birla said. "You?"

"I think we're getting a little too old to be out in the field," John said. "This would be a good one to end on."

"You were very impressive in that house when the situation called for it," Sansi said.

"The adrenaline kicked in and I got lucky," John said. "You can't rely on luck in this game."

"We couldn't have got that child back without you," Sansi said. "I want to thank you too...John." And he offered his hand.

"Name's Lynch," the Briton said and shook Sansi's hand. "That's Sam Bono. Glad to be of service." He climbed into the back of the ambulance beside his wounded comrade and closed the door after him.

The ambulance pulled away and two of Birla's cars pulled up. Annie got out of the first and said: "Please tell me that wasn't Usha."

"It isn't Usha," Sansi said. "She's here and she is in one piece. I will go and get her."

While Sansi re-boarded the plane Annie asked Birla who the ambulance was for.

"There was a mishap getting the girl out of the house and one of our men was hurt but he is going to be alright," Birla said.

"What about Usha? Does she know what's going on? Is she scared?"

"I think she is a little frightened, yes," Birla said. "She was alright on the flight but I don't think she really knows what to make of it all. As you would expect there is a lot going on under the surface. It is going to take time...and patience."

Annie nodded and at that moment Sansi appeared at the top of the steps with Usha. He led her down the steps and Annie went over to her.

"Hello Usha, I'm so happy to see you again," she said in Hindi.

Usha looked at her as if trying to remember her.

"This is Annie," Sansi said.

Usha looked over her shoulder at Sansi. "Am I home now?" she asked.

"Almost," Sansi said. "Annie is going to take you to the place where you will be staying."

"How do you feel?" Annie asked her. "Are you tired? Hungry?"

Usha looked uncertainly back at her.

"*Acha*," Annie said. "The first thing we're going to do is get you to somewhere safe, okay? It's a very nice place, I think you'll like it."

Usha looked at Sansi and he gave her a reassuring waggle of his head. Annie took Usha's hand and led her to the first car. Usha glanced back at Sansi and Birla before the car door closed but that was all. She was resigned to the fact that once again grown-ups were taking her wherever they wanted.

Birla's Mumbai apartment sat atop the most secure residential block in the city. A 20 storey white tower designed for those who demanded the best and could afford it. To the building's armed guards and state-of-the-art security Birla added his own protection. He never traveled about the city with fewer than two bodyguards and he kept two personal security men and a *bei* at the apartment permanently. Ownership of the top floor came with its own elevator to the lobby and the underground parking garage. It was in this elevator that Annie and Usha rode to the top floor with one of Birla's guards. They stepped out into a coolly marbled lobby but when the security man opened the doors to the apartment it was like entering a hill station bungalow though on a grand scale. The walls were white, the teak floors the color of honey and the furnishings a jumble that combined to give it the feeling of a well used home. Intricately carved cabinets and chests, sturdy tables and sofas, enormous potted plants and antique photos of various Indian worthies who may or may not have been related to the Birlas. An enormous sitting area with couches capable of seating 20 or more looked out over Back Bay. Adjoining it was a dining room with a long rosewood table, chairs and buffet hutches that could have served 50. The *bei*, a tiny woman, introduced herself and inquired if Annie or Usha would like anything.

"I think I'm going to show her to her room," Annie said, seeing that Usha was in danger of being overwhelmed.

She led Usha down a wide hallway to the last room on the right. On the door was a full size cut-out of Kapish, a cartoon monkey from Tinkle Comics.

"Do you know who that is?" Annie asked.

Usha stared, expressionless.

"His name is Kapish and he is a very clever little monkey who looks out for all children," Annie said.

She opened the door to reveal a room with a single bed that had been turned into an island of color. It was the smallest guest room in the apartment and Annie had chosen it so Usha wouldn't be intimidated by the scale of everything. The pillows were strewn with brightly colored pillows and on the bed were several pairs of brightly colored girls pajamas. On the nightstand next to the bed was a pink fringed night light and a stack of childrens' comics. On the walls there were posters of characters from Tinkle Comics like Kalia the Crow and Little Raji. Annie also wanted a room with its own bathroom so Usha wouldn't have to go wandering around in the middle of the night and be confronted by one of Ajit's bodyguards. She had also left the closet door open so Usha could see inside. Several types of *salwar khameez* hung from hangars and there were jeans and T-shirts, sandals, sneakers and drawers filled with socks and underwear.

"I had to guess your size," Annie said. "You can try it on later, see what fits."

She reached for Usha's hand. "Would you like to get on the bed and see how soft it is?"

Usha snatched her hand away, alarm in her eyes. Annie couldn't believe she'd been so stupid. A bed was not necessarily a place of comfort to a child like Usha, it was also a place of terror.

"Oh, honey I am so sorry," Annie said her voice faltering. She dropped to her knees and fought the urge to take hold of Usha. "I know how strange all this must be, I know bad things have happened to you and I know..." She stopped herself. "No, I don't know. I don't know what you've been through. I've never been through what you've been through. But I can tell you this, whatever else has happened to you, you are safe here. Nobody here is going to hurt you. And I promise you on my life I will not let anybody hurt you again. Ever." She paused, hoping Usha would believe her. "So, I tell you what. Why don't we just sit here for a bit, the two of us? I'll leave the door open and we'll just sit here on the floor and you can get used to being here. You can take all the time you want." She tucked her legs underneath her and waited. Usha looked around, taking everything in. After a while her eyes settled on Annie. "It's okay," Annie said. "Take your time." And after a few more minutes Usha settled tentatively on her knees.

"You know, you and me never really got a chance to know each other did we?" Annie said. "Maybe it would help if I told you a little bit about myself. Because I was a little girl once and I remember what a scary place the world can be. And how there were lots of times when I had to pretend to be brave and I didn't feel brave at all. The first thing I should tell you is I didn't grow up here in India but I'm thinking you probably guessed that because I have kind of a different accent when I speak Hindi, don't I?"

Usha watched her impassively.

"So, I grew up in a place a long way away from here called California. It's different to India in a lot of ways. I mean, it's sunny and we have palm trees and I grew up in a town on the ocean but there are still a lot of differences. Would you like me to tell you about it?"

There was no response.

"When I was about your age I wasn't what you would call a regular kind of girl. I wasn't a girly kind of a girl, if you know what I mean. I was what we would call a tomboy. Do you know what a tomboy is?"

There was no answer.

"It means I didn't want to play with girl type toys, like dolls and stuff." She paused wondering if Usha even knew what a doll was. "I didn't play with the other girls in my neighborhood that much. I liked to play with the boys because they got to do all the fun things. But, you know, boys can be mean and they didn't want me hanging around and so there were times they would deliberately get me lost and I had to find my own way home. And there was thing in California that was very popular, called surfing. That's where you get a long flat piece of wood called a surf board and you paddle it out into the ocean and you wait for a wave to come along and then you stand up on the board and ride the wave back to the beach. Does that sound like fun to you?"

She thought she saw a glimmer of interest in Usha's eyes.

"It looked like fun to me but girls didn't do that back then. They sat on the beach and watched the boys do it and I didn't want to do that. I wanted to learn to surf. So, there was this boy who liked me a little bit and he let me borrow his board so I could try it out. I lay on the board and paddled it out into the water and tried to do what the boys did and you know what? I couldn't do it. It was a lot harder than it looked and every time I tried to stand on the board I fell off because I couldn't get my balance. And I looked like such a fool and the boys would paddle past me and kind of snigger like I had no chance. And every time I got dumped they would laugh and tell me to give up. But the more they told me to give up the more I wanted to do it. And then one day I got up on the board and I rode a wave. Not far, just a little bit, and then I fell off. And the next time I got up and I went a little bit further and then do you know what the boys did?"

Usha shook her head.

"As soon as I got up they'd cut in front of me or come right up behind me and knock the board out from under me. Because they didn't want me to succeed. And I thought that was really mean but all it did was make me want to try harder and I kept at it and I got better and better and then one day something amazing happened and can you guess what that was?"

"What?" Usha said.

"I saw another girl surfing," Annie said. "A girl from another town who happened to be on our beach that day and I realized I wasn't the only girl in the world who wanted to surf. I was the only girl in my town but there were plenty of other girls doing it at other towns up the coast. And you know, I would have stuck with it even if I hadn't known other girls were doing it. Because I liked it. But it was really good to know there were other girls in the world like me."

She thought she might be getting through but didn't want to push too hard on the first day.

"Are you getting hungry or thirsty yet, because I know I am?" she said. "How about I go to the kitchen and get us some juice and *chiwda* and we can sit right here on the floor and eat them? Does that sound like a good idea? Do you want to come and help me?"

Usha's response was to get to her feet.

"Okay, let's go see what we can find."

This time Usha gave Annie her hand more readily as they walked to the kitchen. The *bei* offered to make them anything they wanted but Annie insisted she and Usha explore it together. It took them several tries before they found a refrigerator that was the closest to a regular household fridge with vegetables, cheese, eggs and drinks. Annie didn't want to baffle Usha with too much choice so she kept it simple.

"How about some coconut water?" she asked. Usha waggled her head and Annie got out an unopened bottle of coconut water. She couldn't find plastic drinking cups and the *bei*, glad to be of service, provided her with two shiny steel drinking cups. As Annie expected the kitchen was stocked with an extensive selection of the best snack mixes in Mumbai. The *bei* set them out on a counter and Annie shook a mixture of nuts, toasted rice and chickpea noodles into a bowl and gave it to Usha to carry back to her room. They settled themselves on the floor for their impromptu picnic and Annie asked Usha if she had any questions about her room. At first she had none but then she got up, went to the nightstand and pointed to the stack of comics. Something she may have seen on the newsstands of Mumbai.

"Bring them over and let's have a look at them," Annie said.

Usha picked up the top magazine to bring it to Annie but when she went to sit down she knocked over her cup of coconut water. She froze, terrified.

"Honey, it's alright, it's only water," Annie said. She got up, went to the bathroom, brought back a towel and used it to mop up the spill. Then, with deliberate carelessness, she threw the towel into the bathroom where it landed on the floor. "See, it's no big deal," she said and gave Usha a reassuring pat on the back. Then she poured some of her coconut water into Usha's cup. "Okay, let's take a look at that magazine."

From Usha's reaction Annie guessed she'd been punished, perhaps severely, whenever she'd made a mistake in Dubai but that was something to be addressed later too.

For now, Annie just wanted to get her settled and to feel safe in her new surroundings.

Annie leaned against the side of the bed and held the magazine so Usha could see it. The name of the comic was Champak and on the cover a young girl was painting spots on a deer. Annie opened it and turned the pages, taking her time so Usha could study colorful image. On one page a boy and girl were planting flowers and there were little speech bubbles above them.

"What are they saying?" Usha asked.

Annie suspected Usha had ever been taught to read. She had probably never spent a day in school.

"Let me read it you," Annie said.

She read slowly and pronounced each word clearly and carefully and Usha listened and took an occasional sip of coconut water and a bite of *chiwda*. Occasionally she would ask a question and Annie would answer so they spent almost an hour going through the whole comic. Annie asked if Usha wanted her to read some more and Usha said yes and brought another one from the nightstand. This time Annie wasn't reading for long before she heard the deep and steady breathing of a child asleep. Careful not to wake her Annie settled Usha on the floor, put a cushion under her head and folded a bed cover over her. And she stayed and watched over her the whole night.

Chapter 9.

Jatkar was not a man to relinquish power easily. In the past two weeks he'd been blown up and shot and each time he'd only taken a few days off work. To hear him it was the psychic wounds of Babala's attack that had hurt him the most.

"He was like a member of the family," Jatkar told Sansi. "I could not feel more betrayed if it was my own son who turned a gun on me. Malti and myself were only ever kind to him. Think of it. He could have killed the two us in our home, we trusted him completely." He shifted to ease the discomfort of the wound in his right shoulder.

On the other side of Jatkar's desk Sansi said: "Those we treat with kindness we only encourage to expect more from us."

"That was Nehru wasn't it?" Jatkar said.

"Actually I think he got it from Lady Mountbatten."

Babala was now in isolation at Arthur Road, charged with attempted murder. Jatkar was overseeing the preparation of a long list of corruption charges against him, the combination of which would likely see him hanged.

"Speaking of trust," Sansi said, "you remember the child I told you about a few months ago? A girl of 11 who was sold by Shiney Borkar's gang to an Arab man in Dubai?"

"As I remember it I told you not to raise it with me again," Jatkar said.

"Well, it has come back in a manner that can no longer be ignored," Sansi said. "I think it would be very much in the interests of this department to make a formal application to the Advocate-General to ask New Delhi to repatriate her. I can give you all the necessary details."

"Do you indeed - at a time when I happen to be especially busy and functioning at less than one hundred percent? I told you the last time it won't go anywhere."

"It doesn't have to go anywhere this time either," Sansi said. "But it is very important that you make the application. You must have it on record that you asked. For your protection and for the protection of the department."

"You want me to begin a difficult and controversial process you know will end in failure so I will look good? You have to give me more than that, Sansi."

"I wish I could, commissioner, but I can't."

"Don't you think my political enemies already have enough ammunition to use against me? Why would I want to give them more?"

"Because, if you do this, it will be seen that you tried to do the right thing and it was the government that stood in your way. It will be them who looks bad, not you."

"I am getting the impression that this is something you and your reporter girlfriend have cooked up between you," Jatkar said. "She wants to make child prostitution into a major cause and pressure the government to bring the kid back from Dubai and she's dragged you in with her. Is that what is really going on here?"

"I have a stake in this, yes," Sansi said. "And yes, I have let it get more personal than I should. But I believe when everything is known what I have done will be vindicated. And if not I am willing to accept the consequences."

"And you are willing to make that decision for me too?"

"Commissioner, you need to be on the right side of this. I cannot emphasize that enough."

"What I don't need, Sansi, is for you to tell me what is good for me and what isn't," Jatkar said. "You will have to disappoint your girlfriend. I won't be making an application such as this on her behalf."

"This is not on her behalf or mine," Sansi said. "All I can tell you is that there will be a major media event very soon and you should position yourself now to be in the right place when it breaks."

"What I want is this case closed," Jatkar said. "You should be trying to find Shiney Borkar not this kid in Dubai."

"This kid led us to Borkar and Pujari," Sansi said. "She is the case."

Jatkar fell silent. Sansi could see from the bags under his eyes that his injuries were keeping him from sleeping well.

"And you want me to take it on trust that you know what you are doing?" Jatkar said. "That you are not allowing yourself and now me to be manipulated by the media?"

Sansi took a breath. "When you asked me to come back to Crime Branch you said it was because you could trust me to do what was right - no matter how inconvenient it might be for you or your enemies. Now, here we are, putting that trust to the test. I can't tell you why you should do this, Commissioner. All I can tell you is you should. And isn't that the nature of trust?" He pushed a folder across the desk with the name and address of Usha's captor in Dubai inside and got up to go. "The time is here for you to decide - either you trust me or you don't."

*   *   *

Annie sat with Usha and held her held throughout her medical examination at the Children's Hospital. Dr. Sopori was thorough but gentle. She was one of few female pediatrics doctors in Mumbai and Annie wanted Usha to be examined by a woman doctor. Usha was apprehensive to begin with but Dr. Sopori won her over with the patience that came from a lifetime of working with children. The most painful moment was when she had to take blood samples. She warned Usha to expect a sting and Usha screwed up her eyes and clenched Annie's hand. When it was over a nurse gave Usha a glass of watery orange juice.

Speaking in English Dr. Sopori told Annie: "There is evidence of vaginal and anal trauma. There has been some tearing of the labia majora, the labia minora, the hymen, the vestibule, the vaginal walls and the anus. There is also some old bruising on her back and buttocks, which may or may not be related to the sexual assault."

Annie thought of Usha's reaction when she knocked over the coconut water and how she must have been beaten for every little thing.

"Healing of the genitalia has begun but there is no evidence that she received sutures or any kind of medical treatment after penetration," Dr. Sopori added. "If there are complications she may need surgery."

"What kind of complications?" Annie asked.

"There may be nerve damage from the tearing," Dr. Sopori said. "Scarring can cause deformity in the vagina and impair its functions so it becomes necessary to remove some of the scar tissue surgically. There isn't any inflammation of the vagina, the cervix, the cervical canal, the uterine canal or the urethra but we will know more when we get the test results. If there is a possibility that her reproductive organs were damaged we will have to conduct a more comprehensive examination under anesthetic. There would have been bleeding from the vagina and the anus when she was assaulted and it is possible that some infection entered the bloodstream. I'll give you a prescription for a narrow spectrum antibiotic to address any low grade infection. I assume you are her legal guardian?"

"Yes, I am," Annie said. "What do the tests cover?"

"Everything," Sopori said. "HIV, syphilis, gonorrhea, chlamydia, hepatitis, herpes, human papillova virus."

"When will we know?"

"We will get some results back in a few days, "Sopori said. "HIV is trickier, it will take a week or more."

"And then?"

"As soon as we know what we are dealing with we can begin treatment right away."

"Is it okay if I ask you something?" Annie said.

"Of course," Sopori said.

"How many rape victims like this do you see in a year?"

"Child rape victims? At least half the children I see each year are victims of rape or some form of sexual assault. I see about a thousand, my colleagues are seeing the same. That includes male pediatric victims. But we're only seeing those children who have somebody to bring them in. The last report I saw said 53 percent of Indian children are sexually assaulted every year. We are only seeing a very small number of those."

"More than half the children of India are sexual assault victims?" Annie said.

"I know, it is an incomprehensible number isn't it?" Sopori said. "It is a major public health emergency but it is not treated as one."

"Why? Because nobody in government cares?"

"There are some politicians who want to do something about it and occasionally we will see an effort to increase the budget to hire more medical personnel," Sopori said. "But it is such a deeply entrenched problem. It is a social problem and it is an historic problem. Prostitution has been part of our culture for thousands of years. Women in India are still valued only as chattels and for the sexual gratification they provide. Female children are considered a burden. And we do not have the medical and educational resources to address it. We are a nation of 1.3 billion people and we simply do not have the means to take care of them all."

Usha was quiet on the ride back to Birla's apartment. Annie wondered how the mind of a child could possibly process what had happened to her. Whether something approaching 'recovery' was ever really achievable. But she wasn't going to try and hurry her along. She wanted to build a bond of trust between them so that in time Usha would come to her. When they got back to the apartment Annie had a *roti* for lunch while Usha had what was quickly becoming a favorite, a slice of bread smeared thickly with Nutella. After lunch Annie had to get some work done and to do that she had to do what she hated and park Usha in front of the TV. She had set up a routine with for the two of them. The first few nights she slept by the side of Usha's bed. When Usha was ready to sleep on her own Annie took the bedroom across the hall but left the doors open so they could talk to each other. Every morning Annie had breakfast with Usha then spent an hour or two with her, sometimes on the balcony picking out places of interest, talking about Mumbai and India and nature, sometimes inside talking about whatever crossed Usha's mind. Rarely did she want to talk about anything serious. Perhaps, Annie thought, she was trying to block out everything bad that had ever happened to her. Though there were times when she would lapse into silence and Annie could only guess at the images that played on the insides of her eyes.

At some point Annie would have to settle Usha down with some comics and cuddle toys in front of the TV so she could write the series about Usha that had a fast approaching deadline. There was nothing sophisticated about it. It was just establishing a pattern of dependability, giving Usha some of the stability that had been missing in her life. Having worked in noisy newsrooms all her adult life Annie had no problem working with the TV on in the background, with the *bei* pottering about in the kitchen, with the cleaners who came in twice weekly, with Ajit's bodyguards who provided security. She had turned the dining room into a work space because it was next to the living area so she could be available to Usha at all times. And, as massive as the dining table was, Annie had managed to cover much of it with notebooks, files, newspaper clippings, reference books and multi-colored thickets of Post-Its.

At the end of the afternoon Annie would take a break and spend a few more hours with Usha. They would eat together and sometimes Ajit was there to eat with them but most often he wasn't. Annie would read to her before bedtime then help her get ready for bed and make sure she brushed her teeth. Annie had got into the habit of brushing Usha's hair before she tucked her in for the night and it was while she was doing this Usha asked her: "When can I see ma and papa?"

Perhaps it was the drive to and from the hospital that had triggered the thought in Usha's mind. Annie didn't think she was ready yet for the teeming streets of Mumbai even with Annie by her side, but seeing the familiar streetscapes might have reminded her that somewhere in this city her parents were still going about their daily lives. But Annie couldn't give her an answer. Not an honest answer. Not yet.

"When I find them I'll talk to them and we'll see," she said.

"And my sister?" Usha said.

"You have a sister?"

"Yes, my younger sister. Her name is Barsha."

"Do you have any other sisters…or brothers?"

"I had two older sisters," Usha said. "But papa sent them away."

"What about brothers?"

"I had brothers when I was little but papa sent them away too."

Without pushing her too hard Annie had tried to get some idea from Usha about where she lived before she was sold. What Usha could remember was plastic and cardboard rooms packed close together, which was every slum in Mumbai. There was a busy road on one side and tall apartment buildings on the other but that too could have been anywhere. She said there was a bus station nearby and a movie theatre that looked like a spaceship. To Annie the movie theatre sounded like the only Imax theatre in Mumbai and the bus station nearby could be the Vadala Bus Depot. She knew the area, a rapidly improving area with a slum in its midst on the way to Five Gardens.

"We will talk about it as soon as I know something," she said.

She put two fingers to her lips and touched them to Usha's head. The closest to a kiss Usha could accept.

When Annie went to go back to her laptop she was unable to work. Her mind had been set on a new trajectory by Usha's question. A question that only led to other questions about the worst in human nature and how massive and insidious it was. What kind of people would sell their children into prostitution? Were they truly evil or victims of an even greater evil? She knew she wouldn't get any more writing done and went to the bar and poured herself a vodka with a lot of ice. She took a fiery swallow before the vodka became diluted then went out to the balcony and sat in the dark and watched the city seethe around her.

Ajit arrived a little while later and had to go looking for Annie before she answered his call.

"Drinking alone in the dark?" he said.

"Is that bad?" she said.

He perched on the arm of a plump sofa. "How is our young charge today?"

"She had her examination today at the children's hospital."

"Oh yes, how was it?"

"She's been raped vaginally and anally. But not recently. There's been some healing. They drew some blood. They'll get back to us in a few days about STD's and HIV."

"How did she cope?"

"Like a little girl who's used to being used."

"Has she touched on it with you at all?"

"I don't think she knows how to talk about it," Annie said. "I'm taking it slowly. If the time comes when she's ready...I don't know...I really don't know."

"There are no guide books for this," Birla said.

"No government guide books, that's for sure," Annie said. "Who knows what this has done to her mind? All she knows is she's been hurt. And that's apart from the injustice of it, the awfulness of it. All this child knows is that there is evil in the world and for a time it had her in its grip."

"I would think her biggest fear is that it may come back and take her in its grip again."

"That's why I'm doing everything I can to make her feel safe."

"Are we any closer to finding her family?"

"From what she's told me she probably grew up in the slum at Vadala. I'll go out tomorrow and see what I can find."

"We have to give them the opportunity to tell their side of the story if nothing else," Birla said. "If they are good people and they want her back and all they need is some assistance to get on their feet we can do that. If helping one child means helping one family then it is worth doing to show the political classes how it can be done. If there is to be any improvement in the lives of this country's poor we will have to show our so-called leaders the way."

"Right now they're not even trying," Annie said.

Pramila phoned Crime Branch to tell Sansi a shipping agent had called to say there were two container loads of books from the U.K. sitting on the Mumbai docks awaiting Sansi's instructions. It was welcome news at a time when little else was going his way. Rushil Pujari was out of reach and the search for Shiney Borkar had hit one dead end after another. Pujari owned too many buildings through too many proxies for Crime Branch to identify them all. Borkar could move from one to another at random and there were probably other hiding places that only he knew about. They couldn't track him through cell phones anymore, he was wise to that. Sansi needed a breakthrough that would lead him to Borkar before the gangster got to him.

Jatkar had been away all day at the *Vidhan Bhavan* testifying before the commission of inquiry into the disaster at the Bharat Petroleum Refinery. With the election in three weeks Chief Minister Athawale had wasted no time in convening a commission that would do as much damage to Jatkar's reputation as possible. Jatkar might be away for days and the burden of Crime Branch's daily operations fell on Sansi. He also had no idea if Jatkar had acted on his advice to lodge the repatriation request for Usha with the Advocate-General. If he hadn't and his appearance before the commission went badly he was doubly damned. His political career would vanish like a mirage and he and Sansi would be stuck with each other at Crime Branch.

Sansi called the agent and made arrangements to cover the landing fees and move the containers to a warehouse in town. He'd had no time to look for a permanent home for his father's library but he had an idea and it required his mother's blessing. When he got off the phone he decided to go home. Agarkar had replaced Chowdhary as Sansi's driver and now that he was acting

Joint Commissioner he merited a second car full of bodyguards. When he got home he found his mother in the roof garden chatting with the General.

"George just got home," she told him. "We have to decide what to do with all your books now."

Sansi changed into *kurta pajamas*, made himself a sweet lime and went outside to join his parents, the bronze urn containing his father's ashes between him and his mother.

"Now they're here do you know what you're going to do with all those books?" Pramila said.

"Well, you know, that rather depends on you," Sansi said.

"All I know is there isn't room for them here," Pramila said. "I thought you might donate them to the university. They'd probably be glad to have them. I can make a call if you like."

"What I thought was that we might use them as a foundation for our own educational institution," Sansi said.

"We don't have an educational institution of our own," Pramila said.

"Well no, not yet," Sansi said.

Pramila turned to look at her son.

"I've been thinking about what is best for Usha," Sansi said. "I doubt sending her back to her family is in her best interests. And while Ajit Birla can take care of her indefinitely I'm not convinced that cocooning her in luxury is the right answer either. We could take her but considering the enemies I have we would probably be putting her in even more danger. Annie would adopt her if she could but she is in no position to take on a child full time. Besides, Usha wouldn't be getting what she needs."

"And what does she need?"

"She needs an education that will enable her to go out into the real world and find her own way when she's ready."

"You're talking about a school of some kind?"

"Yes, a school. A residential school that would act as a refuge for Usha and other girls like her and at the same time provide them with an education. My father's library would be the foundation for the school library. It was just moldering away in England. This way it would be put to a good and lasting use."

"You've given this some thought haven't you?"

"Yes, but the next part really depends on you."

"I thought it might."

"I want to set up a charitable foundation in your name to support the school," Sansi said. "The Pramila Sansi Foundation."

"What you really mean is you want me to raise funds for a girls school, isn't it?" Pramila said. "You want me to be Fundraiser In Chief."

"We can start with the twenty thousand pounds my father left to cover our expenses in England," Sansi said. "And I just happen to know of a firm with a suite of offices that should be vacant quite soon - and it has plenty of bookshelves. And yes, you would be a chief fundraiser. I think you would make a very good fundraiser."

"It would have to be a very small school to begin with," Pramila said.

"As you said, *ma*, if we can help one, we help one. And we would be starting with one."

"It will still be expensive," Pramila said. "You have to find the right staff, you have to pay competitive salaries. We would be doing a lot of fundraising."

"There are government grants and tax exemptions for educational institutions," Sansi said. "And think of all the famous people you know, all the performers who could do benefits. I think once it is a reality we will have quite a bit of help. And I know a good journalist who would be willing to give us some publicity."

Pramila dropped her eyes to the General's urn.

"What do you think of our son's idea, George?" she said. "Do you think it is worth all the time and trouble he intends to push onto us?"

"I am sure he would approve, don't you think so?" Sansi said.

Pramila took her time before answering. "I think it might be a good idea to have a nurse at the school too and a small clinic."

*   *   *

Annie went out in the afternoon in a company car with a driver and, at Ajit's insistence, a bodyguard. The Vadala slum was tricky because they had to drive north to Ambekar Marg then find the narrow entrance to a cross street that curved through the middle of the slum. From there they would have to go on foot. The slum at Vadala was by no means Mumbai's biggest but like the others it filled the cracks and narrows of the city like putty. Annie would have to ask around for Usha's parents and it was impossible to know where her inquiries would lead. Usha said her family lived in two rooms of salvaged wood, plastic sheeting and corrugated iron. She also remembered the front was covered by a blue plastic tarpaulin. But slums had no street names and their dwellings no numbers. She remembered there was a barber who cut hair and shaved customers in the alleyway and a woman who collected plastic bottles to sell for recycling. There were also families with children that Usha and her sister had played with but she couldn't remember their names.

When they reached Vadala the driver parked and Annie struck out with her bodyguard. Incongruously there was a cluster of apartment blocks in the middle of the slum around which the shacks lapped like a filthy tide. Annie carried with her a picture of photograph of Usha and showed it to everyone she met as she and her bodyguard picked their way along pathways where years of accumulated garbage had been trampled into the mud. No-one recognized the girl and no-one cared but they soon acquired a trail of kids asking for money. After an hour and a half of filth and stink Annie needed a break and she and her bodyguard went back to the car. The driver wrinkled his nose at them. "Wipe your feet before you get in," he told them. "You have the smell on you."

A couple of dozen kids stood around the car watching them. Annie showed them the picture and asked if any of them knew the girl in it. A boy of nine or ten pushed forward and said: "I know her."

"Do you know where her family is?"

"I know," he said.

"You take us there now?" Annie said.

"You give me money?"

"Take me to the right place I'll give you a hundred rupees," Annie said.

The boy's eyes widened and the other kids squealed with excitement. A hundred rupees was more than any of them had ever seen. The boy led the way, taking Annie and the bodyguard back into the fetid maze. In just a few minutes they came to a shack with a torn blue plastic tarpaulin out front. There was no sign of a barber but tied to a nearby shack were bundles of plastic sheets and bottles. The elderly neighbor Usha said collected plastic.

"You pay me now," the boy said and stuck out his hand.

"When I know it's the right place," Annie said. She went to pull the tarpaulin aside but the bodyguard stayed her hand and stepped in front of her. He pulled the blue flap open and in an authoritative voice said: "Whoever is in there come out, you have an important visitor."

There was a puzzled oath and a wiry man in dirty shorts and T-shirt appeared.

"What do you want?" he asked. His lips and gums were a deep maroon from eating betel.

"This lady wants to speak to you," the bodyguard said.

The man looked her up and down. A white woman with red hair wearing an expensive *salwar khameez.* She could be money or she could be trouble.

"Who are you?" he said.

"I am a reporter with India Today magazine," she said in Hindi. "I am here to talk to you about this girl." She held up Usha's picture.

"I don't know her," he said. He sensed government and that only ever meant trouble.

"He's a liar," shouted the boy who'd led Annie to him. The other kids joined in, calling him a liar and jeering.

"Get away from here," he yelled and lunged at them and they scattered to regroup a few yards away.

"I'll ask you again," Annie said and held up the picture of Usha. "Do you know this girl?"

"Are you government?"

"No, I'm not from the government."

"Where you from?"

"I'm a reporter for India Today."

"A reporter?"

"I collect information for India Today. It's a kind of newspaper."

"What you want from me?"

"I want to know if you know this girl," Annie said.

"He knows her," the boy shouted from nearby. "He sold her to the goondas."

"You want to ask things, you pay me."

"Do you know her?"

"You pay me first."

"Tell me her name and we can talk about money."

"I know her name," he said. "Her name is Usha."

"How do you know her?"

"She was one of my kids."

"She *was* one of your kids?"

The kids jeered at him again.

"We talk business we go inside," he said.

Annie gave the bodyguard a hundred rupees to pay the boy then ducked past the blue tarp. Inside the sunlight through the blue and gray plastic sheets cast a gangrenous light. It smelled of smoke, piss and rotting garbage. In a corner was a small unlit gas stove with a few cooking pots and bowls beside it. Planks served as shelves on which there were a few small tins of food. The floor was boards covered with more plastic sheets. Squatting at the back a woman watched a portable TV with a girl of about eight beside her. The man shut the TV off and told the two of them to go into the adjoining room. The woman got up with difficulty but he made no attempt to help her. Annie realized she was heavily pregnant.

He turned back to Annie. "You want ask questions, you pay."

Even after he had sold his daughter he wasn't going to miss an opportunity to make more money off her. Annie took a recorder from her bag and turned it on.

"What is your name?" she asked.

"How much you pay?"

"That depends on what you tell me."

"No money, no talk."

"I'll pay you 500 rupee now. If I'm satisfied I'll pay you 500 more when we're done."

"Five hundred rupee?" he hissed derisively. "Five thousand rupee now, five thousand after - or no talk."

"A thousand now, a thousand after - but only if you answer all my questions.

She shut off the recorder and her tone told him she wouldn't be pushed any further.

"Give me money now," he said.

She took two 500 rupee notes out of her purse and handed them to him. He stuffed them into a pocket and waited. She turned the recorder back on.

"What is your name?"

"My name Balbir."

"Your family name?"

"No family name."

"All my questions," she said.

He hesitated then said: "Das."

Das was a common surname amongst Dalits, who were the lowest caste in India.

"Let me see your identity card."

"No identity card."

It could have been the truth. To be a Dalit was close to being a non-person. And, despite efforts by the government in New Delhi to get every lawful resident of India an identity card there were millions who didn't want to be known to the government.

"Are you married?"

"Not married. Marriage for rich people."

Do you have any papers for Usha? A birth certificate, any papers at all?

"No papers."

"How many children do you have living with you?"

"One."

"And one on the way?"

He waggled his head.

"But you have had other children?"

"Some others."

"How many children have you had by the woman you are with now?"

"Some boys, some girls."

"I want a number, an exact number."

He had to think about it. "Four girls, three boys."

"Does that include Usha...and her sister Barsha?"

"How you know Barsha?"

"Usha told me."

"*Acha*," he said indifferently.

"Did you sell your other children?"

"I sell what I have. I have only children."

"Did you sell them as prostitutes?"

"Some for prostitute, some for work, some for servant."

"And the boys?"

"I sell for work."

"What ages were your children when you sold them?"

"I sell them when they can work."

"What ages?"

"I don't know age," he replied testily. "Boys you can sell young. Girls a little bit older. The pretty ones you can sell for more money."

"How old are you?"

"I don't know."

It was impossible to guess his age. He had been hardened by life and he could have been anywhere from his 30's to his 50's.

"And your woman, how old is she?"

"Don't know."

"How long have you been together?"

"Long time."

Long enough for her to have seven children by him and another on the way.

"Have you had other women before her?"

"I have other woman but she get sick and die."

"How many children did you have by her?"

"Four. Five. This woman better. Stronger."

By Annie's count he had fathered a dozen children and had either sold or intended to sell every one of them.

"Did it bother you to sell your daughters into lives of prostitution?"

"No wrong when you are poor man," he said.

"Is that how you make money?"

"I sell what I have."

"How much did you get for Usha?"

"A little money."

"How much?"

"I am not remembering."

"It was only five months ago. How much?

"Two thousand rupee," he shrugged.

"What about Barsha? When are you going to sell her?"

"Sometime."

"What if I buy her from you now?"

"You buy now? What you pay?"

Two thousand rupee."

"Memsahib rich - 10,000 rupee."

"You know what, I'll pay it," Annie said. "I can't stand to have you in my sight another minute. Go and get her."

He pulled aside the plastic sheet separating the two rooms and stepped inside. Annie heard him tell the little girl she was going with the white lady. There was a squeal of protest and he shouted at her and the woman said something but Annie couldn't make out what it was. Annie took a camera from her bag, put it on auto and reeled off a series of shots as he dragged his terrified daughter out by the arm.

"Hey no picture," he shouted. "Picture cost extra."

Annie counted out ten thousand rupee notes and threw them at him. "Take it out of that."

He let go of his daughter's arm to grab for the money. The little girl wailed and Annie bent down and told her: "I'm taking you to see Usha, your sister. She is safe and she wants to see you again."

The child stared at her through a mask of tears and snot. Annie picked her up and stepped out of the hovel accompanied by the bodyguard.

"That man very bad," the bodyguard said.

"He's going to be a very famous bad man when I've finished with him," Annie said.

*　　　*　　　*

By the time Annie got her to Birla's apartment Barsha had cried herself dry. She was bewildered and scared but there was also the dawning realization that nothing dreadful had happened to her. The red haired woman treated her with a kindness she had never known. She awaited her fate in silence, staring at her new surrounds in this palace. Annie carried her through to the living room and called for Usha. The television was on but there was no sign of Usha.

"She was just here" the *bei* said in response to Annie's calls.

Annie went to Usha's bedroom just as she came out of the bathroom.

"I brought someone home," Annie said and put Barsha down.

The two girls stared at each other. Barsha looked as if she might cry again but there were no tears left in her. Usha ran to the sister she thought she would never see again and enveloped her as if she wanted to protect her from all the world's wrongs. The two girls clung to each other till their shock dissolved into awareness that the moment was real. Usha stepped back but held onto her sister's hands. Over and over she said: "You're here...you're here..."

"Where are we?" Barsha asked. "Are we in heaven?"

"Not heaven, but like heaven," Usha said.

"This is the home of a friend of mine, a good man," Annie told Barsha. "Usha has been here for a while and now you can stay here with her."

"Stay here?" Barsha said.

"Yes, honey, this is the beginning of a new life for you," Annie said. "But before we do anything else I think we're going to get you out of those clothes and give you a good bath and then we're going to get you into some new clothes."

Usha fixed Barsha with an earnest gaze and said: "Annie got me away from some very bad people, but we are safe here."

Annie had come close to tearing up when the two girls had grabbed onto each other but this time there was no holding back. Hearing the words she'd been telling Usha since she'd been brought back to Mumbai and knowing she believed them enough to tell her sister she could trust Annie too.

"Okay." She wiped her eyes and tried to keep her voice steady. "Usha, let's get Barsha into the bathroom and out of those clothes." Annie didn't know if 'those clothes' were any more than the filthy tattered T-shirt Barsha was wearing. Her feet were bare and it was unlikely she wore anything underneath. Her hair was also matted and filthy. Usha's hair was clean when they had rescued her because she had been kept to the standard of the household where she was held captive. But Barsha looked as if she'd never had a proper wash in her life. Annie thought the only way to proceed with Barsha was to shave her hair off. First she had to show her what a bathroom looked like. What a bathtub, a shower, a wash basin and a toilet looked like and how they worked. Then she filled the bath half full, took off the tattered rag Barsha wore and set to work washing off the years of ingrained dirt. From the time she coaxed Barsha into the bath, through three changes of bathwater, to when she and Usha persuaded her that her hair would have to come off took a couple of hours. The *bei* came and took away Barsha's T-shirt and the clump of her shorn hair in a kitchen bag and tossed them down the garbage chute. When

Annie finally lifted her out of the tub she looked like a shiny little peanut. Annie wrapped her in a big white towel and told Usha to take her into her bedroom and see if any of her clothes would fit Barsha. Then Annie went to her room, put her clothes in a bag to be laundered immediately and took a vigorous shower to intercept any lice that might have migrated from Barsha to her.

When she'd dressed she went back to Usha's room where she found the girls cross legged on the bed facing each other, so close their foreheads were almost touching. Barsha wore a pink T-shirt with white polka dots that hung loosely on her. They stopped talking when Annie came in and Barsha looked at her with an expression of awe.

"Barsha asked me if you are a princess," Usha said.

"Well, I hate to shatter her illusions so soon but no, I am anything but a princess," Annie said.

Barsha whispered something to Usha and Usha said: "Is the man who lives here a king?"

"No kings or princesses, just people," Annie said. "But I will admit, this is the nicest place I have ever stayed. Now, let's talk about something much more important, would either of you like something to eat or drink?"

Shyly Barsha told her sister she was hungry. Annie had seen how undernourished she was in the bath and suspected she'd grown up on meager portions of rice and whatever else her mother had thrown in it as well as what she'd been able to scrounge around Vadala. She walked the two girls to the kitchen and sat them at the corner breakfast table with its views over the city. Barsha gasped in fright until Usha showed they were quite safe behind walls of glass. The *bei* offered to make them whatever they wanted and Annie said she'd have a plain *roti* with yogurt and honey. All Usha wanted was a glass of juice and Annie decided what Barsha should have.

"We don't know what her system can handle," she told the *bei*. "I think a small bowl of plain breakfast cereal with milk and we'll see how she handles that."

The *bei* suggested puffed rice with a spoonful of shredded coconut. She poured the cereal into a small bowl, sprinkled some coconut onto it and added milk. Annie took it over to Barsha and set it in front of her with a spoon.

"Do you know how to use a spoon, honey?" she asked and dug the spoon into the cereal and brought it to her mouth.

Barsha watched her but when Annie gave her the spoon she held it awkwardly and when she dug in into the cereal she scattered puffed rice onto the table.

"You know what," Annie said, taking the spoon from her and setting it on the table, "You eat it anyway you like and if you want to drink from the bowl you go right ahead."

Barsha scooped a few dripping handfuls of cereal into her mouth before she picked up the bowl and drank noisily from it. The two girls giggled and the cereal was gone in less than a minute. Barsha whispered to Usha and Usha asked Annie: "Can she have more?"

"I don't want to be mean but let's see how she manages with that first," Annie said. "If she eats too much it'll just make her sick. We need to see if she holds that down."

Annie joined them at the table with her *roti* and when she saw Barsha eyeing her plate hungrily she tore off a piece of roti, dipped it in the yogurt and gave it to her. "That will have to do for now," she said. "If you keep that down and you're still hungry in a little bit you can have something more then."

As soon as she could Annie intended to get Barsha to the children's hospital and have her examined by Doctor Sopori too. She would get some advice then on what to feed a malnourished child. Then Usha asked Annie the

question she had wanted to ask Annie ever since she came
back with Barsha.

"You saw my ma and papa?" she said.

"Yes, I saw them," Annie said. "But I only spoke to
your father."

"And you brought Barsha back."

"I thought it was for the best."

"Annie?"

"Yes."

"Why don't our ma and papa want us?"

Given all that had happened Annie knew she
couldn't put it off any further.

"Honey, we can't choose our parents," she said.
"And the truth is some of us are born to the wrong people.
It's one of the worst things that can happen to a little
girl...or a little boy. Because when we are little we love our
parents. And when our ma or papa does something that
hurts us we get confused. We love them and we don't
understand why they don't love us back. And sometimes we
think it must be our fault, we think we are not worth loving.
And you know what? That is the worst feeling in the world
for any child. But you have to understand - you and Barsha
are not the only little girls in the world to have this happen.
It happens to a lot of children. The truth is there are a lot of
bad people in the world and they probably shouldn't have
children at all but they do and they make very bad parents.
But you know something amazing? Being born to bad
parents doesn't mean you have to be bad. In fact, most
children are born good. Most children just want to grow up
to be good people who live good lives. Most of all they
want to be loved. And if they aren't loved by their parents it
doesn't mean there is no love in the world for them. The
world can seem like a big bad place where only bad things
happen but there is more good in the world than bad. I can
tell you that because I know from my own life it's true. I
know good isn't always there when you need it but it does

exist. There are plenty of good people in the world. People who would be happy to be your friend. I know you and Barsha are worth loving and I know you will find friends who will love you just the way you are. It just may take a little time because real friends don't grow on trees."

The two girls looked at each other and giggled.

"And you want to know the really great thing about making friends? You don't have to go looking for them. Friends just kind of happen - it's a kind of magic. So, you just remember that, you Usha and you Barsha. There is good in the world, there is magic in the world and there are people out there who would love to be your friend."

"You're my friend aren't you, Annie," Usha said. "And you can be Barsha's friend too."

Annie leaned forward and put her arms around both girls. "Oh yes," she said. "I'm going to be your friend and I'm going to be Barsha's friend forever and ever."

*   *   *

The India Today issue with Usha's face on the cover was rolled out the following Monday morning. Inside was the first part of Annie's two-part investigation into child prostitution in Mumbai. The lobby at the India Today offices was jammed. Birla had promised a major media event and his publicity department had spent the previous week getting the word out to the Mumbai media. A floor to ceiling screen showed the cover of India Today with Usha's face on it. The photograph had been taken against a grayscale background so that every detail of her 11-year old face stood out. Framed against her glossy black hair her skin was black as tea. Her features were child perfect. Projecting the image onto a big screen made the point that she was incontrovertibly a child. That only the most depraved of minds could sexualize her. She looked directly and frankly into the camera so that her eyes held everyone who saw them. Innocence and accusation combined. The only words on the cover were 'A Child Of India.'

Birla went out first. Flashlights strobed him as he stood beside the blown up image. With a showman's instinct he waited till the crowd had quieted. Without preamble he said: "This is the face of child prostitution in India. We can't tell you her age because nobody cared enough to keep a record of her birth. As far as we know she was born in Mumbai, in Vadala. But, officially, she doesn't exist. She is a non-person. Until recently her only identity was given to her by the father who sold her as a sex slave. She was sold to a man who took her to Dubai. One of between 50,000 and 100,000 girls taken out of the country each year as sex slaves. Because she has no official identity she has no passport. Yet it was easy for a man from Dubai to take her out of the country. As if she was some kind of souvenir. A living trinket to amuse him. To be disposed of however he saw fit when he tired of her. This issue of India Today tells her story in part one of an investigative report written by staff reporter Annie Ginnaro. The report tells how this child was sold first to an escort agency in Mumbai that provided sexual services to businessmen, tourists and government officials. It tells how every adult this child ever knew betrayed her, especially those who were supposed to protect her. Today she is no longer a non-person. Her name is Usha Das and she is a child of India."

A murmur passed through the crowd. Annie had agonized about presenting Usha at the press conference but Birla had insisted that the world had to know Usha was real. So they could put a face to a problem that was otherwise too big to visualize. Annie had tried to prepare Usha by explaining to her what would happen but the only reason Usha went along with it was because she trusted Annie. When Annie led her out into a blizzard of light she did what any child would do and hid her face. Annie picked her up and she buried her face in Annie's shoulder. One at a time the flashes stopped and the crowd of reporters, photographers and TV cameramen quietened. Then one of them began to applaud, then another and another until the whole room was applauding.

"That's for you," Annie whispered in Usha's ear. "Now they know who you are." She turned and carried Usha out of the lobby to where Birla's *bei* could take care of her. "I have to go back out and answer questions," she said. "When I'm done we'll go home and you and me and Barsha will have ice cream."

*   *   *

Sansi knew why Jatkar wanted to see him.

"This is what you were talking about last week," Jatkar said and brandished the latest issue of India Today at him.

Sansi sat down expecting the worst. It was impossible to go anywhere in Mumbai without seeing Usha's face staring out from the newsstands or to turn on the TV news without seeing her picture. Usha's image and her face had gone national.

"I suppose I should be thanking you," Jatkar said.

"So you made the repatriation request?" Sansi said.

"I did," Jatkar said. "But if anything like this should come up again I would appreciate it if you did not let it get quite so far before you come to me."

Sansi thought of the times he'd pleaded with Jatkar to get involved and how he'd been rebuffed each time.

"Well, now you can face the world with a clear conscience," Sansi said.

"I've heard from the Advocate-General already this morning and he accused me of setting him up," Jatkar said. "From what he tells me I can expect to hear from New Delhi before the end of the day."

"They can't do anything to you without making themselves look worse," Sansi said.

"Becoming quite the power couple you and your girlfriend, aren't you?" Jatkar said. "I think it's time I got to know Ajit Birla. Do me a favor and set up a meeting would you?"

There was nothing Jatkar could do to avoid the storm that erupted between the Indian government and the government of Dubai. But he could tell New Delhi honestly that he knew nothing of the India Today rescue mission to Dubai. He also pointed out to the official who called him from the Ministry of External Affairs that Usha Das had been taken out of India illegally by a representative of the Dubai government. The furore subsided as both sides realized they had little to gain by drawing further attention to the matter.

With less than a week to go before the state election the India Today report could not have come at a worse time for the Athawale government. The BJP used the report as a club to beat the Congress Party mercilessly and won the election with a landslide. Within a few days of the BJP taking over Jatkar received a call from Ravi Samant, chief of staff to the new Chief Minister, Vijay Bahl. Samant praised Jatkar for his unrelenting investigation into government corruption and told him they were well aware that the commission of inquiry set up by the previous government was politically motivated and the commission would be scrapped. A few days later the BJP began replacing department heads and appointing new officials to liaise with New Delhi and Adjutant-General Abhay Deshmukh was among the first to go.

Chapter 10.

"You don't touch the money," Shiney Borkar was saying. "All you do is run the girls. You understand?"

He'd finally found someone to run the replacement for Enticing Escorts. She had run one of his other brothels for years and while her former clients were mostly Indian businessmen he thought she could move up to a more international clientele. She was dull but after Madam Lele that was part of her appeal. And he wasn't about to make the same mistake with her that he'd made with Lele. She would manage the girls and the bookings but the new agency would be cashless. Payments would be made electronically through a cashier in a separate office on the premises. The money would go into a bank account controlled by Borkar and the cashier would send him the receipts every 24 hours. And everybody knew what had happened to Madam Lele when she was caught skimming.

Borkar was showing his new madam around the suite that would be home to Exclusive Escorts on the ninth floor of the gold tinted apartment tower on Colaba Causeway. Almost every business suite and residence in the building had been sold before completion. Half the tenants had already moved in and truckloads of furniture arrived every day.

"You can start bringing the girls in Thursday," Borkar was saying. "I want to be open for business Saturday night."

The room trembled but Borkar thought little of it. Workmen were still adding finishing touches to some suites. There was a distant rumbling that swelled to a roar. The whole suite tilted and started to drop. He struggled to keep his balance. The madam slid away from him screaming. The horizon slipped past the window like a floor glimpsed from a falling elevator. The last seconds of Shiney Borkar's life were also the longest.

At Crime Branch Agarkar rushed into Sansi's office to report what he'd just heard on the police radio.

"There has been a building collapse on Colaba Causeway," he said. "They're saying there is a lot of dead. It sounds like Pujari's new apartment block."

Sansi saw the building in his mind's eye when he met with Shiney Borkar to hand over Madam Lele for Mrs. Khanna. A tall yellow clad building supposed to look like gold.

"Tell Commander Wagli to get his men over to Akasha Tower right away," Sansi said. "I want the whole building shut down, nobody gets in or out. I want a helicopter up immediately to keep Pujari from leaving by air. I want a security watch at the airports so he doesn't get on any plane, commercial or private." Next he called Jatkar and told him what had happened. "I'm bringing Pujari in," he said. "They can't get him out of this."

Sansi reached Akasha Tower before Wagli and wasn't about to wait for him. He marched into the lobby with Agarkar and two carloads of armed bodyguards. From the look of the security guards they knew about Colaba.

"Is Rushil Pujari in the building?" Sansi asked a guard at the front desk.

"I don't know sir," the man answered.

"Take me to your security control room," Sansi said. "Now."

Nervously the man took Sansi past the elevators to a door marked private. It led to an area with a generator room, a loading elevator and a flight of stairs. The control room was on the next floor up, a soundproof box enclosed by walls of tinted glass where blue shirted guards watched dozens of TV monitors connected to the Akasha Tower security grid. There was a door with a keypad beside it and when Sansi tried the door it was locked.

"Do you know the code?" he asked the guard.

The man stepped forward and punched in a four digit code but nothing happened.

"It has an override on the inside," the guard said.

Sansi saw two men standing and speaking anxiously to each other, one of them wearing a jacket and tie.

"Can they hear me?" Sansi asked.

The guard pointed to a button atop the keypad.

"Hold that down and speak, sir, and they can hear you."

Sansi pressed the button. "This is Inspector Sansi from Mumbai Police. Open the door or I'll order my men to shoot it open."

The two men who'd been talking looked at Sansi and his armed bodyguards. The man in the jacket said something and the other man came to the door and opened it.

"Who is in charge?" Sansi asked.

The man pointed to the man in the jacket.

"Is Rushil Pujari in the building?" Sansi demanded.

"Sir, I don't know where he is," the man answered.

"What is your name?" Sansi asked.

"Sir, my name is Sandeep," he said. He was young with intelligent eyes.

"Sandeep, what you say next will decide whether you spend the rest of your life in jail as an accessory to mass murder," Sansi said. "Where is Rushil Pujari?"

Sandeep recoiled as if from a blow. Sansi gave him seconds to decide but no more.

"Take him," Sansi said and one of his guards came forward and took Sandeep and cuffed his hands behind his back.

"He left in a car..." Sandeep said but Sansi had moved on.

The control room was deathly quiet as Sansi confronted the man who'd opened the door for him. "Same offer. Tell me where Rushil Pujari is or be charged as an accessory to mass murder."

"I think he went to the docks," the man said.

"Which docks?"

"He has a boat at Victoria Docks," the man said.

"What is its name?"

"The Varuna."

"Put him with the other one," Sansi told his guards. If the man was telling the truth he would be released but Sansi had time for none of that now. On his way out through the lobby Sansi ran into Wagli and his men who were trying to impose order on a crowd of Pujari employees trying to leave the building.

"Have your men take these two in," Sansi said, gesturing to his prisoners. "Then follow me to Victoria Docks. Pujari is trying to get out on his yacht."

Sansi decided they would get to Victoria Docks faster if he went with Wagli in his jeep and his bodyguards followed by car. Wagli kept the sirens and lights on all the way but it took more than half an hour to get through Mumbai's traffic to the docks. They sped along the dock road searching for Pujari's yacht without success. Sansi thought he'd seen a photo of the yacht in a magazine and it was a floating palace impossible to miss. The road turned away from the water and then continued to Princess Dock and Sansi began to think Pujari might not have escaped to his yacht at all. He could be leaving Mumbai by any one of a hundred roads instead. They drove into Princess Dock and found no luxury yacht there either. Only two empty BMW's at the water's edge.

"We're too late," Sansi said.

He got out of the jeep and stared out to sea but there was no sign of Pujari's yacht among the lumbering procession of container ships. He went back to Wagli. "Can you put me through to the Coastguard from here?"

"Of course, who do you want?" Wagli said.

"The most senior man on duty," Sansi said.

He waited impatiently while Wagli went through the levels of command then passed the radio handset to Sansi.

" Chandekar here," the voice at the other end said. His rank was Deputy Inspector General Chandekar but like most military men he went by his last name.

Sansi identified himself and added: "We have a major emergency on our hands and we need the assistance of the Coastguard."

"How can I help you, Inspector?"

"We are in pursuit of a fugitive who is in the process of leaving the country on his yacht. The identity of the fugitive is Rushil Pujari and the name of the vessel is the Varuna. I am at Princess Dock and I believe the Varuna left here within the last hour."   "Rushil Pujari?" Chandekar said. There was a long pause and Sansi tried not to read anything into it. "I know the Varuna," Chandekar continued. "It's a 150 footer and it has engines capable of reaching 35 nautical miles an hour. Do you know where it is headed?"

"I believe it is headed for Dubai."

"*Acha*," Chandekar said. "Indian territorial waters extend for 24 nautical miles. The vessel may already be in international waters."

"I understand that and I repeat: Is there anything you can do to intercept the Varuna and turn it around?"

"We have a patrol vessel in the area that could do an intercept but it would not be for several hours and the Varuna will be well into international waters by then," Chandekar said. "We also have a Fast Interceptor in harbor that could catch it before then but again, not before it reaches international waters."

Sansi felt all the air go out of him.

"If the circumstances are sufficiently important to justify it and there are Indian nationals on board the Varuna we have the authority to conduct an intercept in international waters," Chandekar added. "We know there are Indian nationals on board the Varuna so I ask you this, Inspector; do the circumstances justify an intercept of this vessel in international waters?"

"Yes Deputy Inspector General, they do," Sansi said.

"Do you know if there are any weapons on board the Varuna?"

"I think it probable that there are men with weapons on board," Sansi said.

"Very well, Inspector, on your assurance I will order the fast interceptor to sea but it will be some time before it clears the harbor." He paused. "I think you need something faster. You say you are at Princess Dock?"

"Yes sir."

"I am sending an armed helicopter to your location immediately so you can conduct an aerial pursuit," Chandekar said. "When you find the Varuna you can advise us of the location."

Sansi almost fell to his knees in gratitude.

He heard the thudding approach of the Coastguard helicopter before he saw it. It came in low, skimming the glittering metallic waves, homing in on Commander Wagli's radio signal. With the others Sansi turned his back as the helicopter descended into the car park throwing up a stinging dust spray. When it had settled the pilot beckoned and they ran to it, hunched over, hands shielding their eyes. There were three crewmen on board, a pilot, co-pilot and a door gunner manning a 50 caliber machine gun. Sansi climbed in first followed by Wagli and two of his men. Even with seven men on board there was plenty of room, enough for a dozen passengers and perhaps more.

Pilot Officer Palekar introduced himself and told his passengers to put on life jackets and belt themselves into their seats. When they were ready he lifted off. The helicopter wheeled westward across the city over Chowpatty Beach and out into the Arabian Sea. The thump of the rotors and the rush of wind in the open hatches made it impossible to be heard without shouting. The co-pilot handed Sansi a headset.

"Our orders are to conduct a search and intercept of yacht called the Varuna," Palekar said. "Estimated 25 to 50 nautical miles out on a heading for Dubai."

"Yes," Sansi said.

The pilot grinned and gave Sansi the thumbs up. "Not a problem, sir."

Within 10 minutes they had crossed the territorial limit into international waters. The co-pilot, his eyes on the screen for the forward looking radar, said a yacht the size of the Varuna should be easy to find. But, while the white dots on the screen thinned out, there were plenty of them. Each one a container ship, an oil tankers, a fishing boat or a cruise ship. The pilot took the helicopter down to 200 feet where they could check each vessel visually and began a shallow, sweeping arc. The co-pilot alternated between the radar screen and binoculars. The pilot passed his binoculars to Sansi but the vibration was too much and he preferred to watch through the cockpit. Even with radar, binoculars and multiple sets of eyes it was a big ocean in which to find even a big yacht. The pilot swept back and forth on an expanding arc and Sansi wondered how much flying time they had before they had to turn back. If they returned to Mumbai without sighting the Varuna it would give Pujari that much more time and that much more ocean to hide in. Then the co-pilot pointed to the radar screen and said: "There. Two fifty seven degrees west southwest."

Sansi leaned forward to see and at the top edge of the radar screen there was a clear white dot on its own moving rapidly to the southwest. The helicopter slanted off in its direction and everyone on board scanned the empty ocean ahead. Several long minutes passed with nothing but the endless serrations of white tipped waves.

"Two fifty seven degrees about 5,000 feet dead ahead," the co-pilot said. It was another minute or so before the untrained eyes of his passengers could see the big white yacht cutting through the waves and leaving a wide white wake. The pilot closed in to about a thousand feet behind the yacht.

"It's the Varuna," the co-pilot said and put down his binoculars.

They swooped past the big yacht close enough to see several figures watching them. The yacht was long and sleek with three decks but the bridge was undercover. Pujari would be on the bridge with his yacht captain, Sansi knew, pondering this new and unexpected threat. The co-pilot turned on the emergency broadcast channel.

"This is the Indian Coastguard calling the Varuna," he said. "Bring your vessel around and return to shore."

There was no response. The yacht butted stubbornly ahead at full speed. The co-pilot gave the same order two more times to no effect. "We'll try this," he said and turned on the loud hailer on the underside of the helicopter. He gave the same order three more times, his voice ringing across the waves, only to be ignored.

"Your call, Inspector," he told Sansi. "Do you want us to fire a burst across her bow?"

"Yes," Sansi said.

Palekar banked around once more and pulled up abreast with the Varuna some 500 feet to her portside at a height of 200 feet. The door gunner slid open the side hatch and aimed just ahead of the yacht. The co-pilot returned to the emergency broadcast waveband to issue a final warning.

"This is the Indian Coastguard calling the captain of the Varuna. Turn your vessel around or we will open fire." Again there was nothing. The yacht plowed on in the direction of the Arabian Peninsula four thousand miles distant. The co-pilot issued the same final warning through the loud hailer and the response from the yacht was a wink of light from the lower deck. Sansi thought it might be the reflection off someone's binoculars but there was another wink of light from further along the deck then another and another. A bullet pinged off the helicopter skids followed immediately by a loud double clang as a bullet tore through the cabin. The door gunner opened up in furious response and so did Wagli and his two men. Bullets peppered the Varuna, punching holes in the gleaming white superstructure, smashing windows and splintering the decks. The gunfire from the yacht ceased. Palekar banked steeply away and everyone hung on as the waves spun dizzily past beneath them. The helicopter leveled and Palekar brought it around a couple of thousand feet astern of the Varuna.

"I would prefer we didn't do that again," Sansi said. "I want to take him back to Mumbai in one piece to stand trial."

"We can disable it till the Fast Interceptor gets here," the co-pilot said.

"Let's do that then, shall we?" Sansi said.

While Palekar came around astern of the Varuna the co-pilot ordered the door gunner to shoot out the yacht's propellers or rudder. The helicopter closed to within a thousand feet, well within the range of a Browning 50 caliber but safe from the accurate return fire of most assault rifles. Palekar turned side on to the rear of the Varuna and held steady at a height of a hundred feet to give the door gunner a stable shooting platform. The gunner sighted the 50 caliber and fired off a burst. Spray kicked up in rapid progression as the bullets advanced on the Varuna but angled too far to starboard. The gunner adjusted the range and opened up again. This time the bullets found their mark, gouging great holes in the yacht's transom and marching down below the water line. The gunner squeezed off one burst after another and while his fire was finding its mark it seemed to be having no effect. The Varuna charged through the water its speed undiminished. Sansi thought the yacht must have a reinforced hull or protective propeller casing. The gunner fired again and again, the racket inside the helicopter ear numbing. Sansi tapped the gunner on the shoulder and he paused. At last it looked like the yacht was slowing. Sansi was right, its speed had lessened. The churning wake subsided and the yacht slewed to starboard describing a slow semi-circle until it stopped dead in the water. Agitated figures appeared on the deck overlooking the stern. Men were running. Some tried to lower a motor launch on the starboard side. On the port side someone threw an inflatable into the water and jumped after it. Wisps of smoke drifted out of the yacht's interior. Someone grabbed a fire extinguisher and disappeared inside while others signaled frantically to the helicopter.

"It looks like we hit the engines," Palekar said. "It's on fire and it's sinking."
Sansi saw Palekar was right. The Varuna listed steeply and black clouds boiled up from inside.

"We have to help them," Sansi said.

"Two minutes ago they were shooting at us," Wagli said.

"Get in closer," Sansi shouted to Palekar. "We have to do something."

Palekar nosed the helicopter forward and closed the gap to around 500 feet then hovered while they surveyed the scene. There was a fiery tinge to the smoke that now engulfed the yacht. Men struggled in the water but the motor launch, with only two men in it, sped away. The one man in the inflatable was paddling frenziedly, trying to put some distance between him and the yacht.

"It looks like there's oil in the water," the co-pilot said. "We must have hit the fuel tanks."

Sansi borrowed the co-pilot's binoculars and focused on the men in the launch, neither of whom was Pujari. Next he turned to the man in the inflatable and that wasn't Pujari either. Pujari might be one of the richest men in India but when it was a matter of life or death it was every man for himself.

"Get in closer," Sansi said. "We have to find Pujari."

"I can't get in too close if that yacht is going to explode," Palekar said. He eased the helicopter to within 200 feet of the yacht. An expanding black stain around the Varuna was visible to everyone on board the helicopter.

"Do you have a rescue cradle or a ladder?" Sansi asked.

"We have a ladder," Palekar said.

"Lower me on the ladder and get in as close as you can," Sansi said.

"Inspector, you'll be completely exposed if that boat goes up."

"I am taking that man back to Mumbai," Sansi said. "Put me over the side."

Reluctantly Palekar ordered the gunner to deploy the rope ladder. Wagli put a restraining hand on Sansi. "Don't put your life at risk," he said. "Not for a man like Pujari."

"I have to try," Sansi said. He grabbed the topmost rung of the ladder, swung out of the helicopter and started to work his way down. When he reached the bottom rung he put his legs through the ladder, hung on with one hand and waved to the helicopter that he had to get in closer and lower. Palekar took the helicopter down to 50 feet and circled the burning yacht, trying to avoid the oily smoke. Sansi swung wildly at the bottom of the ladder whipped by wind and spray. There were fewer men in the water now. Some, blinded and covered in oil, had drowned. Sansi twisted around trying to make out the few swimmers he could see. The oil was breaking up in the waves and under the downdraft of the helicopter, giving some men a chance to swim clear. Sansi swept past one swimmer and then another but neither of them Pujari. Despite Sansi's best efforts he realized Pujari might already have drowned. He motioned Palekar to go lower still but the closer the helicopter got to the surface the more it whipped up the spray and the less Sansi could see.

He heard someone shout his name and he looked up but it wasn't coming from the helicopter, it was coming from below. He squinted through the spray and saw the oil spattered head and shoulders of a man in an orange life jacket waving at him. It had to be Pujari. Sansi signaled urgently to Palekar to close in on the man. It wasn't easy to fine tune the positioning of a helicopter in these conditions and twice Sansi was carried past the swimmer. Palekar inched in again, Sansi wrenched the ladder around to keep himself from spinning and this time he saw that it was Pujari. He was down to a white undershirt and shorts and was streaked with oil but the lifejacket had kept him afloat. Sansi leaned toward him, his arm outstretched but he was carried over Pujari's bobbing head. Palekar brought Sansi in for another try and Pujari lunged desperately out of the water but their hands missed by several feet. The smoke was getting thicker and starting to settle on the water.

Behind it Sansi heard the ominous crackle of flames. He signaled to Palekar to try again but knew he hadn't much time left. The helicopter came in again, so low this time Sansi's feet touched the water. The rope ladder was 20 feet long. Sansi couldn't ask Palekar for anything more. He reached out again as a wave lifted Pujari up and this time their hands locked.

Sansi saw the fear in Pujari's eyes and through them he saw the fear of his victims. He saw the fear in Usha's eyes, in Mrs. Khanna's eyes and in his mother's eyes. He saw the despair in Chowdhary's eyes as Sansi in his incoherent rage accused him of betrayal. He saw the thousands of unknowns who had known the same despair he saw mirrored now in Pujari's eyes and Sansi loosened his grip and let Pujari fall back into the water. There was a whooshing noise and Sansi looked toward the yacht. Blades of flame sliced through the smoke and ignited the oil in the water. Palekar veered away just as the flames reached Pujari. A fiery claw reached up to snatch Sansi from the ladder but too late. Sansi felt himself carried into cool air, the only sound in his ears the rushing wind.

*   *   *

"Athawale called me this morning to say he hoped there was no ill will between us," Jatkar said.

"Remarkable how amenable politicians become when their power is taken away," Sansi said.

It was the end of a slow day and Sansi was leaving for home early. The drive was more relaxed since Shiney Borkar's body had been pulled from the rubble of Pujari's golden spire on Colaba Causeway.

Jatkar's phone rang. "Yes?"

Sansi got up to go.

"I'd forgotten about them," Jatkar said. He signaled Sansi to wait. "Take them back to Arthur Road and put them in with the general population." He put the phone down. "That was Commander Wagli. He asked if we still want Aadekar and Dubade in isolation. I'd completely forgotten about them."

So had Sansi. Like him they were no longer under threat from Borkar or Pujari. There were no more deals to be made. They would be prosecuted for frequenting under age prostitutes like all the other players.

"It might teach them some humility," Sansi said.

He went home, ate a light supper and went to bed early. Prolonged stress took a toll and he was feeling the effects of the past six months. In the morning he poured himself a mango juice and went out to the roof garden. His mother was going through her yoga exercises. One precious day at a time their lives were returning to normal. Mrs. Khanna brought out the morning papers and asked Sansi if he wanted *chai* or coffee. He picked up The Hindustani Times and read about all the other disasters that had afflicted India while he was preoccupied with his. An article halfway down page 3 caught his attention.

"Oh," he said.

"I'm not sure I like the sound of that 'oh'," Pramila said.

"Do you remember when I was at the law firm, I told you about a Mrs. Deshpanda?"

"The name is familiar but I'm not sure why," Pramila said.

"She came to me and asked if I could arrange for a professional hit man to get rid of her husband for her."

Pramila straightened up, her face slightly flushed but her breathing steady. "I remember that," she said.

"There is a piece in the paper here that her husband, Parth Deshpande, the head of Deshpande Electronic Systems has gone missing."

"Oh," Pramila said.

Paul Mann is the award winning author of 10 novels, two novellas and numerous short stories. He is married with three daughters and lives in Maine.
For more information visit: pauljmann.com

Made in the USA
Middletown, DE
24 March 2020